SCRAPBOOK OF MY YEARS AS A ZEALOT

Scrapbook of My Years as a Zealot

Nicole Markotić

ARSENAL PULP PRESS | VANCOUVER

SCRAPBOOK OF MY YEARS AS A ZEALOT
Copyright © 2008 by Nicole Markotić

ARSENAL PULP PRESS
Suite 200, 341 Water Street
Vancouver, BC
Canada V6B 1B8
arsenalpulp.com

The publisher gratefully acknowledges the support of the Canada
Council for the Arts and the British Columbia Arts Council for its
publishing program, and the Government of Canada through the Book
Publishing Industry Development Program and the Government of
British Columbia through the Book Publishing Tax Credit Program for its
publishing activities.

Book design by Shyla Seller
Editing by Brian Lam
Editorial assistance by Jon Fleming

Printed and bound in Canada

Library and Archives Canada Cataloguing in Publication

Markotić, Nicole
    Scrapbook of my years as a zealot / Nicole Markotić.

ISBN 978-1-55152-248-7

    I. Title.

PS8576.A7435S37 2008   C813'.54   C2008-905495-4

I dedicate this novel to my
mother, Margarete Markotic,
for her tough character, for her
strength and wild curiosity, and
for her constant love. She forever
supports her family's passions
and pursuits, she taught me to
love gardens and reading, and
her incredible spirit continues to
inspire and motivate me.

—N.M.

Liebe ist Heimweh. (*Love is homesickness*)

—Sigmund Freud, "The Uncanny"

As Man is, God once was;
As God is, Man may be.

—Mormon couplet (*The Articles of Faith*,
James E. Talmage)

Everyone
Will explain to us
How to do
The wrong things
The right way

—Louis Zukofsky, *"A"*-12

Latter-Day Saints

I used to pray the missionaries would come save my family. All three of us daughters had Mormon friends, but only I truly believed. Every time I'd see those pairs of dark suits and white shirts walk up our street, I'd hold my breath. But every single time something stopped the miracle: My parents happened to leave for the annual Croatian cultural banquet as soon as the missionaries reached the next-door neighbour's house, or my mother bustled with her garden shears into the back yard where she couldn't hear the doorbell, or someone—other Mormons—invited the suited and sweating boys in for a full meal, and by the time they emerged it was too late for conversions.

At what point can any of us claim we are truly adults? When we first move out of the parental home? When we marry? Become parents ourselves? Turn twenty-one? Thirty? One hundred and seven?

To paraphrase from *Catcher in the Rye*, I don't want to relate my childhood. I don't want to reveal where I was born, how many toes I had, or what my first day of kindergarten was like. I'd get bored. But some details are necessary, the reader demands clues. "I'm telling!" we used to say when boys horked out a spitball or deliberately snapped your pencil in two. "I'm telling!" we'd complain through clamped teeth. But we never did. "I'm telling. I *will*."

"Go ahead," the boy who'd shot elastics at your ear always said, "see what happens if you do."

* * *

When my oldest sister Ruth gave up cola, six months before deciding to move to Israel to live in a Kibbutz in Jordan Valley, she made Jana and me give up cola, too. Forever and ever, Amen. Ruth preaching to Jana and me about the Angel Moroni when she turned seventeen and became a Mormon for almost two months; during that summer, she was the strictest convert ever. Then she discovered communism. Then when she got married, she converted to motherhood, and her prayers focussed on absorbent recyclable diapers.

I was eight years old, and hadn't met my best-friend-to-be Vera yet. I loved the way pop made my nose hurt the first time I tried it. Ruth, old enough to act like my mother, was strict, so that summer I drank my cola in the backseat of our dad's station wagon parked in the alley. No one surprised me there. Back then, no one, not even our mother, could drive except our dad. He'd just bought our first television, black-and-white, and our mom only let me watch fifteen minutes of *The Friendly Giant* on the mornings I stayed home sick. But once our father had settled down to watch *Ironside* and read a million newspapers from Europe, once he'd angled his coffee mug against the lip of the card table he used as a desk, I'd sneak his car keys from his jacket hanging upstairs. And I'd sneak a glass bottle from where I hid them inside my winter boots. When I'd drained the bottle down to its cola dregs, I climbed into the front seat and rehearsed steering. Our father grew up in rural Croatia, where kids drove rural roads on their own by the time they were eight.

He'd let us grab the wheel on straight highways, despite our mother's "Ach, no!" So in the back alley, I'd hunker down in the parked car and shake the wheel so-so-slightly, yet rapidly, like real driving in the cartoons.

I pretended to drive and I drank a brown-flavoured pop that Ruth insisted was forbidden. No one could see me. No one knew. Except God.

Boomerang Love

Four days. That's how long I've been back in my own apartment, this time from Philadelphia where my boss sent me for a three-month stint. I attended conferences and workshops on the North American Teen. I gave talks on "Delinquency and Prevention" and "Social Worker or Parole Officer: Who Tends Our Teens?" for social workers in the States who wanted to model their program after ours. I ran a ten-week seminar. I took notes when others gave papers. I observed Pennsylvania delinquent youths, and compared them to Alberta delinquent youths. And now I've returned to Calgary. Again.

Mutti—my mother—you say it like "rookie," except she's anything but. She's the expert Expert, the practical Practic—or is that pragmatic? Whenever I fly away, when I leave town in an absolute way, Mutti recedes till I can't quite make out her face, can only see her figure standing on the doorstep, waving goodbye. I live in the same city as my mother, but we haven't bonded as two adults, as two women who may be related but also share a friendship. She is my mother and I her youngest, always the youngest, daughter. She never forces me, she never pushes, but her words do the pushing for her. Is Mutti wise because she has given birth or because she has attained widowhood or because she refuses to cover herself with a religion security blanket? I don't know the answer, because I am not wise, and both Mutti and I know I am not. I leave and I return, I ask her advice and resent when she offers it. What travels with me are her words, her advice. *Ad* meaning from, and *vice* as in vice squad: "You make your own bed, or don't lie on it ever again"; "Two's company, five's a family"; "A friend in need is a friend in need."

Words, in my mother's hand, are like a kid's plastic toys—squeaky and adorable and irritating. But in my hands, words are what get me in trouble: "Home is where the heat is"; "Eat, don't drink, and marry young"; "Something old, something new, something borrowed, someone blue." And where the hell was that penny in my shoe? Words claim me far tighter and more often than I claim them. From my ears to my brain, from my mouth back into my own ears again. "Step on a crack, break your mother's back"; "I'm your Mutti, you're my cookie"; "Fly away Peter, fly away Paul / come back Peter, come back Paul."

"He never will, you know," she told me. Why did she have to?

Mutti calls me the Boomerang Kid: I keep throwing myself away from her, she keeps enticing me back. First it was from home, *her* home: I'd move out, lug boxes spilling over with jeans I'd had since I was in grade seven, and a month later I'd be back, same boxes, same 70s jeans, same no-window room in the basement. The only time I didn't boomerang back home was when Darius and I split. I got my own apartment, then, and finally lived as a grownup. A grownup alone. As a teenager in Mutti's house, sleeping in a windowless room was the only way to tolerate the sun. So I chose the basement, despite Ruth's, and then Jana's, empty bedrooms upstairs. When Darius and I lived in an apartment on the thirteenth floor and I started working nights, I taped black construction paper over the bedroom window every morning, so the day could slice through only after I was already awake.

I was a caseworker for junior delinquents—that was the legal term—and I was willing to work nights. Seven nights in a row, three off. My rotation had been nights for so long that I only thought about movies in terms of matinees, romance in terms of seven a.m. quickies, and teenagers in terms of caged apathy. I'd sleep mornings and afternoons, slam awake to both alarm clocks, cram cereal into my mouth at three in the afternoon, and then cycle off to work again when others in the building prepared for bed. Then I graduated to administration, and I worked at a desk and from regular morning till regular late afternoon. I'd been a good caseworker, and my boss started sending me to conferences and seminars. I'd fly off for the weekend, and then boomerang back, a swinging-door policy on my apartment, a catch-up meeting at the Teen Centre first thing, the Monday after. Mutti, in contrast, had shot straight as an arrow: pointed and sure and buried so deep inside her bull's-eye destination that she never left Canada again. She never aimed herself back toward Germany, not once, never stopped believing how much she belonged in her adopted country. As a kid, I'd thought that she was too busy being our mom to visit her brother. But when Ruth, then Jana, and finally even I left home, Mutti stayed put. My two sisters travelled and moved and wandered again. And, except for visits back home, they stayed away, giving birth to their lives abroad as if that were easy. But I kept my boomerang habits: leaving and arriving, driving off, zeroing back. Arrowing myself into Mutti's kitchen. Just in time to be the last one left at the dinner table.

Mutti warned me that Darius wasn't returning, back when I thought his leaving was a mere interruption, one to match my own hesitant departures, back when I thought he'd boomerang back as easily as I did, reaching out. For me. Back when I was young enough to believe in Darius, reaching for my arms as if I was his home.

❋   ❋   ❋

As soon as I return from Philly, Gabrielle phones me for advice about her love life. No, not advice exactly, she calls so we can hash out who said what to whom. My apartment's stifling. Gabrielle told me that it's been a freezing and snow-heavy winter, but a March Chinook hit just as I landed. Guess the apartment's been empty too long this time, because opening the windows simply stirs around the asparagus-scented air. When the phone rings, I let the machine answer. I know Phil's going to call soon, he wants the three of us to partake in a road trip. But when I hear Gabrielle's voice, I pick up. She's in the midst of a full-blown crush. She told me a little on the phone, but she wants to see my face when she reveals the rest of her story. She's fallen, hard, for a Mennonite from Manitoba. I think she likes the alliteration as much as anything else. "Why don't you just say Winnipeg?" I ask, knowing she likes to act sarcastic about her own heart.

"Tell me what to do." They started seeing each other while I was gone. I agree to pick her up for coffee, and she asks me what to do as we zig-zag our way through traffic and construction to Kensington for chocolate lattes where we'll parse her love letter. Three times. One letter.

"What do you like about her?" I enquire, watching Gabrielle

15

manoeuvre her wheelchair around cement cracks and thawing dog shit. End of March in Calgary is the worst time for wheels—baby carriages, wheelchairs, extreme cyclists, shopping carts—worse even than January-polished ice.

Gabrielle re-adjusts her left foothold. We progress forward again: slowly. "Everything. No, I dunno. Well, she's really sarcastic. She makes fun of my job, which everyone else in the world pretends is elaborately dignified." Gabrielle nods to herself.

When she says the word "job," Gabrielle means the thing she does to pay her rent, she doesn't mean her painting. Though she won't call painting work, Gabrielle's been written about in visual arts journals and been asked to guest lecture at the art college. She's had a few group shows in Calgary, and submitted a canvas for a Paris show in which she imbedded woodchips into paint stroked on directly from the tube. And a curator in Berlin has invited Gabrielle to exhibit her "Off Ramp" installation piece, but *that*'s not what she's talking about. Her "job" title is "secret shopper"; companies pay her to spy on their employees, though they don't call it spying. Gabrielle pretends to find her job irritating and a bore. She'll wave her hand in the air when someone asks her what she does ("They're just so surprised that I have a job at all," she whispers to me), talk about the reports she stabs out on the appropriate forms, or the sales analyses companies have hired her to perform. But with me, or with Phil, she offers details about the stunned shop workers or grumpy managers who quickly lose patience with Gabrielle's needs. They don't know she's there to spy on them, to see how they respond to a customer in a wheelchair, a customer who can't decide between a café mocha or a caramel macchiato but who *must* have skim milk, a dizzy customer who can't remember her own bra size. They don't know she's there to tell on them. Gabrielle rummages around in her bag for a shopping list, calls a fictional husband to confirm burgundy-beet or eggplant drapes, demands better ramp access ("though I'd do that anyway, nobody has to pay me to be cranky about not getting *in* to a place"), changes her mind mid-order. She used to let me go with her, depending on the job, but I tended to cramp her style. Hard for her to pretend to be helpless when she had an overzealous friend in tow who kept cracking up at her dramatic crankiness.

"Shut up and let me work!"

Gabrielle used to believe she could convert me to her cause, that I'd end up being "good cop" to her "bad cop," and the manager, or assistant, or underpaid part-time clerk would then give us free cookies or spa treatments to cover for the misunderstanding. Instead, I jostled the arm of her chair and grabbed the twenty-percent-off coupon before she could refuse it. The last time she let me tag along, she wheeled out of the vacuum cleaner store so fast I had to run down the mall after her. "Sorry, wanna grab some lunch?" I begged, once I caught up.

"Not on my nickel," she shot back. So I don't get to accompany her at work anymore, but I still get to hear the details.

* * *

Gabrielle loves the performance, rolling into a stationery store and complaining that none of the Valentine cards are at chair-level, that "help-yourself" fast-food joints place their counters

17

far too high for her to reach. She's not a complainer by nature, but her job pays her to nag, to make sales reps flush red and repeat themselves, to become the whining mosquito customer they'd rather swat away than bend down to talk to. She's excellent at demanding the one item they've run out of, or loudly pointing out that the access bathroom has a toilet against one wall and toilet paper on the opposite wall. In other words, she's a semi without brakes, a battery-operated transformer whose wheelchair can be a demolition derby hot-rod. Or a space shuttle shooting for Mars. Or a crucifix.

"She doesn't make it to Calgary often." Gabrielle's voice brings me back to March in Calgary, to me still a tad jet-lagged, and our current mission. "Manny fell onto my knees when the bus we both rode curved around Memorial Drive too fast." Gabrielle's not shy, but even she can't believe a story where the girl literally falls into her lap. "She makes fun of the way I call customers kittens," which is Gabrielle admitting to me that Manitoba Mennonite has already been invited into a great deal of Gabrielle's life, a great deal of conversation which Gabrielle does not waste on one-night-stands.

"So what's the problem?"

"C'mon, she's *Mennonite*. All we do is kiss. *You* tell *me* what the problem is. *You're* the expert on these people."

"Darling," I begin patiently, "except for the upper-case-letter M, there is *no* crossover between Mennonite and Mormon. Zilch."

"Oh, c'mon. They're both radical religious-type religions. No drinking, no sinning. You're familiar with the type." She leans sideways at me. Why is it that my friends always think I have

18

answers? They should know I don't even have the right questions anymore.

"Yeah, yeah, Mennonites fear sex cuz it leads to dancing," I say in reply. Gabrielle waves away a mosquito and my inevitable punch line. I navigate around a deep sidewalk crack that her motorized chair rides effortlessly over.

"Yeah, and I didn't ask for a 'lame in quotation marks' joke." The mosquito, of course, moves to feed on my flesh. In order to populate the entire city this summer, it's getting an early start. I swat it dead, and it smears red across my forearm. The Chinook blows insects and light gravel at us, and any answers I might have taste like dust in my mouth.

A gust of roasting beans, and Gabrielle's electric chair rides over the lip of the coffee shop doorway. If she could get front-wheel-drive, she'd be able to roll over a regular-sized curb with no trouble. When Gabrielle's in her manual chair, she calls it Emmanuel, and then she lets me push the chair over bumps, around cracks. Mostly, though, she drives her power chair, navigating around pedestrians who only stare straight ahead, cracks jokes with kids whose parents ignore them and Gabrielle.

In the coffee shop, the lone barista wears a bright red bow-tie and white vest. Gabrielle leans toward the counter. To flirt, I'm sure. She rests her chin on the counter, gazes up into green eyes. "Two mochaccinos, double whipped cream, lots of chocolate sprinkles." She has memorized my weaknesses.

The clerk turns to make the drinks, ignoring Gabrielle's gaze. "Double whip on both?" she asks me.

"Yes, like I said," Gabrielle answers, turning her chair away from the counter. Small tip for this one.

"Over there." Gabrielle points at three waydowntown suits abandoning their Styrofoam cups and crumb-decorated table. We arrange the chairs to leave more room for her power boat. "You were telling me a story about your chosen people," Gabrielle prompts me. She wants to get to her love letter, but she can't resist my crazy mixed-up German-Croatian-Mormon childhood reminisces.

I can. "Look, I'm not a member anymore. And, except for a few Jack-Mormons, you're either in the club or you're out." I wipe coffee spills and swipe crumbs off the table. "For me, trying to be Mormon was like trying to become American: all or nothing. Like being an astronaut: either you've been to the moon and back, or you're just a pilot." Gabrielle licks some whipped cream off the rim of her mug.

"Are you trying to convert me?" she says, ridiculing my earnestness. I recognize my own preachy oration. Gabrielle loves it when I lose my stern atheism and wallow in dogma like the rest of what she calls "those of us destined for a lesser heaven."

"No. I'm trying to encourage you. Go after this Mennonite with your mind. And your lips and your thighs. You obviously want to. But if she's all twisted around because of religion like I was, I can't help you." I take a sip of my chocolate spiked with coffee, smearing whipped cream all over my chin. "Look, Gabrielle, I don't live anywhere near Christianity anymore, wouldn't even recognize the stop if my bus went right past. I don't speak the language, can't dress Mormon anymore, don't even bother to cross the street to avoid paired missionaries cycling through my neighbourhood." There was a time I could spot a Mormon girl before she'd said one word. That was long ago, when I thought

I could also be that girl. When I thought believing was the same as doing. When God lived in my head and accompanied me to school or bike-riding or when I couldn't resist buying an ice cream on Sunday.

Gabrielle immerses a finger into her whipped cream, spoons it into her mouth. She's ready to dive into Mennonite Manny, but my teenage zealotry boomerangs in my head. God used to be a puppy who needed constant stroking, and who could bite down hard if I stepped onto the street in front of an oncoming car. He listened to my thoughts about Jana's new boyfriend's forearms, He ruled on my motives for helping Mutti plant the garden, He kept a scorecard of the Merry Miss sing-alongs I attended with Vera. And in exchange, He saved me. From stealing nickels from Mutti's purse. Or from doubting what Vera told me about invisible underwear and condo-living heaven or that Adam and Eve lived in the US, in the North American Garden of Eden. Vera was my best-best friend in the country called childhood. Her family was authentic Mormon, and mine the conversion project from Europe. Vera knew all the rules about what length skirt to wear, who was going to get to the best Heaven, and how God only loved real Mormons. When God set up house in my head, I prayed He'd save me from wishing *I* was the real Mormon, without having to pass the entrance exam. That *I* was the authentic Latter-day Saint, and Vera the one who needed saving.

"No," I answer Gabrielle, though she's silently tracing initials on her chair's armrest. "Don't ask me about religious freaks, because—except for me—I don't know any."

Wooden Wants

In junior high, Lyle Nimzowitsch mouthed "fuddle-duddle" from the back row, and teacher sent him out to bring back a skyhook. Teachers frequently sent troublemakers out on errands. When they didn't legitimately need a prop, teachers would dispatch a boy (and it was always a boy) to fetch a skyhook. From Mr. Wiebe, the caretaker. From Mr. Nusantara, the science teacher. From the librarian. Each request duplicating itself: the principal took it to her office, the phys ed teacher left it by the mats in the gym; each teacher sent the boy on to another teacher. The skyhook was always in the next classroom, down the hallway on the other side of the school. Until the bell rang, and the cursed wanderer had to return empty-handed, and admit defeat.

There was no skyhook.

But in junior high, endings are possible. The sky is a roof, a blue ceiling that shuts off continuous expansion. In junior high, teachers created a holy-grailed time-out.

The skyhook eluded us, eluded Lyle Nimzowitsch.

We never hooked on to the never-ending chase from janitor to teacher to secretary to skyhook.

We believed in them because of a teacher's say-so and right to send students off on errands. We believed in practice that followed theory. To not be able to hook into the sky pulled too much authoritarian rug out from under our adolescent feet. If we could reach up and up and not touch bottom then what were we standing on?

Now: unhook that image.

So what if the student later finds out he was hooked by a non-hook? *He's* the one who got to skate down empty hallways while the rest of the class (and teacher) stared at the extremely unblue ceiling.

In junior high, I never had to hunt down skyhooks. I got straight Bs, I crossed my legs at the ankles, I wore a mood ring, and I rolled fat curlers in my hair at night to help straighten it.

In junior high, Darius became provincial chess champion and took his first sip of beer when Bobby Fischer trounced Boris Spassky. He told me that chess inspired him—to study, to train, to concentrate. "And to never take holidays," I complained.

"X-marks-the-spot-Mass is a holiday. Ramadan is a holiday. Labour Day and Thanksgiving aren't holidays, they're long weekends." Then he'd smile his wonky smile. I used to be the kind of person check-mated by wonky smiles.

"Okay," I conceded, "we never get long weekends together. Which means we don't get any time off together. I work nights and sleep days, and you say you can never take a weekend off because of med school." I stretched out a hand to caress his cheek, trying to stroke the wonk brighter onto his face.

But instead, his wonky smile evaporated. "I don't *say* I can't take weekends off, I can't actually afford to lounge around on weekends. I need to study. All the time. It's *med* school, not flower-arrangement school." Why did he make those asinine comparisons? Why did I just shrug when he did? "Besides," he brought up his ace move, "it's not like you get weekends off yourself." This was true. Back in the 80s, I worked seven days in a row at the Teen Centre.

But I did get days off, just not the same ones every time. No matter that I drew up my schedule every week using a ruler and placing giant XXs through my days off, Darius could never commit to time-off plans. "Let's go to Banff, let's drive to Lethbridge." I was forever trying to drive Darius into the mythical Road Trip.

In junior high, my dad and I drove all the time. Weekends or after school, we'd jump in the station wagon and careen out to the foothills, to the farmer's market in Millarville, to abandoned campsites, to fields of wheat stubble. Once he dared me to try to lift a compressed hay bale. "You'll never do it," he challenged. "It may look like loose straw, but it's too heavy for a girl." He himself was safely seat-belted behind the wheel, but I bolted out of the car and leapt over the fence. The hay smelled like fresh-cut grass, and my fingers grabbed the cord that bound the bale. I tugged, but the thing rooted itself to the damp ground. I thought I heard Vati laugh, so I wrapped my arms around each end, hugging it to my chest. The rectangular bale had appeared small and compact from the car, but now strained my arm muscles to bursting. The hay scratched my arms through my shirt and I nearly fell forwards onto my head, but I managed to raise it four inches from the ground. I sure showed him. "See," he said when I huffed back into the car, "I told you you would barely lift that thing." He started the car, hands at ten-and-two, shoulder checked, pulled back onto the highway. "You've been eating too much Cochrane ice cream," he testified. That ice cream parlour had been the day's destination. One hundred and one flavours in the three-flavour 70s. "We'll tell Mutti you lifted it over your head," he granted.

We called Dad "Vati"—*Fah-tee*—which made no sense when we should have used the Croatian word for dad, not the German, but the nicknames in our family tended to the German side. Vera would hear me call him that and repeat it as "Farty."

"Why don't you call your dad, Dad?" she asked me once. "It sounds so rude saying it like you do." Then after calling me rude, she invited me over for double-cheese pizza and lemonade. That Sunday after church, when Vera was busy having brunch and prayers with her family, Vati and I drove to Big Hill Springs. When we turned off the main highway, he let me lean over from the passenger side and steer. Sometimes, if we were on a flat enough dirt road, he'd let me sit behind the wheel and drive on my own.

But Darius never became smitten by the idea of the holy Road Trip. His legs would start to twitch and he'd pull over and I'd drive so he could lift his knees to his eyebrows and flex and un-flex his leg muscles instead of just sitting. As opposed to when he sat in the apartment and studied anatomy or chess. Then, when his legs started to twitch, he lifted weights. Sometimes he curled dumbbells as he read. Once, he bench-pressed my body. When he raised me up, I felt my bones grind into his thick fingers. Darius lifting me made me feel as if I'd balloon away if his hands weren't holding me. But I wasn't a challenge for him. The muscles in his upper arms were smaller than his bulging forearms, and the first time he tried out for a weightlifting match, he didn't come near close enough to winning. His arms grew to Popeye proportions the first year we lived together, but although he could lift heavy barbells smoothly, he couldn't hold the bar steady while he straightened his legs. His arms slackened, his legs trembled, and the bar threatened to slip from his fingers. He threw it down like the bar itself had let him down. Darius, the youngest student in med school, was used to being ahead of the fray. Far ahead.

"What kind of a chess player lifts weights?" Phil asked when Darius first invited him over for a chess game one Sunday night. Mutti was off visiting Jana in Toronto, so there was no Sunday supper that week. Darius didn't invite any other students over to study together, as med school was a different kind of competition. Phil was the first friend of Darius's I met. I knew Phil's remark was a trick question. "Chess players are supposed to look scrawny and intamalectual," Phil said, trying to poke Darius in the abs, trying to find *give*. Darius and Phil both planned to register for the Victoria Day Chess Match. Darius wanted to register as an international grandmaster and Phil as a FIDE master, but they needed to adjust their scores first. So they arranged a private game, to help them achieve their desired national ratings. I didn't understand, back then, how chess players can orchestrate their preferred ratings, so that during serious tournaments they could either play better opponents in order to improve, or worse ones in order to win cash.

Phil did and didn't entirely look like a chess player, either. He was small and wore glasses, yes, but he smiled too much. And his lips—red and smoochy—curled up into dimples even when he lost.

"Strong body, strong mind," Darius replied. He pulled out his nylon chessboard and pine chess pieces. "As long as we don't have to play with plastic men, we don't care about the rest of the decorations." When Phil showed up, he had a matching bendable board, and a wooden chess timer.

"Won't you be bored?" Phil asked. Darius looked up quickly, thinking the question was for him. Phil curved his luscious lips up toward his philosopher glasses.

Darius told me Phil was in his fifth year of a four-year degree. "History, or something equally useless." Darius, in contrast, was blitzing through med school. He wanted to be a doctor *now*; he wanted to save lives before they all slipped through someone else's less-than-deft fingers. In junior high, Darius played chess and football and volleyball. He won provincial chess games and lost volleyball games and football matches to other schools. When he started pre-med, he stopped playing team sports. Chess games and weightlifting competitions. Darius was big and chunky. Not someone you'd picture holding a scalpel. But his bigness made his way for him—introduced his body into the world before he had to introduce himself. He had wide shoulders, a thick neck, and was tall even when sitting down. He was big-hearted, he was solid, and he was sometimes immovable.

"I won't be bored for long," I replied to Phil, who cackled at my words. "I mean," I clarified, "I won't be here tonight. I've gotta get to work. I'll be out of your hair in a few minutes." Phil may have wanted to ask what kind of job pulled me away late on a Sunday night, but I turned into the bedroom before he spoke.

"Bishop to queen-4."

Their words drifted into the bedroom where I was matching socks and folding t-shirts. What Darius loved about chess was winning. What I loved about chess was its vocabulary. I imagined the bishop and queen in a secret tryst, meeting at four o'clock, the bishop coming to the queen's chambers. Like the beginning of a gothic novel, prickly with robed intrigue and royal infidelity. When I peeked into the kitchen, I could see that green checker field filling Darius's eyes.

"Pawn to king-6." The next sentence compounded the mystery, the king gathered his pawns, his six bodyguards, to surprise the queen. Soon, the castles unfurled their talents, and the knights advanced. The only really useless players in my narrative were the players themselves. I counted nine socks with no mates, a new record. They must have been studying a game from the recent issue of *En Passant* because they switched to chess lingo derived from the mathematical layout of the board, rather than each piece's relationship to its sovereign ruler.

"C-4, and my queen destroys your rook."

"But if I sacrifice the E-pawn?"

"Nuh-uh: F, D takes F, K to H2. Forced." And Phil grunted in agreement. No arguing once the endgame is forced. I tucked away the paired socks and shoved the singles into the same drawer, but way at the back. As soon as I threw one out, its mate would appear, clean and lonely.

"Pawn takes knight."

"No, that's weak, push the G-pawn instead. Then castle on your left."

"Push, push, and then equal."

"And you end up hanging a piece—double exclamation mark!!" Hanging wasn't just good, it was doubly good.

They dove into another endgame, not forced this time, and the pieces snapped across the board. Push, protect, variation. Protect, push, variation. I grabbed my backpack and two crossword puzzle books and pulled open the apartment door.

"I'll call in a couple of hours," I reassured Darius over my shoulder.

"Okay, honeypie," Phil answered, as the apartment door swung shut behind me.

Merry Miss

The Kimballs never locked their door when home. Just turn the knob and shout out "hello," and you were in. Safe. No need for barriers of protection, God was protection enough. The Kimballs didn't talk about Jesus much, mainly it was "Heavenly Father," or "the Lord, our God." Jesus remained the curious son of a demanding Jewish father. Joseph Smith turned that Biblical Jehovah into a Heavenly Dad. And Joseph Smith came from the proper birthplace of Christianity: America.

"Hello, it's me," I'd say, and push the door wide open, then slam it shut, reminding myself that there was no need to lock it.

"We're in the kitchen." Making popcorn after school. Snow-blown sidewalks outside, but the popped kernels reminded me of the Primary School song about spring blossoms on an apricot tree.

Sometimes, we'd melt caramel and pour it onto the fluffy kernels, then pack them tight as Alberta snowballs. In winter we needed to believe in a Utah kind of spring, a spring that reminded everyone of godly blooms and holy-ghost buds, even those of us who'd never been. Popcorn balls and toffee pulls, mini-hamburgers and patio picnics. Vera's brother Sheldon went to Brigham Young University and wrote letters home about meeting girls who majored in marrying returned missionaries. He also made fun of girls who majored in physics, but then *minored* in home economics, "so they'd have something to fall back on." I didn't get the joke.

I'd enter the Kimballs' front door and there'd be no piles of cups beside the kitchen sink. "Can't you just use *one* cup a *day*?" Mutti would demand, grimacing at the mountain of glasses and mugs with bewilderment, every evening surprised at their multiplication tricks. There was no sisterly coven at the Kimballs to try to break into either. When Vera's sisters visited, she blended in among a herd of nephews and nieces, some of whom were her own age. At the Kimballs', we politely mentioned God when a meal ended as well as when it began. As if God were *there*, had just stepped out to the corner store to pick up a litre of milk. Elohim, but don't use God's name until you get a Temple Recommend, until you baptize for yourself and for dead family members, until you know for sure which of the three Heavens you're going to end up in.

My mother never—as far as I could tell ever—believed in God. Any God. "It's a crutch," she'd say, waving her arms. She'd left God behind in Germany after the war. The war had taught her to unbelieve, she said, but wouldn't speak about the war or after. "For me, I am Canadian, and we start with no gods, no perfection." I didn't get it, but I didn't push it, either. Instead I argued that we *all* need crutches sometimes, which made her angry enough to sweep the front steps so hard dust got into our eyes. "No, you need a crutch if your leg's broken or hurt. Or missing. But people shouldn't rely on the invisible, we have trouble enough believing ..." She didn't finish. The only details I'd ever get about Germany was the gorgeous Potsdam gardens or fresh rye bread. When I asked why she never went back, not once since she moved to North America, the dust swirls increased so frenetically that I dashed over to the Kimballs', pushed open the unlocked door, and hid among the herd.

❋ ❋ ❋

When you're just a kid, grownups tell you not to run across the street, but they don't tell you why. They don't say anything about tripping and car drivers not noticing a horizontal body. They offer rules in good faith, but they don't explain them. "Don't ask questions, just do as I say." They give you a rhyme wherein "y" is sometimes a vowel and sometimes not. They tell you that exceptions prove the rule, but they don't say *how*. They say let sleeping dogs lie, but then they tell you lying is wrong. They say don't talk to strangers, but they also say always be polite to grownups. They tell you don't talk to strangers, but then don't teach you how to stop strangers from talking to you. They crush rules into shards and chunks like a nutcracker, but they never explain which part is the shell and which the meat. They say loyalty is vital, but don't jump off a cliff just because of your friends.

Mutti never prepared for reverse peer-pressure—me waking in a sweat because I'd prayed in bed instead of on my knees after the lights were out and the floor was freezing. Or getting itchy skin whenever Mutti swore, *Scheiße*. Or waiting every day for the missionaries to come to our door and explain to Vati how he could get his own planet. If he would just follow the rules, they could save us.

❋ ❋ ❋

"You can't just do what you want, when you want, you have to stick to the rules!" My mother, deciding to fight church with church. At thirteen years old, I'd been going to Mormon Church with Vera for two years. Mutti tired of waiting for the phase to end. She enrolled me in the United Sunday school classes that started an hour after Mormon Church let out. "Fighting fire with matchsticks," I heard her say to Vati, so I pounded down the stairs loud enough to wake several saints. But in my room, with the door slammed shut, I didn't know what she meant. Two fires burning at the same time—one inside the other—just like the Ezekial song. I rejoined the argument.

"But I don't want to go to United Church for Sunday school. It's not as fun as the Mormon ..." She'd set a booby trap, but I wasn't sure how to avoid avoiding church. "Don't you think I get enough church on Sundays already? You think I need *more*?"

"You need sand in both hands if you want to create glass," my mother said, grit between her teeth. Suddenly Mutti, my atheist mother, cared about the local church. She marched me from the house to the building that welcomed a Catholic/United mix, with a roof that slanted from the ground to an elongated peak then to the ground again. A generic A-frame with a pagan cross painted on one side of the ever-slanting roof. We skipped the church service and arrived in time for Sunday school. Mutti didn't stick to the rules; we were supposed to go to both.

"You can't *do* that," I tried to explain, but Mutti just kept marching me along. In some twisted Mutti-world, this was for *me*. "How come Jana and Ruth didn't have to do this?" I demanded. "How come you only make *me*? It's not fair," I ended with the archetypal kid's lament, knowing as I said it that Mutti never gave a *Scheiße* about "fair."

"Come," she said, "it'll be fun."

Mutti thinking religion was supposed to be fun. "You just want me to hate church like you do, that's why we're friggin' here," I accused.

In Mormon Church, we weren't allowed to swear, and especially not take the Lord's name in vain. Speaking the Lord's name without reverence was worse than saying "fuck." At the United, Mutti and I entered after the sermon, the minister talking to parents whose kids had already moved downstairs for Sunday school. I heard the minister say, "Oh my God," to a woman whose hand he grasped when she told him there was a fire at her neighbour's house. Mutti waited in line, then signed me up for their Sunday school. In the basement, I joined the other pagan kids, selling smokes in the corner or playing board games on a Sunday.

Afterwards, I ran from United Sunday school to Mormon Church. A bike would have been faster, but my dress had to make it through two dress-up events; it had to please two denominations. Mormon girls were all pink and yellow and mauve taffeta dresses. Billowy, light. United church girls wore dark colours and heavy sweaters. At Mormon Sunday school we memorized the *Book of Mormon* bit by bit so the words travelled through our blood into every crevice. Of the lost tribe of Lamanites: "Wherefore, as they were white, and exceedingly fair and delightsome, that they might not be enticing unto my people the Lord God did cause a skin of blackness to come upon them." Of the Devil's mocking us: "Wo, wo, wo unto this people; wo unto the inhabitants of the whole earth except they shall repent; for the devil laugheth and his angels rejoice." Of the birth of angels: "And it came to pass that Moroni died also." We were not just ladies, each girl was a Merry Miss; we traipsed across the room balancing books on our heads, we passed around platters of cheese to one another, politely offering, politely taking only one cracker. At the United Church Sunday school, we read *Go Ask Alice*, and talked about teenage runaways and unexpected pregnancy.

Our Mormon Merry Miss class raked leaves in October and shovelled walks in January and February. We saved our earnings for July's Pioneer Day Fair, where hamburgers cost a nickel, and all the girls wore bonnets with ribbons tied at their chins. I needed to borrow a dress from Vera, who'd outgrown every dress her mother made for her that past year. Now Vera sewed them herself, to make room for extra bosom. Vera's dress smelled vaguely of bubble-gum and delicate farts. At the fair, some of the women carried parasols, and the men displayed hats twice as tall as their heads. The fair was inside the gym, but was supposed to look like a small town in Old Utah. Real wooden planks doubled as saloons selling root beer and a sheriff's office. Boys had painted all the phony housefronts that the women's Relief Society designed all week. I wanted to grow up and live in one of these old-fashioned houses, one with painted yellow roses and forever-green bushes, marry in the Temple, give birth to five impish boys and four dainty girls. I stood at a store façade with holes cut into the cardboard so I could talk to Vera's mom standing on the other side of the window. Vera and I bought twelve hamburgers, each one the size of newcomer Tommy Cardinal's eleven-year-old palm.

Tommy Cardinal had just arrived, Vera's new Lamanite foster brother. Her parents said, when they told Vera that Tommy was coming, that "now Vera's not the youngest." But Tommy Cardinal didn't count, Vera told me. Because he was a boy and because Brigham Young said his skin was a cursing. At the fair, Tommy Cardinal stood in the gym, back to the wall, watching boys slide across imitation barnyard floor, staring at white people dressed up as long-ago pioneers. Tommy Cardinal didn't know the rules to the games here, but when he tugged at her sleeve, Vera told him: "Only cowboys are welcome in this town."

No teams played in the gym that day because the basketball lines were all sawdust and fake manure. We bought lollipops and maple candy and threw them back and forth over Tommy Cardinal's head. I kept forgetting I could catch things in the skirt of my dress, in a ladylike way. I read in *Tom Sawyer* that boys squeeze their legs together to stop the ball, and girls widen their legs so that their skirts can catch the ball for them. Tom Sawyer would never guess I was a girl. The ribbons tore from my girl bonnets and my Vera dress had an outline of dirt. The women and Merry Miss girls stayed after to sweep up the fake manure and gnawed lollipop sticks.

At the United church, we painted an oversized closet in the basement sea green so we could use it as a rec room, and served each other tropical punch and peanut butter cookies. The minister provided the paint, "as long," he said laughing, "as you don't choose purple and green together—nothing too disgusting." Every Sunday for a month I wore Ruth's old jeans that were too big but already had paint stains, and carried my Mormon dress in a plastic bag, the sash flopping over my bike handles and dragging in the alley. The paint dripped all over, and my hair sparkled emerald by the end of each Sunday morning. First we cleared out a ratty couch, large pieces of what had been school blackboards, and every broken thing that hadn't made it to the trash. Then we washed the floor and walls. We scrubbed and we sloshed and we wiped, and my jeans got soaked and grey from so much dirt on the walls. I'd thought the room was black, but it had been cherry—smoke-stained from years of kids sneaking puffs in the utility closet. And graffiti scrawled all over the back wall. Somebody wrote, "God is dead—Nietzsche" and "Nietzsche is dead—God." "Kenny sucks cock." "How do you make marmalade? Go ask." In *Church*! We painted one wall every week, and every week I dashed to Mormon Church, with my grass-flecked hair announcing that I'd sinned on Sunday.

The United church organized a field trip to see the movie *Jesus Christ Superstar*. Mormon Church said I wasn't even sup-posed to say the title out loud. Hollywood forced everyone to take the Lord's name in vain. Everyone except Mormons.

Mix together cowardice and a mother's love, and you get me at thirteen. I did not swear. I walked lady-like into Merry Miss classes and sat with my ankles crossed. Saturdays or after school, I drove around with my father and chatted about ice cream and hay bales. I envied my grownup sisters for spend-ing more time with Mutti voice-to-voice on the phone than I did face-to-face in person. I prayed to the Eternal Father every night, but silently, and on my knees if the floor wasn't too freez-ing. I wouldn't dream of mixing green and purple. I believed Joseph Smith spoke to the Angel Moroni when he was around my age and converted his own parents by telling them the ghostly tale. I did not convert Mutti—I sprinted from United to Mormon Church, from blasphemy toward the devout. I usually arrived sweaty and sloppy, my mother winning that round.

* * *

Besides Sunday school on the weekend, Vera and I attend Primary School on Wednesdays after regular school. There, I am a Merry Miss, but only Mutti calls me Miss Mary. The dresses I wear are always slightly too dark, and my shoes don't match my dress. I wear leotards instead of nylons and have no eyeliner. Nylons are not necessary, but all the Merry Miss girls wear eye makeup. My eyelids are too Croatian, I have no eyelids to speak of. I paint bright green eye shadow onto my lids but, as long as my eyes are open, no one notices. Vera tells me to add some to my lower lid. "It will highlight the green on your eyelids, even just a thin line beneath your lashes."

"You've got to be kidding, Ver, I'll be a clown." Laughing on the outside …

"No, really, it'll put colour into your eyes."

"My eyes have colour, they don't need a circle outline though, okay?"

"Whatever suits," she sniffs at me. Now I've offended her. Merry Miss Lesson No. Kazillion: Do what Vera says, then offer thanks.

"Okay, I'll try it. Thanks, Vera." And we're pals again, one with makeup, the other with Chuckles-the-Clown eyes.

Not until long after Darius has come and gone will I cater to my Slavic skin and features: no wonder Barbie-doll makeup never cut it for me. I skip the eye shadow entirely, don't let *extra* grease anywhere near my skin, and stick to deep, dark burgundy and cinnamon lipsticks. I may colour my hair the same United Church paint-a-thon shade, but never again my eyes. My birth certificate says my eyes shift from green to brown to green again. Depending on my mood, depending on what part of my Slavic-German-Hungarian-Gypsy-Jewish non-Mormon non-United heritage wins out. Today.

✳　✳　✳

Other non-Mormon friends that Vera had invited to church dropped off over the years. She'd invited all the non-Catholic girls from the neighbourhood to Primary School—Catholics were a lost cause, according to Vera's dad, Brother Kimball—but I was the only neighbour girl still attending, still faithful. Every Sunday, church and Sunday school, every Wednesday, Primary School lessons.

Before Wednesday services, Vera and I ran through the gym next to the chapel. During services we had to sit solemnly, fixed, proper. No talking during church, no squirming when a returned missionary told his story about no indoor plumbing in rural Peru, no singing off key.

That was the worst of it for me. The singing. Mormons leap out of the womb singing with perfect pitch. Perhaps singing should have been my clue to stop. Everyone in my family is a terrible singer. My sisters and I learned how to mouth words for school choir. My music teacher used me as an example of how well you could participate by smiling only if you couldn't carry a tune. To prove her point, she put me front and centre. But in Mormon Church, everyone sang, and singing off-key was rude. Church songs I could sometimes fake, because voices have a way of getting lost inside hymns. But I couldn't hide inside Primary School songs. Some were just for girls, some just for boys. Some verses were for particular classes, so no way I could be one of only seven girls singing and not squawk. My favourite song consisted of popcorn bursting from apricot blossoms.

Who's blessed enough to have an apricot tree in Alberta? And what Mormon miracle nurtured popcorn onto its branches instead of fruit? At our house, Mutti just shook a big pot of kernels over a hot burner. Told stories of how, right after the war in Germany, an American soldier gave her family a bag of popcorn. *Will increase twenty times its size!* the English words on the bag promised. Mutti thought there'd be enough food for weeks, maybe months. But when she boiled the contents, the small kernels merely turned soggy, and only lasted one meal between Mutti and her older brother. In Vera's world, popcorn sprouted from trees, already sprinkled with pink sugar. These mysteries stayed frosted and the voices of the Mormons around me proclaimed them powerfully and joyously. And when I sang off-key, Sister Kimball, Vera's mom, gave me stern warning looks: sing in key. Smile like a lady. Look tidy. Be nice.

One week we had a lesson about how ladies cross their legs: *not* one leg stretched across another, spreading your groin was always in bad taste; *not* one knee pressed on top of the other, as this was too manly. I'd never seen a man cross his knees that way—up until that day in Primary School, I thought crossing at the knees was only for women. "Ladies gently cover one ankle with the other, and press both legs demurely beneath a chair." Crossing at the front was aggressive, tucking beneath a chair puts your legs out of other people's minds. We always rehearsed modesty.

Another week, Primary was about politeness versus rudeness. The teacher passed out cookies she'd piled on a serving platter. Chocolate chip she'd baked herself. She took a bite of one cookie, then placed it delicately back onto the plate she passed us. After we'd each eaten one cookie, she quizzed us on etiquette and made us list all the mistakes she'd made as a hostess. I put up my hand and pointed out a tear in the teacher's nylons. Miss didn't call on me again for two weeks.

We each got a *Book of Mormon* wall hanging for our bedrooms. On it were painted twelve quotations with an empty round space below the words. "Joseph Smith is like Jesus," Sister Lauren Salmon, our Merry Miss teacher, told us. "And Brigham Young is Moses—he led his people through a barren wilderness in order that they might find the Promised Land." Each week, we'd recite the sayings and at the end of every month, one of the Elders tested us. He'd appear at the class doorway, Miss would get up to sit at the back, and the Elder quizzed us one by one, frowning when we hesitated, only passing the absolutely correct answers. If we got it right, exactly, with no hesitations, he'd give us a glass bead to glue inside the empty circle on the cloth wall hanging. Inside the glass, tiny paintings depicted the scenes we'd just recited. Exquisite beads

41

full of the angel Moroni coming to Joseph Smith at night, of Joseph translating the gold tablets, of the Zion temple built in what's now Kansas City.

One morning, I brought my wall hanging to school after Primary because I had volleyball practice, but being late, I rolled the cloth up and shoved it into the back of the locker. Then I piled all my other things carefully on top of it so it was firmly wedged in, wouldn't move or wrinkle. By the following week's Primary, the locker had swallowed it; I had no clue where it could be. I collected my beads anyway, waiting for the miraculous cloth to magically unroll before my eyes. I started praying hard, going over old wrongs in my head, trying to fix them. I trudged around with Vera's brother Corey, for no fee, snapping elastics around newspapers so he could toss them expertly at front doorsteps; I mailed Ruth her 45-single I'd borrowed with "Hair" on one side and "What is Happy, Baby?" on the other. She said it arrived in one piece, but bent, like a sad pancake. I insisted to Vera that we invite Tommy Cardinal to play Crazy Eights with us. But no sign of my religious hanging. I couldn't understand why God would want to punish me by taking away Church teachings. But I also had no trouble believing he wanted me punished. What did I expect? I wasn't a real Mormon. There was no plethora of scripture hangings on my parents' walls. Instead of Joseph Smith's portrait, my mother hung intricate macramé planters from ceiling hooks.

Joseph Smith. An artist in his own time. A trickster, a confidence man, a lover, a cheat, a charmed one. In Merry Miss classes, Vera and I studied his Life and his Beliefs and his Faith and his Ways. We learned more about Joseph Smith than we ever knew about Jesus. Vera had pictures of Donny and Jimmy Osmond on all her bedroom walls; I had pictures of Joseph Smith. Church drawings of him as a fourteen-year-old, kneeling on cold ground. Awaiting the Light of Heaven.

Joseph was a kid who could have been in my grade. He could have been the boy who kept a Pet Rock in his locker, and brought it out when someone paid him a dime, just to touch. He could have been the guy who sat behind me and shook his feet against each other so hard during geography that my desk wobbled. A kid, like Vera and I were kids.

At night, when Vera was several houses removed, and Mutti's words were safely stowed under the dinner table, I sometimes believed I could be Joseph Smith. I lay in bed and prayed to God, "Choose me." I prayed to God to let me make the Word new again. But at least once a week, I forgot to pray at all, or else did it lying down, instead of scrambling out into the cold to kneel on the basement floor. I'd stopped correcting my sisters every time they swore—not because it was hopeless, but because they called me Goody-Two-Shoes, even though Mutti told them everybody had two shoes, *na und?* But even Joseph Smith had flaws. He tried to avoid school *and* chores. He went out at night without his parents' permission, and he talked back to his mother at the dinner table. God knew I *wanted* to be good, he knew I *could* be good—even Vera used slang and kissed boys during recess—but could a prophet be female? And carry a European last name like mine? Not even close.

✳   ✳   ✳

It's not nice to call someone an imbecile, it's not nice to cheat on exams, it's not nice to talk in church, it's not nice to take God's name in vain, it's not nice to hang from a tree in torn jeans if you're a girl. Sugar and spice. At Mormon Church, we played Boys Chase the Girls. Girls never chased the boys. Once I ran away for real. I didn't want to get put in the dungeon. When a group of boys finally cornered me by the entrance to the deacons' rooms, I scratched with my nails and jabbed with my elbows. One of the boys bit through my skin down to the bone. I couldn't scream or we'd be banned from gym before Primary. Boys chase the girls. And girls better like it.

Summers in Calgary meant Mutti sending me to bed before the sun disappeared. Meant complaining about the stewed cabbage because it was *too* hot for July. My sisters disappeared into jobs and boyfriends. I tried to disappear into the Kimballs' kitchen and Primary School homework. "Come into the garden," Mutti would say. "Help me weed the butter lettuce." Each of us daughters had a few feet of Mutti's garden that was ours to plant as we wanted. I put down mini rows upon rows of Yukon peas. No carrots, no radishes, no potatoes. Then I'd let them grow thick and fat and chew them through their skin. "Ugh," Mutti said, "why do that when you can pick them sweet and tasty?" We had a difference of conviction. Mutti wanted her vegetables as close to verdant as possible, and I just wanted *more*. The fatter, the better. The fuller the pail, the happier I was with my own distinct backyard corner of earth.

We planted mint along the side of the house. "Later, I'll show you how to make tea from the leaves," Mutti said, digging her blunt fingers deeper into the stone-ridden dirt. The sun blazed through the clouds while I ever-so-painstakingly pulled weeds up from the base of their roots, up out of the ground they clutched. Mutti wanted me to weed out my thickly clustered peas. "Pull out half that row," she'd instruct. "They need room to flourish, Schatz, you have to separate them or else none of them will grow bigger than the size of your thumb." But I didn't want to pull out a single stalk that could harvest something edible. My corner section grew trimly, though crowded. Too many peas shoved in together, and not enough eggshells or compost. I wanted my garden to seem *neat*, and feeding the earth properly was too messy. I think Mutti dug crushed eggshells into my corner when I was at church. My peas climbed nearly to my waist, and I spent evenings reading with bags of pea pods at my feet.

When the mint reached as high as my knees, Mutti told me to pick the leaves and lay a single layer on a cookie sheet. I pulled the bigger leaves away from their twigs one by one and filled the entire cookie sheet. No immediate eating, no cooking, just a wait period. Waiting always the hardest. Vera's dad said I'd never get to Heaven based on patience. I checked the mint every day, reaching a hand up above the fridge where we'd placed it out of reach of the cat, and fondled the leaves carefully. I didn't want to damage or bruise a single one, but I didn't want to miss when those leaves changed from being a plant to being what kids drank in Germany after cross-country skiing.

When Mutti pulled the tray from above the fridge a week later, I was afraid we'd left it too long. I could barely smell the mint, and the fat leaves were completely withered and shrunken. I stared, my throat tight, my hands getting ready to throw the whole mess away. But Mutti poured them from the pan into a wide bowl, said, "All we have to do is crumple them." Deliberately decimate what I'd tried so hard to preserve. I crushed them like she showed me, my fingertips smelled minty all day. Then we slid the remains into a jar I labelled "Peppermint Tea," though the "pepper" was an exaggeration. "That's it," Mutti informed me. "You've just made tea."

"But it doesn't look like much."

"Forget looks. I can smell your fingers from here. That's what it *tastes* like."

"You mean it's ready? I could make a mug right now?"

"Yup."

Mutti boiled the water and I phoned Vera. "Come over! We're making mint tea like Mutti drank as a kid in Germany. Hurry. It'll be ready in no time."

"Mormons don't drink tea."

I stopped dead. "But ..." Vera already knew I loved to drink hot mint. I'd told her that last winter after a freezing hike up The Three Sisters mountains, Mutti gave me a nose-clearing mint tea she'd stashed in the car. "But ..." I didn't know how to argue. "It's not *real* tea," I finally managed, whispering into the mouthpiece, forced to take away some of its thrill. "It's a drink for kids."

"The Teachings tell us we shouldn't drink tea. You're drinking tea, right?"

"I'm about to drink *mint*—it doesn't have any caffeine. The reason you, *we* don't drink tea is because of the *caffeine*, right? No coffee, no tea, no cola."

"You know good Mormons don't drink tea."

Good Mormons don't.

I was a Mormon by the skin of Mutti's European teeth, as it were. Vera didn't come over that day, and the next sheet of mint remained dried up in curls on top of the refrigerator.

* * *

Mrs. Kimball came over to Mutti's place only three times. The first time was right after Vera and I had just become friends and I was stay-home-from-school sick. Jana had already puked for days and finished off all the flattened pop on the planet. Mutti phoned up Vera's mom and asked if she had ginger ale to spare. I'd seen that the Kimballs had cases and cases filled with jewel-bright glass bottles lining their basement shelves. Their entire basement pantry chock-full with enough canned food and drink containers to last the Kimballs a year, maybe longer. Church ordinance. By asking for this favour, Mutti demonstrated our own unpreparedness.

For two days, I barfed up everything, crawling from bed to bathroom. And when crawling wasn't possible, I stayed in bed and turned my head sideways, trying to hit the bucket Mutti had planted by my chin. My lips were as dry as crackers and my eyes stung along the edges. My family's faces blurred, in and out, and even though Jana sat on my bed and laid out the cards for Double Solitaire, I was useless for any game, even whining.

"Of course," Sister Kimball said, with Christian graciousness, "I'll bring a bottle right away." Mutti must have been afraid to leave me, though my upchucking by then was all style and no substance, my gut wrenching emptily, my face hovered over the bucket. The flu tore me from the inside out. A purge. After three days, I felt entirely righteous, my body having expelled all sin.

"God, she's praying to the can!" Jana had yelled out two nights before, then took off for the evening with two Mount Royal College pals. I was, too. Holding steady and praying I'd not pass out or topple. My arms around the porcelain coolness, my tongue thick and empty. My sister laughed when Mutti put the thermometer in my bum. Throwing up days of food might make a person feel holy, but that thermometer took away my delusions of becoming one of God's apostles.

"Don't move," Mutti warned. As if I could.

I nibbled dry toast, then gagged, no saliva to swallow with. That's when Mutti phoned Mrs. Kimball. "Do you mind terribly?" she asked. "Only if you've got some to spare."

Once she got there, Mrs. Kimball stayed for milk and apple strudel. With Vera's brother Sheldon just gone on his mission, she would have only four phone calls from him over nearly two years: one each Christmas, and one each Mother's Day. She wouldn't miss an important overseas call today. When she got to our place, she poured me a glass of ginger ale and Mutti stirred it with a fork until it was too flat to entice my nose. Both Mrs. Kimball and I sipped our drinks while Mutti pre-heated the oven and then jammed Jana's hockey sticks, blade first, into it. Jana had ten minutes to get home before Mutti removed the sticks and started baking. Home for lunch, Jana would grab Mutti's oven mitts, and bend and warp her wooden blades to a perfect curve.

*　*　*

The second visit came after Vera decided we had to get our ears pierced. *The Best of Bread* resonated from the radio, short shorts were back in style, and you could get your ears pierced at K-Mart. Vati had told me that his mother and both his aunts had had their ears pieced when they were babies. I asked Mutti for permission. "Vhat could a few more holes hurt?" Mutti said. "If it's okay with you to stick needles into your own body, then it's okay with me." Mrs. Kimball rang our doorbell the following morning.

"Frankly, I'm worried," she told my mother. She had on a dress dotted with blue and red flowers, a purse that matched her shoes. Mutti wore an old shirt of Vati's, stained with dirt and compost. Mrs. Kimball crossed her ankles primly and brushed them discreetly beneath her chair. She put the glass of water Mutti had offered her down on the orange crate beside her. "Vera's too young. I'm afraid she'll get it done and then stick inappropriate talismans in her ears." She peered around for a plate of cookies, but Mutti hadn't baked yet this week.

"So don't let Wera pierce them," Mutti's practical reply. I almost corrected her pronunciation, except I didn't want them to know I could hear.

"But I was counting on *you* as an ally!" Mrs. Kimball took a quick glance at Mutti's pants, at all the orange crates in our living room, draped with thin Hungarian veils and speckled scarves. "You're usually so strict." I put my thumbs to my earlobes and felt where the needles would go in. Was piercing less Christian than clip-ons? I was supposed to be downstairs reading. In fact, I'd deliberately taken my book and made a show of clumping downstairs when the bell rang. I knew what was coming, even though Mutti didn't. Mrs. Kimball hated saying no to Vera. I did, too. Since Mutti didn't understand lax North American ways, she usually laid down sterner laws than the Kimballs enforced. If I was restricted from piercing my ears, Mrs. Kimball could line up behind Mutti's ruling, and the brunt of Vera's displeasure would hit my mother. I had to be home hours before Vera, wasn't allowed to attend sleep-overs unless Mutti knew both parents, and my clothes came from Ruth and Jana who'd given them up years ago. Clothes being out of fashion wasn't a reason to buy new ones, according to both Mutti *and* Vati.

When the kettle boiled and whistled, I crept up the left side of the staircase so they wouldn't hear it creak, and settled into our large front closet. I was safe until Mrs. Kimball left. I'd figure out my escape route later.

"Oh, Bev," Mutti said. She was tired today. She didn't even make the faux pas of offering coffee or tea, just poured them both a mug full of orange juice from the fridge. "They're *teenagers*, for God's sakes. They're not drinking, they're not smoking, the needles are going into their earlobes not their arms, they just want to dress up. I don't put holes into my body, but I also don't push my heels up my ankles and walk on my tiptoes all day." I heard Mrs. Kimball scrape her high heels deeper beneath the chair. "What do I know about being a teenager in America? As long as they go to a good place, clean, this seems harmless."

To my parents, the entire continent was "America." There

were US Americans and Mexican Americans and Canadian Americans. They assumed when an announcer on the radio said "American," he meant all three countries, maybe even both north and south continents. My parents had immigrated from Europe to "America" via New York City. And, as Vati liked to say, since they never moved back to Europe, America must be where they still lived. And now they had teenage daughters growing up American and requiring an un-European kind of parenting.

"That's it, then?" asked Mrs. Kimball, her fingernails tapping on the orange crate. "We just let them do whatever they want?" Her tone was plaintive, cajoling. But Mutti's Europeanness was not there to please Mrs. Kimball.

"That's all I say, Bev, what do you want?" Mutti swallowed her juice, and then, without warning, went to the closet and yanked out a coat from above my head. She didn't see me crouched below. "You probably shouldn't let her," Mutti turned and helped a surprised Mrs. Kimball on with her overcoat. "We each have to let them do what we think is okay, and we have to *not* let them do what we think is a problem, yes? *I* think it's okay. You do not, yes?" But Mrs. Kimball was already out the door and down our steps. She marched resolutely down the path, and turned from my sight. Mutti closed the door, then slammed the closet door, hard, nearly clipping my toes. Why did Vera's mom give up so soon? Was this the Eternal Father testing me? My gut told me that a decision to wear earrings might have Mormon implications. And that I *had* to pierce my ears, now that Vera's mom wasn't protesting any longer.

But if this was a test, did I now have to stand up to Sister Kimball *and* Mutti? And Vera? I pulled the winter coats closer around me, wishing we had a basement full of soda pop.

That week, Vera and I took the number ten bus to the mall, pierced our ears, and bought gold-plated miniature hoops to decorate the holes. They had to push the earrings through the holes while the needles were still inside our lobes. When the needle went in Vera's ear, she sang Roberta Flack's "Killing Me Softly." When the needle pushed into my tissue, I felt cold metal inside my body and thought of nails on the cross. I'd always thought Jesus felt burning hot metal piercing his palms, but maybe he felt an ice-cold blast that transformed the inside of his body to the outside. My cheeks burned because I'd blasphemously thought I could feel what Jesus felt. And over vanity. Vera saw my face go nuclear and thought the piercing hurt. She held out her hand, and sang, "we're being killed softly," until the needles were out again. At home, we rotated our gold rings every night and every morning, dousing the scabbing skin with rubbing alcohol that smelled so illegal I held my breath while I poured it onto the cotton balls.

For Christmas, Mrs. Kimball bought matching pearl earrings for herself and Vera. "I got mine done, too," she declared, "since it's becoming such a fad."

❋　❋　❋

Mrs. Kimball's third visit cost Mutti her faith in her daughter and should have cost me my allowance for a year. Vera and I were at her place after Merry Miss, bubbling over with stories of Joseph Smith who saw the Lord at our same age. We turned on the stove and poured oil into the cast iron pot, then dropped one kernel of corn in to gauge how hot the oil was. When that single kernel popped, we'd add a full cup of kernels, melt margarine on top, and shake salt over the bowl in rhythm to Vera's favourite Osmonds record. We sang, "One Bad Apple (Don't Spoil the Whole Bunch Girl)," as we grabbed ingredients from the cupboards. Vera was going to date Jimmy Osmond because all the teenage girls liked Donny, so Jimmy was free. And because Jimmy had freckles. She wrote him letters and pasted pages from *Tiger Beat* on her wall, *no way* I'd let Mutti catch me at that game. "You want to write, you write to your cousins in Germany," she'd say, if she caught me composing letters to American pop stars. Didn't make a difference that *she* never wrote to her brother, that she never visited Germany and he'd never been to Canada, that she only ever phoned him when Vati went into the hospital for an overnight checkup. Vera wrote to the Osmonds because they were Mormon and once came to Calgary for a Fireside meeting with true believers.

We burnt the popcorn kernel. It popped, then charred, the oil angrily hopping around inside the thick pot, ashy smoke seeping out from under its lid. We were downstairs playing Vera's Edward Bear LP. She sang loudest to "Masquerade," but I wanted to hear "Last Song" over and over. I liked Edward Bear more than the Osmonds but didn't say so. Vera told me about the new boy in her grade who was also Mormon. When we finally smelled burning, we leapt up the stairs to the kitchen, grabbed the pot, and slid it onto the countertop. I burnt my wrists where the handle grazed my skin, then Vera shrieked, pointing, and we watched the countertop rise, rise, rise, like the popcorn in the Jiffypop package that we should have used that would have kept us at attention by the stove, whereas now the counter rose up to meet the pot, the pot floated upwards, the smoke crept out, down the sides, hung onto the surface of the countertop, and glazed the entire flowery pattern a dark dull grey.

One burnt kernel, and Mrs. Kimball needed to replace the entire counter on both sides of the stove, because she couldn't find a pattern to match the other counters. When she first heard what happened, Mutti just stared at our countertop that she'd grouted herself with leftover tiles from the bathroom. The pattern didn't match our kitchen cupboards, but Mutti had learned all about angles and balance and grouting. Her face showed me how likely it was she was ever going to do *that* again in this lifetime.

"Ach, Bev," said Mutti. "I thought I raised a daughter who'd never burn food, let alone burn a kitchen." She shook her head. *That's all I say*, I could hear her thinking.

"Mine, too," Mrs. Kimball answered. "They were listening to music and busy talking about *boys*." Suddenly, Mutti and Mrs. Kimball were conspirators, suddenly they were best friends.

"Of course, we'll pay. I pay you now, and she'll work until she's earned half the new countertops, paid for them right down to the penny." Mutti sat up straighter in her chair, her apron hung loosely around her belly, she absently pulled at the ties behind her back.

"Oh, don't worry about it." Mrs. Kimball actually laughed. "I wanted an excuse for a new countertop anyway. These silly girls just gave me that chance." And just like that, Vera's mother saved me.

* * *

The fourth visit never happened. Mrs. Kimball never came over to visit Mutti years later, when I was in my last year of high school, when I was too big for hiding. In physics class, our teacher informed us that Pluto now had a new satellite, Charon. Somewhere in Switzerland, thieves had absconded with Charlie Chaplin's corpse, though police found the coffin a few miles away. I didn't hear about this fourth visit, even when I stopped going to Mormon Church. Mutti hoarded this story, like she hoarded many of her stories, to protect the long-gone people who'd lived them. And to protect the listeners. I'd left the Mormon Church, but Mutti knew I still needed to believe, at least a little. Mutti only told me Vera's mother's story years later, in an airplane. We soared above international borders and could believe anything, by then. But way before that mother-daughter flight, Mutti drank peppermint tea, listening while Mrs. Kimball sat crying, makeup streaking down her face, her hands balled together like they were trying to keep each other from sinning.

Mrs. Kimball telling Mutti that she was having an affair, that he was in the choir and that the two of them sang together often, that love had crashed and shattered into her life too late, that she was a grandmother, for gosh sakes. Mutti putting the coffee pot on, Mrs. Kimball still refusing caffeine as a lesser sin she was capable of denying herself, her hands refusing to let go of themselves, her shoulders heaving into Mutti's arms, her voice wailing, "He's Mormon, we still want to be Mormon, but together." Then she raised her face to Mutti's stern European one, gulped, tried to explain the real dilemma. "But we want eternity, too," she said, wiping her sleeve across her face, lipstick smearing onto the yellow daisy pattern. "Loving a person means being together in the next life, too, and if he can't bring me into Heaven, I won't get there."

Mutti patted Mrs. Kimball's shoulder, but she must have had no clue what Vera's mom was talking about, that Mormon women need men to escort them into heaven—like prairie bars in the olden days—your husband or your father or your brother. If she left him, Mr. Kimball wouldn't take her, and her family would no doubt agree with him. A new husband couldn't take her, not without a Temple Sealing, which was impossible for a second marriage. That left her sons. There was no way Sheldon would forgive her. Corey might, but would Sister Kimball be willing to risk eternal life on a maybe?

She sat there, sobbing, grabbing onto Mutti—as a woman? as non-Mormon? as sudden outsider?—and sobbed and sobbed because she was a middle-aged, middle-class woman who fell in love for the first time without realizing that falling included hitting ground. "What should I do?" she moaned at my mother, the only person she could tell, the only one who wouldn't tell on her. "Tell me what to do!"

Mrs. Kimball came to visit Mutti three times. The fourth trip not a visit, but only a lipstick smear on a milk glass, a smudge of defeated crying. An as-yet-untold tale dormant inside my mother's brain, gossip that hibernated deep inside Chinook-free winters. Along with Mutti's other buried stories that never happened.

Husha-Husha

Saturday afternoons at the Cardston Temple, the Church baptizes for the dead. Seventeen times the Bishop pushes Vera underwater and seventeen times she emerges, hair plastered against her skull, eyes scrunched shut, having saved the life of a lost soul. Every time her head is dunked in the sacred water, another soul flies into heaven. After the final time, the sacred vessel releases her. Her white gown drips rivulets of holy water and when Vera looks over her shoulder, wet shiny footprints follow her on the blessed tiles.

At regular church, she sits in her pew, knowing she's been made sacred times seventeen.

"What else shall they do who are baptized for the dead, if the dead rise not at all?" demands the Sunday speaker, Brother Hawkins, who shrugs his shoulders as he speaks to the congregation.

Vera nestled between her parents on one side, and me and Tommy Cardinal on the other. I haven't been saved. Not dunked for myself and not for any dead souls. Vera keeps her arms folded across her tummy and her feet crossed at the ankles, just like a lady. The missionary back from Kuwait is up at the pulpit. Before church, Vera and I and Tommy Cardinal and her at-church-only friend Tracy Alekhine chased each other around the stake centre, because it was God's rumpus room. But the pews furnish God's parlour.

Vera and I never call Tommy Cardinal anything but Tommy

Cardinal. Never Tom, never Tomkins or just Tommy, but first and last name always together as if we need reminding from whence he came. I never met a foster child before Tommy Cardinal: not adopted, but somehow still "son." That's what Sister Kimball announced when he arrived: "You're part of the family now, Tommy Cardinal, *we* are your family." But Tommy Cardinal has two other sisters. And cousins. Some in Calgary, some at the reserve just south of Edmonton, and an aunt and grandfather in Vancouver. I learned this later; at the time I believed—as Sister Kimball said—that Tommy Cardinal was grateful, once lost, now found. A descendant of the Lost Tribe, who the Kimballs took in to save. During church, Tommy Cardinal concentrates on his hands, building staircases with his fingers. He crosses his middle finger over his pointer, then the ring finger over the middle one, then the baby finger on top. He builds his right hand into a set of stairs first, then manages to use its twisted form to build the left staircase. His hands fold in his lap like layers of people's legs crossed together, the thumbs skulking beneath them. I try, but can only do one hand, and even then my baby finger slips off. But Tommy Cardinal holds the position, wiggles his thumbs around, then snaps all his fingers apart at once. I miss most of Brother Hawkins' talk practicing Tommy Cardinal's finger exercise.

"Verily, I say unto thee: Except a man be born of water, he cannot enter the Kingdom of God." Sister Salmon told our group that Brother Aaron was baptized in a cloud and in the sea. When Tommy Cardinal goes to be baptized in the temple, his skin will lighten and he'll ascend into the best heaven with other Mormons. "Then I can baptize my whole family, too?" he asked Sister Kimball after church service.

"You can have your ancestors baptized right now, Tommy," Sister Kimball told him. "Just give me a list of names—all the grandparents and great-grandparents, all the cousins and any-one on the reserve who has passed over." She patted his arm. "And I'll make sure they receive vicarious baptism."

"No no no," Tommy Cardinal tried again. "What about my sisters? They're still Catholic."

"Tommy, that's so sweet." Sister Kimball beamed, her face red and moist from baking. "Why don't you invite your sisters to church on Sunday? They'll be welcomed, just like you are, with open arms."

Tommy Cardinal stared down at the scuffed tips of his sneak-ers. "Uh-uh," he grunted. "They can't come on Sundays, they gotta go to mass." He lipped his fingers one over the other. "We have to wait till they're dead, too, I guess," he finally said, com-pleting the second staircase, then leaving his fingers open, with-out a dramatic snap.

Tommy Cardinal is two years younger than I am, and three years younger than Vera. I drew a snail-shaped version of hop-scotch on the Kimballs' driveway, and brought over the board game *Mensch Ängere Dich Nicht* that my cousins-I-never-met mailed from Germany. Games designed for two or four players. Tommy Cardinal could play if he brought a fourth in. Sometimes Vera's brother Corey was around. Sometimes Tommy Cardinal stayed in his room.

Sister Kimball said we should treat him like a little brother who'd been lost for days. "And, just when you think he'll never be back, there he is! Think of the relief," she said. I sometimes wished Tommy Cardinal and I could trade histories. Then there'd be hundreds of Mormon arms reaching to hug me the minute I chose Christ as my Saviour. Immigrants don't get special stories of how we once belonged but then lost our way. Tommy Cardinal didn't stop being Catholic, but that didn't stop him becoming Mormon, either. The Lost Tribe was magic, the Lost Tribe was the prodigal son times a hundred jillion.

But the Lost Tribe were also Indians, and every time Tommy Cardinal returned from visiting his family, Sister Kimball's face did the opposite of beam. When he scrambled off the Greyhound bus steps by himself, her face turned off and off and off. Until his questions about baptizing his family turned him back from a lonely Indian boy into a gift recovered from the Lost Tribe. What if the Mormons had never found the Lost Tribe? What if Tommy Cardinal's skin never lightened?

His first year in the family, Tommy Cardinal got hot dogs and a pink and green Co-op bakery cake for his birthday. I ate two hot dogs, my sister Jana kept dropping hers, and Sheldon, who said he'd been starving ever since he'd been called to his mission in Thailand, devoured four in a row. I asked him if people there spoke English, and he said no. I asked him if they would thank him for the food and clothing. "Mormons aren't that kind of missionary," he said, wiping hot dog juice from his mouth with a balled-up napkin.

"We spread the Word," Sheldon said, "and we learn every different language in the world to help people." He crinkled his nose at me. "We don't build bridges or teach people about irrigation or pass out American jeans." He then reached for another hot dog. "We're not like other Christians, we don't join in. We're preachers, we speak for God and Joseph Smith. Vera, fetch me the ketchup, will ya?"

Vera told me later that missionary pairs had to always be together, for two years: no music, no TV, no help from the Church. People in the countries often gave them supper because they didn't get any money or anything from the Church, because going on a mission showed their devotion. Sheldon must have been mad at me for thinking he would have extra food to give away, when he probably would have to ask people in Thailand for free supper. Tommy Cardinal said he wanted to be a missionary, too, back at his reserve, where he could convert his whole family into Mormons. Sister Kimball clapped her hands and said, "That's a lovely idea, Tommy, but you don't choose where you go. You have to be willing to trust the Church to send you to those who need you most." Then she brought in the store-bought cake, decorated with blue and mint green icing flowers. We sang and gave Tommy Cardinal a photo album, a tic-tac-toe book, and a candy necklace he could eat.

The next month was Vera's birthday, and when the Kimballs woke up to discover friends had toilet-papered their house, they laughed and took pictures. At her party, Vera got homemade cupcakes with singular and spectacular icing, each cupcake a different character from the Bible. I ate Samson; Vera got to eat Jesus. Fifteen friends, streamers from the ceiling, an Ice Capades theme. We brought skates and Mrs. Kimball handed out old-fashioned hand muffs at the door. Tommy Cardinal joined us girls for the angel food cake that took centre stage on the dining room table, surrounded by the spiritual cupcakes.

The returned missionary from Kuwait breaks into my thoughts:

"Heavenly Father. We are thankful to gather here today." Vera's thigh touching mine, I sense her blood spreading through her circulation system. She's thinking: missionaries always travel in pairs. "Brother Palmer and I ask for the Saints' help and prayers that God be here with us today." Vera's head bobs up and down. But where's the other one? Her head swivels in search for the other body in the pair. "And we pray for guidance that we may do right by the Lord." The missionary's tongue licks at the edge of his lips. His voice hangs over Vera's gyrating head. She hears the sprawled-out vowels in his Utah *g-eye-dance* and *r-eye-t.* "Those Saints who neglect the doctrine of the Salvation for the Dead do so at the peril of their own salvation." Vera nods vigorously.

"And we say these things in the name of Jesus Christ, Amen."

❋   ❋   ❋

Amen, Vera thinks. Shouldn't it be *Aman*? Her hair settles down against her ears as she spots the brother missionary on the front pew, his own head properly bowed.

On Wednesday, Vera rushes home after school. Not to gulp down a whole glass of chocolate milk, and not to tumble out to the backyard for play time. And not to pet the St. Bernards who live behind the grey house with yellow trim, or to pick lilacs from the alley for her dead cousins who already live in heaven. Today is Primary class. Vera throws off her sneakers and shorts and pulls on a mauve dress.

Vera spies Tommy Cardinal sitting cross-legged in her parents' room, pulling kleenex from a box. "You get out of there," she says, her voice chops the air. "Mom and Dad don't let sinners in their bedroom." Tommy Cardinal unsnaps his legs and follows her into the hallway. She pushes him back with the heel of her hand. "You're not family, you know." Tommy Cardinal knows. While Vera's in teenage Primary, Tommy Cardinal goes to baby Primary. He learns the same lesson there Vera tells him every day. "You're a Lamanite—a transgressor against brethren." Tommy Cardinal stubs his sneakers against the first step. Could he tangle the fingers from both hands together to form one continuous stairway?

Vera is a Merry Miss. Primary is Sunday school for weekdays. Partly it's church, and partly it's a social group with other young ladies and young gentlemen. During the church part of Primary Vera prays and sings. During the Merry Miss part, Sister Salmon teaches manners, like how not to eat with your elbows on the table, and to always use a knife dinner. She teaches the history of Mormons in America. Vera's favourite story is about the Lost Tribe and how God wants the Lamanites back. Sister Salmon holds up a picture of people draped in tattered blankets and staggering through snow. "The land was a menace to the people, but they had forsaken their God and knew not whither to go." Some of the people in the picture have red paint streaking their faces. Vera shivers. "We must discipline these lost Saints and permit their children into our homes." Vera hugs herself so hard she can feel her shoulder blades jutting. She leans in to listen harder.

"Vera's family welcomes a foster boy," Sister Salmon announces. Vera crosses her legs ankle-to-ankle and tilts her head back. Sister Salmon pours smiles all over her and Vera feels her eyelids shiny on the inside.

Tommy Cardinal moved into the guest bedroom when he was still a heathen. Vera has to help him get into the best heaven. Tommy Cardinal is eleven years old. Eleven years dumb, Vera tells him. Her parents permit him at their breakfast table, give him a slot for his toothbrush in the toothbrush holder, fold him into Family Home Evening every Monday. The Kimballs want this chance to save Tommy Cardinal's soul. He's their chance to save a whole family of souls. Tommy Cardinal is still a Lamanite, trudging barefooted through the snow. Tommy Cardinal can't ascend into the Celestial Kingdom until he's so pure his skin turns white again. His whole family needs Vera's family for salvation. Tommy Cardinal's the first. So far, he's failing. Vera prays harder and harder for this heathen. Vera tries to pinpoint the red ant crawling lazily inside her heart. Brush it away. An impure spirit cannot perform vicarious baptisms. Vera has been baptized seventeen times. Tommy Cardinal says his priest baptized him, but Vera tells him, "Catholic equal sign pagan," except Tommy Cardinal's also a church treasure. The red ant slips down an artery, tirelessly begins the slow crawl back toward her heart. Vera grinds her forehead into her knuckles praying for Tommy Cardinal's lost soul. "God help the lost peoples regain the Celestial Kingdom."

On Vera's birthday, her parents give Tommy Cardinal a present, too. A brown jackknife. The Bishop tells Vera she should call Tommy Cardinal her little brother. Her father calls him "Tommy Special." Vera repeats these words over and over on the way to school, after supper washing dishes, in bed through the crack in the door. "Tommy *special*, Tommy *special*, Tommy *especially* special!"

On Sunday, Vera's dress blends into the row of pastel-coloured dresses. She sings lustily to every song and mouths Brother Palmer's sermon about seeking out the dead. The Church doesn't encourage girls to become missionaries, but Vera could travel to South America and convert the Indians there. They are the Lost Tribe, too. Vera will save them all, one by brown one. Many of the Saints in her ward have children with brown faces. Tracy Alekhine, Vera's church friend, has an older foster sister, Marilyn, who's sixteen. Marilyn has asked permission to baptize her dead grandfather Gordon Tailfeathers. Marilyn's lived with Tracy's family for three-and-a-half years. But Vera calmly assesses escalator hands scaling the pew in front of her. Tomorrow's Hallowe'en and Vera plans to dress up like an Indian princess. Tommy Cardinal, Vera thinks to herself, will be out the door by Christmas.

❋ ❋ ❋

Vera on the way home from Primary: "Did you hear the Church Fathers are thinking of declaring a Heavenly Mother?" Usually, Vera's parents drove us, but today they needed to drive Sheldon to the airport. We spotted ladybugs and hopped over sidewalk cracks. Vera continued: "If there's a Father, there *must* be a Mother, right?" She sneaked a peek at my reaction. "Together, Holy Father and Holy Mother live on the planet Kolob and make spirit babies that come to live on Earth." Primary wasn't for another week, so Vera knew I'd have six and a half days to think about what she said. A week to pass her test.

"His own planet?" I snorted. "That's science-fiction blasphemy, right?" Though a grade beyond me, Vera read books too young for either of us. "Sounds just like *The Little Prince* to me."

"God lives on the planet Kolob," Vera scolded me, "where Heavenly Father and Heavenly Mother's spirit children populate the earth." She'd opened this topic gingerly, but then ploughed her faith smack into mine. "I mean, God wouldn't be *gay*, would He?"

What was she talking about? *What* was she *talking* about? "I didn't hear that in church," I mumbled.

"Oh, not in church," she told me. "This is higher up. My dad's a high priest, you know."

"But *everybody's* father is a priest. Practically every Brother in church." Vera knew this as well as I did. Better. Best.

"Not *your* father," she snapped. End of that conversation. I never got to hear about a typical day for Our Mother in Heaven. Maybe she helped Santa with his cookies, and washed God's underwear.

❋   ❋   ❋

One winter, the Church prohibited playing cards. We could play Old Maid with the deck from the Old Maid and Lying Cousin board games, but we couldn't play with face cards, not even for solitaire.

Vera stored them in a gold-foiled chocolate box. After dumping my books in my bedroom and wiping down Mutti's banisters and batting the sofas a few times so the room smelled like I'd dusted, I went to Vera's. We were going to set up a Double Solitaire tournament. The snow outside was sharp and crusty and I dawdled on the way, tip-toeing over the crusted-over parts. The air caught in my throat every time I stepped out onto a snow mound and didn't sink through. I walked on snow, one of God's versions of water. I tried to float each step above winter. Deep into winter, I tried to step across the snow's light crust without cracking through. That's what Mutti meant when she said being around Mrs. Kimball was like walking on egg-shells. Heavenly, delicate, fragile. "Don't try to be Jesus!" Vera said when I taught her walk-floating on the way home from school. Her voice peeled away the clouds from the snow, as her shoes tramped through the path of weightless righteousness. The snow was settled enough that I could walk its crust and not fall through. If I concentrated. This must be what Jesus felt like, though his water wasn't frozen. I carefully measured half my weight on each foot before I moved another step. I figured out how to make the snow trust me. How to move stealthily, furtively, so that the snow didn't quite notice me perched on its surface. On such a floating day, the snow trusted me all the way to Vera's, but it took me a long time to get there, though there were only three neighbours between her house and mine. Levitating takes time. And when I rushed in their back door, she was already packing away her face card collection.

I ran inside the Kimballs' house without knocking and threw my kangaroo jacket into the closet. Usually we'd sip hot choc-olate and slam our cards onto the rug when we won trump.

Double Solitaire and then Speed and then Hearts and maybe even Cheat for the finale. Except this time, when I got to her room, Vera announced the new rule: No tournament. No cards.

"But *why?*" I kept asking. How could card games be okay one day and not the next?

"People use face cards for gambling."

"But *we* don't gamble, we play Crazy Eights and Go Fish."

"Cards are not faith-promoting. We can only use board game cards now." Vera said, her mouth firm, smoothing the wrinkles in her lap, calmly plucking a loose hair from the material and dangling it over the trash can. "Nothing with royalty or numbers."

"But what about *Hearts!* You *love* Hearts." Her favourite card game. The evil queen ruled. "And your cards are shaped like triangles and ovals and each Jack has a different expression on his face! It's a collection, it's not gambling."

"Big whoop," Vera snapped. "Church *says*, okay? We can still have hot chocolate," Vera said, "and then we'll play Old Maid."

"But you could gamble with Old Maid cards," I protested, outraged for *her*. "You could bet five bucks on who's going to win."

"No," Vera said, her arms pinned piously to her chest, her shoulders in Church posture. "I can't believe you even think about betting when you know it's a sin." Her skirt fanned out behind her as she swung down the hallway and around the corner to the kitchen. She clanked out two mugs from the cupboard for hot chocolate.

"*I'm* not going to gamble. I'm just saying that anyone could bet on anything, right?" Why wasn't Vera mad? Gone was her prized collection of Mediaeval Kings, Queens, and Knaves. Gone, the cards sparkling with portraits of famous painters. Vera had round cards and cards in triangle shapes. She owned cards embossed with braille and cards double the regular size. She had cards from England and Syria and South Africa, and now she had to throw them all away. She plugged in the kettle and I spooned the chocolate powder into our mugs. "As long as *you* don't gamble, why can't you keep the cards?" I persisted. "What does the Church have against Crazy Eights?"

"That's why," she said. Her smile was Bertollini's Madonna as the Queen of Diamonds. She showed me an old Chiquita banana grocery box filled with her collection. "These cards make you think you know better than the Church," she said as she swept a pack from her sock drawer into the grocery box. "This is trash," she told me. "You aren't even a real Mormon yet. *You'd* better figure out what you want to fight for." I was furious for her, but Vera was beatific.

We were *never* going to play cards again. For years. I'd loved the portraits staring back at my plotting. Vera refused to bend even one miniscule angle. She was playing through to the end, cards close to her chest.

After that day, whenever my family played Schmier, I felt the cards heat up my hands. I should have been saving them, I should be telling them it was *forbidden*, I should have taken a stance. Where were the Mormon missionaries when I needed them? Why not go to the Croatian Catholics? Vati asked. Why not join a synagogue? Mutti ignored it all, still waiting out this phase, the way she had waited out my sisters' infatuations with boys they spoke of in code. My father listed off European religious architecture while Mutti bid "Schmier" on only one Jack and a three.

Mutti saw my church-going as teenage-related. "Just wait till she meets some boys," I heard her tell my father, before he could head down to his television. I crouched inside the closet, heard her say to him: "Just wait till she tries to give up boys." My father opened the closet door to hang his jacket, but his hands couldn't hold the hanger properly. It kept slipping without hooking onto the pole, and I thought for sure he'd see me. This was the third time he'd found he couldn't get his body to perform a simple task. He slammed the closet door shut. Mutti opened it and straightened up his jacket, pulling the sleeves down toward the shoes. I pointed my feet out so that she'd think I was just another pair of sneakers. She gently pulled the closet door shut again, and their voices retreated to their bedroom, not talking about me anymore. My shoes sagged against each other. Vera could kiss all the boys she wanted, I was going to be *good*. Better than I'd been, better than Vera. My tongue tasted the blasphemy rising in my throat, and I ran out of the closet and spit into the kitchen sink.

For the rest of the winter, Vera and I played Monopoly and Risk and Sorry! and World Domination. Games with dice, but no face cards. And when Vera came to my house, we didn't use pennies to keep track of who was ahead and who was losing. We drank hot chocolate whenever Mrs. Kimball let us. "Just don't get too roly-poly," she'd warn, and turn on the TV for her exercise show. I wanted to watch with her, but Vera yanked me toward her bedroom. Vati had just bought our first colour television set that he kept in the basement. His favourite show was CBC's *This is the Law*; Vati cheered for the eternal lawbreaker, but I rooted for the hapless constable. During commercials, Vati told me about other obsolete laws: In 1655 England, a mad Quaker claiming to be the Messiah was sentenced to having his tongue bored through and his forehead branded with a B for blasphemer. That in Alabama, it's illegal to wear a moustache if it makes you laugh in church. That Charlie Chaplin once came third in a Charlie Chaplin look-alike contest.

"That's not a law," I complained.

"Shh, the show's back on."

Vera's family had three televisions—all colour—and Vera knew, sinner that I was, that I'd get hooked on anything, even *The Buckshot Show*.

A decade later, when I'd converted from Mormonism, converted to *not* Mormon, Lila, a co-worker at the Teen Centre, mentioned how rigid the Mormons were. Even then—slurping down the New Coke—her words surprised me. It all seemed so much *fun* at the time: pioneer fairs, matching dress to shoes to hair bows, boys chasing girls, sitting in Primary class with our knees exactly so, singing about popcorn and paint-by-numbers colouring. The rules were for *us*, I'd thought, and following them was part of a perplexing and elaborate game. And the prize at the end was heaven—eternal and everlasting, the top dog, exceptional, reserved heaven—forever and ever and.

"But what about *pleasure?*" Lila asked, and I didn't have an answer. Following the rules was the pleasure, was the fun. Catholics may give up chocolate for Lent, but never forever. Half the Catholic kids in our block smoked and drank at parties, and they didn't even hide it. Once they were over sixteen, the mothers stopped yelling that they were wrecking their lungs or would turn out just like their fathers. My mom didn't let us smoke, but maybe she would when we were eighteen. She changed a lot of rules—growing into ourselves, she called it.

My sisters transformed from big-mouthed teenagers to strangely calm grownup women. "They're done," Mutti said to me about my sisters. Then she nagged me about washing the dishes and cleaning up the scraps of Styrofoam and broken light bulb in the alley, and that if I wanted to be just like Vera, then why not join *her* family? Mutti said she trained her daughters to be grownups. Except I never got to grow out of the rules, even though there was no chance that I'd ever come home with cigarettes smoke in my lungs or alcohol on my breath. Perhaps *because* there was no chance of that. With my sisters, my mother's rules waned and then evaporated, leaving three equal women who called each other long distance, and didn't care if they were sisters or daughters—the telephone held them together, cancelled out decades of living in the same house. But with me, Mutti continued to be the European mother: stoic and opaque, doling out advice, holding back her own childhood anecdotes until I was long past mine. Around the Kimball family, her accent thickened and she spoke fewer English words. She wouldn't let me miss five minutes of school to attend a church fundraiser, but she let me pierce my ears and go to grownup

European movies, like East Germany's *Jakob, der Lügner*.

Vera's rules: no smoking, no drinking, no heavy petting, no coffee, no cola, no jeans in church, no lipstick, no swearing, no tea—not even peppermint—no mocha-chocolate, no mixed parties without grownups, no working on Sundays, no playing cards, no friends who weren't Christians, and Catholics don't count.

In between Vera's home and mine, three Catholic families lived in a row—French, Irish, and French-Canadian—and by going to church with Vera, I became the Protestant kid in the neighbourhood. Even my father's Catholic Croatian upbringing didn't give me a passport into the baseball and soccer teams those Catholic kids created and populated. Kids from these three Catholic families pitched in to hammer together a jointly-owned Go Kart on weekends. When Vera's cousins invaded her house, I sat on my doorstep pretending to read, but covertly watching them connect a floorboard to the axles, cutting out a square piece to attach later as rubber-coated brakes.

Vera joined me one day. She wore a blue pastel dress, so she didn't sit down beside me. Her socks were pastel pink with images from the *Book of Mormon*. The socks were embroidered with the hickory handcarts Mormon pioneers pulled into Utah, fourteen-year-old Joseph praying in the grove, and an open *Book of Mormon*. "You know," she began, and I heard in her voice the beginnings of another lesson, "the Pope has the symbol of the devil on his forehead." I pictured a cartoon crimson naked man with an arrow-tipped tail, blazing between the Pope's eyes. She meant something more mediaeval; Vera always knew blasphemous tidbits about Catholics that Vati never passed on.

"A birthmark?" I asked. "Or a stamp in the shape of the devil?" Perhaps Catholics, in their misguided attempts at Christianity, had got the symbolism wrong.

"No, you can't see it," she said, lowering her voice so the Go Kart builders couldn't hear this truth. "666 right underneath where his white tiara sits." And then I wasn't sure if the devil was on the Pope's skin or his mitre. How much clearer could God be with this message? And why hadn't my father ever told me? Numbers mean more than words, sometimes, and 666 added up to Evil.

Vera and I leaned against the house watching the Go Kart transform from a pile of wood and discarded car parts into floorboard and steering wheel and red racing sides. We listened to the Guess Who and Trooper on her parents' stereo, with the front door wide open. Even with 666s tattooed on their foreheads, Carmen and her brothers and all the other kids prayed just as hard as we did—I'd seen them at softball. They skipped school and smoked and bought beer for the younger kids in the neighbourhood—no way Vera's mom would let us play with them after school. "Roman Catholic," she always said, as if they might pick up at any moment and move back to Rome; or as if they'd emerged, as a group, from ancient classical times, and were still somehow to blame for messing up early Rome-Christian relations.

I watched the boys rev the motor while the girls screwed hinges onto the door flaps. You'd think having a gazillion siblings would put Vera into their club. But Vera's sisters were so much older, married and moved to Provo or elsewhere in Utah, which nudged them outside the sphere of teenage politics. As for me, I'd long ago joined the Mormon team. Catholicism seemed to me an ornate and rigid religion. Too many saints—all dead, not like Vera's family who were Latter-day Saints, and still alive—too much paint on chapel glass. When Vati invited the Croatian priest over for supper, Mutti cooked boiled cabbage dripping with onions and tomato sauce. The priest sat across from Vati and spoke to us all in Croatian, even Mutti, even though we couldn't speak more than a few words back. Around his neck, he wore a big cross with red jewels studded at each end, which waved across his food as he intoned. He seemed to me altogether too papal, too European, too staged. On December 24, Vati dragged us to the once-a-year midnight mass, and the spikes all around the crucified Christ jabbed my eyelids awake. No Jesus-my-friend in that church. Only poor, tormented Son-of-God Christ staked to the beams that loomed over the priest's echoing words.

Catholics drank real wine for communion. One week before the Go Kart was finished, Carmen Molero asked me to suntan on her deck. Suntanning was like reading on the back porch, but without the books. Carmen lived between Vera's house and mine. She wore a bright pink boob-tube and matching bathing suit bottom, and her mom handed us popsicles made of frozen ginger ale. When Vera opened the gate to my parents' back yard, I called out from Carmen's, but my stomach bunched. Was the truce for both of us? Carmen straightened her boob-tube when she sat up, announced that she had a slow-pitch game in an hour, and that we could come too, which we did. The coach wore a silver cross around his neck and made the sign of the cross on his chest whenever our pitcher wound up. I'd seen

Vati cross his chest during midnight mass, but never the rest of the year. Would God really help out at a softball game? Vera didn't want to wait around to find out, and pulled at my sleeve for us to leave. "But it's just a *game*," I tried punting my words to her. She let go of my sleeve, and flounced away from where the coach stood. I followed, and whispered, "Softball isn't the same as church." She didn't lecture me about Jesus Christ, but grabbed my shoulders with both hands. "Do you know it's still perfectly legal to kill a Mormon person in the state of Missouri?" she screeched, then ran home. I felt a trembling coagulate in my gut, but I still wanted to play softball.

Later at her house, Mrs. Kimball handed me dishes to set the table. Their kitchen counter was littered with two toasters, a blender, a juicer, and a fruit dryer, and with different-sized wooden spoons and a clock in the shape of a sunflower. I placed the plates close enough together so that Vera's eldest sister and her seven kids could join the supper table that night. "You see, honey," Sister Kimball began, "Christ is your most precious friend of all, a better person to play with than any neighbourhood girl." I nodded. "He died on the cross for your sins," she continued. Perhaps I'd sinned again by playing Catholic slow-pitch? "He didn't die on the cross just so girls can attract boys with blasphemous jewellery around their necks." She moved one of the plates so it was more evenly centred.

"But the coach ..." I knew I shouldn't finish. *Why* Christ was being disrespected, and by whom, wasn't really the point. The point was, I had lingered around sinners, while Vera righteously left.

After that first slow-pitch game, whenever Carmen invited

me to her place, I sneaked out the side door and ducked under the hedges along the sidewalk. And every game we lost was God's reply to the coach's prayers.

✻   ✻   ✻

On Sundays, you were supposed to rest. This meant not working or doing anything to cause others to work. Meals had to be cooked or baked the day before, though Vera and I still washed dishes Sunday night. No sewing, or singing, or games that led to shouting. We could play Old Maid, but not Twister. Sunday was for quiet reflection. And for praying. On Sunday, Vera and I usually memorized scriptures for our wall hangings, or finished our math homework. This was a no-no. Sister Kimball strictly forbade homework past Saturday at midnight. I was afraid she'd catch us, and faced the mirror so I could keep my eye on the door handle at the other end of the room. Vera scattered her books and papers across the bed. She must have known that her mother didn't really mind. Vera and I caught up on school work on those nights, and then we'd settle, one on each end of the couch, in the family room to watch *The Bionic Woman*.

"What about TV?" I asked. "People work at the station."

"No. The shows are all programmed—they'd have to pay too much overtime for people to work on Sundays." Vera always knew the details of this kind of God-negotiation.

"But *somebody* has to be there," I insisted. "Somebody *has* to be down there at the station making sure our shows come through at the right time, and that the commercials don't go on forever." Why didn't I just shut up? Why couldn't I leave the questions alone? The Six Million Dollar Man was torn up inside that the Bionic Woman didn't remember him, now that her body was filled with metal and plastic. He'd been too late to save her, completely; she was like him now, but without him. True Love foiled by good intentions and machinery.

"No, it's all pre-programmed. The station's empty, except for portraits and voices." Nobody there but shadows. Just watch the Sunday night movie, *They Call Me Trinity*, and forget the rules.

Because of my United church Sunday school, because of playing softball with Catholics, chocolate addictions, and the occasional desperate need to take one little sip of Jana's cola slurpee in the middle of August, I thought I'd never make it as a real Mormon. But surely using the telephone caused someone to work? Watching television *did* cause people to work. Other people, but not Mormon people. Mormons never worked on Sundays.

✳ ✳ ✳

A week after Christmas, Vera decided I had to lose weight. She was fifteen, I was fourteen, and we both had to think of our figures, she said. Her body, too, was the wrong proportions—I was 105 pounds and she was ninety-five, though taller and bigger boned. We agreed that 100 pounds was the perfect balance. She had to gain five pounds and I to lose five—easy. "Sacrifice is something you give up now for something you'll get later," Vera quoted our Merry Miss teacher. But sacrifice—giving up roller-skating to attend Mormon Church functions, or giving away an old skirt to charity—had been easy. We "gave up" drinking coffee, smoking cigarettes, and even, though older Mormons like Vera's brother Sheldon never offered, drinking alcohol. No drugs, no cola, no wine in the white sauce, no cussing. Except for furtive sips from Jana's slurpee and make-believe swear words that rhymed with the real thing—*hamnation, slit, hugger-cough*—we managed okay.

But Vera now expected me to deny my body German chocolates sent by my never-met-them cousins. Vera taped her message—*Sacrifice is something you give up now for something you'll get later*—to her refrigerator door and told me to do the same. "Then you'll see it whenever you have a craving."

"But cravings are messages," I'd say. "They're codes. They say: I'm hungry! Eat!"

"They're the wrong messages," she answered. From my body to my brain and back to my body again.

Cravings were what made me sin and lie to Vera. "Sorry, I'm busy," I'd say, when really I was just reading the second-to-last chapter of *A Train for Tiger Lily* and *had* to finish. Years later, cravings kept me going to Mormon Church months after I'd begun to think of ways to break away, escape routes that would lead me out of the bewildering maze of Mormon faith. When I missed a Sunday, my guts curdled and complained. Even thinking about missing church caused me to make up words to accommodate my body's need to be there amidst the pews, singing off-key, and watching Bradly Manners' jaw as he sang. "Teach me to Walk in the Light of His Love / Teach me to Pray to my Father Above."

My sisters chomped through the German chocolate. "Chocolate is going out of style!" I tried to shout at them, but they thought I was trying to get their share from them so I could have more. And I couldn't let them know I'd completely crossed over the edge, had wavered between being German or Mormon, and that God had won. Ruth and Jana were back for the holidays. They lounged in the kitchen with Mutti, chocolate foils scrunched on the table, clamping their lips shut when I entered. It wasn't enough that they slurped ice-cold cola in midsummer, waving their glass bottles in front of my eyes. Now with the winters crusted with ice, I'd given up the comfort from chocolate that my German genes screamed out for.

I didn't eat chocolate on December 24 or December 25 or for a week after. My stomach made it to the day after New Year's. I lasted eight days without chocolate, my first sacrifice. Then Jana noticed that I wasn't reaching out my hand for more, wasn't trying to wheedle her portion away from her. "You're not eating," she said, assessing me with a squint. "Can I have some?" It was a trick, of course. Even when we were too overdosed to take another bite, we never gave it away. We hoarded it till later, or stuffed it in anyway. Nobody handed over chocolate. Jana set up a test to prove I would give away chocolate, just to release me from its temptation. "Mom!" she yelled into the kitchen where Mutti chopped chicken livers. "She's on some sort of Jesus-kick about chocolate now!" Mutti stopped chopping, turned to the both of us with bits of brown meat hanging from her fingertips, the "what now?" expression on her face.

Jana was seven years older, but still a tattletale. She'd gone to Mormon Church with one of Vera's older sisters twice, then stopped because she met a cute Catholic guy. Even though she'd obeyed Ruth years ago when Ruth forbade us from drinking cola, whenever Jana caught me praying beside my bed or humming when she swore out loud, she called me a Moonie. She knew she couldn't complain to Mutti that I didn't like swearing, but not eating German chocolate would prove to Mutti that this American religious kick was taking over my body as well as my mind, and her European foot would come crashing down through my faith. Jana knew it. I knew it. I walked over to the stove and flicked on the light because Mutti hadn't noticed how late in the day it was getting. I held up a piece of Lebkuchen, soft gingerbread coated in chocolate, and popped the whole thing in my mouth. Jana smirked. Mutti went back to her chopping.

So it wasn't just temptation, I told myself, I had to protect my faith from my heathen family. I had to sacrifice the sacrifice for the sake of God. My tongue curled around the succulent pastry, stroking each nut embedded in the spongy cake. Then the chocolate lurched into my stomach, swirled bits into my blood, evaporated out my lungs until my skin secreted chocolate sweat. Like mint tea on my breath. Vera would know.

My failure was pre-ordained. I stared at the slogan on the Frigidaire and tried to think what else I could give up eating. But the real shocker wasn't my failure to halt the German chocolate, it was Vera's inability to *increase* her intake. Vera didn't gain a pound. "Yes," she shook her head sadly, and her curls patted both cheeks, "I try, and try, and try, but I'm just too slim. Like women on TV. I wish I had your ability to finish each meal, whether you're hungry or not." She sighed then, and her shoulders sagged visibly. "I'll pray for help—God must have given me this body for a reason."

That spring, in the last months of junior high, trying to reduce my weight made me really notice my body for the first time. I was short, I barely had breasts, my legs had no curves but were still stubby, my fingers weren't as long as my sisters', and hairs on my forearms stuck out at all angles: a catalogue of faults and imperfections. Vera was thin, but also what her mother called "well-developed." "Boys like that," Mrs. Kimball told Vera when we put on our swimsuits for the pool, "so be careful." Vera began dating—walking home with boys after school or to Primary. Necking.

"What about sacrifice?" I'd say, when she came back from lunch with messy hair, having consumed too many boys' lips.

"Kisses don't have calories," she'd retort, looking me up and down, straightening her skirt, and marching off to class. Vera knew which rules bent and which ones broke. I knew how to follow rules or fall by breaking them.

Driving Home with Father

My father's thin, translucent body can barely steer the car, his hands at ten and two, his eyes dart to the road, the dashboard, my sneakers.

"The road, Dad, eyes on the road." I can't help saying this, even though his hands tighten.

"You can always walk," he says, then we glare at each other, and don't speak, and I've missed another chance with him, another minute.

That afternoon, we drove to my junior high school to play catch. We stood twelve feet apart in the bitter wind—my father throwing, me catching. He wasn't wearing a mitt, so I tossed the ball back underhand. He threw to me, the ball arcing in the wind, I tossed it back. He threw, I tossed. Then he drove us home, idling at green lights, accelerating through yellow ones.

We're doing a lot of that these days. Little excuses become Big Moments. I don't usually go for the sport-bonding stuff, but tossing a softball is as easy to count as anything else. When he was a boy, my father played soccer in the streets of Zagreb with a ball made out of a rolled-up old shirt. That was fifty-two years ago and he hasn't really used his body since. Until me, the youngest daughter.

Both home for a week, my sisters are so used to the grownup role of confidant to my mother, they forget to be Vati's daughters. At breakfast, Jana leans over and pours orange juice into my cereal. "Keeps you healthy," she whispers, "you'll need it."

This is the understood joke: Father and I are playing; I am the only one young enough to be fathered.

That I am an equal accomplice, that I desire this father-daughter thing myself, is something my two sisters do *not* understand. Neither of them can believe it. Sometimes I don't myself. My sisters, when they come home to visit, dump their suitcases in the front hallway, cram the closet rod with their coats and purses. They slap my arm as they pass me standing by the front door, hanging up my jacket and Vati's. My arrivals and departures are suspended there in the doorway—coming or going, in between motion—my sisters are lightning, travelling too fast to hear the thunder that echoes their hurry. They have already grown up and out and away. They pat my shoulder because I stand there at the door, in their way, an icicle melting too slowly to dampen the path, but dangerous if ignored for too long in the blazing frozen sun of winter. They pat my arm to reassure themselves that I am still there, that they still move past me and beyond, out into the world of engineering, and dating a violin player, and a husband and pre-school bake-sale, and tromps through Europe. And short visits home.

Vati and I play at being father and daughter. My sisters are scandalized by Patty Hearst's kidnapping and bank robbing. They marvel at Nadia Comăneci's perfect 10 at the Montréal Olympics. They inform me that the Episcopal Church in the US has ordained a female priest and they ask me, when will Mormons accept women as priests? Then, my sisters each pat my arm, reach out to the air suspended beyond the front porch, and evaporate into the next year. "I won't live past Christmas," Father tells Ruth, packing to return to husband and child. "Talk to me about this engineering thing," he says to Jana, who will fly back to Peterborough the next day. "Pretty soon, I won't be able to give you advice." That my sisters don't ask his advice, that they never would even if Vati lived to be over 100, is not the point. They move out, and I grow up and sideways under his roof: an only daughter, the youngest of three.

"You're not that old," I tell him, which is a partial truth. He could be my grandfather, but he's not that old. "You don't look old." This one is the lie. My father, at sixty-seven, looks over eighty. His hair's white, though most of it has crept up beyond his hairline and taunts his face. His knees pop when he climbs in and out of the car. His face isn't exactly wrinkled, but the skin sags and stretches around his eyes. I often get the urge to pull at his lids to see how far they'll reach. A bit too old to still be father to a teenager. Still, he shouldn't be dying.

In his face, I see a young immigrant boy trapped inside slouching skin. I see a boy catching a soccer ball made of worn cloth. I see him kicking it, hard, over the heads of the other boys, way over the goal, no chance of winning now, the ball rises and rises and, when it drops back down, it unravels and catches in the wind and lands in the street, chest-down, a flattened torso.

My father's wheezing gives him away, the effort to bring oxygen into the body, to circulate, to expel the carbons again. His breathing belongs to an old man. To a great-grandfather, surrounded by adoring generations of progeny. To someone who needs to be driven.

"Well, I feel old," he says, voice vibrating his throat. One sentence, and his breathing labours out of his lungs' control.

It's his heart, of course it's his heart. Men my father's age are enslaved by their hearts. Their hands reach tentatively for their chests, fingers press in to the soft pulse, the elastic beat. They avoid sudden shocks, open their mail gingerly, skip war movies on TV. Not once do they allow themselves a wild scream for a winning sports team, or an outburst at the guy who cut them off at the intersection, or running of any kind. They elude heady joys that belong to the living.

My father is no exception. Once stern and direct, he has become hesitant, or worse—accepting. He no longer storms from my mother's dinner table, raging that no one talks about what he can understand, or that my mother and older sisters are a coven. He no longer stares down at his youngest daughter, as if wondering how he produced such a North American, only to walk determinedly away, his eyes pinned to a magazine. Instead, he stays put, pretending an intimacy with Jana's math assignment and upcoming calculus final. His eyes bounce off the ceiling, the walls, my sisters' faces, but his mouth smiles slowly, trying to catch our words.

"Let's do a movie, Dad. Let's drive down by the river," I offer, after Jana's stubborn refusal of his math help.

More than his heart stopping, or even the pain itself, my father fears the process of becoming nothing: the operations, the drugs, the lack of control. The end. His body, inactive and unnecessary, is not what he grieves. But he fears the taking of it, without permission. He cannot forgive this. Forgive whom? I want to ask. But I am too nice. I retrieve my question from the air and store it in the back pocket of my gaucho jeans.

Being "nice" is one of the legacies left me by the Mormons: "Do unto others …" But being *nice* was not something I learned from the Kimballs.

Vera dealt herself three sets of friends: school friends, neighbourhood friends, and church friends. I thought I belonged in all three decks. She played with packs of girls who made up a set that she fit into snugly. Tommy Cardinal didn't count. Neither did younger neighbourhood girls. Vera walked to school with me, though we weren't in the same grade. Later, we didn't even share the same school. At church, my role was perpetual outsider, though I sweated much harder than Vera to follow the rules. Tommy Cardinal practiced his finger staircase, releasing them in a cheery bust of snapping. He could touch the tips of his thumb and baby finger behind his knuckles. Vera couldn't ignore him if he was concentrating on bending his bones. When he left the Kimballs' foster care, I peeked into his room for a goodbye, but then didn't have words for the boy who should have been my companion outsider. I didn't want to just learn God's lessons, I wanted to follow the Mormon road all the way to the whitest heaven. I wanted to feel holy water all around me, bathe myself in water so pure I didn't even get wet. I wanted to dunk myself again and again and again, until my sisters were Mormon, until Mutti and Vati and my never-met cousins with their boxes of illegal chocolate were Mormon, until the whole world turned Mormon with me.

Sometimes, Vera would quiz me on Church history and decorum: "When did Joseph Smith first see the angel Moroni?" or: "How many True Believers followed Brigham Young all the way to Utah?" These were usually questions covered in Sunday classes Mutti made me miss; facts about Our Church every Mormon was proud of. I memorized the weekly *Doctrine and Covenants* assigned passages days before Vera did, and I always read our Merry Miss homework twice. But some of the answers fell right past my grasping fingers. Usually I sideswiped the questions easily enough, diverted her before she really got going. She'd quiz me right before Primary classes and I'd try to distract her. "Line race!" I'd yell. "Black is all colours, Blue is true," and then we'd be playing tag, running in the gym without letting our feet leave the coloured markings for basketball and boys' floor hockey, tagging other girls who ran across a corner without looking, or forgot that only the girl who was IT could run on the blue lines. Even in our games, we were dominated by rules. Even in our playing.

I studied for Vera's questions and the quizzes Miss gave our class at the end of every month. When *did* Joseph Smith first see God's messenger? Was it that first time when he knelt in the woods? Or was it in the dream that sent him there? Which counted more—dreams or visions? I'd ask Mutti during supper or right before bedtime, or Vati during *Bonanza* commercials.

"Oh, Schatz," Mutti said once, "you don't have to be Catholic or Mormon, you don't have to be anything. If there is a god, such a deity already loves you." Mutti thought throwing in that "if" would wedge open a door in what I wasn't old enough to realize was just a wall. But for teenagers, especially teenagers whose parents mispronounce friends' names—"if" is too big a word for so few letters.

"If? *If!* Mutti, if you don't accept Jesus as your Saviour, you might not even get into second-best heaven!" Once I was old enough to get baptized, I'd spend eternity living in a different heaven from my parents. The Mormons baptized Shakespeare, Mao Zedong, Elvis, but that didn't guarantee a place in the top-tier Heaven. "We might not see each other ever again ever, IN ALL ETERNITY, even if you're *good*," I tried to persuade Mutti. "Don't you care?"

She kissed my forehead then, and suggested, "Well, you could try to be just a little bit bad, no?"

Vati was worse. When I began going to church with Vera, he claimed he was 49 percent of every religion. When the Kimballs came for supper, he was 49 percent Mormon. When Mr. Bloos stopped by to collect for the Salvation Army, my dad was 49 percent Protestant. Even the Catholics got less than half of Vati's faith, so it was pointless asking for help to get 100 percent on my Primary School quizzes.

One day my father's heart did a few flips-flops when he was driving, and he was suddenly 49 percent healthy. The Croatian priest came by more frequently, and Vati kicked me under the table if I tried to joke about fractions. I thought then that Vati and I would at least be able to talk about God stuff, being the only two believers in a house taken over by the coven. But Vati didn't want just God, he wanted a whole package deal.

❋   ❋   ❋

In my family, no one was allowed to say the word "relax." Unspoken rule. A rule we all believed in and never bent. Because

Vati used to drawl its syllables whenever anyone got excited or frantic or mad. "Rah-laaaaax," he'd say, as he drove me to kindergarten, or to my screaming sisters as they searched through the house for their high school presentations. "Rah-laaaaax," when my mother grabbed her purse in panic because her wallet wasn't anywhere. And: "Roll-axe," when I tried so hard to sew my first-ever Primary dress for the girls-only dance where we'd learn real ballroom dance steps. My fingers bunched the shoulders too much and tears smeared the fabric of my sleeves. I couldn't sew to save my life. Pathetic and miserable, I tore out the daffodil thread from the spool and started again. Mutti's machine worked by pedal, and my right foot pumped as fast and as evenly as my mounting distress would allow.

"I can't sew," I mumbled into my sleeve, "I can't sew I can't sew I can't sew I can't."

"*Typisch*. Of course you can't, if you're going to keep feeling sorry for yourself." My mother's wisdom didn't help the situation. "Don't be such a perfectionist. Don't keep starting over, just *do* it." She poked her head into the laundry room, appraising my tangle of yellow thread and tan cloth. "Once you realize that, you'll be able to sew it."

"I *can't*, I don't know how!" Teenage histrionics ruled. I threw down the fabric and hurled the scissors at the wall where they chipped into the paint. I was waiting for pity, but pity didn't live in our house. This was my "homework" and my choice, and Mutti wouldn't interfere.

"Roll-axe." My dad's voice pushed through the doorjamb. "Don't get excited, it's just a dress."

Mutti shut the door firmly. "Give me that," she said, pumping the sewing machine pedal evenly with her right foot, and feeding the dress material to the machine's teeth. Mutti saved my life.

*　*　*

On Easter Sunday, the Croatian priest gives his sermon from Amos: "I hate, I scorn your festivals." This strikes me as an unusual passage for a Catholic to read—isn't ritual part of the plan? "I take no pleasure in your solemn assemblies." But then again, I haven't been to a Catholic church since Christmas Eve six years ago. Father wanted us, all five of us, to observe a Catholic mass.

These were his words: "I want you to *witness* a mass." That we two are here, again, years later, is a symptom of his dying.

If I were to lean over, ever so slightly, and whisper into my father's ear, if I were to say, "Remember last time?" Father would frown and nod, irritated at the interruption, and pretend that he *did* remember, knew what the hell I was talking about. If I were to continue, to say lightly, "You wanted us as witnesses to God's mass," he would smile a tight line and nod vigorously. To show I was still interrupting, and to agree with the notion of his child as holy witness.

That he really does not remember his earlier intention is another symptom of his dying. And that I can predict his response is the most telling symptom of all.

So I say nothing. I don't want to remind him I can remember what he cannot. And I don't really want to prove my predictions accurate. That: he will take a pro-Catholic stance, even though he's only half-Catholic, even though he hasn't thought of this place as *his* church since long before I was born. His eldest daughter Ruth married here. And we two are here, now, because he needs to believe in more than just his dying.

"And that day, saith the Lord, I will turn all your feasts into mourning, and all your songs into lamentations." Father perks up at the sermon. *More than usual*, I would like to say, but of course that is not possible. More than he should, is what I mean. The priest takes a long time to expound on Amos. When he waves his arms, he's showing us how hard he's *trying* to understand God.

I disapprove. God is not from the 60s. I don't think He cares to be *understood*. Every time the priest makes a point, he taps his fist on the open Bible in front of him. There is a small "thud" as his hand connects with the Holy Book, and then an escaped breath *en masse* from the pews. After all the arm waving, I can't believe the priest's restraint.

"He that calleth for the waters of the sea, and poureth them out upon the face of the earth: Jehovah is His name." For all the priest's performing, I can't help running my eyes over the ornate carvings and woodwork around the church. The saints ignore me, fixed upon their own burned-at-the-stake martyr problems. They're not like the statues I've seen in other Catholic churches. They've got a definite Slavic style—the angle of the eyes, the cut of the robes.

My mother would say this is nonsense. "They're all made here in Canada. Besides, saints don't have fashion." She would like to believe that all the Catholic churches in the city display statues made from the same factory mould. All the churches of any denomination. Not out of a particular distaste for churches, but because that would be an economy she'd approve of. It would not be as much of a waste. "Their beauty isn't what's supposed to matter," she'd say of the statues.

Mutti doesn't fret about Father and me in Catholic church. My oldest sister Ruth has reduced her job to part-time because of their toddler. Jana changes cities every week, it seems. In the weeks when Vati and I almost share a Christianity, Mutti thinks about reupholstering the couch. She wonders, should she write a letter chastising Anita Bryant? Should she phone Jana again or wait another day? Do Ruth and her husband need money but are ashamed to ask? Should she shove some coupons into the next letter? Should she suggest another visit? Mutti picks up the phone and dials.

The mass causes most to close their eyes and slip onto their knees. But I'm not the only one squirming. Perhaps the priest notices. He leans over the pulpit and pauses his fist mid-air. "Prepare to meet thy God," he quotes, and then, "Let us pray."

Father insists on driving home, even though I just got my learner's. I almost yell, "You can't shift properly." I almost say, "You don't even signal when you turn." I'm dying to tell him, "Traffic lights are there for a *reason*." But today is Sunday, and my father has just been to church for the first time in six years. It's not Mormon Church, it may not be *mine*, but it's still God's living room.

My father forgets intersection restrictions, forgets who has the right-of-way at a four-way stop, forgets to put the car into gear when he parks, though he himself taught me this trick. His hands, once sure on the steering wheel, roam, stroking the inner ridges as if he were reading braille.

"What are they doing?" he asks me, referring to the other cars waiting their right-of-way turn. "Why don't they just *go*?"

❋ ❋ ❋

For years, my father sat comfortable and confident in the driver's seat, the radio set to Radio-Canada, his coffee cup balanced between the newspapers and rolling pencils. Cars were a second home to my father. Every holiday we crammed into the car: three daughters, one mother. And Vati, the only driver.

Content to drive all day. Happy to slow down at every curve in the highway and lecture us about the land we passed. "See where that mountain appears caved in and rumpled?" he'd ask, as we stood in line before the outdoor toilets. "That's where two different plates of the Earth met. That's how mountains grow." Or he'd explain how on the prairies warm winds pushed down from the west, and where wild grasses grew before farmers cultivated acres of land. "Watch that water on the highway," he'd say, pointing at a huge puddle. "See it evaporate just as we get there?" And he'd laugh when we begged him to catch up to the errant puddle, its waters miraculously landing just so far ahead of us.

"Stop the car, Miko," my mother would finally burst out. "We all need a little air." And Vati, sighing volubly, would pull into a gas station or, better yet, a Historical Point of Interest. There we got the lecture about an explorer who came through this exact mountain pass, or the politician who'd bribed his successor to give the area his name. Vati mentioned so many dates and places that we all filed voluntarily back into the car, back into the driving, back into the lecture voice that at least travelled forward, speaking toward the shimmering TransCanada.

* * *

"He was talking to me," my father says, stopping at a green light.

"You can go," I urge him, rocking my body forward to propel the car into motion. "Who?"

"That priest. He sees me dying. He was warning me." And my father's hands wave round and round the steering wheel, never resting, never actually steering.

"Vati, that's ridiculous. Watch out for that car!" I shout, which swerves around us, my father not noticing the bumper near-miss. "The priest couldn't even see us," I add. I sneak in a shoulder-check. "And you're not dying." An afterthought.

Vati runs his hands along the inside grooves of the steering wheel. Not answering me, because I refuse to take his dying seriously.

I give in. "Warning you about what?"

"Prepare to meet thy God." Vati slams his fist down against the steering wheel rim and the car veers to the right. I feel the tire beneath my feet gently scrape the curb.

Every muscle in my arm aches so as *not* to grab the wheel. The curb slides farther away. "Which God is that?" I ask. Vati steers on.

When Vati and I pull up to the house, safe, I look up the Amos passage in the Bible. I cannot find the priest's words. Was he possibly mistaken? This is not a question I can ask my father or my mother. Or Vera.

I seek out Vera's brother, Corey. He's older than both of us, but the youngest of two boys, after a long series of girls. Five daughters, all of them grown and living in Utah. And then came Sheldon, and then Corey. And then Vera. Both Vera's brothers are basketball players. One in high school, one a year into university. They are exactly the same height. At supper, they have to sit kitty-corner or else they'll get tangled up in each other's legs. Even though they're three years apart, people confuse one for the other, even Vera, sometimes. Not me. Sheldon stands in the driveway in front of their house, feet apart, shoulders tense, practicing hoops.

"Bugger off, fag," Sheldon says to me. "We don't need short-stops in this game." He goes to university in Provo, but he's home for American Thanksgiving. First time I've seen him since he came back from his mission. Sheldon had expected to go to Norway or Finland—he's blond blond blond and had pen pals in both countries. The Church sent him to Thailand. Corey told me Sheldon hated every day, every minute, couldn't even play basketball with his missionary-buddy who played baseball with local teams. Sheldon wrote letters home about going back to school, being the star at Brigham Young University, getting back to being young again.

"He shits raisins, that one," Mutti said to me about Sheldon, knowing I wouldn't tell Vera. Or Corey.

But playing basketball in Provo is harder for Sheldon than playing in high school. He's no longer a lone star, just another fairly good player on a spectacularly good team. Plus, some of the other universities are refusing to play against BYU because Mormons won't let black men be ordained into the priesthood. This is an edict from God and, until He changes His mind, Mormons and sports no longer fit together so snugly. Since he went on his mission, Sheldon has transformed into a righteous man. He's actually a nasty shit, but I only say that in my head, even though God can hear thoughts. I sit down on the curb and wait for Corey to finish playing. I watch them shoot the basketball against the metal hoop, matching each other's skills. Sheldon's older, but he's not better; Corey plays centre for his high school, headed for the provincial finals. Three American universities have been sending brochures to him. But before Corey goes to Brigham Young to be a basketball star and get his MBA, Vera tells me, he's going to spread the work of the Lord to underprivileged heathens.

Corey's the brother I can talk to. He takes a shot that swooshes in dreamily. Sheldon scowls. He's behind by seven points. Sheldon grabs the ball and bounces it off the neighbour's garage. Then Sheldon twists suddenly and flings the ball at the hoop. He doesn't even hit the backstop and I giggle from the sideline. A mistake. The ball whips past my left ear and across the street. "Fetch!" he yells. And I do.

When they're finished, Corey yanks off his shirt and wipes his forehead and armpits. Sheldon heads for the house and shower. Corey grins and shoves my knees over so he's got more room on the curb. "Nice way to treat a *sister*," I begin.

"Just ignore it," he replies.

"How come you put up with him?" I really want to know. He shouldn't have to put up with anything. Ever since they hit the same shirt size, the brothers haven't fought. Not with each other. Not that I know. "Is it because of basketball?"

"No." He shakes his head and sweat splatters my legs. He passes me a fast one and I catch it before I realize he's thrown. Then I hug it close to my chest so he has to pay attention. "He's the eldest son," and then he pauses for a long time. I hug the basketball tighter. "That's kind of an excuse."

Vera said the same thing, once, but when I pushed her for details she had nothing else. "He's going to be an Elder some day," and she added, "something you can never be. Never. Even if you do go on a mission."

You can't be an Elder, either, I wanted to say. But didn't.

✳   ✳   ✳

For as long as I've been hanging out with Vera, her brother Sheldon's been a vicious brat. Especially so once he moved away to Utah. And for just as long, Vera's other brother Corey has defended the meanness, even when he's right there, even when he tries to change the angles. "Duck," he once yelled to me when we were goofing off at a church picnic. I froze. Mashed potatoes landed on the side of my face. Even Vera's mom cracked up. Corey just handed me a dishcloth, not even an I-told-you-so. And if I *had* ducked? If the mess had hit Mrs. Kimball? Or nobody?

"You're a better basketball player than he is," I want to tell Corey. But he'd just swipe away the compliment, even though it's true, even though he'll soon have to admit it himself. Instead, I tell him about the sermon and my Father's reaction. That's another thing about Corey—he doesn't get paranoid that my dad makes me attend Catholic sermons sometimes. He won't tell Sheldon. Or Vera.

Corey smirks when I repeat what my dad said about the priest. "Look," I tell him, "I read the whole Amos chapter and I can't find what the priest said anywhere. Did he make it up? I don't get it. Dad thinks the words are direct from God and they're not even in the Bible. Should I tell him? Would that be worse?" I run out of questions and hope he can figure out what I'm really asking.

It is, after all, just one sermon, delivered by just one priest. And a father who has never, until this summer, given any credit to God or his consorts. Vera's brother could have pointed all this out. He could have told me that Catholic priests lie because they're in the employ of the devil, or that I should forget it, just forget it. And I would have. Maybe.

"Try a different Bible," he suggests.

At supper, we all wait to eat until Vati has said a Croatian prayer. Our new family ritual. His contribution to the meal. My mother doesn't fold her arms, but she doesn't roll her eyes like she does when Sister Kimball talks about Her Saviour. Tonight, after supper, Vati and I are going to a lecture. He invited Mutti and Jana and Ruth, but only I said yes. "New Technology in Medicine." We're going out of pure interest's sake, it has nothing to do with Vati's operation, the one he isn't having. I asked Vati if I can drive on the way back. He said, "We'll see."

Mutti will stay home, wash the dishes, paint the kitchen cabinets sunflower yellow. My sisters will chat with her while she paints, Ruth offering mother-woes regarding her three-year-old, Jana describing her latest "the one" for Mutti's approval. He's from Toronto, always said he'd never date an Alberta girl, then he met Jana.

The lecture will be forty-five minutes long, with a fifteen-minute question/answer period. Afterwards, my father will talk to the professor, ask him questions one-on-one. Heart pacemakers and scalpels and fridge magnets that time themselves with the radio. If the professor gives the right answer, I'll be allowed to drive home.

✳ ✳ ✳

"So, people of Israel, I am going to punish you. And because I am going to do this, get ready to face my judgment." What the Bible at home says. How was I supposed to recognize the priest's ominous words from *that*? The problem is that the only Bible I could find in the house is the *Good News*, which Mutti bought at a garage sale when I was in grade two, because she thought we should at least know it existed. The *New Jerusalem* I lugged home from my school library. It says, "Prepare to meet your God," which is close enough. Does Vati know that different Bibles say different things? Or was I supposed to seek out another version? If you find the same idea in different words is it a different idea?

The lecture concerns the great success surgeons have had recently with double, triple, and quadruple bypass operations.

Once they've removed a vein from your leg, they can use it to bypass the heart's arteries. These replacements last up to seven years before you need another operation.

Vati does not need bypass surgery. His problem isn't his circulation, it's his valve. Nevertheless, we sit in this lecture hall. Listening. All around the room, people rest two fingers on their wrists. We throb, in unison, to the beat of lung capacity, chest cavity, maximum expectation. The professor's words drum against our bodies. I feel like the inside of a basketball. Vati rests both arms at his side. Tonight, Vera's brothers play in earnest, and Corey will beat Sheldon by eighteen points, will beat his nasty shit older brother by a long shot. When he does, Sheldon will strike out at the only other person in reach, the one person who will never tell, not even me.

The professor has finished his talk, and is taking questions now, and my father is impatient to get this over with, to talk to him alone. He leans back in his chair, rasping air. The professor peeks at his watch. A long line of independent questioners has already formed. At home, my mother's painting the trim on the cupboards, wondering what's taking us so long. What could possibly be so fascinating about unrequired surgery techniques?

It's Vati's turn. Slowly, he gets up, though his knees wobble before he's stable on his feet. He limp-steps to the end of the line and pulls out his car keys. Then puts them back in his pants pocket. When the last person in the line leaves, he waits for the room to empty. The medical professor has picked up his file folder and slaps it against his palm. He turns to also leave the room and Vati steps forward.

He asks about valve replacements and pig parts versus mechanical. He asks how long he'd be under and how much anaesthesia his doctors will apply. He tilts his head toward the professor so he'll be able to hear over his own breathing. I can see the skin beneath his eyes droop toward his lips. At this minute, I despise his oldness. The professor shrugs and reaches to dim the lights as he leaves. Vati, no steering wheel to grab onto, gropes in his pocket for his keys.

No Photo

I've ripped this page out.

I've ripped out the photo of the open casket, the pressed Casablanca Lily, the hand-embroidered invitation. Everything from this page is gone except, of course, I can smell the lilies. I can picture the embroidered announcement. I can hear the Croatian priest's words, hear him pronounce each careful syllable, even though I cannot understand the words, even though I don't want them humming in my ears.

Baptizing the Dead

I live as a dual citizen in language, a thief who steals nothing but colour from a map, commas from a sentence, nationality from nations.

When Vati died, it hit me how irrevocably I'd lost my father's country: Croatia, reconfigured as Yugoslavia. Mutti had reinvented herself as a translated Canadian. Like many Europeans, her English-speaking memory only touches back to 1946. When Vati died, the dying was fast, the death a surprise despite his defective heart valve, despite the doctors' repeated words, despite his own body. My father's archaic heart pacemaker had seemed to me a mere obstacle en route to his living forever.

I told Vera that my father was from Yugoslavia because, during the ignorant and lucky 70s, no one knew what or where Croatia was.

"Vladimir?" Vera asked, if ever I spoke my father's name, "like Lenin?"

"Yes," I said. "No," I said. "Well, once."

Croatia is where my father always said to say he was born. Croatia has become a name that Canadians recognize. We still don't know exactly where it is, but a few years ago it came to mean the fallout from the end of Soviet communism.

Like Mutti and Vati, I have an immigrant tongue, a tongue ragged and loose at one end, locked and hinged at the other. A tongue that will not behave, will not pronounce the words the way they lie on the page. English is my second language; this is true of many Canadians. English comes second (or third, or fourth) to many of us. But, I don't mean that I have come to English after first learning Mutti's language, or Vati's. Like lots of immigrant kids, the lack of English—that gap—is my true first language.

My father told stories of learning theology from the priests, of sneaking into early-day movie theatres every Saturday, of paying the town doctor with a chicken. But he didn't like to tell me a single story that took place between 1939 and 1945—for these stories, I need to seek the words in another language, inside the shape of other people's stories. Time has a way of stopping for offspring who come to know too much about strangers who have become their parents.

I read my father's handwriting with an accent—either his or mine—and hear in the English a tinge of the Croatian tongue I do not speak.

❋　❋　❋

After I left the funeral, Vera took my hand in hers and we walked from the church to the cemetery. Late November, the weather hovered between winter chill and Chinook damp. No snow, but the ground is ice-hard, with spurts of grass still sprouting among the gravestones. Mutti said she chose a spot where he could be the fourth member inside a cross-shaped grave, with three other Croats buried at each end. Vera knew I needed to listen to her chatter. "Tommy Cardinal says he wants to be ordained in the priesthood when he turns eighteen, but he should know Lamanites aren't white enough for the Church." Vera wore a dappled grey dress that clung close to her knees, a sash at the waist, a bow at her neckline. For once, my too-dark dress made me look, at the funeral, like I belonged to the right church.

The priest had thrown out Croatian admonitions and prayers and burial rites. Mutti nodded her head occasionally, but Ruth and Jana and I sat helplessly in the front pew, trying not to crane our necks at the rest of the congregation for cues about when to stand, when to kneel. When to file past the coffin, lid open, Vati's lips moist as if he'd just spoken. Or was about to. The priest threw out more and more and more Croatian words, until I thought he'd used them all up, but he hadn't. The church sweltered and ceiling lights beamed down on the altar, spilled over our laps.

Jana grabbed onto her Toronto boyfriend's slippery hand. Ruth sat between her husband and daughter, Cassandra, who was three and had only met Vati once. She squirmed over her mother's lap, turned to stare at the people sitting behind us, crawled beneath the pews, and dug plastic cars out of Ruth's purse. She kept leaning her head back to stare at the massive Christ that hung from the ceiling beams right to the floor. This Jesus was twenty-five feet tall, at least, and his toes that scraped the floor were the size of my outstretched hand.

"The giant's bleeding! The giant's bleeding!" Cassandra screamed when the priest first started his sermon. Ruth picked her up and folded her into her arms, suffocating the girl's screams and her own crying. Ruth's husband reached out, but only held on to her shoulder, not sure what to stroke in a church. I could sense the Kimballs behind us, wanting to cry out as loudly as Cassandra, but sitting there, nevertheless, and

107

understanding as little of the Croatian as we did, even less of the Catholic. Cassandra closed her alarmed eyes for a while, but when she woke up, she eyed Jesus as if she didn't trust how the blood pouring from his side hadn't increased a drop while she slept.

What seemed like decades later, we stood and turned to file out of the church. "No," Mutti, whispered, "go on up to the coffin." I couldn't. "Come on," Mutti said, and grabbed my elbow and marched me to the front of the church, to stare down at waxy Vati, staring up at the ceiling lights, melting his face. "You can kiss him if you want," Mutti said, but I pulled my arm away from hers, pulled away from my sisters, toward the front doors. In a minute, Vera was there. In another minute, she was holding my hand, leading me down the hill to the gaping hole waiting for my father.

Back in September, Vera and I sat on the porch behind her house and plucked wet grass that grew high past the garden. "I'll show you a trick," she said to me, and I thought I was in for another Jesus-lesson. School had just started and I already had exams in social studies, language arts, and Merry Miss classes.

I wanted to be Mormon so bad I could taste dust on my tongue when I thought of Christ pacing through the desert. After Merry Miss, two boys teased me that my navy blue dress was too sombre—better suited for attending a funeral. "Yeah," said the other, "it's fall, not winter, learn how to dress properly." Chastened about fashion by boys, I wasn't in the mood for another lesson.

Vera plucked the fattest stalk of grass she could see, and lay it along her left thumb until it touched her wrist. "This works with any grass," she told me, "but it's best in fall, when the grass is thick and reedy." She placed her right thumb neatly against the left, folded her hands over one another, and showed me the thin green line peeking between her knuckles. "Now, listen," she commanded, and brought her thumbs to her lips to kiss, but instead blew a note out of her fists, blew out the "Families Can Be Together Forever" song.

This wasn't a bad lesson. I plucked my own blade of grass, and blew holes into it the first time I tried.

"Keep it flat," Vera instructed me, "and press it as straight as possible." She held my fingers together and helped me position the fluttering green blade until I blew a thin, hollow note out from between my fingers. "Next time you need a song in your heart," Vera told me, "you've got an entire orchestra right outside your window."

A few months after this music lesson, Vera and I stood in the cemetery beside my father's grave-to-be, the cemetery strewn with greying snow and mucky leaves. We'd managed to miss the reception line-up after the ceremony, where Calgary Croatians gave condolences in my father-tongue. I stood, eyes closed, so I didn't have to stare at the empty hole. Vera took her hand out of mine, put her entire arm over my shoulder, and said, "They'll be here soon. I need to talk to you."

"Thanks, Vera." I tried to smile at her, tried not to look at the mound of earth piled between two spokes of the four-person cross.

"Let's sit," she guided me down beside her. We sat on a dry patch, but the earth was bitterly hard and cold.

"But your dress ..." Mutti always said grass stains were near impossible to get out, and who knew about multi-coloured leaf dye? What would Mrs. Kimball say if Vera stained her dress during a funeral?

"Never mind the dress, I'll rub it with white vinegar and molasses." She checked over my shoulder at the gently sloping cement path. "Listen, what was your father's middle name?" She found a blade of grass to pluck, slid it down along her thumb and wrist. Perhaps she meant to whistle? Maybe she knew a good funeral dirge that would make me sad, but hopefully face the future? Perhaps I should blow on grass, too, so we could vibrate in harmony?

"What? I dunno. I mean, he didn't have a middle name." *My parents couldn't afford it*, he said, when I asked him once.

"If you give me his middle name, my mom can pass it on to the bishop, and he can be baptized next month. Sooner, if you want." No whistling, then, this was another quiz.

"What?" I could still see Vati's nose balanced beneath his eyebrows, his eyelids glued closed, his lips sutured together. "No, Vera, he really didn't have a middle name. I mean, thanks. I mean, that's really great of you to offer, but Vati never wanted to become more than 49 percent Mormon." If even that, I thought to myself, but didn't want to hurt her feelings. She was ruining her dress on wet grass with me. For me.

"That doesn't matter," she smiled comfortingly, patted my back. "You know he doesn't have to be Mormon to be baptized." Then she closed her eyes, tilted her face toward the sky, and recited: "Behold I say unto you that ye shall have hope through the atonement of Christ and the power of his resurrection, to be raised unto life eternal."

"Moroni, Chapter Seven." We'd studied that in Merry Miss class. "You left a part out," I told her, "that verse continues: 'And this because of your faith in him according to the promise'." I giggled. Here we were, practicing the *Book of Mormon* at my father's gravesite. "My dad never made any promises to Christ, certainly not Moroni's Christ." And I grabbed at a wilted blade of grass, perhaps if I blew a strong enough note, we'd move on from today's lesson.

"Well ..." Vera knitted her brow. "Maybe it was Chapter Eight, then." She shrugged. "The point is, he doesn't have to have chosen the Mormon way to be baptized *now*." Then she thought for a moment. "It'd be better, of course, if he'd converted on his own. He won't get into the best heaven this way." I could see Vera thinking about the afterlife's levels of reward. She had a father, brothers, multiple sisters and nephews and nieces, and would sooner than not have a husband to bring her into the top level paradise. Was she worried for Vati or for me? "And when you marry Mormon, you'll be with your husband, not your father, during eternity. But at least he'll be in a heaven of sorts, at least he'll be saved."

How to explain my family to a Kimball? "Look," I began slowly, "I wish I could have talked him into Jesus while he was alive. Your Jesus. *Our* Jesus. But when he got sick, he became more and more Catholic." I took a breath. "My father doesn't want to be Mormon," I hugged her. "Not before he died and not now. Not ever."

"I don't think you understand," she hugged me back, "all we need is his name." She pulled back and tried to guide her smile into me.

"And for him to be dead, right?" I spat out the words. "You can't baptize him against his will when he's alive, but now it's open season?" I threw a clump of grass down, and the wind whipped a few of the blades away from where we were sitting, over to the dugout cross that would soon enfold my father. "He doesn't want to be Mormon. Understand this simple thing. He's Croatian, not American. He's Catholic, he believes in priests and saints and the Virgin Mary." I had no idea if Vati had actually believed any of those things. Or if, just before he died, he was hedging his bets with a religion that brought him closer to his Croatian childhood. "He believed in crosses, for *God's sakes*, we buried him in a grave the shape of a Catholic cross!" The first time I ever swore. "Let him stay dead in peace, okay? Leave him alone!"

Vera picked herself up, brushed leaves off the back of her pale dress, and left the grave site. She continued up the asphalt road in the direction of the cars with their headlights on, all descending toward me and my father's ready grave.

Such a little argument, such a minor episode of swearing. But *goddamn it*, my father's the one who died, my child passport into heaven who went first, leaving his family all alone.

Tournament Score Card

The first purchase Darius and I made together when we moved into our apartment was our dog. And not just any crossbreed, Darius wanted a purebred Great Pyrenees. Chatterly's Circus Clown. Long-haired, white, and huge. "That's not real alliteration," Mutti said when I told her the name. "You may write it with three Cs in a row, but they each sound different to the ear." Darius spent days and days taking Circus for morning walks, brushing his thick coat, hunting down dairy farms that sold rank cottage cheese, cheap. Circus was good at lying around on the kitchen floor. His coat was too warm for prairie summers, or heated, indoor prairie winters. He should have been high in the Pyrenees—or at least roaming through the Rockies—scrambling over snow, padding across thin bridges of ice. But house signified pet, just as apartment signified "shacking up." Darius, the Mormon boy who didn't go on a mission, who went into med school instead of dentistry, who pierced an ear and wore jeans on Sunday, Darius wanted a house and a dog and a legalized spousoid. I knew Vera thought "living in sin" was a sin, but I didn't know Mormons could boomerang back to childhood values just as fast as immigrant kids. Faster, in this case.

When we took Circus out walking, Darius tried to teach him to sit, heel, stay, sit, no sit, sit *sit*. After a while, Darius conceded he was too busy with med school and weight training to walk Circus every night. I'd come home from the Teen Centre, crash on the couch for an hour, rouse myself enough to stir-fry peapods and carrots, lie on the couch for an hour digesting, then walk Circus into the night. Nobody tried to talk to me or walk beside the path as long as this big, lunky dog loped along beside me. Circus snuffled wet grass, dusty newspapers, clumps of dandelions, garbage cans, rows of hedges, other dogs' asses, and the corner of every building. The walks took hours, but we never wandered that far. A drop of pee here, a drop there. Circus rewriting his route, outlining the radius of his leashed nightlife.

* * *

Darius and I called each other "lover" and "spouse" in ancient Greek. We could do this in front of most people without revealing our gushiness. "Hey, Gunike, pass the salt, eh?" he'd say, and "Sure thing, Aner," I'd reply.

When Darius travelled, he wrote cards, love promises I would read only after he'd already been back for days.

Where are you when I need you?! This seminar has turned out to be pure garbage, in my humble opinion, I have nothing but contempt for the pathetic, deluded, intellectually stunted groupies that constitute the better part of neurologists, these guys are really putting one over on us. Most of these morons worship brain surgery.

On his first day of med school, Darius and the other students found notes in their lockers detailing their study schedules, their on-call schedules, even how often they should wash their white lab coats. Included was an invitation from the coffee shop across the street from the hospital for free coffee. "You are entering the most important career a person can choose," said the note. "We respect how busy and overworked doctors in this city are. Please walk right past the line-ups—no matter how long—for a free coffee. Any time, as long as you wear your lab coat as an indicator of your new medical status." The note was signed, "The Management," and punctuated with a happy face. Every year, the hospital interns put these notes in first-year med students' lockers. Every year, at least one greenhorn believed wearing lab attire deserved extra privileges. Darius came home his first day, complaining that the teenager working at the coffee shop threw a Styrofoam cup at his head when he butted in front of four other customers.

The tournament is a blast, The Minch has won seven in a row. Phil doesn't even stay for the after-game analysis anymore. I should place second or at least third, the judges have let three cheats by unnoticed, there's one woman Grandmaster, but it's rigged.

My scribbles back were fragments of: *I miss your hair. I miss the veins on the back of your hands. I miss your fill-in-the-blank.* I was in love in love in love, but I wasn't deluded; the letters didn't arrive at his hotel until days after he'd checked out.

Hey Gunike, the tournament sucked but the brick houses are cool. To adapt one of Bruce Lee's finer attempts at profundity: discussion is like the finger pointing to the moon, look not at the finger pointing, but at the splendour of the moon being pointed to. Now that's po-tree!

Then the Teen Centre sent me to my first conference. The Alberta government funded a study comparing our Teen Centre to American-run institutions. My supervisor was overloaded with court appearances and *her* supervisor was off for three weeks. I got along with my boss, wrote reliable reports, and not one kid had ever "run" during any of my shifts. That was luck, but shone as a gold star in my file. That, and my night supervisor promotion gave me the authority to represent the Teen Centre at conferences. Nothing happened during night shift, except when everything happened at once. The kids slept heavily, not usually waking even if there was a disturbance. But if there was going to be action, it would come in the middle of night shift. Any staff member who fell asleep during shift was immediately fired. Kids waited till after three a.m. to try to break out. The promotion to administration took away the danger. And the excitement. At the conference, nobody talked about "kids," they were all "clients" and "subjects."

Darius, naturally, expected letters, but I didn't have the gift. I bought postcards depicting a twenty-foot-tall donut and the LA freeway at night, then read my Simenon mystery. *I miss you. I miss you. I miss you. Kiss the Clown for me.* The next day was filled with panels discussing the Delinquent vs the Offender. I added, "Americans are crazy," in a quick P.S. When I got home, I slipped the thing through our mail slot while Darius was busy pulling my bags out of our old beater.

❋   ❋   ❋

Easter, and a chess tournament loomed in Montréal. At the new Media Centre. Usually, in Calgary, the chess club met in community centres, the boards set up on tables that very recently entertained bingo. But this Montréal tournament presented itself as classy. "It's because of the European connection," Darius told me. "They're even giving hotel discounts for the players."

"Quite the step-up from the hallowed hockey change room we had to play in last time, eh?" Phil nodded his head slowly, closed his eyes, and sniffed the air to give off an aura of contemplation. "International Chess Masters of the World: come squat and hunch over our skinny rec-room benches."

Darius took the bait. "I still can't believe that kind of a double booking. And then the-powers-that-be gave the *boy scouts* preferential treatment over a serious tournament." Darius *always* took the bait.

"I think that was the idea," I wanted to turn Darius's objection into part of a serious discussion, and not just that he'd tripped into Phil's sarcasm pit. "You know, because they're young, they don't have the patience and concentration of you guys." Say what you want about chess players, they can sit and stare at inch-long square rows for *hours*.

"Yeah, sure, take the kids' side," Darius retorted. "You always take their side."

At the tournaments—whether it's a crowded hockey change room or an official hotel conference room—lines and rows of chess players sit beside concurrent games and study a checkered, square-inched world. The players themselves look like a chess board, so full that not a single piece can move. Until several hours pass, a few of the games end, and those players who are triumphant or else ousted push their chairs back, stretch their arms above their heads, and creep around the room peering at the other games. The players still playing may not move around, but they are far from immobile. Some twitch, some scratch repeatedly, some knock the first pawn taken against their arm or leg or the top of the table, if their opponent will let them. I used to think chess players were just neurotic. But during the week-long international tournament in Montréal, Phil pointed out that it was a very particular kind of neurosis.

"It's all about luck, m'dear," he explained. "Chess freaks are creatures of habit, polar bears pacing figure eights in the zoo. Some have lucky shirts, which is why a chess tournament has such a refined aroma by the third day." Phil sniffed the air again.

"Don't exaggerate," I warned him. We were just getting to know each other. It was the sixth day of a seven-day tournament, and Phil usually managed to finish his games early. Because he didn't care about winning and because he was good enough to wipe away players whose scores were artificially higher than his. Players who, like Darius, got their scores bumped up just before a tournament, but unlike Darius, weren't good enough to pull off a win. Right after a tournament, Phil wanted to lower his own rating again, so no one would accuse him of being a "professional" chess player, which was a joke Darius and Phil made about some of the players who tried to live off the paltry winnings available to chess players in Canada. After his games, we'd hang around together till Darius not only finished playing, but finished analyzing each play. We were all starving by night's end.

"You think I'm making this up?" Phil asked. "Darlin', a person does *not* have to make up weird stories about chess players, dig?" Then he ranted away, without checking to see if I dug or not. "See Juan Capablanca over there?" He pointed to a corner near where we stood. "Well, he forgot his saline solution back in

Peterborough. Not a big problem, he just didn't take his contact lenses out the first night. Then the drugstores were closed on Sunday, so he played another day without taking them out. By Monday, he'd won every game he'd played, and now he can't change anything, right? I'm surprised he can even see his opponent's moves." Sure enough, Juan Capablanca's eyes were glaringly red, protesting this abuse.

"But that's absurd," I said. "I'll go buy him some saline solution right away—that boy could damage his eyes. Not to mention how much they must hurt." Chess players aren't human, I thought.

"Don't bother, he won't use the stuff." We watched Juan Capablanca set his knight down beside his opponent's king. "He's a champ, d'you understand? He's won every game since he got here, and is going to make big money this tournament." Phil pulled at my wrist. But I couldn't take my eyes off Juan Capablanca's scalded red eyes. "Even if he loses *both* games tomorrow, he'll still place second, that's how far ahead he is," Phil told me. "He's playing Darius first thing in the morning and he's better than Darius." I had learned that chess players never complimented or insulted each other's skills. Phil wasn't being an unsupportive friend, Darius would have said the same thing. Phil motioned that we should grab a drink. "Chess players aren't human," he advised me. "Don't you know that?"

✳ ✳ ✳

Back then, back when Phil played chess, he'd play with me as well as with other professional players. Just for fun. Except that chess players never really play for *fun*. They play to pre-pare for tournaments, or they play to increase their World Chess Federation rating. Sometimes they play to decrease their status, so they can qualify for tournaments against less-skilled players. Phil would get together with a younger player who was trying to work his way up, and they'd agree to play, keep track of the moves, and mail the game in to the national chess federation. Where they'd be recorded as legal games, counting as much as tournament games. As long as both players signed the game score sheet, it counted toward their standing. Sometimes, Phil would agree to fill in the scores without actually playing a game—what was the point, if they both wanted the same result? It was cheating, but everybody did it, right? But usually, the two would play an actual game, because filling in the score sheets was much easier than making up a series of moves never played.

Sometimes, so it wouldn't take all day, the two chess masters would play speed chess, giving each other three minutes per move. Speed chess was a good way to practice, as it got the game into a tight position fast, and then left each player little time for anything other than reacting to the situation. But speed chess didn't count as tournament-regulation games. Three minutes, and the chess clock would bounce back and forth and the players' hands would sweep across the board, choosing this particular gambit, rejecting that particular sacrifice. I could fol-low for about fifteen moves, but no more. When I played speed with Phil, he gave me four minutes per move and gave himself ten seconds. It never helped.

"Hey!" I complained once. "Don't use *my* time for your thinking."

"I'm not stealing time from you, you've still got nearly four minutes left."

"But I only have a chance if you *don't* have four minutes!" I protested.

"Oh, honey," he soothed, "you don't really have a chance anyway. You know that, right?" he said, slipping his queen to safety and threatening two of my rooks at once.

"Thanks, friend." I conceded the game, but wished I'd at least come close to winning.

"But you're getting better," Phil reassured, in spite of the huge pile of my pieces by his elbow. "Besides," he told me, "you know this game's all about cheating anyway, right?" When I twisted my lips to one side of my mouth, Phil explained: "During tournaments, players must write down their moves after hitting their clock. But during blitz moments in the game, they don't want to waste precious seconds writing, so usually wait for a lull to record what they've played. Got it?" Sure, they don't want to bother with the paper work. "So a weaker player can take advantage of that, you see?" I didn't see. "Look, if players repeat the same moves three times in a row, that position creates a draw. A weaker player wants to draw; the stronger player wants to win. You following?"

"Yeah, weak players want to claim they tied with a strong player. So how is that cheating?" Even breaking the rules in chess was complicated.

"Because, if the stronger player has neglected to record every move and the weaker player writes down false moves, claims a repeating sequence took place that never did, the judges side with the player who's kept a record." I nodded then. Someone should write a book called *How to Cheat at Chess*. It'd be a best-seller with tens of readers.

"Always get it in writing," Phil concluded his lesson, scratching his nose.

Phil taught me many different ways to cheat at chess. But when I tell people this, they assure me I'm lying. "Chess," state all non-players authoritatively, "is a game at which one cannot cheat." Right. You can *always* cheat, Phil taught me. You just have to want to.

※　　※　　※

When Darius attended chess tournaments without me, or I flew off to give a teen seminar in another city, I usually dreamed about us going kaput. When I finally told him about the dream, he said I was predictably Freudian. He finished his one-month rotation in the psych ward and, on Labour Day long weekend, he flew to Toronto to play in the Canadian chess championship. I dreamed that we threw plates at each other's heads, and then he got together with Gabrielle. So I kissed Vera, whose belly protruded under an elegant pink mini-skirt. "Is this all you ever wanted?" I asked dream-Darius. "Is this all you ever wanted?" dream-Vera asked me. In the dream, I worried that the baby might be mine, and then I'd be stuck playing Old Maid and having missionary sex with Vera on top for eternity. But when Vera said, "No, it's not yours," I hurried to catch up with Darius, trudging away from me in his get-your-coffee-free lab coat.

※　　※　　※

Never ignore a mother's advice. Admittedly, a mother's advice shouldn't always be heeded, but I should never blatantly ignore direct instructions from the one who bore me.

So I guess I invited trouble.

"Come in," I said, when Vera knocked on our apartment door in her white sweater covering a white sleeveless shirt, and dress slacks that covered her—I had no doubt—white-on-white specially blessed underwear.

"Even vampires have to be invited into your home," Mutti said at our weekly Sunday meal. I was lining up the glasses with the forks, she was poking the roast with a serrated knife. She said it as if she were telling me how many more minutes till the roast was done.

"What? You don't watch TV, you never go to horror films. Is that a metaphor?" I plonked a plate down at her setting. The glassware shook.

"That's all I say." She grabbed three potatoes from the oven. "Don't break the dishes."

That's all I say—Mutti's favourite adage when she hadn't, yet, said anything. At least not clearly enough for me to get more than a gist. *That's all I say*—as if whole sermons had flooded past her lips and now her voice was spent, her throat raw.

It's not that I deliberately ignored my mother's words, it's just that I didn't always know how to interpret them.

"We're getting married," Vera announced, stepping into the living space that Darius and I used as front entrance, kitchen, dining room, and TV rumpus room. The bedroom fit our double bed and not much else. I worked nights, and Darius spent too many hours at the hospital. We didn't need much room.

In junior high, Vera invited me to a sleepover and Mutti said, okay. Seven girls. Blankets and pillowcases and duvets all piled on the rumpus room floor. Then we played the tickle game. All but one of the girls lie in a row, arms straight down beside our bums. The remaining girl moves along our heads, reaching to tickle our faces, our arms, our chests. The first one to move loses, becomes the tickler. I was fourteen with no boobs. Vera had practically full breasts and the other girls had at least the beginnings. When the second tickler started to reach down our nighties to make us gasp, I laughed right away so she wouldn't feel my prairie-flat chest. Then I was supposed to be the tickler. I stroked arms and bellies and under the girls' chins. No response. Now it was my turn to tickle some Mormon chests and I felt like the boy Vera dated who couldn't get her bra open. What was I supposed to do?

"C'mon," Vera urged me, the top button of her nightie already unbuttoned from the last tickler.

My fingers hesitated above her nipples. "Can't we play Risk or something?" I said and knelt beside the TV to dig out the board game. "There are enough of us to make Risk really exciting." The other girls bounced up to play, and then the tickle game was over. Vera lay on the floor among the blankets for a while, but eventually buttoned her nightie and joined us. She mouthed something to Tracy Alekhine that I was glad I couldn't lip-read.

Now, in my apartment, mine and Darius's, Vera's "we" reverberated around the front room and sank into the fraying couch. Not: "I'm getting married," or: "I'm marrying Joe Missionary," but "we" as if I'd know that of course she was a *we*, of course "we" would get married, and of course these should be the first words she said to me since I moved in with Darius.

"Yes," I answered, as if she'd posed a question, throwing my arm out against the front wall, inviting her to the couch beyond. "Don't mind the milk-crate coffee table." Shit, I shouldn't have said "coffee." Shit, I shouldn't have thought "shit."

"In December. In Cardston." She sat, stared at her white legs against the burgundy fabric of the sunken couch. She picked at the fraying cushions, and then said, "I want you to be my bridesmaid. Matron maid, whatever you call yourself." Matrons are married, and maids don't live in sin. When I wasn't in the same room as her, what did Vera call me?

I walked around my bike propped against the coffee table, filled the kettle for tea, then remembered. And only cola in the fridge. "Do you mean you want me to pretend to be married or you want me to pretend to be single?" I was making it hard for her, but I really didn't know what she meant by this proposal. Sister Kimball would not approve.

From her slumped position, Vera shrugged.

I took down two glasses and filled them with tepid water. "Vera." I said her name, but she continued picking at the couch fabric, as if ripping it off evenly would help its appearance. "I'm not. I don't. They won't." Somehow I couldn't say it. That I was a Jack Mormon, a Jacqueline Mormon? She shook her head in response. First a proposal and then forgiveness. What was next, confession? I barked out a laugh and Vera pulled her sweater tighter around her arms, stretching the material past her wrists.

"I know you've left the Church," she said, her voice sinking to prayer whisper. "You can't come to the wedding, it's at the temple," she looked up, finally, but out the kitchen window. "But I'm having a reception in Calgary the next week. You can be bridesmaid then." And she looked at me, right into my head where dozens of denials were racing to get out.

"Of course," I nodded, "I'll be your bridesmaid." Make or buy an expensive dress, and not even attend the ceremony. But what choice did I have but to agree? I had invited her in.

Night Shift

Before I ascended to administration heaven, I was one of the front-line workers at the Calgary Teen Centre for Junior Delinquents, which is what we called them before the courts converted the kids into Young Offenders in the mid-80s. The Teen Centre had two group homes, two detention holding pens, and two long-term lock-up facilities. We worked in rotation shifts, in teams. We were all cynical and callous and tyrannical about kids lining up in front of the office before breakfast, before lunch, before after-school hanging out in the rec area. Four cigarettes a day at the max, one swear word or inappropriate hand gesture or unwillingness to put the lights out when told subtracted one cigarette. They were legally too young to smoke, but none of us wanted to deal with thirty pubescent nicotine addicts freaking out from withdrawal at the same time. Besides, we had no other means of bribery: they wanted cigarettes and they wanted out, nothing else.

The year Darius and I brought home our dog, they promoted me to night supervisor. We'd walk our new puppy, then when Darius did 120 sit-ups and 80 push-ups, I strapped on my helmet and cycled off to work. When I wheeled my bike back into the apartment after seven a.m., I'd find Darius curled into a warm body covered with long white hair all over the duvet, barely room for me to scrunch in beside them. I spent the whole winter working detention, trying to convince my body that dawn was dusk.

＊　＊　＊

My dad had a life-long struggle with pillows. For years, he sought the perfect pillow—its shape, its insides, its covering. Mutti bought old winter down jackets at garage sales, tore them open so she could sew down blankets and pillows. The richness and give of those pillows reminded Mutti of Germany. You could sink your head into a pillow and disappear for the night— secure in that pillow's tender grab. But Vati fought even with those dream cushions, pushing and twisting, one piled upon another, so he could get the angle right for reading or drowsing or blocking out noise. My father, clasping one pillow inside his right elbow, his left arm curled around the oval pillow covering his head. These days, I jam against the headboard, my mother's down pillows piled on top of the flat Styrofoam ones I buy cheap at department stores, wanting the height so I can make notes while I work in bed. Working night shift wrecked my body for nighttime sleep. Instead, I sit up in bed, plan the next day's meetings, try to zonk out with a mystery novel, watch the clock: 1:15, 1:27, 2:04. I slip under the covers and move pillows from beneath my head to over my head to between my thighs.

I trained my body to stay awake all night and my body obeyed, even when I didn't want it to. By spring, the sun slanted onto my page long before I stopped reading. I paused, turned the page, read on. Once Darius accused me of sleeping all day while he worked hard, and I thought he was joking—I never see the ending until it's long past. When I was eight, I read the last paragraph of *Pippi Longstocking*, and was half-way through the author's bio before I realized that the book was over.

I entered the apartment, and Circus started yapping at my bike spokes. Darius woke up when I crawled into bed. "What's it like?" he asked, his voice lazy and full of syrup.

"Boring," I whispered, nuzzling his neck. "Go back to sleep."

"You always say that," he complained, pulling the blankets to his side as he flipped over. "You never tell me stories about work."

"Yeah, well, we're not allowed to tell their stories. We lock our words up with the kids when we leave in the morning." I pulled the blanket back toward my side, and tried not to hear the rush-hour traffic building outside.

The stories *were* boring. Boring, repetitive, and full of shoving and blood. After my second promotion, when I permanently moved into administration, working mostly with well-adjusted adults, I left my last night-shift sweating relief because I'd made it all those years without any kid dying. I didn't even know I'd been thinking that, but I fumbled among the pillows that morning crying.

✳ ✳ ✳

Friday night in detention, staff choose four boys to stay up late. Late night for the kids means one movie or two hours of TV. No raucous pool or foozball. I arrive at the Teen Centre seven minutes before eleven p.m., see two male co-workers amble to the downstairs dorm as I climb upstairs to the girls' dorm. Boys and girls don't mix after ten p.m., except the late-night boys have permission to watch TV until one a.m. The girls' dorm rooms surround the TV area, just as the boys' dorms surround the pool table and breakfast area downstairs. I turn down the sound, and the late-night boys hiss. Only two girls reside here tonight; I peek my head in each girl's room. Sound asleep. I haul myself down to our staff office which sits on the landing between the two dorms, read the communication book standing up. We need to be able to observe the dorms if we're on the telephone or filling in reports, so the staff office is almost entirely plexiglass. The room is barely closet-sized, but two people could fit among the binders, and video cassettes, and coffee maker—one standing, one sitting—but only one adult works in here at a time, and no teen may trespass. Ever. The office is crammed with court files, staff jackets, confiscated make-shift weapons, papier-mâché sculptures, and meds and meds and meds. I glance out and see the day-staff pull out their keys. They wave, but there's no time to chat. I pull out the communication book. Not much activity since I got off this morning at seven:

Afternoon kids had free period outside. Some passing teenagers threw rocks over the fence. Bobby threw them back, got an hour time-out.—Jake

Leroy and Steve got into a shouting match after supper. ½-hour time-out each in their rooms. They should also not be allowed late-night next week.—Reg

The nurse will set up in the upstairs classroom tomorrow, 8:00-11:00. Morning staff should make sure she examines every kid in Groups B and C.—Reg

Jerry got a phone call from a female claiming to be his mother. She sounded 15. He wasn't allowed the call.—Lila

Duncan's on tonight. I exit the office so he can read the book.

He's worked at the Teen Centre longer than I have, but we've only overlapped shifts for the past month and a half. He reads and I hover on the landing between dorms. Duncan's back from three days off, and so reads the communication book backwards from tonight. I can see the late-night boys, and most of the dorm rooms from the landing. The VCR blinks 11:01. Lila, the last of the day-staff, grabs her ski-jacket from above Duncan's head, and backs out the staff office doorway.

"Why did Jerry still get awarded a late-night?" Duncan asks Lila when her jacket sleeve brushes his forehead.

"Actually, he wasn't involved," says Lila. She steps away from the staff office, unlocks the heavy detention door leading to a public waiting room, pulling it open with her key. "We didn't tell him about it, so he's not upset. No problem." Then she hustles out. We never collect overtime in this place. Unless the kids riot. The exit door swings shut behind her.

"Bloody idiots," Duncan slams the book shut. He pours himself a coffee then joins tonight's temp worker, Tim, downstairs. There are fifteen boys in detention, only half asleep, and Tim's not used to working the lock-up unit. I close the office door, making sure the door clicks shut, step upstairs where the late-night boys wait for their movie. "What are we watching?" I direct the question to Jerry, slumped on the sofa, but it's Luther, the littlest, who answers.

"MuchMusic."

"No," Jerry says. "*The Warriors.*"

"Yeah!" the other two boys agree.

I already have it in my hands. "You realize I've seen this video a thousand times," I complain, shoving the video into the VCR.

"MuchMusic!" begs Luther, but he knows it's hopeless.

"We sold our cow," sings one of the boys sitting next to Jerry, deliberately taunting Luther. "We sold our cow. We have no use, for your *bull* now-ow-ow ..."

"Enough." I press play and gangs wearing leather uniforms and whipping chains face each other onscreen. Jerry gets up and clicks off the lights. I check the girls again, and since they're both asleep, let Luther make popcorn in the microwave. The boys devour it like they've had no late-night snack tonight, no supper tonight, no food all week, but I don't let them have another batch. Boys choose this movie every Friday late-night, but most fall asleep before the end.

One by one Duncan kicks their feet to send the boys down-stairs. Luther first, his eyes don't even open at Duncan's kick. "But I'm still awake," he pleads. Twenty minutes later, Jerry's the only kid still watching. Duncan stays on the couch with him while I go to the office to start tonight's entry in the com-munication book.

Luther to bed at 11:47, Tony and Rupert at 12:03. One batch of popcorn. No problems with Tony's shot. Tony has to inject insulin into his stomach in front of the staff. He usually tells staff that he's already done a shot with the previous shift. If he shouts that he wants to take the needle to the bathroom for some pri-vacy, we administer the shot for him. He hates that more.

I prop the office door open with a winter boot while I write. This is against the rules, but it's stifling in the tiny office. Even the communication book pages curl.

Just after Duncan and I started this rotation together in February, the detention kids planned a riot. They heard the heavy detention door slam shut behind the day staff, waited five minutes, then a bunch of boys rushed at Duncan. He was savvy enough to throw his keys into the staff office and slam the door shut. Then he turned and faced thirteen hostile boys, plus three screeching girls.

Beyond the heavy door leading to the waiting area, another locked door separates this building from the street. The kids wanted staff keys. Some of the boys were twelve years old, many of them around seventeen. I was on the other side of the detention door, in the waiting area admitting an Overnight Courtesy. Besides me and the lurching drunk boy, two cops leaned against the desk, but none of us heard the shouting through the thick walls. "Courtesy" meant a kid who was too drunk for the cops to charge officially. He couldn't or wouldn't give a home address, so they brought him to us. The rioting kids couldn't break through the plexiglass in the office, though they pounded and threw chairs. They wanted out and they knew that I'd be back. Duncan couldn't get into the office to call me at the front desk, the kids couldn't get his keys. They surrounded Duncan, but didn't hit him. His back against the wall, his mug flung down when they rushed him, coffee seeping into the carpet. They all waited—a riot of waiting.

But unfortunately for their better-than-usual plan, the Courtesy was not only drunk, but crawling with lice, too. I called Duncan to get the kit ready. He'd have to take the kid into the shower while I covered the dorms. Duncan wasn't picking up the phone. I called again. No answer. Shit!

I left the drunk kid passed out on the desk, ran into the parking lot after the two cops. Then the three of us, plus a confused drunk teenager I manoeuvred by the elbows, shot through two sets of locked doors into the dorms. The rioting boys scattered at the sight of uniforms. The cops hung around until a couple of yawning on-call workers clocked in. Duncan and the cops stood downstairs, I made sure the girls upstairs didn't budge from their rooms. Next day, staff put every kid on permanent time-out for two weeks solid, and Duncan got a letter in his files for not maintaining hold on his set of keys, though if he'd tried to hold them those boys would have yanked at his fingers, bending back the digits that clutched his keys in a fist. Duncan calculated all this while dorm doors slammed and feet rushed up the stairs. At him. He was quick enough to figure out a way to safely lock his keys inside the staff office. If it'd been me, I might have tried to reach the office and the telephone, to push the door shut from the inside. Who knows if I'd have made it?

The Teen Centre's board promoted me. For being scared shit-less, I guess. And for bringing in the uniforms. So I had two more weeks left of my detention nights rotation, then it would be permanent days in administration. Not just a promotion in pay, but also outside my area of expertise. That's where doing good work gets you.

I pick up the popcorn bowl, dump the unpopped kernels into the garbage can. Duncan comes upstairs one last time. "You got a phone call today, Jerry," he tells the boy. Jerry's fixed in his seat, Duncan bent over the couch. "Sounds like it was Doreen."

Jerry shifts in his seat, but doesn't look away from the screen. A good number of the Warriors get eliminated, one by ragged one. Jerry shrugs. "She shouldn't even try while I'm stuck in this joint," he finally says, then follows Duncan down to the dorm without watching the end of the movie.

Jerry has been admitted to the detention unit often, knows all sorts of tricks for getting around the rules. Duncan wants to set up trust, and lying to the kids won't get him there. "What's the point?" he asks me. "They find out anyway. There isn't a single street tidbit our kids don't hear about within twenty-four hours. And when they do, they think we always lie." Day staff don't see it that way. Easier to just nip trouble in the bud. "They aren't exactly tulips," Duncan tries to argue, but he's splayed up against the bureaucratic wall. One of the reasons those boys last month didn't attack Duncan physically is they wanted to escape without assault charges. But another reason is that they *do* trust Duncan. He's always straight with them. "How else do you get them to grow up, for fuck's sake?" he demands.

Duncan will never get promoted.

For the rest of the night, we alternate our rounds with the new on-call staff, Tim. Used to be one worker on each floor, but since the riot, it's been me, Duncan, and one on-call worker every night.

Quiet night, I write at 4:32 a.m. *All kids asleep by 1:25.* I check to see the girls are all sleeping, not missing, not hanging by their sheets, not slipped down into any of the boys' rooms. A boring night is a good shift. I fill out the paperwork on court stats for the morning. Three for Juvenile Court, one for Preliminary. I make a note in the communications book: *Two of the kids are from Group B, they should see the nurse first.* But the morning staff—who have to wake up the kids and get them off to school all within forty-five minutes—will not read it until after the court van has hauled kids downtown. I should remember to tell Nora. I stick a post-it on the office plexiglass. Then I open my mystery, the bookmark stuck exactly in the middle. Working nights, I can read three a rotation. In less than two weeks, it'll be day after day of administration paperwork, no stretches of time for solving mysteries.

When the phone rings a few hours later, I'm still reading.

"Hello." I open the communication book, in case I have to record another "mother" calling late, who just has to speak to her darling boy. "Detention unit."

"This is Sergeant Coe at the front entrance. We have two Courtesy Holds for you—one girl, one boy."

"Be right there, thanks." Shit, *two*. And it's almost 5:30 a.m. I press the bell and Duncan meets me at the detention door. "Duncan, hi, we got two Courtesies." I look down the stairs. "I'll need help admitting them, but we shouldn't leave Tim alone on the unit. He hasn't done many shifts in detention." But I don't enjoy pulling rank on Duncan with so few shifts together left to us.

"He's never done a Courtesy before," he says, meaning he'd rather leave him alone with fifteen sleeping boys than send him down to admit one drunk and disoriented delinquent.

On the other side of the door, two police officers are each handcuffed to a teenager. The woman to a girl with blue hair, the man to a larger boy who thrashes violently when Duncan unlocks the door. The boy's shaking, and his legs kick the air. Only the cop's weight prevents the boy from banging against the cement wall. The policeman hugs the boy against himself, twists the boy's arms behind each other, and drags him into the waiting room. The policewoman and the girl follow.

"She's just drunk, but he's high as shit," the policeman shouts. "Chain him to a bed or something."

"We don't tie them, we don't chain them," I tell him.

But it's much too late for cop/caseworker banter.

The cop lets go of the boy, who staggers and hits his head on the doorknob, nearly passing out. Duncan grabs him and wraps his arms around the boy's chest. The girl starts crying when the policewoman uncuffs her, so I hold her by her free wrist and we head toward the detention door. She stinks of puke, but doesn't resist. "You guys should take him to the hospital for a detox," I say over my shoulder. Duncan gives me *the look* as I unlock the door to detention and lead the girl in.

Charlotte's charged with being drunk in a public place. Since that's all, the court will probably release her to her parents in the morning, once she's sober. I'll add her to the court list, but she and the boy might have to wait a day, if the court roster is already full. She follows me to the showers. "Who else is in here? Is Tina here? She's a riot. Where's my phone call?" she asks. Now that she's free of the cops, she cheers up, and her voice sails around the dorm, the smell of scotch leaking into the air.

"Where's my phone call?" she yells out while she showers and changes into clean Centre nightclothes. When I point her toward one of the dorm rooms, she screams, "I get my phone call, bitch," then stumbles onto the bed. She makes retching noises, but then passes out without vomiting.

I note her belongings in the communication book. Charlotte has pink jeans, a pink sweater, black bra, no underwear, and twenty-three cents in nickels and pennies. In the morning, she'll swear she came in with a black leather jacket and a twenty-dollar bill, and where the hell are they? I write down what time we admitted them, and what time Charlotte passed out, and then my initials. 6:04 a.m. I poke my head into the other two girls' rooms. They've thrown off their covers, but otherwise don't look like they've moved since my shift began. Charlotte's already asleep, too, so I go down to the boys' dorm.

Duncan sits on the Courtesy's bumping legs while Tim tries to hold the flailing arms. The boy's face-down on the carpet, not screaming, but his body jerking. "Goddamn cops aren't supposed to dump the psychos on us, right?" Tim looks up at me for confirmation and gets an escaped elbow in his face. The boy's arm rips from Tim's hands, and he scuttles into a corner. Duncan yells at Tim to hold his arms, dammit, just his arms, but Tim remains out of reach, holding onto his own jaw with both hands.

I kneel down on one of the boy's arms, and try to grab the other one. "It's too close to seven in the morning, Tim. A hospital admittance takes too many forms, which means the cops wouldn't be able to bring him back till past seven." Duncan's trying to hold the legs still. "They want him to get a court appearance as soon as possible. And since it's Thursday morning, if they took him to detox for a night, he might end up here all weekend. We can't keep kids locked up that long without a court appearance." As supervisor, I have to explain, but Tim should already know all this, he's probably just dazed from the slugged jaw.

"This kid's 180 pounds and crazy stoned!" Tim wants to argue the justice of us taking on kids we're not equipped to handle.

"Sometimes it just doesn't make sense," I add. I push my

knees against the inside of the boy's elbows. Duncan's managed to sit on both legs and hold his back still. He's yelling, but his voice comes out more of a gargle than a scream. I don't want to be mean to Tim, but there's no arguing about the rule book when things don't go the way they're *supposed* to. Not in this place. Not on night shift. "Go up to the girl's dorm and stand in the TV area. The new girl's passed out so shouldn't be a problem, but make sure she doesn't wander out of her room, okay?" Tim shouldn't be alone in the girl's dorm, but we've got a situation. "Tim, if *any* girl wakes up, call me immediately, okay?" I turn back to the struggling elbows. So far, none of the boys have woken up.

Tim unfolds himself from the corner, moves past the boy battling to flip Duncan off his legs. I'm solid on his arms and Duncan now lies across the boy's entire body, his legs on the boy's legs, his chest against the boy's back. We're both sweating, but the boy's shakes seem to be subsiding. Slightly.

"Don't go in unless she starts banging or something," I manage to say to Tim, before he leaves the room. "And call me if she does. *Before* you go in." I try to give Duncan *the look*, but he's holding on for the ride, his face lost in the boy's wide shoulders. If even one boy wakes up and tries to run, we'll have another riot, but detention kids can sleep through earthquakes.

The Courtesy's winding down and Duncan sits back up, still holding the boy's legs. Maybe he'll pass out until it's time for court. I ease off his elbows and he doesn't react. Then a thumping from upstairs and Charlotte howls. No words, just supernatural howling.

"Shit. Can you hold him by yourself?" Duncan nods and I

stand slowly, like maybe the boy won't notice. Duncan places his own arms overtop the boy's. The ride seems to be over, but he lies back over the boy's torso, just in case. They look like one person from the top of the stairs, then I turn and rush to the new girl's room.

"I just went in to give her an extra blanket," Tim explains apologetically. "Then she started that terrible noise." Tim's a new temp worker, so he's not completely up-to-speed.

"Tim, don't disturb a Courtesy who's already fallen asleep—it makes no sense. When they wake up, they don't know where they are, they don't know how they got here. And all they see is *you*." Tim's used to the open policy at the group home where no doors are locked. "If that boy starts up again, you'll have to go down, okay?" Tim nods, but I hope it won't be necessary. At least Charlotte isn't hurting herself—just wailing—but Duncan shouldn't be downstairs alone, pinned to one boy. "Charlotte!" I shout, then walk toward the figure rocking on the bed. "It's okay, Charlotte, you're in detention. You came in a few hours ago. You'll attend court in the morning." I reach out for her shoulder.

"You fuckers won't let me phone my mom." Charlotte knocks my hand away. "I'm not shit-faced, I had one beer, them cops pick me up for *nothin'*." She assesses my reaction, which hasn't been one. "You bitch. *You* don't care." I let my arm fall back to my side. She won't take comfort, then. It's going to be nasty. Her crying is half gulps, half screams. She jumps up and stands on her bed. "You fuckers won't let me phone my mom!" Her voice gains momentum, then she falls ass-down, like she's on a trampoline. "You tell the cops I'm drunk but I'm not! My boyfriend finds out, he'll kill all of yous. You *pretend* you care, but you don't care. None of you care *shit!*" Then she spits, forcefully and accurately, onto my left cheek. She freezes, shoots a hand up to stop what she thinks will be an incoming blow. I stand completely still, don't even wipe at my face, and Charlotte collapses in a heap. And then she's sobbing normal sobs.

"Okay, she'll just sleep now," I report to Tim, who's wiping his own face as if the spittle could fly out the door and around the corner to where he stands. I wipe the spit off my cheek with my sleeve and say, "I'll be downstairs."

I don't have to tell Tim not to go into Charlotte's room again. He squats by her door, elbows on his knees, his back rigid. The effort of her breathing wafts the stench of alcohol down the halls. The Courtesy boy starts gargling again, but no thrashing. I rush toward the noise, leave Tim crouching by Charlotte's door, rubbing his jaw, wiping invisible spittle, and waiting for the morning shift to release him back into day.

Since the Depression

I met Darius at a church dance. My last. After Vati died, I stopped going to church regularly, I stopped risking a swear word near Vera's ears. But when I passed her house, my eyes would probe the windows, trying to pick out each Kimball during Family Home Evening, playing Old Maid without gambling that the loser had to wash the dishes. Then, just as I finished high school and she came back for the summer from her first term at Brigham Young University, Vera invited me to a dance. I hadn't been inside her ward in over a year. The convicted murderer and Mormon-born Gary Gilmore had chosen execution by firing squad in Utah, a revelation from God changed church policy to now allow black men to be ordained into the priesthood, and temple garment fashion switched from a one-piece long underwear style to a two-piece. Given all that—what to wear?

I showed up late so she'd arrive at the dance first. She waved when she saw me, didn't seem surprised or disappointed. Or pleased. We hugged and she asked the boy standing with her to get her some punch. Soon as he left, she pointed. "Jack's here," Vera said, introducing me to the cute guy with longer hair than most Mormon men, but a smooth face, sipping from an orange soda, emphasizing his drowned-out-by-music sentences with his free hand. I could see he had a hole in his left ear, but nothing dangled there. He wasn't wearing a suit, not even dress pants.

In fact, we wore the same Roadrunner jeans, except mine were recycled into a skirt, years before recycling became the trend. Mutti wasn't about to throw out perfectly good clothes just because my inseams frayed. I put on the skirt because it was a Mormon dance and I had to show up in a dress. The other girls wore icing-cake blues and hospital greens. As usual, I was halfway—unwilling to dress up like a doll, but not brave enough to risk spreading my groin in slacks. The cute boy stood comfortably in his jeans, which made me wonder why he'd go to the bother to come to a Mormon dance without the uniform.

Except it turned out his name wasn't Jack, he was a "Jack Mormon," no longer going to church, yet not entirely divorced from his faith. "You two have a lot in common," Vera told me, then whizzed away toward her own boy, leaving me to ask silly "what's it like not being Mormon anymore?" questions of a boy whose name I'd gotten wrong before I even talked to him. The music was loud enough, and dancing took care of a good part of the evening, though Darius wouldn't dance the slow ones. But just before eleven o'clock he leaned in and whispered through my hair. "Let's be bad," he suggested. "Let's you and I go get a coffee."

❋　❋　❋

Darius was the only guy I've ever been with who had intercourse without touching his partner. "Let's green-Smartie it," he'd say, squeezing a wisp of his hair from behind his left ear. Pushing the hair back behind his ear again. Letting go. He stood on one side of the bed, I on the other, undressing. I used to think it was me undressing that sent the Smartie message that it was time for intercourse. I was young then.

We lived in a typical Calgary high-rise: walk in, closet on your right, kitchen on your left. Straight down the hall to a square living room. On one wall, a door to the bedroom, on the other a bathroom door. Given my income back then, we should have been living in a basement rental, like everyone else we knew, but Darius wanted a place near the hospital. And with a good bed. "If I work nights, I need to get home and to bed, fast." I worked nights then too, but we didn't live near the Teen Centre. "You work until seven in the morning, so it's day already." He pointed out the kitchen window where night stared back at us. "I work thirty-six hours in a row and come home at four a.m., sometimes, and then have to go *back* at seven." So we lived in a building with grey-haired joggers, newly-invented yuppies who couldn't afford a house yet, and the occasional papa-supported student.

When I nodded to his Smarties proposal, Darius would leave the lights on, climb over the sheets to my side, and grab my breasts—one handful per hand. Grab and twist just a bit. Then he'd roll us onto our sides, so we faced each other. "So we can gaze into each other's eyes," he said while I pulled the blankets over me. He wasn't cracking a joke. In those days, especially with how low Darius kept the thermostat, I thought not touching was a novelty, that we were developing our sex life by focusing on romance. I was young then. We'd lie shoulder-to-shoulder, him gazing, and me chewing words instead of saying them out loud. I could smell his apricot shampoo. Only his stiffened penis rubbed against me. Then he'd cock a leg and pull down my panties with his big toe. Sometimes they'd get stuck at my knees and I'd squirm around until they flipped off. When I did that, he'd arch his back so my knees didn't scrape his.

Still lying on our sides, I'd lift one leg and his penis would go in fast. Facing his face, I'd stare at his tear ducts, their red rims reassuring me he'd had enough protein today. I could smell cinnamon and oranges from the apartment above. It made me think of our old-lady neighbours drinking tea, sitting side-by-side watching *Mary Tyler Moore* reruns. They were two women who'd been friends since the Depression, now living together. To share the costs of rent and groceries and cable. I was young then.

For music, Darius liked the Beach Boys, partly for rhythm and partly to make sure those spinster neighbours heard nothing else. "People aren't stupid," I told him. "It's the only time we ever turn on the record player." I drew the fingers of my left hand along his right thigh. He let me. Our bodies lay stiff and parallel. I slipped down the bed a bit and leaned my belly into his left thigh. He inched toward his side of the bed. "If they even care," I added. While I reached over to turn down the noise, he just hung onto my breasts.

I didn't try to pull away; grabbing my breasts during intercourse was the only time he touched my nipples. "They may *think* they know what we're doing. They may *guess*," Darius conceded, repositioning our bodies so that we rhymed again: two lines close, but not quite touching, "but they don't hear anything but 'good good good, good vibrations'."

The two spinsters lived right above us. Sometimes Rose got off on our floor and walked me to my door. "Calgary's first oil boom lasted three-and-a-half months, did you know that?" she asked me the first time we found ourselves both digging out our keys at my door. But it was more of a ruse than forgetfulness, Rose trailing me. She liked to finish a story she'd started in the elevator. She was born during the roar of the 1924 Turner Valley oil boom. "Middle of the night, on the way to the hospital," she told me as she dropped her key into her clasp purse and turned away from my door. "My parents said the sky lit up like it was the middle of the day. From oil flares at the rigs over twenty miles away! Boom lasted three years, that time. Everything was hot." I imagined Rose's apartment as blazing hot, the two women wearing undershirts and not needing covers at night. "The companies started burning oil in the fields, to drive the price up." The next time Rose and I met was in the laundry room.

She said her life was an arrow from one twentieth-century self-indulgent decade through to another. "The early 20s to the early 80s—people wanting money more than food," she said, as we folded our matching old-lady panties. Hers at least had flowers decorating the elastic bands. Mine had elastic bands so loose they looked chewed. What was the point of sexy underwear if Darius just stretched and dragged them off with his toes before he even saw them? He'd slip his penis inside, rock back and forth, making sure his stomach didn't touch mine. I'd push my chest against the palms of his hands and gyrate so his calluses from lifting weights would chafe my areolas. Then I'd moan and he'd come. I picture Darius in those days leaning away from me in a January wind. I wanted to swallow him whole, inhale the base of his pores, warm my skin by entering his.

Rose and I chatted sometimes when she stood in the lobby waiting for her ride to yoga class. She'd started yoga a few months before, on the day she turned sixty. She didn't talk about the present much; instead, she talked about the Depression as if it would come back and swallow the city. "People think they know what those times meant," she told me as, shivering, I pushed the thirteenth-floor button for me and the fourteenth for her. Most buildings skip the thirteenth floor, but the developer must have been a realist. Rose wore a sleeveless top, jacket in her left hand, yoga mat in her right. The skin on her arms wobbling enthusiastically as she breathed out peppermint tea and hot chocolate. "But they can only picture farmers in dustbowls, hobos lining up for soup." She stepped spritely off on my floor so she could finish her sentence. The elevator doors closed, and she pressed the up button. "But not getting enough was a condition we all shared, those of us on farms and those in the cities." The elevator chinged open and she stepped in. "The first time I ate a pomegranate, I was eighteen years old." She held the door open with one hand. "Best sex I ever had." The elevator punctuated my wintry intake of breath.

Darius didn't love his own body. He loved the *idea* of his body—its potential, its ever-more-bulbous body-building prospects. In between work and chess, he trained for weightlifting contests. He was the best chess player in Alberta, but only fourth Strongest Man. He'd oil up his skin after a shower and stare at his triceps. Twist around and clench to make the muscles bigger. "No pain, no gain," he said, when I asked why he lifted more weight that he could safely carry. Or when I suggested we turn up the heat. "As long as you don't think about your body, you can make it take anything."

Not thinking about his body didn't mean ignoring the essentials. Pasta and vegetables and diet-shakes every day were vital for bulking up. But food was also for shunning: no donuts from the shop beside our building, no chips from my shopping cart, not even popcorn at the movies. There were try-outs every month, and a big tournament twice a year. Darius ignored his body enough to gain seven pounds two months after we moved in together. I lost that amount from shivering alone.

"You need willpower," he cautioned. "Move around more. Get into an exercise routine."

When we first met, I'd just read an article about how the mythic green Smarties don't make you any hornier than any other colour. The rumour that they *did* made it onto the evening news. Darius and I had heard two radio guys making innuendos about "the green ones" on the drive to our seventh date. He'd borrowed his dad's Pinto and had to be home by ten. Not much time for making out. And talking about chocolate-induced aphrodisiacs was a bit dicey of a topic for a not-quite-yet-a-couple. It was that "not quite" that had me worried. Maybe he wasn't interested? Maybe he was dating someone else? But then why keep asking me out? At the Italian pizzeria, we ordered pesto and I got giggly about the "green Smarties" code. "Yeah," Darius said, picking at his anchovies, his doctor-to-be voice scathing about the genius who wanted to market green-only Smarties, "the chocolate that helps guys score!" And though I was willing, he just dug into his pizza and drove me home.

On our eighth date—another movie and another pizza joint— I gave him a fancy gift-wrapped ring box when he walked me to Mutti's door. In a sexy voice I said, "For next Friday, wink

148

wink," except my voice came out a cross between a nineteen-year-old's and a ninety-year-old's. In other words, Eartha Kitt's Cat Woman, with a rising squeak. "Consider this an after-dinner delight." Then I took a chance, pecked him on the chin, and bolted in the front door, not caring if Mutti heard.

For the record, green Smarties in the early 80s were a *rarity*. Every box offered lots of red, a ton of brown, some pinks, and a few yellows. Often a box had *no* green ones, two at the max. I had to buy fifteen boxes just to collect a miniature pile of nine.

My older self is proud of my younger self. After seven dates with no kisses, I'd made a move. Then, after yet another martial arts movie, Darius drove up past the Mormon Church across the street from Puckers' Peak, parked overlooking the river, and showed me the box he'd unwrapped already. "Are you trying to propose to me?" he said, and I saw that he hadn't shaved that day, scruff crawled across his usually infant-smooth face. He was so young then. I giggled because I'd used up all my clever with the Smartie, just undid my jacket, but stopped there. I wasn't sure what our bodies were supposed to do next. After a few minutes of just looking, Darius reached over and undid my blouse. Before he even kissed me, I'd managed to fog up the windows. If any deacons stepped out of the church, they'd see nothing but foggy windows and a slightly shivering form leaning across the handbrake.

Darius had my bra up under my chin before I even knew he'd unsnapped it. I leaned over to kiss him, my lips just beginning to taste his lips, when he stopped me. "I've got a sore throat," he said, "better not." So I kissed his neck and cheeks and shoulder blades and my nipples lit up like elevator buttons and turned as red and hard as pomegranate seeds. For a while, I kissed his neck and he grabbed my breasts, and then he drove me home. It wasn't until I was inside the door—shoes off, breasts on fire, and sneaking down the stairs without turning on the lights— that I realized that Darius had used my Smarties invite in a half-assed way, but we hadn't actually eaten any. No donuts, no chips, no chocolate—not even to "help a guy score."

By the time we moved in together, Darius's sore throat was "permanent." I gave up asking for a stroke or a lick, and just touched myself. He'd let his penis in, and keep his hands on my breasts to push the rest of me away. I was allowed to stroke his chest or shoulders and his abs a bit, but he only clutched my breasts. Not that we were unaffectionate. We'd hold hands when we walked, or hug hello and goodbye at the door. But naked bellies against naked thighs were like food during the Depression, that kind of want just didn't happen in the Darius world. Naked was for sex, sex was for coming, but savouring chocolate on the tongue was a language he'd bite his lips against. When he was done, he'd allow one moan into his pillow. I'd grab his buttocks and pull his groin against me until I came, which wouldn't take long if his calluses still pressed into my nipples.

With the lights on, I could see out the bedroom door as I came. Darius lay his head on the pillow, his eyes on mine. I found I could look around at our apartment and he didn't notice. Crappy carpet covered by crappy furniture we bought at garage sales, a crack in the wall that grew an inch or so every month. My bike scraping tire marks against the kitchen wall, the thermostat set at sixteen degrees Celsius. The door to our bedroom faced the hallway that led to our front door, and I sometimes pictured Rose walking in by accident, her key perfectly fitting our lock. A scarf draped across her collar bones, a pink gerbera adorning her blushing hair. "Sorry, so sorry!" she'd say, leaking in warm air. Then she'd back out, pulling the door closed behind her. But not before she saw our two young bodies, pressing against the bed sheets, though not pressed against each other. "No pomegranates here," she'd declare, edging back out to her own Beach Boy-free apartment.

Darius liked fellatio, too, I think now because that required the least touch of all. His penis inside my mouth, my teeth threatening a gentle bite, his eyes closed, and his arms grabbing fistfuls of sheet and pillow. But when I asked if blow jobs went in both directions, he said, "Don't be crude." When I asked if I was to be the only one who tasted sex in my mouth, he let go of my breasts. "What's sexy about where you go to the bathroom?" he complained. And then he slid his legs over his side of the bed and got up.

I wanted to shout the perfect word at him. Icicle or Popsicle. Or melted Smarties. I wanted to spread my legs and aim the V-point at him like a porno shot. I wanted the bed to be small enough that if he let go at night he'd fall onto the cold, bare floor. But Darius was already through the hallway, turning into the bathroom, closing the door so he could discreetly pee.

The needle of the record player tick-ticked to the centre of the LP. Song over. With the end of the record, I could hear the elevator hum past our floor, delivering the spinsters to their temperate apartment. Keys and Smartie-red pomegranates in their hands.

Salvation by Proxy

Vancouver is grey with wet sleet that becomes a river the moment it hits the streets, pellets of rain that slap my face. I've rented a bed-and-breakfast for this post-Darius, post-Vera, pre-Xmas seminar week. The day I land, I lug a duffle bag filled with t-shirts and running pants and a week's underwear into a laundromat on Davie Street. Once my belongings are steadily gyrating, I cross the street to an Italian café; inside, the barista tops my latte with snowy foam in the shape of a leaf.

Back at the laundromat, I pull out my Marissa Piesman paperback and fall into a narrative of detecting-by-gossip. Just before I left town, Darius moved from our apartment to house-sit for one of the hospital anaesthetists in Marda Loop. Now, when I picture him, I have the wrong floor map in my head. I can't remember on which side of the kitchen the hallway exits. Or enters. Perhaps that's the point.

Mutti has tracked my phone number here via my boss in Calgary. No one can resist her charms, and he handed over my B&B's phone number without question. "She's your mother," he would say, if I confronted him. I press my forehead into the book's pages, obsessing about Darius, about Mutti, about Vera. I'm away from Calgary, again, but about to boomerang back. But to what? My clothing swishes and rolls and people unload their jumbled heaps in front of my chair, but I don't look up from the page. There's something dangerous about a woman with a book.

I find it comforting to read in a crummy room where everyone is a stranger and the phone will not interrupt me. Back at the B&B, I climb the stairs to my room, and flop down on the single bed hugging the farthest corner from the phone jack. Who was Jack, anyway? I wonder, tossing my keys onto the bed. Some guy. What Vera used to call Darius. I reach over the futon's edge, pull the cord toward me, and call him.

Even though I swore I wouldn't. Right after the "divorce," I fled here, glad of the excuse the seminar gives me. The Teen Centre pays thousands for another study on youth crime, or for uncountable conferences on the subject of disengaged teenagers, but can't shell out the money for more caseworkers, to give the kids the time and attention that all our studies recommend. So I run away from my ex-home, still bruised but somehow hopelessly hopeful. I get our—his—answering machine. He's not in. I breathe out evenly. Then leave a message for him not to call, but I'll be in all evening.

Our final end-game, but it seemed endless. An ending, less. Darius's hands chopped the air every time he repeated that it was over. No. I'm beginning to make it up already. He only did that chopping thing once with his hands, it was his exit-line that he tripled.

I want to blame it on the house-sitting, though we broke up in our own apartment. But two months before, we'd had a huge fight. About sex. Or not having sex. Or something to do with sex. We were house-sitting for Thanksgiving, a long weekend in a doctor's house as a last-ditch effort to "make what could have been great, great." But I didn't know that yet.

"Why?" I'd asked him. "Why don't you just say it? Come right out and *converse*, for God's sakes." Taking the Lord's name in the opposite of vain, taking it on *purpose*.

"Because ..." and his hand waved back and forth, not violently, but exasperatedly. The backs of his fingers patted the air.

"Shouldn't you be doing a karate chop?" I suggested. His knuckles fascinated me—they cringed at each sentence as if being rapped.

"Huh?" His argument drained away.

"Your hand. You're waving it, but not at me, at the ceiling or something."

"What do you mean? I'm not waving or anything. I'm trying to *tell* you something." He sounded genuinely perplexed.

"Yeah, well go ahead." My own knuckles look the same.

He slumped onto the doctor's king-sized bed. "I don't even know what we're talking about. What are we talking about?"

"Same thing we were talking about last night. Remember, when you wouldn't cross from your side of the bed over to mine?"

"Are you joking? Did I stop you from touching me?"

"You avoided my spine," I informed him haughtily.

"And your *spine*? What did your spine have to say about all this? And how about the rest of you? Ever think about where the rest of you was?"

"I don't know what we're talking about." His knuckles no longer interesting to me, I closed my eyes, experimented with squeezing out a tear or two. Nothing. My throat was dry, my back tired of holding itself rigid. I crouched across from him on the bed, pulled one of the pillows into my lap. "I don't think we're fighting," I finally said. Looked at him for longer than half a second.

"We're not fighting? Right *now* we're not fighting?"

"That's right." And I smiled.

"Whew, that's a relief. Because all yesterday while we hadn't been getting along I mistakenly believed we were fighting." He *did* do the karate-chop thing then, but absentmindedly, like he was trying to figure out my tactics with his body. "Same thing today."

"Well, there was fighting all right, but it wasn't *us*."

"Is this more Gabrielle nonsense?" he asked.

"Listen, I think the fight is all this house. House-sitting comes with the owners' emotional baggage." I raised my hands up in the air. "Don't get me wrong, it's great having a yard for Circus and storage in the basement for your extra weights, but I think there's a strange vibe here. I think we're having another couple's argument. The asshole anaesthetist and his wife. Did you see the way he grabbed her arm when she was explaining how the stove works?"

"So you're saying this isn't even us, it's the house making us fight?"

"Sort of. I don't know who we are, but I know we're not fighting like *us*. We're not even caring about what we usually care about. Last night I told you their lampshade was an unbearable mauve, and we ended up sleeping in separate rooms." The tone of my voice became high and thin.

"Maybe it's us fighting, but someone else's anger," he said, then sighed. "Well, they can finish their own damn argument, so let's just stop."

And I thought we had. Until almost two months later, when we had somebody else's divorce.

* * *

Gabrielle kept Darius on edge. Her humour or her art, I wasn't sure which. "Neither will earn you a living," Darius sneered, when he thought she'd already wheeled into another room.

"As opposed to the lucrative career of lifting weights?" Gabrielle threw back over her shoulder. Darius glared at me.

When we were alone, he said to me, "That girl's so sharp, she's going to cut herself some day." Then he said he thought Gabrielle was a pervert. *Oh, no*, I thought, not him, not my beautiful muscle boy. But it wasn't homophobia, as I feared, it was just plain old misogyny. "According to what you told me, she can achieve orgasm forever. That's not normal." That night, we went to sleep on opposite sides of our bed.

Gabrielle told me she'd figured out how to masturbate when she was five, when brushing up against chairs became more fun than crawling past them. When I was taking social work courses, I read a sociology textbook that said most girls start early, earlier than boys, but none of my other friends ever admitted to such depravity. Back then, Vera still got her kicks from combing dolls' hair. At that age, my doll could fly and had thick wool hair that didn't invite combing.

"What are you, a freak of nature or something?" I laughed at Gabrielle when she told me.

I'd just confessed to her that I was "really young" when I started. "Twelve—Mutti caught me when she walked in to collect my school clothes for laundry day. She kinda noticed I already had, um, changed out of my school clothes."

"I saw other girls doing it, you know. I wasn't the only kinder-garten kink," Gabrielle claimed. "Not that we talked about it or anything, but obviously it can't be that weird." I couldn't tell from her tone, was she proud or unrepentant or embarrassed or just matter-of-fact?

"No wonder you're a sex maniac," I concluded, but elbowed her in the arm to show I was more jealous than critical. "You were obviously masturbating up against your mother's placenta when you were a foetus. Sicko."

"Oh, that's nice. I'm the sexual pervert, but you can be crude and shocking."

"Not me basking in my childhood transgression," I laughed, remembering Vera trying to get girls to feel her up under her nightie during sleepovers. "Not me bragging about my nasty infant sins."

"Sin it is," Gabrielle agreed, "which is why I'm having such trouble giving it up now. Haven't had sex in four months. Quite a stretch, you know."

"Poor baby," I told her. Gabrielle was notorious for her short stretches between girlfriends. No point waiting for "the one" when several "ones" were all around. "Besides," I continued, "I thought we were talking about *orgasms*, not about *sex*."

Gabrielle sometimes said she had a convincing disregard for the latter, but that could just be a hangover from her hetero-sexual days when she still slept with boys who didn't care or even know if she came.

"Didn't care if I was coming or going," she said, then laughed because she found her own jokes infinitely rewarding. Gabrielle loved her own jokes. Mostly I did, too. But even when I didn't, there was always at least one of us laughing.

Vati, too, would laugh at his own jokes, no matter how much we bugged him, or how many times he told the same one. His favourite joke was the one where a woman shouts out seemingly random numbers, and people sitting in the room either laugh or groan accordingly. "What's going on?" asks a novice to the group. "Oh," his friend explains, "they're all such old friends that they know each other's jokes by heart. So they've numbered the jokes and just call out the numbers to save time." 'What a great idea,' thinks the novice, and immediately joins in by calling out "thirty-four!" Nobody cracks a smile. "What happened?" he asks his friend, "you guys must have at least thirty-four jokes to choose from." "Well," the friend explains, "it's not that—you just didn't tell it right." Then Vati would crack up and we'd roll our eyes to the ceiling. "What's up there?" he'd demand. "What's so goddamn interesting about our roof?"

"Vati! You shouldn't swear, you know." I could complain about swearing, Mutti didn't want any of us speaking sewer talk, nothing to do with religion. She didn't want our neighbours to think immigrants sat around all day eating cabbage and swearing. I didn't want that, either. Vera already made fun of the way my parents called her *Wera*.

"Can't your parents pronounce my name?" she'd ask, then add, "it's so cute the way they say it. What else do they say?"

"And it's not a roof till it's *outside* the house, okay?" I'd lecture Vati. My parents were always getting words wrong in public and then Ruth and Jana and I would squirm. A store clerk once asked me to translate what my grammar-perfect mother was saying; a bus driver mimicked her accent. Not knowing how to speak properly is a sign of not belonging. Belonging was my theme. I didn't want to get in, I'd wanted to already *be* in.

*   *   *

True confession: I chose sex with Darius because I was a virgin. And because we were both ex-Mormons, I thought we could freak out together about breaking the "no sex till we're married" rule. I was afraid regular guys wouldn't take it slow. Darius took so long just to make a move, I knew intercourse would be gradual. Gabrielle says you need lovers who can follow directions. In bed, she says, she's a traffic cop: "Left, no right, turn, turn, down!" I'm no dictator; I was mostly afraid of boys who couldn't find their way, but didn't even realize it. I wanted to reinvent the rules, but I was afraid of garburating them.

"If *they* have a blast the first time, then *you* should, too," was Gabrielle's best-friend advice, which became my virgin motto. I must have assumed that biology was negotiable, a haggling point. In my teens, I inserted two fingers past my vulva, reaching as far as I could. I was determined, even at an age when I still believed in the colour white, that my first time having intercourse as a married Mormon would not hurt. What else could a virgin do to prepare herself? Mormons don't indulge in *any* sex before marriage. Come the wedding night, it was all or nothing. By the time Darius and I had intercourse, we'd already been dating for weeks. It wasn't biology I needed to adjust, but definitions.

Darius fit perfectly—his body the length of mine, his penis rounded at the tip for easy insertion. We explored and fiddled for months before I finally went out and bought condoms. "Tonight," I said, "okay?"

And it was fine. Or at least it was okay. He liked sex on his side, and I could come as long as he pinched and tweaked my nipples while he thrust in and out. And then the next day we had a monumental fight that lasted a week and nearly forever. During the seventh night of silent resentments and nuanced slights, he fell asleep while I was telling him, finally telling him, that I hated how he fell asleep before I did and I knew it was crazy, but why couldn't he just keep his eyes open for thirty-two more seconds? I needed to trust him to listen to me, and could he understand that? With no response except the sound of his breathing, I flung off the blankets with such fury that he woke up naked and shivering. He caught me, literally caught my arm as I was diving out the door with the small bag I'd packed in a purposefully loud hurry. If he hadn't stopped me, I would not have come back. Such is the nature of pride.

When he caught my arm I didn't want to struggle, I'd used up all my anger on the bedclothes, but he'd fallen asleep while I was complaining about him falling asleep, so I had to remain mad. He didn't tell me to stay, or ask me not to go. "Leave if you can say you don't love me." It was too early for love, we'd only just consummated an "us" I hardly believed in. But I couldn't speak that negative either. Be nice, I kept thinking to myself. Be nice.

✻ ✻ ✻

Turns out, ours was just another love story, nothing special.

And like all love stories—one person loved more, oh so much more—than the other person. Gabrielle says, "When two people love each other exactly equally, that's not a story, that's science fiction." The problem with growing up Mormon is that you tend to cling to a belief in eternity. Even when I parted my lips to taste Blaise, even when I deliberately risked my Darius love story with the delicious Blaise interlude, I couldn't let go of Darius as my destiny. It's hard to get out of the habit of wanting. Even after leaving the Mormons, I couldn't get out of the habit of waiting for my eternal partner, searching for a love story that would usher me into the highest heaven.

En Passant

I was fading from the Mormon Church and its faith-promoting customs. A couple became pregnant with the first "test-tube" baby in England; the Mormon Church excommunicated a woman for supporting the ERA in the States; "O Canada!" achieved official national anthem status.

I'm all grown up, the youngest daughter of three, and I don't know what my mother's favourite flower is. "Don't trust anyone who doesn't read or tend a garden," she used to say to me. I heard, but I didn't listen. I don't have a living plant in my apartment—they all die when I go to extended out-of-town conferences—and I've given up reading anything but mysteries. It's too hard to pay attention. I start a novel, even get into the characters and their myriad of problems (how to balance the ex-husband, the joint custody, the new love-life, the rotten job), but then my own job intervenes. I admit a thirteen-year-old girl who is pregnant and strung out on heroin into the Compulsive Care unit, I go to court, I counsel the same family for eight days straight, I take off to Seattle for a few days. Or Montréal. Or Moose Jaw. Or East Coulee. When I get back, the characters in whatever book I'm in the middle of are cranky; they don't like being abandoned any more than my plants do. They refuse to tell me what they were arguing about last week or who won the toss to coach the ice hockey team. They get belligerent with an inattentive reader and retreat back into their private fictions, and the book goes back on the shelf, half-read, with all the others.

But when you lose your place in a mystery, you still know what's going to happen. Somebody did it, somebody gets caught, the detective transforms into hero. The characters don't care if you forget about them, in fact, they *count* on it. Simple clues like soap on the bedroom door handle slip easily out of your mind and slide into the detective's brilliant deduction that he's *glad* went undetected by everyone else. The best mysteries end with a secret you already knew, but didn't know you knew. I read the clues, I forget the details, and I find out the solution along with the other characters. No muss. No thinking.

After Vati's funeral, my mother started reading. Novels about birds that swear, poetry that plays with gender cases. Mutti, the true immigrant, favours local and national literature. She hears Nicole Brossard or Robert Kroetsch or Michael Ondaatje on the radio, and she's ordered their books before bookstores have them in stock. She gives me gift certificates in my Xmas stockings, and leaves books by Marian Engel or Betty Lambert or Fred Wah by my bed when she comes over to water the dry twigs that used to be plants. "I don't have time, Mutti," I try to tell her, but my mother is a newly-minted Canadian *and* a true-blue Albertan. She coaxes tomatoes to grow through June snows, she hikes the Rockies on long weekends, she reads any author she hears on the radio speaking their words into Peter Gzowski's ears. My mother the saint. My mother the practical practicist.

Gabrielle's favourite flower is the tulip. "You know me," she said when I asked, "I always go for the double lip action!"

* * *

Nine is my favourite number. Nine has both secular and spiritual significance. I admit here that my attachment had its origins in a much more practical creed. A Mutti-like creed. When I was nine years old, I got tired of changing my favourite number every time I celebrated another birthday. What was I supposed to do, I thought, keep going till my favourite number was 87? 92? 113? Until I was eight years old, I didn't know how to choose a favourite number except as my own age. But I was also just beginning to be old enough to recognize that my love was inconstant. Perhaps that was the moment of conception, for me, the moment of choosing loyalty over transience. Once I recognized that my affections shifted yearly, my affection for change ground to a halt. Nine I was, and nine I stayed. My favourite number, my favourite game, my favourite time of day, my favourite days left before summer holidays, my favourite age, my favourite grade—for always.

I still believe all the magic I believed when I was nine: godmother wands that can rescue you at midnight, my innate ability to teach dolls to fly, telepathy with best friends, water monkeys that transform from bacteria into pets, Uri Geller truly bending spoons with his mind. But never Santa Claus, nor horoscopes. No enchanted forests growing outside the city waiting to trap lost children. Telepathy is possible because it *should* be, every kid knows that, but there's no guy in a suit handing out toy guns or computer desk sets. And God, of course. I'd got rid of him, by making a religion out of non-belief. Then Gabrielle brought "Him" back.

We were listening to the latest Kilgore Trout album at her place, and she was teasing me for still being Christian enough to stumble when I casually tried to slip swear words into a sentence.

"I'm *not*," I insisted, swigging down some cola just to prove her oh-so-wrong. "I'm not a Mormon anymore." I sneezed when the bubbles went up my nose. "I don't even believe in God." That would show her.

Instead, she pretended to tip her chair over. "How can you *not* believe in a god?" she asked, when just a minute ago I'd been the one she called a Molly-Mormon. "The way you were brought up, you'd think it'd be easy." Then she looked at me like she'd proved a point, hands crossed over her chest, one eyebrow raised in perfect Spock.

"Yes, well, it's *because* of how I was raised, don't you think?" I countered.

But Gabrielle still tried to convince me that her Murphy's-law-Almighty was the god to fear. "God is out to get us all," she told me, "so just don't royally piss him off."

✳ ✳ ✳

My belief in flying comes and goes. At nine, I decided to levitate my doll, but never managed more than short across-the-room flying bursts. I'd shut the door to the rumpus room so Mutti and Jana and Ruth couldn't walk in and surprise me, surprise my *student*. I stood at one side of the room, and the couch on the other side provided the perfect landing pad. That the doll did land, every single time, didn't stop the lessons. Santa Claus, who appeared in shopping malls only, and in multiples, was an obvious fraud. But flying reindeer, invisible, were a definite possibility and I listened for them all through winter. Mutti told me she could play songs on the piano just by hearing them one time, but I never could. She taught me that churches are taverns for people too thirsty to drink. My mother promised herself that we'd learn North American and that I'd grow up to be a good atheist, but she didn't keep her promises, and I grew parched for the taste of holy water.

According to my mother, no one can see the future. Practical Mutti rejects the idea of predictions: "It's insulting," Mutti says, though I point out that often the cosmos isn't above a small insult or two. "If someone can predict even one minute of your future, then you have no choice. And if you have no choice, then you have no *you*."

"But what about mothers?" I argue, determined to provoke her. I, too, have no faith in those who offer a beaten path-already-taken. Where's the fun in *that?* "You used to tell me all the time that I'd be sorry if I went out without mitts, that Vera wouldn't call when she'd said she would, *you* guessed Ruth was pregnant when she hadn't dropped a single clue. What about *that?*"

"Oh, poo," is my mother's sophisticated response. "Ruth's my daughter, no? That's not the future, that's just *common sense*." Common sense reigned in my mother's home. We could all follow, or stumble along at a slower, more perilous pace. Common sense told my mother who would call when, who was reading under the blankets with a flashlight or crawling out the window without one, and how many pennies there'd be left at the end of the month for cherry strudel.

Sense, uncommon or otherwise, is what I strive for, what I

am determined to acquire from my mother, who has more than enough to spare. Where does she store it? Why does she hoard it? When I ask Mutti how she knows things, she huffs away my question, like she huffs away questions about her family in Germany. I figured out how to leave the Church of Latter-day Saints: by making unbelief my new religion. But how to have faith in losing faith? If I asked Mutti, she would say, "Just be practical." Advice against advice. "Just be."

❋　❋　❋

My father taught me to play chess. Chess was European. Nobody in elementary school even knew the rules, and playing chess, instead of tetherball, meant you were too smart for your own good. I was good at tetherball. Best in my grade, best in the neighbourhood. Until I entered an official tetherball contest. Best except when the game included referees, who doled out demerits for playing by our school rules. No catching the ball and "tagging" it on the pole so you could hold it, long as you liked. Holding a tetherball, in competition, was against the rules. I floundered to keep up with girls who knew these rules by heart, who bounced the ball away from their fingers as if it were a volleyball, who were already experts at what I'd only just discovered. One round and I was out. On Monday, I told the other kids that we played "wrong." But instead of practicing the official game for the following year's tournament, we stuck to our schoolyard rules. Official or not, *our* rules were what we knew and what we wanted: playground rituals, capable of granting tetherball immunity.

I am the same now when I play Hearts against my laptop. Gain 100 points or more and you lose. In fact, everyone except the player in first place loses. With live people, there are ways around this rule. If any player reaches *exactly* 100, her score is halved. *Every*one knows this. Everyone I know plays this way. A method of losing to gain first place. But my computer won't allow me to cheat.

In chess, my dad taught us about *en passant* and how to get out of it. "When you get stuck," he explained, "just switch these two pawns. Like this." Then he'd whoosh his large fingers around the plastic pieces, and the black and the white pawns traded sides. "*En passant!*" he'd cry, like it was *en garde!* The game would then continue, and we looked for more opportunities to lock our pawns into impossible positions. This was because *en passant* could get you out of a mess when your opponent was about to descend upon your queen or rook. One flick of the wrist, and a checkmate game could turn. The entire back row was yours, a whole field of squares awaiting double kinging.

In junior high, teachers came up with the ingenious plan of testing the math skills of all the grade seven students every Thursday. Anyone who achieved 80 percent or higher on the weekly quiz could skip math class on Friday and play chess instead. Suddenly chess was the desirable school sport, though I had to pretend several times that I could lose quite drastically, especially to Robbin Tarrasch. He wore pink shirts and the other boys threw dirt at him during recess and I saw him try to wash off the stains in the water fountain. And the safety pin inside my chest snapped open and the only way to close it again was to never *ever* beat Robbin Tarrasch playing Friday chess. But I could beat all the girls I wanted, and did, until Miz Gillespie caught me performing my *en passant* move, and sent my cheating self back to the dummy math classroom.

By mid-term break, half the class was skipping math on Fridays. And by February, two-thirds. For the first time ever, the girls were as good as the boys in math, though I noticed that girls never beat boys at chess, not even backwards chess, which the teachers, as they walked from row to row and looked on at our games in self-satisfaction, could not distinguish from the real game. In backwards chess—also taught to me by my father, which years later I generously tried to pass on to Darius and his friends—all the same rules apply to how the pieces move, but the object is to *lose*. Knights crash in front of rooks, queens commit suicide before normally impotent kings. Last person with a chess piece loses, doesn't matter which piece. Checkmate gets you nowhere; pawns march purposefully to their deaths; and *en passant* can still get you out of a tight corner.

In junior high, when I found out that Vati had been wrong and *en passant* wasn't the magic move we had played it as, I abandoned chess. Instead of being able to switch white and black indiscriminately, *en passant* is a fixed rule, legal only when players achieve a specific position, and only if they play one exact move. And you don't "trade" white for black, you "take" a piece from your opponent, moving your pawn to the in-between square. Not because both pawns are stuck facing each other, but because capturing a piece is the move to make. We learned that chess does not allow sneaky moves—we also had to *warn* our opponents they were moving into mortal checkmate, which Vati never made me declare.

Chess insists on chivalry and sacrifice and mathematical winnings. Vati taught me chess was ancient and cunning, my teachers that it was noble and mathematical. And Darius taught me that chess was competition. But it was Phil who taught me how to cheat.

✳ ✳ ✳

Twice Phil saves me. Once by driving toward my voice, when I'm practically dying of an overdose of conference boredom in Montréal, and once over the phone, when I dive, then sink into bleak and soggy Vancouver.

The seminar I'm to attend that December is more like an intensive course, one that I'm supposed to give other caseworkers. I'm booked to stay until December 23, but moping in laundromats grows less appealing by the day. I'm supposed to deliver my talk exactly one week after my "divorce," but the title has more words in it than I have in me: "Dysfunction Family Dynamics and the Teen Who Knows Better." I skip my own seminar. I stop phoning Darius. I stop washing the clothes I'm not wearing when I don't go out. I curl up on my bed at the B&B and try to read whodunits where the clues inform me how to figure out the climax, how to know who done it.

Mysteries used to comfort me with their clear plots and looming solutions. Now I notice that they conceal love stories within their sleuthing pages. I'm not ready for storied love. I give up on men. I give up on reading mystery books that prominently feature men, give up going into stores where men shop. That decision leaves me taking cover in my rented room, ordering

delivery from the vegetarian restaurant around the corner. I behave so unprofessionally in Vancouver, I'm positive they'll pro-
mote me again. So finally, I phone Phil.

❋　❋　❋

With Phil, who tutored me in the rules of cheating, I could be
honest. Before I bonded with Phil, I'd given up on men, even
as friends. Lovers stay on top of your skin. At least, Darius did.
Friends get under your skin. My skin. "The minute you start
sleeping with a lover, you start lying to him," Gabrielle's wisdom. "My advice: tell the truth to your friends, but maintain a
healthy set of lies with your lovers."

Phil makes everyone call him Philip, no nicknames or acts
of condescension. So of course I call him Phil, and of *course*
he doesn't deign to correct me. That's why I love Phil: he's an
enigma, wrapped in a mystery, wrapped in bacon. A good friend,
if you don't think about it too hard. He used to be a philosopher—degree and everything. Then he played chess while he
was a social studies teacher. He quit his job to play more chess.
Then he checked facts and wrote indices for a scholastic publisher in Toronto. Then he stopped playing chess. Now, his job
is all about driving through Ontario as a book jobber. He does
three cities a day, has a left-armed tan, pretends he's in the biz
because of books, but it's all about the driving.

Because he and Darius had been friends, I'm not talking
about Darius to Phil. He probably got the scoop already from
Gabrielle. That's fine; if he has the details, then I don't have to
try to muddle through them myself: *What happened? I have no*

idea. Why'd you guys break up? Well, we had a big fight weeks af-
ter we moved into his boss's house. Will there be a reconciliation?
No, spells cast three times in a row stick in your hair, stay in your
blood, pumping through your arteries and veins until they find
your heart and rest inside that rogue organ forever. Eternity.

"Hey, chicka," Phil greets me, when he figures out who the
throat-clearing at the other end is. "Give me some lowdown."
So he hasn't yet heard my news, which means I have to tell him
myself. Why can't my friend be telegraphs when I need them
to be?

"Too much low to tell, Phil," I confess. "Lots and lots of low,
a vista of low, a cornucopia of low."

Phil laughs, and in the nicest way possible. "Just as long as
you're not *sad*," he declares. Now *that* would be tragic."

*　*　*

Phil never asks me about lovers. Maybe because he's convinced
I'll tell him anyway, but also because then we'll have to trade
stories and he's been single a bit longer than he likes to admit.
Or he's been quite celibate lately, and he doesn't want me to
know just how long it's really been for him. Better to keep up
the mystery.

"Oh, you wouldn't be able to handle the truth if I told you,"
he sidesteps when I question his evenings or make suggestions
for weekends. "You just don't get it—it's not about getting a
date, it's not about getting laid, it's about getting *heard*." Like I
don't know about being ignored. "No," he explains, "that's not
what I'm talking about. I get plenty of attention when I want,

even when I don't want." Poor guy, I'd like to interrupt, but stop myself. Phil continues. "I don't get to say what I need to say, to have the other person listen and hear and digest my words."

"I don't understand," I confess. "You don't want attention, you want a tape recorder? You want someone who just listens and can then regurgitate?"

Phil sighs. "Let's just say my loving is of the glacial variety, slow but steady."

My turn to sigh.

When I repeat this conversation to Gabrielle, she acts like I'm the one who's out of it. "Look," she explains. "You and I hear Phil the blabbermouth, but in relationships he's a pretty quiet guy." I wait. "So when he does say something, he means it entirely. He's not just making conversation. Weeks later, whoever he's with has to remember just how vital the El-Mayor Bakery is to our young hero." Even Gabrielle can't keep the sarcasm out of her explanation.

"If *your* girlfriend tried that shit, you'd dump her on her able-bodied ass," I declare.

Gabrielle doesn't deny it. With her girlfriends, she's pleased as a bull-dyke in a femme shop, as she likes to say. "Of course I would," she agrees, which surprises me. I thought she was on Phil's side for this one. "Look, sweetie, Phil's the greatest *friend*, but who'd want to *date* him?"

"That was my original question," I protest, but the conversation's over. Gabrielle wheels around so she's facing the elevator and I retreat into my own conundrum-less apartment. I must be asking the wrong questions.

✳ ✳ ✳

"Of *course* you're asking the wrong questions," Mutti told me later that night. Why did I adore Gabrielle's flippant sarcasm, but shun Mutti's acerbic wisdom? She let her other daughters grow into their adult selves, but I was the one in need of parenting. In need of correction. Like the kids in the correctional facility, who still needed grammar or moral or street lessons. Me: a work in progress. Mutti: the mother forever ladling advice.

✳ ✳ ✳

In February, the sun starts to set at four-thirty, but for me, with my body tuned to years on night shift, the days easily slip into near-morning. Nights, I may sleep, or I may get up and cook. Then I set the alarm to interrupt me a few hours later, and try to stay awake all day. There are only so many options, certain obvious choices. A movie's perfect for utter exhaustion, but then there's no chatting. Coffee shops are perfect for gossip, but then the caffeine sits in my bloodstream for too long all night, all day. A walk would be great, if I still had Circus to accompany me. And there's always an art opening, with wine and cheese to follow. I'll let Gabrielle decide.

"How about the LAWNS show?" she decides. And I'm stuck with it.

"Not another bloody installation!" I protest. "Those artists never know when enough is too much. And they'll all be dressed in grey and black tight things, their backs to the walls.

Nobody actually looking at the art."

"So you don't want to go to this one?" She's being sarcastic. It'll be a good show, I concede, but it'll also be irritating.

"Oh, we'll go all right. We just have to hide in a corner and complain about artists who are convinced that snowflakes are the perfect metaphor for just about everything. I expect you to look at the *walls*, you understand? not just the *people*." An art opening with Gabrielle is an invitation to hang on her elbow like a lost girlfriend, girls envying me because they've slept with her already, boys pitying me because they don't know her rep.

Gabrielle and I met at her first opening. Darius was actually the one who suggested we go. We still hadn't slept together, and were running out of appropriate date pastimes. He'd read in the newspaper's *Entertainment and Religion* section that an exhibit called "Dumbbells" opened on Friday at the Stride Gallery. He thought there'd be photos of weightlifters and their equipment. Instead, Darius got to ridicule the installation which featured mangled walkers, canes, and wheelchairs, and I got introduced to the artist. At LAWNS, Gabrielle and I discover more text than tactile pieces. It's grassier than green, a comment on colonial traditions imbedded within a resistant prairie. I read every wall, and on the drive home Gabrielle is the one who complains about pickle-up-their-butts art novices.

My best talks with Phil take place while driving, his car or mine, cross-country or interstate. When Phil hears I'm conferencing in Montréal, he decides to show up the next day. "Look," he shouts into the phone. "I'll be at Carlton and Ottawa, and then I have the weekend before I need to be at U of T. Why don't I pick you up at your hôtel-de-semaine, we'll drive for a few hours, and you can fly back to Calgary from Toronto? We can do a road trip!"

The Road Trip. There are no better two words in the English language to invoke adventure and junk food. Road trips soothe the prairie heart. Road trips are for going all night without sleep just to break your previous highway record. Road trips are for later, when you can brag about doing Calgary-Winnipeg in just under twelve-point-five hours, scarfing down chips and chocolate bars, and skirting past the RCMP radar.

When I turned fourteen, my twenty-one-year-old sister Jana and I headed out to Québec City, where her bilingual-incentive eagerly awaited her (and the return of his car, which he'd rashly lent her at the end of her summer immersion). I was Jana's last choice, but all her friends were deeply busy with boyfriends of their own, and even Ruth, our eldest sister, was just married and starting an auto-service job that she couldn't even temporarily abandon. Mutti wouldn't let Jana go alone. Period.

"But Mutti," Jana begged. "It's only a week, we'll head straight for the airport as soon as we get there, we'll drive so slowly, and you know what flying stand-by is like this time of year. Come on, it'll give us a chance to bond, you know, like sisters."

"Well …" Mutti was stubborn but not unreasonable, and she didn't like the way I'd started calling Jana and Ruth, *them*. "… go ask your father." The ultimate parent procrastination manoeuvre.

Vati was a whole different story from Mutti. Vati could take you to a movie way past your bedtime, but he could also refuse to let you go over to a friend's till your entire *week* of homework was done. Vati would let you borrow money for ice cream anytime, but you couldn't watch more than half an hour of TV a week. "Let me talk him into it," Jana said. Vati sat at his card-table desk, and Jana recited most of the story except, in this version, the guy who owned the car was a mutual "friend" of several of Jana's friends. "We'll pay for everything ourselves, including the stand-by flight home." Wrong move, in our house, each person *always* paid her own way, it wasn't a virtue we needed to stress.

Vati tapped his typewriter keys and j's and f's crawled across the blank page. He hadn't said anything at all yet, which meant he wasn't completely opposed, just that he didn't like it. "Vati, you *have* to let us," Jana urged, not understanding a thing about timing.

"Look, Dad," I cut her off, despite her tug at my armpit, "it's a road trip. You love road trips. And Jana and I have never been on a road trip, just the two of us. And Vera's brother will bless the car, he did before we all drove out to Cochrane for ice cream last week. Come on, Vati, it's a *road trip.* " And my father, the converted Albertan, the road trip devotee, stopped tapping his keys and nodded his head instead. Emphasizing "road trip" in front of Mutti would have been put the brakes on Jana's plans, but it worked with Vati. Road trip—a call to luck and the sun blazing into a car without air conditioning.

"Way to *go!*" Jana said, cuffing me on the back of the head after. "Like I always tell you, it's all in the timing."

＊　＊　＊

Montréal isn't truly on Phil's book route, but Ottawa is, and that's close enough for a two-hour detour to come rescue me from overly sincere child care administrators—with jobs focused on delinquent teens, we should have been making oxymoronic jokes at the seminar, but we weren't. We were very sincere and self-righteous. God save me from the earnest.

After his last Ottawa appointment, Phil speeds to Montréal. As soon as his truck—impractical, but very Albertan—pulls in, I sneak away with him. After our hug, Phil says, "I'm sick of driving. You take over, okay?" Phil is *never* sick of driving, he just wants to torture me with Montréal.

"No way," I tell him, "I'm from Alberta, remember? I can handle any highway, and any city except Montréal. Montréal freaks me out. You can inflict your cowboy directions on me tomorrow, tonight we take the metro."

I keep my room for one last night, and we spend the evening at Phil's favourite Portuguese restaurant downtown. After, we walk to the lesbian bar Gabrielle recommended, the Chic Pub, and Phil points out that we're sipping pepper martinis across from the St. Denis Chess Club. We can see them from where we are sitting, a row of earnest Darius- and Juan-types, tensely huddled over their square benches and malleable boards. Phil shrugs and sips the dregs of his martini like a bored tourist, not like someone who was once a member of the chess brotherhood.

* * *

The next morning, Phil and I hop into his truck, me behind the wheel. I get to rediscover that driving with Phil means listening to his lectures *and* his punk rock. Phil-the-Driving-Instructor offers highway advice like he's a genuine teacher, not just another Albertan with a truck. "When going around a curve, always take the lane on the inside," Phil advises.

Just after Saint-Zotique, we cross into Ontario. It's only been an hour, but I've already hit lesson overload.

"I don't mean to sound ungrateful, Phil, but don't make me trade you in for the company of a childcare *administrator*, okay?"

"My car, sister," he says. "These are good tips—you should thank me."

"As if." But I push in my favourite Leonard Cohen tape, hoping to lull Phil with genius lyrics and Canadian pride. It works.

"This *shite!* The guy has a monotone voice and we throw money at him." He leans over to switch the tape.

I swat his hand away. "Driver's prerogative," I say, invoking one of Phil's own rules. "Besides, it's not just Canadians who love Cohen. He once got nineteen ovations for 'Take This Waltz' in Barcelona, and he was even on an episode of *Miami Vice.*"

"Big whoop," Phil says. "Here. I just bought this tape in Ottawa, how's *that* for national pride?"

"I'll be agreeable if I get to be the passenger," I bargain.

"Fine." We stop and quickly trade places. Crossing into

Ontario has reminded me I'm heading west. Again. "I can't stand that 'Infamous Blue Raincoat' any longer." So now Phil careens across Ontario, skipping what he calls his "re-edumacation" lessons. "Let me know when you want another turn behind the wheel," he offers, "*without* Mr. Tower of Torture," then pushes the vehicle from first to fourth in 3.2 seconds. Phil will babble away even when he's driving, but this way it'll be conversation, not just instruction. We listen to his new tape, Furnaceface, and I shut my eyes, cuz I don't want him to know that I'm actually liking them. We drive for about an hour like this, Phil speeding to the tune of Ottawa punk, and me just rolling with the "She Thinks She's Fat" vibrations. The car rattles a bit, but it's nothing like my beater in Calgary, or like the old dinosaur Phil used to drive around. Back in his own Darius days.

"Remember your Flintstones car?" I ask, laughing at the memory of a car that had more rust and duct-tape than it had original paint job.

"That was Gabrielle's nickname for it," he replies after a long pause. Even though he mentions Gabrielle, his voice is chilly. Usually, Gabrielle is the inviolable catalyst that melts all ice. But for some reason, Phil's icing over. Instead of trying to joke him out of it, I sink back into faux-leather car seat.

For another hour, I watch the same set of skinny trees dash by again and again. Trees, trees, trees, curve. Trees, trees, trees, curve. We've been driving a long time with only music pounding out of the speakers. Dammit. I've never been a big fan of sullen Phil, I've gotten a lifetime of sullen from delinquents at work. We pass by rows and rows and rows of fences bordering the highway. Even when the road is straight, you can't see more than a few feet in either direction. And people say the *prairies* are boring?! Give me open fields any day. Give me the drive from Calgary to Saskatoon, yellow billowing out on each side, slivers of rust peaking out from creeks, shades of wheat, gold, burgundy reflecting off the ground. The sun setting gloriously behind me, me pumping the accelerator to break previous records.

"Hey, Phil, did I ever show you that series of grain elevator photos that I took between Calgary and Winnipeg?" But Phil's still gone. Maybe I should demand to be let out at the closest bus station. I lean back and concentrate on Furnaceface. The road curves and Phil changes lanes every time. Ahead, nothing but trees and a gas station. Another curve, and more trees. Way in the distance, a large cement bridge arches over the highway. I don't see the roads that lead to this bridge, it seems to grow out from the trunks of the trees. It has no cars on it, but a few dark spots bounce on top. Like several follow-the-ball singing commercials, but out of sequence. I squint and see that the dots are three men, dressed entirely in dark clothing. One of them stops in the middle of the bridge and gets down on one knee. He lifts a black tube about a foot long and aims it right at us. All this must take four seconds because we still haven't reached the bridge yet. Phil's facing the road and only the road.

"Phil!" The man holds the gun steady, aimed right at us. I try to grab the wheel, but Phil fights me. "Philip! A *gun!*" He won't let go of the wheel. One more heart beat. Then. My chest opens from the inside.

But we're under the bridge, the car still intact, and I remember to breathe. I check out the back window and see police cars nestled against bushes below the bridge. A speed gun. The cop was aiming a goddamn speed gun at us. Shit, if I'd been driving, Phil and I would be crunched against the meridian by now, with four cars piled behind and on top of us. What kind of police force poses as gunmen in order to nab hasty drivers?

"Okay, you can tease me about that from here to Toronto, but you're still the one who gets a speeding ticket in his mailbox." No reply. I'm sweating and still shaky, but this time Phil's re-action—or rather his *non*-reaction—sinks it. "Phil?" What the hell is up his butt? He should be cracking up over my law-abid-ing panic. "Phil!" and I tickle the inside of his elbow. Nothing. This time, there's no heart-racing Hollywood crisis, but Phil-my-friend has turned into Phil-the-zombie. At 120 klicks per hour.

"Phil," I start out softer, "I am obviously the most gullible person in all of Ontario." He keeps his eyes on the road. "But this is really not a great time for a practical joke." I stroke Phil's face. He doesn't blink. Please please please let this be a practi-cal joke, I pray. We pass by a few houses and more trees and another gas station. Maybe the safest thing is to wait till we run out of gas, sort of glide to a stop in the midst of all the other hurtling chunks of metal. I lean over and see we've barely dipped below F—brilliant me, insisting we fill up every time we stop for a pee.

Phil grips the wheel, his neck locked into forward position, and his eyelids have disappeared. His lips are gone, too, there's only a grim line left where his mouth used to be, a scratch above his chin. Phil is gone.

Insulin shock. Of course it's insulin shock. This morning I came into the bathroom of the motel and Phil still had the needle in his belly, though he says he usually shoves it in his butt. He pricks his finger every morning before he even takes a piss, and swipes the lonely drop of blood onto a glucose strip. Then he shoves a needle somewhere into his body that isn't already bruised and jaded.

This morning, Phil passed on toast cuz he's only allowed one piece of bread a day. Sitting too close to him in the cab of the truck, I have the clue, but I don't know where to put it. Did he take just a smidgen too much insulin in that needle, or was there too much sugar in the cereal? In the St. John's Ambulance first aid course I took for my job at the Teen Centre, we did a section on diabetes. "If the patient's breath smells like nail polish remover, then she's got too much sugar in her system and needs insulin; if her breath smells like apples, then she's taken too much insulin and needs sugar." Maybe if I leaned over during an extremely straight stretch of road, Phil wouldn't even notice, but keep heading straight for whatever destination lives behind his forehead.

"Forget that doctor crap," I remember Phil advised me once when we went camping together. I'd wanted him to know I was prepared for any emergency, even one emanating from inside his own body. "Like you could ever handle an insulin pen properly." He hoisted his backpack onto his shoulders and slammed the car door shut. He carried the portable stove and tent poles for both of us. "Or even come close to guessing how much insulin to load me up with. I'd be dead in less than a minute, you poking needles into my lifeless carcass!" He looked at me like I was ten years old, wanting to play nurse. "Here's what you need to know," and he waited for me to catch up, because Phil adores playing teacher. "If I need insulin out here, I'm pretty much a goner, okay? Besides, it's much much more likely that I'm low on sugar, right?"

"Yeah, sure." My backpack was already cutting into my shoulders.

"And if I start getting sleepy while we're walking or act weird—you know, kind of wonky—then feed me a chocolate bar. I've always got something sweet around. Just dig around my knapsack. Got it?"

"Aye-aye, sir. All hail your great excuse to eat chocolate."

He'd said then that he always had sweets around. I search the truck's glove compartment, where Phil actually keeps leather work gloves. Nothing else but old car insurance and leaky pens. Phil follows the yellow line, though he's stopped changing lanes every time we go around a curve. His knuckles are yellowish—a symptom or his grip? I grab Phil's burlap bag from the hole be- hind our seat. No chocolate, not even stolen sugar cubes from the last diner.

But, as if in preparation for another camping trip, Phil's got several bags of mountain mix—granola and sesame seeds and almonds and raisins and pistachio nuts and, thank-the-lord, chocolate chips. I slip them inside the crack that used to be Phil's lips, one by melting one. He curls the chocolate into his mouth and his Adam's apple bobs when he swallows. Eventually, his neck unstiffens for the first time since the would-be gun- man. "Hi, Phil," I say. "Can we stop and buy some chocolate bars?"

184

At the truck stop, I hug him and try to dance the two-step in the parking lot. Phil gracelessly refuses. He piles three bags of chocolate hearts and a dozen Kinder eggs onto the counter, then passes me the bag while he's in the restroom. I shove the bag into Phil's burlap bag, slide behind the wheel, and leave the passenger door wide open. I am the hero nurse after all. Phil climbs in the passenger side.

"Now maybe you'll drive for a while?" he demands. "And no bloody Leonard Cohen, it'll make me OD on the sweet side!" Phil, my crabby but mouthy friend. I notice that the truck cab now smells like sour green apples.

Postcards from Away

I accept the gig in Philadelphia because I need an excuse—after getting a postcard from Germany—to get out of town. Two years since Darius split, and I was positive he'd entered the past tense. After I'd spent much of that December hiding out in Vancouver, by the time I returned, Calgary was keen with Winter Olympic zeal. In February, Eddie the Eagle made ski-jump history. While other skiers took wing all around him, the Eagle finished far last, "ski-dropping" into legend. I changed apartments; a year later, Salman Rushdie—although British, an author Mutti also favoured—panicked religious leaders with a novel. I geared up to confront Mutti about her tightness with my sisters, her looseness with me. That summer in Tian'anmen Square, Tank Man faced an army of military tanks alone, the day after a government crackdown against students. And then the Berlin Wall came falling down in Germany.

I attended more and more conferences, and I should have guessed I'd have to leave for longer, at least once. My boss, who rarely left his desk during the day, gave me the Philly invitation in person: "The powers-that-be request your presence." To contrast his words' highfalutin embroidery, he dumped six extra thick problem-kid files on my desk. With a January bonus and paid flights, he crated me off to Philadelphia to research inner-city programs in the US, sure I'd boomerang back without pulling any muscles. And, of course, to attend a plethora of teen info seminars and meetings about who was responsible for what and for how much money.

My role in Philly is as bridge between Canadian and American methods. A three-month gig, perhaps longer, perhaps shorter. "Guess that depends on how desperate they are to get rid of me," I joked to Gabrielle.

"At least you're lucky enough to leave in January," she said. "It'll make you nostalgic to come home." But I was already nostalgic, could already anticipate missing Gabrielle and Phil. Longing for advice from Mutti, though she'd be sure to ladle out several helpings over the holidays. "Who's going to shove me around now?" Gabrielle laughed.

I arrive in Philadelphia two days after New Year's. There is no snow, and my hosts predict there will be none this year. Here I don't have to worry about bumping into Mormons who think they know me. Or Darius. So this is what it is to live in American anonymity. This is what it means to not care that you don't care. From my suburbs, the Septa train whisks me past burnt out buildings and boarded up shop windows, to a downtown that's at once populated and vacant. Perfect, because I'm on vacation, I tell myself. I don't need to know anybody. William Penn built four parks and placed the city of Philadelphia inside them. The four corners of civilization. Train tracks carry commuters like me to and from and through the grime and deterioration that other people inhabit. I don't mean the city's filthy, but it lacks a good washing down, a true optimism to wipe away the grey.

It's not until I stroll down South Street that I feel the wrench of homesickness Freud says we confuse with love. In the neighbourhood where I'm staying, the houses are all colonial stone. I rent a room in a three-story that has two stairways—one regular and one for servants. The garage used to be the servants' quarters. The attic has a higher ceiling than my Calgary apartment. In the lonely Philly suburbs, no sidewalks or paths interrupt the streets. My hosts wake me up with mango loaf and rye bread and roiboos tea. But I have nowhere to wander after I finish working. Once the Septa train deposits me back at my stop, I aim for the shops or for the house. In my rooms, I read mysteries or write letters to Gabrielle, Phil, my sisters, and to Mutti, eschewing the jocular postcard. Or else I fall asleep hours earlier than I need to, only to awake abruptly in a chair, my head pillowing into the desk, in the middle of the night. My body still not trusting bedtime. A neighbourhood so safe you leave your doors unlocked, in a city so unsafe you don't dare carry a wallet downtown once the sun sets.

The parks end south of Walnut, so I usually don't venture past that edge. At lunch, I buy a Philly cheesesteak from one of the gleaming metal trucks set up around town, and settle on a bench in one of the downtown squares until the afternoon cycle of meetings, lectures, and counselling sessions. The downtown's narrow streets, the hallway-width alleys, corner nail salons, and beige-coloured stone boutiques draw me in. In the February sun, I chew on my sandwich; I almost chirp, dressed in short sleeves and out of bounds of a single winter carnival.

One day I finally resist the urge to hop on the Septa. Instead, I head away from the train station and downtown, aim toward south instead. East is New Jersey and west a cluster of universities. North reaches past the museum and old penitentiary and on and on till my train stop. But I've failed to take the routes south, so today I face the sun through narrow streets till I discover what has to be a supernatural occurrence: an oasis of second-hand clothing stores and bookstores and coffee shop after coffee shop after coffee shop. Calgary's Mission district opens out before me, Edmonton's Whyte Avenue, Winnipeg's Corydon. Except all rolled into one. Jungle motifs plaster the buildings. Arcades, historic signs, street vendors crowd the one-way street. My lungs twist, and I feel truly alone for the first time since moving. Who to share this with? Who to tell? The couple I rent from must already know South Street, so my news won't be miraculous to them. The outer walls of buildings are studded with bits of glass and porcelain and murals that cover the graffitied walls. A feast of colour.

I tell Gabrielle over the phone. "You won't believe the two bathrooms in the one coffee shop I sat in." I picture her raising one eyebrow. "Yes, of course I tried the men's, these bathrooms are *amazing*. Each one decorated individually, each one a piece of art." I can't contain my gushing. Gabrielle lets me gush. "The walls have pieces of mirrors and tiles and kitchenware sticking out of them, you should see it!" But she won't. Gabrielle can't afford to fly to Philadelphia just to check out the local coffee shop bathrooms. Somewhere along the line, my work associates have fallen in love with meetings; away from home, I'm falling in love with a city and that makes me homesick.

❋   ❋   ❋

The word *gift* in German means poison. Two years after I un-believed in Darius, I got a work offer for a three-month stint in Philadelphia. While I was deciding, I received a postcard from

Berlin. A regular-sized postcard, with a thick, plastic bubble embedded into the cardboard. One square centimetre of the Berlin wall rattled inside the plastic as it whirled across the globe, reaching out for me.

Cities and their monuments. Receiving that postcard aimed me toward Philadelphia, to instruct fellow Teen caseworkers, to pay homage to the British Quaker whose statue lives on top of the city.

"I want my mind to be dull as a lover's," Darius had written on the postcard. No way to deliver words back at him.

Secret Shopper

A week after we first moved in together, Darius bought me a no-reason gift. He made me hide in the bedroom so he could set it up properly, but I saw the empty box lying on our bed. A hot-air popcorn popper—neither romantic nor useful. I made popcorn every weekend in the overly-heavy iron pot my mom gave us when I moved out. Why would he spend money on a contraption that had only one purpose?

"C'mon," he called, and I entered the kitchen and feigned surprise and glee and immediately popped us a batch. The salt wouldn't stick to the popcorn because the popper didn't need oil, which was the point of popping it in the iron pot. I resented this health-minded loss of decadence.

"The perfect gift," I told him, making my grateful face.

Fact is, I grew addicted to that popper. Tonight, I'm slack-brained from a day of organizing dysfunctional teenagers and Pennsylvanian parents into groups. Learning groups. That's the theory, the reality is the kids want to hang out with their friends and the parents want to be home drinking beer and watching *Hill Street Blues*. Forcing them to talk to me is sometimes a waste of time, a cruel joke on the one kid who'll get picked on when a Canadian like me is not around to hold the familial hand. That's one of the reasons they've sent me here, though I'm more here to train other staff and try to let them train me. I'm a caseworker-turned-administrator extraordinaire, sent to homes where the parents are often more of a problem than the kids. But you can't tell them that. You can't tell them anything but positive action words: "focus," "strengthen," "achieve." I hang around and make discreet throat noises. Sometimes the noises work and the parents care more about what I think than they realize. They don't want a bad report card, they don't want a police file, they don't want their kids taken away even though they quite often don't want their kids. And that's how it works—I scare them into believing they should stop scaring their kids. But today's *strengths* didn't *achieve* positive *focus*; I've had it with trying to convert delinquent parents. Really, I'm here to observe more than change, but that role depresses me more than failing to reach parents. I want to be back in Calgary, choosing a movie with Gabrielle. But even a long-distance phone call isn't going to happen, because tonight Gabrielle's line beeps busy for hours, and then there's no answer at all.

I glance in my mini fridge—a raw steak and three wilting carrots. I want to bend open the cover of a new mystery, flick on the TV. I think of that popper as I shove a flavoured bag of buttered corn into the microwave because I'm too lazy to shake a heavy pot over the stove. I swirled corn in that popper for years and years, even kept it after Darius left, right up until its cord frazzled and shorted. I should buy another popper, though I know I won't. The microwave popcorn is good enough, though not great, not even close to movie quality. And you have to stop the microwave before all the kernels are popped or they'll burn. But buying another popper would somehow feel like a betrayal. The perfect gift, and I popped it. I turn on the local news and settle down to focus on other people's problems that are not mine to solve.

Although I'm not allowed to speak of individual teens or mention specific names that come through the Teen Centre back in Calgary, if Gabrielle were available for chatting, I could complain about the Philadelphia Learning Group I'm here to train, about the extremely short kid with knife scars on his back, the parents who showed up thirty minutes late "to teach him a lesson." The staff behave as if knife marks on a twelve-year-old are routine, don't even add that case to my seminar discussion group. I could tell Gabrielle all this, because she wouldn't know these people, would never meet them, there'd be no breach of confidence. And Gabrielle would give me her day, the stationery shop she visited where the clerk wouldn't help her with the too-high Valentine cards, "Because he didn't want to insult me," she'd say, "because letting me poke a stick to shove one off the top ledge is preferable, dignity-wise, than him simply helping." An assistant who assists, what a concept.

I sink into the rented couch and dial Gabrielle's line again. Busy. Busy, busy, and then no answer. No answering machine, even. Ignoring me or her Manitoba Mennonite? Gabrielle's not cement-hard and lemon-bitter, but she prefers her girlfriends to think that she is, rather than think she needs them. She once went for an ice cream with a girl who pitied her. A long evening of a near-stranger asking her if she needed to go to the bathroom, if she wanted more to drink, if she felt comfortable in her chair. At the end of that date, Gabrielle got the impression she was supposed to thank the girl. Instead, she wheeled herself up her ramp while Charity Girl pushed her needlessly. Gabrielle unlocked her door, let the girl hold it open for her, grabbed a half-filled can of mauve paint and a camera from her studio.

She wheeled back outside, down the ramp, and flung streaks of purple all over Charity Girl's car. "Thank you," she said, taking a few polaroids, "thanks so much."

I try to imagine her day. I go through images of Gabrielle painting in the morning, then her paying job in the afternoon, and an evening lusting for her out-of-town girlfriend. Suddenly, Gabrielle's day bursts fully-formed from my head, an Athena-narrative. My best friend's story:

✳   ✳   ✳

Before heading for work, Gabrielle has to decide whether to take her power wheelchair or the manual. She lets the type of workplace that she has to evaluate that day make the decision for her. Which chair she chooses on her own and which she chooses for work are almost always exact opposites. When she's sent to evaluate coffee shops and restaurants, it's usually Emmanuel, because there's always some waiter who tries to move her around without asking first. A sudden shift in her landscape when she's rudely hauled away from her table. *Nobody* can move the power chair. But when her job was to evaluate a car rental agency, she took her motorized chair because the "oh-yes-we-have-absolutely-exactly-what-you-need" guys had to figure out how to rent a van to someone who could drive, but who couldn't lift a chair that weighed nearly as much as a car into their vehicle. You're either mobile, or you're not, end of story. The idea of a ramp she could use to drive her chair right up and into the back of the van had never occurred to them before. But, hey, if she wanted to bring her own, that would be great.

Each of the two chairs leads people to yet another set of assumptions about her body and what they think it should be able to do. Or shouldn't. Once she used her foot to punt a nerfball to a kid in a toy store and his mother glared at her like she was stealing money from the Sunday collection plate.

Today, she's got sexism as well as the crip-factor to provoke, wonders which one will win out, which will prove to be the more pervasive prejudice. She chooses her motorized chair, because at least one guy in the shop will then assume she doesn't have use of her arms. She spent the morning working on a new canvas, and by 2:15 has the afternoon free for this job. But the report has to be in by tomorrow, so she better not have too much fun.

* * *

At five to three, Gabrielle rolls through the automatic doors toward customer service. The guy working behind the high counter doesn't see her so she has to reach up and knock on the particle board.

"Oh. Hey. Can I help you?" The guy bends forward onto the counter so his belly rests against its flat surface and his chest leans into her face. "Hi, I'm Gabe!" his nametag declares. He's smacking a wad of gum so large it garbles his words.

"Hi, Gabe!" Gabrielle imitates his tag's enthusiasm. "We share a name!" His eyelid does a sudden twitch, so she just continues. "Well, I'm here to buy your deck kit, but I need advice on the height sizing." Gabrielle points to the flyer she's brought with her, displaying a bright new back deck, complete with husband at the new barbecue, wife and kids eagerly waiting to be fed, dog happily curled up in the newly-painted corner.

"Oh. Hey," says Gabe. "We prefer if the guy assembling it comes in. Maybe you can come back with your husband when he gets off work?" He blows a bubble and leans down a bit more. Gabrielle is tempted to snatch his nametag and wheel off in the direction of the manager, but her job is only just starting in this place, she hasn't even talked to the hardware guys yet, just this front man, whose magenta bubble has slid down over his nose. He sticks his tongue out, licks the pink goo back into his mouth and waits. In all fairness, Gabrielle thinks, most salesclerks never assume she'd even have a husband.

"I'm not married," Gabrielle says into the next expanding bubble. "And your flyer says anyone can do the construction, 'no professional experience necessary'." She quotes from the flyer, folds her hands over her lap, and waits.

Gabe blows another bubble, letting gum fill the space where his words should be. Hey, he's in charge of customer service and he *knows* you can't tell crippled people they're not as capable as normal people. But no way this chick can build a back deck by herself, must be a brother or uncle helping her. Gabrielle can see Gabe's thoughts inside a cartoon bubble hovering beside his forehead. He's not going to push it, she might be some sort of women's libber. How's she going to hammer a nail and not end up propelling her wheelchair backwards at the same time? He looks at her for real now, taking in her nose ring and burgundy-tinged hair. Same age as him, he'd guess, cute in a mousy way, except what's with those billowy neon yellow pants, don't cripples cover their knees with grey blankets? He pulls his hands behind the counter. He wants to touch those slacks, they look like they're made of parachute material. He gets the feeling this woman could float out of the chair, if he blew a big enough bubble. Maybe he should offer to help her with the deck construction, except that's against company policy. Only the hardware guys work assembly, and then the store charges customers by the hour. No sitting around drinking a beer, yakking about what kind of accident was she in anyway, and how come she wears so much yellow?

Gabe's sister used to tell him that yellow was a colour you should never risk. "Very few people can pull it off," she'd say to him, arranging her own layers of muted blue skirt and metallic green blouse. "A real woman has to be confident, work on having perfect skin, and figure out what in her closet might go well with banana." Gabe looks down at this woman's skin, but he can't tell what qualities his sister would look for—perfect shade or perfect smoothness? Gabrielle just sits there, waiting for him to say something, without twitching her fingers, without tapping a toe. Oops, even with her sitting in a wheelchair right in front of his eyeballs, Gabe keeps forgetting that she can't tap her toes, or hop up and poke his bubble with her fingernail, though she looks like she wants to. He lets his bubble sag and spits the gum into the garbage. Shouldn't be chewing at work, anyway. He knows what he has to say to this customer, knows the exact words to offer her. But as soon as he says them, she'll wheel away, and then he'll never get to see her yard, nor what colour a woman who wears tropical pants will paint her deck.

"Hey, you wanna build in February, I'm not the one to stop you," he says, his first words in minutes, and points her toward the Handyman aisle. "The guys down there will help you choose a deck kit to fit your yard." Gabe watches Gabrielle back up and turn with the flick of her index finger, only now noticing that her chair is powered. Perhaps she can't even lift her arms? Shit, how's she going to nail two pieces of wood together, let alone a deck that will hold the weight of that chair? But then she waves at him behind her head, and he realizes she knows he's still staring. Maybe she's got extra good senses, because of her handicap? Or is that just blind people? Gabrielle turns into aisle seven, her hand still waving behind her, and Gabe gets back to work. Next guy in line wants to know if they sell measuring tapes! Geez, what a moron.

Gabrielle comes to the end of aisle seven, waits for the two guys at the back to stop chattering and ask to help her. There's no counter here, they can see her perfectly. She can smell freshly-cut cedar and pine and maple as well as paint and metal shavings and plastic and oil lubricants. Maybe she should pick up something for Emmanuel's squeaking wheel? The one guy's bragging about how he treated his kids to a skiing weekend, dropped $600 bucks just on ski-lifts and lunch. The other guy, sprouting a pimply forehead and scraggly chin, nods, sure, sure, kids cost a fortune. Two nametags: "Hi, I'm Jim Cardell!" and "Hi, I'm Tod!" Older guy must be a sub-manager or something. Gabrielle turns to him.

"Excuse me," she says, and the older man stops mid-sentence. "I'd like help choosing and sizing a deck for my back entrance."

"Sure thing. When do you want it ready by?" Jim Cardell squats down so their faces are level.

"Not sure, your guy at the front desk seems to think February's a bad month for building." Gabrielle inches her chair back a bit. "Think I should be able to get it done by May? The brochure says it's easy."

"Are you kidding?" Jim Cardell says. "I can have that done in no time." He shoots Tod a look, which ricochets right back at Gabrielle. "Don't know why Gabe said February's bad. With a good Chinook I'll have that baby built for you in two weekends." He gets up. He's speaking to Tod, but points at Gabrielle just in case there's any confusion. "You get the specifics of her yard, including back steps, Tod, and I'll get the service book." Gabrielle has to raise her voice to catch him before he walks away.

"Excuse me," she says, and raises one finger. I picture her nails manicured a Philly-style studded blue. "I understand some customers hire you to construct the job, but your brochure says anyone can build this deck themselves, 'no professional experience necessary'." She holds out the flyer. The mother in the photo is beginning to look like maybe she should just go in and make a sandwich and forget about her husband's raw hamburgers that take him an entire Sunday afternoon just to burn on the outside and serve stubbornly pink on the inside.

Jim Cardell does an about-face. "Miss, this is men's work. Even a *normal* woman couldn't build this deck by herself. No offence." And there it is: the crip-sexist moment she's been waiting for. Time to wrap this up and head for the C-Train so she can get her notes down safely before she forgets Jim Cardell's sandpaper voice. This evaluation will write itself.

"You're the manager?" Gabrielle asks. She can't pull out her notebook in front of them, has to remember his name by the time she gets out of the outlet, and hides among masses of seated commuters.

"Assistant Manager," Jim Cardell announces with forced heartiness, then points to Tod. "But he'll tell you the same thing, and so will my boss—no way can you hammer a deck together all by yourself." He takes a breath, like he's been through a difficult mission. "Well, it's noble of you to try, noble that you want to do things on your own, but some jobs are just too tough, and that's why *we're* here to help." His legs spread to secure his solid torso. "This just isn't a job for someone with special needs." Gabrielle fiddles with her steering mechanism to distract herself from whipping out a caustic retort. "You need muscles, lots of them," he says, and flexes his own as if she may not, quite, understand his word choice. "You need to walk back and forth just to hammer different ends." He stops, checking to see how she's taking the news that she has a disability.

"You know," Gabrielle says slowly, "my entire backyard is cement. So I guess I could wheel back and forth, rather than try walking." She catches Tod's lips twitch once, then settle back into a smooth line.

"Look, miss," Jim Cardell says, "you don't understand." Gabrielle waits for his impeding explanation. But Jim Cardell shrugs his shoulders. He's finished sugar-coating this handicap-handyman business. "This is a *big* job. You want a *beautiful* deck, let us build it for you. Otherwise, you buy the material, you get it delivered to your front yard, and it sits there." Jim Cardell means to let out a cynical chuckle, but it comes out a burp instead. "Sits there annoying your neighbours because you can't even lift the wood into the backyard." Then Jim Cardell shakes his head sadly, agonizing for the hard-done-by neighbours.

Gabrielle moves her chair in a bit, grazing Jim Cardell's slacks at the cuffs, and stares up at both of them. "*Look,*" she says, carefully imitating Jim Cardell's intonation. "Is that your selling point? Is that how you manage it, get customers to sign up for the labour as well as the material because you convince them they're feeble?" Gabrielle loves using the word "feeble" with such reckless abandon. The two guys each take a step back. Jim Cardell shrugs again, but this time he says nothing.

When Gabrielle powered into this hardware store, she felt like a secret agent, like a rogue: paint smells permeated the building and the aisles were wide enough to navigate her motorized wheelchair without worrying about tight corners. All the floors were cement and incredibly even—people would be surprised how warped some store floors can be. But she's only eleven minutes into the job and she already knows how her report will turn out. May as well get home and start writing. "Salesclerks intimidate customers into buying more service." Shit, what if that's exactly what the company *wants* to hear? Gabrielle actually thinks her job is important: sneaking up on service people, asking for assistance when they know the boss isn't around. But she's heard rumours that she's just an extremely underpaid market researcher. What if the company *wants* to hear about their employees tricking customers for an extra buck? She loves her job but today her stomach sours at the thought of opening herself up to more offensive slights and slurs. Bone-headed twerps like Jim Cardell insult her to her face and aren't even smart enough to act embarrassed. They just blink a few times before pawning her off to the next clerk. Her lips ache from smiling, and she's suddenly pissed off at her own act of folded hands as if she's some sort of holy lady. She unclenches her body.

The two men huddle together without her. Gabrielle wheels away, down the light-bulb aisle, past the hammers and screwdrivers and wrenches. She snags a child's balloon with her handlebar, grimacing with satisfaction at its wet *pop*.

Tod finds her grasping handfuls of nails, ¾" in her left hand, ½" in her right. He speaks for the first time: "You follow the instructions, you'll have no trouble with this kit," he tells Gabrielle, walking back with her toward the hobby section. "But the wood planks are super heavy, and someone has to hold the other end while you hammer, no matter what. It ain't just you, even I couldn't assemble this kit single-handed. Cardell couldn't, either." He looks around to see if his boss will come charging back into the sales pitch, but way down the aisle Jim Cardell is barking orders into his walkie-talkie.

Gabrielle's tired of today's assignment. Of *course* these clerks are going to be condescending and manipulative, it's her job to catch them at just that. They sell the extra features, she plays her part of handy-handi woman. They don't know she's a spy, a plant, a devious mole. Bottom line is, this is Man's World, even when the male customers wandering the store will also be tricked and manipulated into buying manual labour as well as pre-assembled parts. Focus on the job, she tells herself.

"So," she snaps at Tod, "the brochure *should* say, 'beware: at least two semi-professional people required for assembly'?" She waves the pamphlet in the air in front of his crotch. "Just tell me this: if I pay you guys to put it together for me, do I have to pay for just one of you or for both?"

Tod looks back down the aisle at his absentee boss, who busies himself lining up two-by-fours so that the red painted ends are spectacularly even. "Actually," Tod confesses, pointing his chin in the direction of where Jim Cardell slaps at the sawed wood, "a team of us come out, usually four or five—we get it done in two days, depending on the weather, and you pay by the hour, times five. But it's *never* just one guy." He hands back the store flyer to her, not able to preach its words or promise its photographs. Tod wears the hardware uniform: grey coveralls with the store logo printed in orange over the breast pocket. He's also got one ear pierced, and wears his hair longer in front than in back. His hands and fingernails are clean, way cleaner than Gabrielle's, which are always encrusted with paint flecks.

"So, there aren't as many handymen in Calgary as your store likes to suggest?" Gabrielle is amused again. She's had rotten service and she's had service so patronizing she can see the snot forming in the salesclerk's nostrils, but she's never had service this honest before. Perhaps it's a new trend. Forget the negative report, maybe she'll write a fan letter about Tod. "Okay, in that case, I'll take the construction workers as well as the kit." She pulls out her credit card, and miraculously, Jim Cardell is back, ready to step in and close this deal.

"Here," Jim Cardell says, handing her a piece of orange cardboard. "We fill in the model number you want. Then take this to one of the tills and they'll bill you there. You can choose a week-end date when you get up front." Having closed the sale, he's done, does not want to even risk being the foreman in charge of building for a crazy lady in a wheelchair who will probably want to mess up their workman rhythm by "helping." Gabrielle stuffs her wallet into the pocket behind her backrest, redirects her chair to the front of the aisle, lets them believe they are free, that she's gone, the deal done, the deck already gleaming sunbeam yellow in a February Chinook.

"Uh, one more thing," she says, halting her backward motion. Just when they think it's safe to come out of the hardware aisle. Jim Cardell raises his eyes to the ceiling, he has suffered enough for his carpenter's talent. Now he knows how Jesus felt. He squats down beside her chair again.

"What else can we do for you?" He wobbles a bit, but his body remains at exactly her height.

"Oh, I almost forgot." She gives a "silly-me" laugh, to show: how could she ever forget such a thing? "What about a ramp?" she asks. "Your brochure says you offer a variety of deck kits—designed for *everyone's* needs." She stares straight into Jim Cardell's eyeballs, because really, it's about time he earned his salary, rather than leaving all these details to a subordinate who doesn't make enough to drop $600 on one day's skiing. "Obviously, I'll need a ramp rather than stairs."

"Um …" Tod starts, but Jim takes this one for the team.

"Noooo, that would entail much more wood than kits that supply the normal three steps. A ramp would need about twelve times as much wood, in fact." Jim Cardell's pleased with his answer.

"Oh, I'll pay for a more expensive kit," Gabrielle reassures them both. "I just want to buy one flexible enough to include a ramp." She drums her fingers against the metal frame of her wheelchair in a staccato beat. "You can do that, can't you?" she asks the air. "And, you know, absolutely make sure it will hold the weight of a motorized vehicle." She refolds her hands; she *is* a holy lady. If only she could include pictures with her final report.

* * *

When Gabrielle visits Paris, the art gallery that invited her only has escalators, the curator and two men lean her backwards into the steps and hold onto her armrests as they all ascend. At night she crashes with Jana, who lives close to the gallery, and whose apartment building has an elevator wide enough for Emmanuel. Aside from her show, Gabrielle's main tourist objective is not the Louvre but the Père Lachaise cemetery—row upon row of granite and marble marking names engraved onto their stones. Antiquated cemeteries seem to have been designed for wheelchair access. Gabrielle zips along the main paths, humming an updated tragic-lesbian version of Dr Hook's "Sylvia's Mother." Paris streets have nearly defeated her, filled as they are with cobblestones, unwary traffic, and fresh, rained-upon poodle shit. She wears gloves all day, buys seven replacement pairs during her short stay. Gabrielle pays tribute to the graves of Molière and Colette and Oscar Wilde. "Wilde's ornate headstone is covered with a thousand lipstick kisses," she writes to me in a postcard, "and over it all looms a large sphinx with its genitals knocked off!" When she returns, she tells me she left a stone on Gertrude Stein's grave. "I intended to leave my bra," she admits to me, "but I didn't think I could top Wilde's lip tributes."

Gabrielle's deep secret: bitter, twisted, pessimistic Gabrielle was once a fallen woman: in love. She fell long and hard and didn't get up again for eons. The expression, "her heart was broken," is inaccurately passive—she smashed her own heart, slamming against it so hard it burst.

Burst from the falling. From the hard concrete landing. Long ago, we were both balancing up there on the tightrope. But Gabrielle could see that they were already taking down the tent. I thought I was an acrobat, but actually I was an obsolete astronaut—living on the thinnest stream of Darius's love, holding my breath to make the minutes last. Counting seconds. At the end of the countdown, there waited Gabrielle: broken and restored, destroyed and pieced back together again. A perfect Bible story.

Day Shift

"*Cops Running Loose!*" Charlotte shrieks. She's stepping over newly-melted puddles in high-heeled sandals, fingers clutching her shopping vouchers, the March Chinook fluttering the paper in her hands. She's shouting to celebrate the outside world she's been shut away from for these last six weeks. The licence plate she's pointing at reads: "CRL 827." Charlotte's informed me countless times: all cop cars in Alberta—marked or under-cover—bear the same first three letters: CRL. I'm supposed to believe a thirteen-year-old girl from kiddie-lock-up is three steps ahead of the Calgary police?

She's pointing at a beige TransAm. Not exactly police-stan-dard-issue. "Sure," I say, grabbing Charlotte's elbow to stop her from bee-lining across the intersection. "No jaywalking, Charlotte. Cross at the stop sign." The TransAm's splattered with chestnut mud, has been parked in this same spot for my last three shifts. "You're telling me this is a car where detectives sit on the hood and whistle at girls?" Charlotte thinks that in high school I wore bobby socks and skirts and ruby red lipstick. She thinks I danced the jive. I don't tell her I'm younger than her current boyfriend, who shows up at the Teen Centre weekly to offer chocolate bars and smokes. He yells he has the right to see his girl, but the staff keep her cloistered in the library Friday afternoons, so she won't hear the front buzzer, won't lose her cigarette privileges by begging for an unvouched-for visit.

Out here on scratchy pavement, I find it difficult to imagine the Charlotte of nighttime streets. Her blue hair matches the blue baby whale tattooed on the inside of her left forearm. She's unzipped her thin kangaroo jacket and wrapped it around her neck. The wind whips the jacket so its ripped arms wave at every empty car we pass.

I don't want to dump on what Charlotte's convinced is an inside scoop, but I'm not naïve. Charlotte has her network. Other girls in the lock-up unit volunteer to skip snack time, to comb their hair for twenty-five minutes in front of the one window that mirrors the front entrance, just to report to Charlotte's eager ears that Kevin swung by in his pick-up, that today he wore tight black jeans, a black t-shirt cut off at his nipples, and a brown leather bomber jacket, unzipped. Grateful Charlotte gets enough news about Kevin to last her another week, to believe he's out there waiting for her. That they'll get married, make money fixing farming tools. That she'll become a grown-up, mature into Kevin's adult girlfriend. Except Kevin doesn't want an adult girlfriend, he doesn't date girls over fifteen. But Charlotte's too much of a street kid not to believe in snow-scattered fairy-tales.

"I know what kind of cars cops drive," Charlotte says, as she scoops up some lingering snow, pelts it at the innocuous TransAm. The wet snowball knifes across the car's antenna. Charlotte's showing off her street creds. "You just ain't never gonna believe me," she says. Street kids know it all, know more than I'll ever scratch away. Holy shit—like an ex-Mormon caseworker's going to delete teenage STDs, B&Es that they rely on to stave off withdrawal, pimp jive that thrives. But I'm eager to stop Charlotte from elbowing me away from her already bitten heart. I've moved up the job rank, from childcare cases toward administration, but I don't want this kid thinking I don't give two shits. I take her shopping, I attend her family therapy, I buy her Mountain Dew and sit on the rec room steps frowning at her boasts about where the drug deals go down, how to recognize cop cars by their licence plate initials, how to crack a safe, how she could run from the Teen Centre in a minute, if she really wanted. Streets kids know what they know. Pimps lock up eleven-year-old girls in motels. Wimp-sized stepfathers beat up their wives' seventeen-year-old hulking sons. Their world "ain't never gonna" change.

"You say it's a cop car, I believe you, Charlotte," I promise. A passing bus cruises too close to the curb and sprays us both. What does it hurt to let a street kid play street-smart on her first day back on an actual street in thirty-seven days? I glance over my shoulder at the TransAm. Beige with a mauve stripe along its hood, tan interior. Empty, parked on the street two blocks up from the Teen Centre. We've passed it on our way up to North Hill Mall where we'll shop for a new jacket, court clothes, new underwear. Charlotte's made it all the way to day-passes in just over a month. When she first arrived, she was a drunk maniac spitting on me, then climbed the slow incline toward the one-cigarette-a-day privilege, then two, then three.

The Chinook wind knifes my lungs. Ahead, out of breath and legs quivering, Charlotte sprints away from the Teen Centre up the hill, hair stroking her shoulder. She runs to keep ahead of me, but Charlotte's I-don't-give-a-fuck demeanor suffers from lungs too used to smoking and too unused to air that smells like ice cream and a good mood. I inhale the fresh Chinook, and notice the sidewalk looks like it's covered with clumps of melted brain.

Thirty-seven days ago, the police had brought her in after five in the morning, along with a boy stoned silly, so neither of them made it onto the court roster the next day. The next afternoon, the day staff told me that a woman with raspberry hair, tight 50s-style skirt, and a lipstick-coated cigarette marched up to the front desk, demanding to see Charlotte. Mom. The file said she was thirty-one, but Lila said she looked fifty-eight trying to look thirty-one. Mother and daughter spent fifteen minutes alone in the conference room, and Charlotte came out having swallowed her hangover, and zipped her mouth for the rest of the day. By eleven that night, she was asleep, her lips ragged like she'd been biting on lollipops. Next morning, in court, she broke two chairs.

Turns out that when she came to the Teen Centre, her mom had promised Charlotte she'd show up in court, vouch to the judge that if Charlotte was allowed home, Mom would stay put. Charlotte had run before, but only because her mother didn't come home for two weeks. Her mom had scooped Charlotte's hand into hers, said, "We'll blast the past, together, okay hon?" But the next day when the judge asked Raspberry what she thought of her daughter's chances, Charlotte's mom fingered her new boyfriend's lighter and said, "Hell. I don't want her. I'm *go-an* on the road with my old man. That kid'll zip off faster than the end of this sentence." Charlotte leapt three rows before the guard even knew a starting gun had blasted. The judge sentenced her the maximum. Then I graduated to Administration and gave Charlotte the one-step-at-a-time talk. She's been adding privileges ever since: a cigarette every two weeks, late-night videos, lipstick and eyeliner, blow-dryer. Right up to today's shopping voucher.

We crest the hill and scale the overpass above the train tracks. Charlotte and me, her pretend mom, while the real one's somewhere in California, trucking through the night, sleeping in a muggy rig during the day. At the peak of the overpass, Charlotte turns to take in the city centre. Downtown's parked towers mirror the Chinook arch. Charlotte informs me she'll move into Kevin's pad when her sentence is up. She's crumpled her shopping vouchers into balls, goosebumps congregate on her arms. Odds are, the judge will send her to a group home. Where she needs to be. So I'm here pretending to believe in Charlotte's street diploma, hoping that the new bras she'll pick out this afternoon will make her look too mature for Kevin. I'm wishing for another scratch against her loosening heart.

The walk from the Teen Centre to the mall is less than fifteen minutes, unless you're Charlotte, winded by stairs and enchanted streets. We cut across the police station parking lot that elbows the TransCanada, hugs the mall parking lot, and Charlotte again picks up the pace. Two hundred metres away from new blouse and leather jacket, she dashes toward the mall entrance. I straggle after her, walking past a line of marked police cars in a row. Hey. Every single one, including the paddy wagon, has an official licence plate starting with "CRL."

Charlotte Renounces Lollipops.

I bite my lips, and catch up to Charlotte—just another

thirteen-year-old from kiddie-lock-up, sprinting three steps ahead of the cops. And me.

* * *

In her version of this story, how does Charlotte describe *me*? What major or minor character am I to her? I cannot think myself into Charlotte's head, into hearing in court that my mother would rather take three weeks with her boyfriend of four months than invite me back home. Mutti nags that I spend too much of my psyche on the Teen Centre kids, that I wasted too many years pining for Vera, that I should cradle Vera now that she's in crisis mode. How does Mutti know Vera's in crisis mode? Is Vera truly in trouble? Are Mutti's psychic vibes working overtime? I can't think like Charlotte, but maybe I can remember how to think like Vera. I can try to remember my way into the Mormon girl I was. Or at least wanted to be. Darius said Vera appeared at our apartment door last night, but he didn't know where she was staying, didn't know if she'd call, didn't have any kind of message from her. Did she walk here to Calgary from Utah? What major or minor character am I to *her*?

Vera Says

We hadn't seen each other for over a decade. Why did I end up at her doorstep, out of all the doorsteps my feet could've aimed me toward? I know why, all right. There aren't that many people who know my world but aren't in it. She's the only one both in and out. She's left the Church and won't judge me as a fallen and crushed woman.

I remembered the place from years before. The phone was in his name, and the apartment, too. Like he wanted her to be invisible. Like I was invisible. When she wrote me letters it was always to: Ms. Vera Kimball, like she'd forgotten the "Mrs." Craig always grimaced when he saw the envelope, "If she's your best friend, how come she doesn't even know your name?" he'd ask. Best Friend. A name from when we listened to the Osmonds and wore boob tubes and schemed about who we'd marry when we grew up. Best Friends. Except when I moved to Utah, she stopped wearing dresses, wrote to me once a year. Or wrote to someone who used to be me. I wrote to her once with her first name and her Jack-Mormon boyfriend's last name on the envelope and the letter came back unopened. So much for subtlety. But right now I needed a Best Friend. Needed someone who wouldn't call my mother, wouldn't send me back to Utah, to in-laws, to church ladies. Right then I needed a doorbell to ring, and hers was where my feet and my huge belly took me.

I was going to call. Make out like I was visiting and maybe had time to drop in for a glass of juice. What a riot—come all that distance for grape concentrate. In for a penny, as my papa used to say. My fingers closed the phone book and my feet took me right to their apartment building. An older woman in tights was just exiting, so I grabbed the door and rode the elevator up to the thirteenth floor.

I stood in front of her door and waited for inspiration. Nothing. I rang the buzzer.

I could hear him thumping around in their apartment—didn't he know where his own doorknob was? Then he pulled it open with a whoosh and I could see his shirt on backwards. What a thing? Maybe it was later than I thought. Maybe I was interrupting a bit of nonsense, I thought. After all, they weren't married, legally, so they probably went at it all the time.

Jack pulled a face when he saw me, like you do when it's the Jehovah's Witnesses ringing your bell. "You remember me?" I asked, with a bright missionary smile I hadn't used since I was fifteen and still dreaming the wrong dream of becoming a girl-missionary. There I was, nearly midnight, behaving as if I wanted to sell salvation. His forehead started blinking a neon "No Soliciting" sign out into the hallway.

Inside, they had Christmas lights strung up over the kitchen, except it was a string of hot peppers instead of holiday bulbs. I started humming "Away in a manger ..." then stopped myself mid-chorus. For the love of laundry, why couldn't I just ask for her?

It was obvious, though, I mean, wasn't it? My belly sticking out of my jacket, two duffle bags at my feet. His eyes blinked red-green-white red-green-white and I wondered if she strung the lights up or if he did? Jack had once been in the Church, he'd

once lived in Utah, most of his family members were still Saints.
How do people act like heathens all year and then celebrate the
most Christian of all days? I guess I expected her place to be less
deck-the-halls, less festive. Red-green-white. Red-green-white.
We'd been standing there for eons, me waiting for her to appear
and him waiting for me to sell God to him.

My lungs filled. "It's Vera." My lungs emptied again. As if that
was all I needed, to say it out loud. As if saying my name was all
I had to speak in order to conjure Best Friend there between us.
Get her out of bed and into some inside-out shirt of her own.

"She's not here." He gave me as many syllables back as I'd given
him. He didn't invite me in, he chose not to see the bulging belly,
the bags at my feet. Red-green-white. Red-green-white. Guess I
wasn't the only abandoned woman who needed shelter. Guess
that was that.

※　　※　　※

That wasn't that. Vera was never very persistent, but where else
do you take a belly like that when you're home for the holidays?
It was the Mormons who taught me Christ was born in April,
but since the calendars all got it wrong, they celebrated along
with other religions. Darius said the shift to December must
have been some sort of Byzantine version of the boardroom
decision: A bunch of robes sitting around headhunting for ways
to rid the world of pagan rituals without a peasant revolt. "Move
the friggin' date," I hear one of them exclaim. "We can't *stop*
the plebs from celebrating, but we can tell them *what* to celebrate; we can make them go to town over *our* version." Or:

"Hey, they're rigging up dried berries and wrinkled apples this time of year anyway, may as well link it to the baby—candles for the Virgin. Like that." So go the large conversions. Such perversity comforts me.

There is no Santa in Mutti's Europe; instead, St. Nicholas comes on December 6 walking from house to house, filling shoes with oranges and nuts and home-baked chocolate balls wrapped in wax paper. Every year in mid-December, Mutti dragged the potted avocado plant over from the window to the living room corner to serve as the Xmas tree. No way Mutti would let anyone chop down a living plant just for a holiday week. "And who cleans the pine needles that get everywhere, you?" she asked my sisters, then me when I got older. "That's all I say." Every January, she moved the pale avocado back, just another plant in a house full of vegetation. Vera thought our house was a jungle. Back in the 70s, nobody else had more than a box of geraniums or African violets growing discreetly beside a bay window. Mutti's hothouse tomatoes and peek-a-boo plants and kung pao peppers made our place come across like we lived in a greenhouse. I said this out loud at dinner once, and Vati looked over his glasses and pronounced, "People in green houses shouldn't throw dirt." Years later, I tried keeping plants when I moved in with Darius. By the mid-80s, the plant craze had caught up with Mutti's tastes, and there were many species to choose from. But I didn't inherit my mother's green thumb, and the only plants that survived me were miniature cacti.

One December, when I was still Mormon enough to want to celebrate Christ's birthday commemorated with a pagan tree and antediluvian Yule logs, Mutti tried to dig up an evergreen for re-potting. "You know you're crazy," I told her, as her shovel tip barely dented the earth. "It may be Chinook weather, but the ground isn't fooled." I was teasing her, but I was also protecting myself from having to pitch in. "Why don't we just buy a fake tree, like everyone else?" Even the Kimballs had set up a huge silver evergreen, exactly in proportion, no hauling out to the trash the day after New Year's.

"I'm not replanting, I'm rescuing." Mutti pointed to a gash in the trunk. "The thaw hasn't gone deep yet, and my bleeding hearts think the sun's telling them to peek out." Sure enough, Mutti's perennials were beginning to bud. By January, they'd all be frozen mid-bloom, tricked by the weather and their own longing.

"I think trees have lived through winter before," I reminded Mutti. "Isn't it enough that your bedrooms are filled with orphan tomatoes?" In some ways, Mutti was more Albertan than any of her daughters, except when she defied the geography that insisted tomatoes needed a long, moist growing season.

"Come the revolution, you're going to waste away, waiting for someone to bring you a glass of water," Mutti grunted. We disagreed on the subject of gardens. "My own daughter doesn't listen to the weather report?" she commented. "There's going to be rain tonight, sheets of it." She stopped pawing the patch of dirt to point all around. "By tomorrow, everything frozen, decorated with frost." She bent back to her task. "No snow, no winter, everything beautiful Alberta brown, except white trees. Most of them will break." And I felt a drop.

"God's always on your side," I joked, "which is really unfair given your history of denying him." But I bent down, tried to wrestle loose the tree's roots, and help Mutti dump its under-side into the waiting wheelbarrow. Mutti let my God comment slide by, and I wondered how God *could* be on her side so often, when she didn't even believe in him, when she and Vati drank Glüwein all through the holidays.

✳ ✳ ✳

Over a decade later, Vera showed up a few days into December, after years of no phone calls, no visits, just the occasional post-card and cross-border missive. She married at twenty-two, late for a Mormon girl. She followed her husband around like a puppy with her leash trailing from her neck. I knew all this because Mutti told me. My mother spent her years trying to release me from Vera and the Mormons, and then she wouldn't let me walk away.

"A friend is a friend," Mutti told me. "And Vera needs one."

"Wrong, Mutti. Vera has barely spoken to me since I moved in with Darius. She won't even call him anything other than Jack, because he's a Mormon fallen from grace. Either she's morally offended, or just jealous that I got domestic before she did." I was defensive, after all those years of defending Vera to Mutti. "I phone, she doesn't phone back. I send a birthday card, she doesn't send a thank-you note. But on Jesus' birthday, I get a group letter—*we* did this and *we* did that—those are the rules of etiquette, Mutti, and she's not playing." Why did I have to explain myself to my own mother? The mother who tried to extricate me from fundamentalism, but now urged me toward tolerance?

By the time she was twenty-six, Vera still didn't have children. A near-scandal, according to what Mrs. Kimball told Mutti. I sent sepia-toned postcards I bought at second-hand shops, and she sent me mass-letters, addressed to "Hello out there!" She moved to Provo, Utah; I stayed in Calgary. Darius and I lived too high for a garden, too high for insects, even. Ruth and Jana trekked around the globe, babbled for hours on the phone with Mutti, but my working nights meant I could never coordinate their countries and my schedule. I sent retro postcards to Ruth and Jana, and now Vera, my third estranged sister.

✳ ✳ ✳

Rain in December. Rain that anticipated me taking cover inside Vancouver weather. Calgary rain that washed away dirt and mud and would freeze into jagged snow the next day. Snow that left its tracing on the outer edges of north-facing lawns. We didn't dance in the rain, but the night of our big fight, Darius and I both walked Circus together. Proving we could get along when we weren't getting along? Circus pulled on the leash and Darius pulled his hood on tighter. He hadn't spoken to me since he offered another religion as ending. "You know Mormons think Christ's b-day is nowhere near now," he said, "Mormons say Jesus was born in April."

"Mormons, Muslims—are you an expert on Mennonites now, too?" I asked. Did he need reminding that when we met I still wore a dress to Mormon dances, while he waltzed around in jeans? Glancing up at his hooded face, I wondered why he'd started this conversation. I thought then it was to reconcile.

And it was, but not with me.

"Excuse me if I'm getting too intemellectual for you," he huffed. Then he walked ahead, yanking at Circus to follow.

"No, Darius, I'm sorry, it's just ..." but he was gone, running with the leash held tightly in one hand, the slack bouncing and tautening between the two of them. They weren't heading for the apartment, which meant they'd both be soaked when they got back.

A manic dinner, a huge fight, and what I hoped would be a make-up walk. I arrived back at the apartment drenched, Darius still out. When he marched through the door, Circus wasn't with him and I panicked that we'd be living across town in the doctor's house when Circus found his way back to our apartment building. I panicked into the past tense, forgetting I was leaving for Vancouver in a couple of days, that I wouldn't, ever, move with Darius again. Clots of matted hair trimmed the choke-chain Darius carefully hung on the coat rack, but no words from Darius, and I couldn't choke out the questions tangled in my gut. Questions he stopped with a flick of his hand, reminding me that there no longer was an us. Then the doorbell rang and Darius stepped into the shower. I should have followed and confronted him, but I'm too European to ignore a late-night summons—what if someone has died?—so I opened the front door.

* * *

Her pregnancy filled the threshold that divided where we each stood. Instead of examining her belly, I noticed her cracked lips and wide upper arms. "Craig's gone," Vera wailed, and I pulled her quavering shoulders into a hug, and pulled abandoned Vera into our soon-to-be-abandoned apartment. In Mormon circles, babies need a father. Vera moaned and wept, refused to sit down, paced the front hallway as her teeth chattered. "I came yesterday, but Ja—Darius said you were at work." Darius forgot to tell me the details of Vera's belly. And the duffle bags she was dragging around with her.

She was dripping wet. Her coat clung to her belly and her legs, the rain had soaked her hair, her shoes, her not-so-dainty skirt. "Come in, come in," I said, waving her from the hallway into the living room.

"No, I can't," she said, pointing at the soaked carpet beneath her shoes. And then I got it. It wasn't the rain that had drowned her feet, it was her impending avalanche.

❋   ❋   ❋

Vera didn't want to know whether she was going to pump out a girl or a boy. "It doesn't matter," she said, "I just want it to come out. I just want one friggin' thing to go right, and I don't want to start hoping too soon." For months, she hadn't shown. Her doctor worried, her parents worried. Craig too departed to worry. Without a husband, Vera couldn't dwell at home, couldn't bear to see the ragged grass he wasn't mowing, the rows of soda pop he wasn't drinking. She wasn't getting any bigger, perhaps the baby had departed too? Her doctor told her that was nonsense, she just needed to eat properly. She needed to heal. But Vera didn't crave recovery, she yearned for escape. In Utah, the sun shone, the grass kept growing; in Calgary, winter smothered the city. She trundled home, then grasped at me instead. And then her water broke. I called a cab and stuffed one of her bags with a hot water bottle, tennis balls, a nightie, and mitts. Neither Darius nor Vera made a move to clean up the gunk that slowly seeped into our carpet.

Darius could have driven us to the hospital, but offered instead only med-student observations: "Could be she's not in labour yet. That liquid could be pee." And: "If her water did just break, inform the obstetrician that her fluid came out light green." Craig had never particularly liked me, but had I shown up at midnight, in labour with no husband, he'd have bundled me into his car *glad* to be able to help a heathen in trouble. But I wasn't allowed to talk about Craig. Vera wouldn't even let me say his name. "I hate him," was the only sentence she'd let escape as the cab careened the three blocks to the hospital. "I can't help it. I can't forgive him." And then we arrived at emergency to see if we could book her in for a birthing.

12:52 a.m. Her water had broken about a half an hour before, and now the waiting began in earnest. Despite the dramatic hallway pronouncement, this baby was in no hurry to get born. At 1:34 a.m. we heard that Vera was dilated two centimetres. At 2:27—two centimetres. At 3:44—the same. Vera and I paced the corridors. Outside I saw only night, but heard rain hitting the tenth-floor windows, puncturing the white icing that covered the city. "I can't take it anymore, I really can't." Vera leaned heavily on my arms. "I just want to stop, I've changed my mind. I don't want Craig's fucking baby!" Great. The first swear word I'd ever heard from Vera. If Craig had been here, she could've yelled at him, blamed him for her bloated and constipated body. Made him take responsibility. Screamed the pain back in his face. Raged about men and how easy the giving birth was for them. Instead, she got me: the supportive Best Friend from when we were both still kids, really. Not exactly what the doctor ordered. More like a Sort-Of Friend. But I was there to coach Vera when Craig wasn't.

"Listen to me, Vera," I said, holding her face in my hands. We hadn't seen each other for years, and now she needed to see that I was there, that I wasn't going anywhere. "You're a marvel, do you know that? You're stronger than this and you'll beat the devil at his own game, okay? You're strong, stronger than you think. You're going to deliver this child tonight. So don't stop now, cuz the main event is just around the corner and you really don't want to miss that one!" She stuck out her tongue, but grabbed the hallway banister and started another circle round the corridors. 6:14 a.m. Some contractions started coming, weakly. Vera and I: together again.

✳ ✳ ✳

I ponder the word *delivery*. Vera's brother Corey delivered newspapers for years. Sometimes I got to help. On those days, I'd rise before dawn, struggle to the depot pulling Corey's wagon, and then we'd deliver right to every doorstep—no hurling an already unravelling bundle—as if every day were a holiday and who knows how much they might tip? For a year, Corey gave me a cut of each doorstep, and then I treated my whole family out to dinner at the Ponderosa.

Delivering. Vera, in the delivery room for hours and hours and hours. Waiting to deliver life from her own body. It didn't seem miracle-like in the middle of the night when I was sweating and she grunting. The nurses chat about delivery date and delivery time and what time Papa Sandro's stops delivering pizza.

"If you don't let me deliver this thing here and now I ain't keeping it," Vera gritted between her teeth. They must have believed her because even though she wasn't dilated much at that point, they let us stay through the next day. I offered to call Vera's mother, but she shook her head. "No family, not yet." Cupped one against the other, I braced myself all night, all day, all night again behind Vera, my hands rubbing her rounded belly. She wasn't crying much. That would come later.

When Darius and I used to lie together, his hand brushed against my stomach. "I don't mind a little flab," he'd say, squeezing a fold of skin. That a man could exist who said he *liked* chubbiness was to me a miracle. He'd study all day, work all night, lift weights for tournament training. That didn't leave us time for much play, but he was such a marvel I didn't complain. And when I'd ask, he'd always say. "I don't know why I love you, I just do." I loved his confidence. I grew up believing policemen were always right, fathers were for listening to, God had a plan.

"How do you do it?" I said to him. "I always yield at a four-way-stop, I always say sorry when somebody spills juice on my shirt, I really believe the kids I work with will go back to school, use condoms, learn to believe in more than the present tense." I kept the faith despite what I knew could go wrong. "Except with you the plan *doesn't* go wrong, it goes the way it goes." I stroked a vein on his arm. "How do you do it? How do you keep on believing?"

"I have a daemon," Darius whispered in my ear. "It protects me, lets only good things come to pass, makes sure the bad moves on to someone else." His words resonated inside my head. I believed him. I believed *in* him. But believing in the tooth daemon is the same as believing in the tooth fairy—what happens when you grow up? Darius may have not been to church since he was a teenager, but he was still a Mormon. If I walked back into church that day, my dress would shout out the wrong era, my shoes the wrong colour, my ribbon-less hair would look naked, and my nylons would bunch at the ankles. If Darius walked into church, he'd chat with friends on the wooden pews, remember the words to all the songs, would soon be called to the priesthood through prophecy. The daemon is a mythological intermediary between the gods and men: an inferior deity. Not a daemon, just history.

✳ ✳ ✳

People think it's easy becoming an atheist, all you have to do is *not* believe in mythical beings. But for me it was hard work, it was reverse-faith. After Vati died, I wanted to believe in God more than Vera could have guessed. But I knew that Vati dead was the same as Vati alive, and 49 percent was all any religion was going to get of him. I started asking questions—of myself, and not Vera—and the answers didn't lead me back to faith. To fervently not believe in God, especially when he used to accompany me to a school dance, to buy rubbing alcohol for my neglected earlobe holes, to the bathroom, was as impossible as handing God an eviction notice, and it was that impossibility that made me need to try. He'd lived in my head for so long, he practically owned the place. And it wasn't as if anyone else wanted to move in. Darius had a daemon, a good luck charm to take up residence in God's apartment. I had only a vacancy, and a determination to spring-clean God's bungalow. Hard work and utter conviction.

✳ ✳ ✳

Vera groaned and tugged my arms around hers. The large-faced hospital clock insisted that five minutes had passed since the last contraction. Daybreak. We squatted on the birthing room floor together, my legs wrapped around hers, my chest pressed into her back. "You're doing *great*," I cheered. "You're doing *fine*. We're getting birth-in-the-taxi close, Vera, I can feel it." Vera shut her eyes against my words. She no longer believed. Her labour had begun just after her water broke and by the time we got to the hospital she was feeling weak contractions. Nine hours ago, she was two centimetres dilated. Her calve muscles tensed and another spasm hit us both. Other than the cables of pain, no change. In another minute, the nurse coerced Vera onto the bed to check her cervix. "Two centimetres," she told us, yet again, and Vera groaned into her pillow while I glued my right butt against the edge of the foam mattress, massaged the heel of my hand against her spine. All I had to offer was Darius's inferior deity. Where the hell were Craig's camp songs now that we needed them?

"When my doctor told me I was pregnant," Vera told me, "I actually hooted like I was the Devil character in a Punch & Judy puppet show." She and Craig had had so many miscarriages. She told me this as she lay strapped to a foetal monitor, the nurses watching every minor blip. "It's stupid," she said, "but getting pregnant, finally, was like approaching a green light." She lunged to her left to handle a contraction, then straightened almost immediately. "I mean, if it's red, I know I'll have to stop, but when it's green I never know when it'll turn amber. I could go sailing through, or I could slam on the brakes. It's only when I'm halfway in that I know if I'll make it or not." She squirmed around on the bed while I fed her ice chips.

When the nurse left, Vera and I turned out all the lights and unhooked the monitor probe. The straps kept it rigid against her abdomen, and when we undid them, the machine stopped sending signals to its base. "I hate this thing," she said, trying to climb off the bed. "It's too tight. I need to move around." The nurses had connected her to the monitor because nothing was happening. Contractions, but no progress. They checked again, and she was still only two centimetres dilated. They said the monitor was routine, "just to make sure the baby's not in distress." Vera was convinced they planned a C-section. "Whatever happens," she said to me, "don't let them put me under. I want to be there when it comes out. *If* it ever comes out."

The nurses changed shifts, and the new rotation began all the tests again, hooking Vera up to the foetal monitor that bound and chafed her. When they left us alone again, I massaged her forehead and rubbed ice along her neck and earlobes. "Here, unstrap it, and I'll hold the probe-thing against you. As long as you don't shift too much, the nurses won't know." I helped her sit up on the birthing bed. Three minutes passed till the next one hit. Vera's husband would have been good at this. Craig could have held her face in his hands and sang goofy camp songs. "Purple People-Eater," or "Down by the Stream." Vera says he was a camp counsellor and offered these songs when they had a fight or the pipes leaked all over the bathroom. But now when she needed them, she couldn't remember the words. Two minutes and forty-five seconds, and almost lunch time.

Until I met Darius, I wasn't lucky at all. I didn't have any myths to replace Our Father in Heaven. But, unlike Vera, I *had* someone. At the time, I thought that was enough. At the time, I didn't realize: I made him up.

Yet another shift change, Vera and I still pacing the halls. The sun set so early close to the winter solstice, it was already dark outside. In slow motion, Vera shuffled back into her room. "Thank the stars!" she groaned. I pressed both palms against the small of her back and pushed down. "It hurts, oh it hurts! Hurts hurts hurts." Her words became breathing and I urged her on: "hurts hurts hurts," we repeated together, until the words no longer meant themselves.

That December, I was invited to a week-long seminar in Vancouver, a last-minute replacement. The day before we were to move in to the doctor's house, Darius and I ordered sirloin steaks at the Almond Garden, the most expensive place we'd ever been to. He told me Vera had been to the apartment looking for me the day before, but not that she was pregnant. I could make out bits of broccoli in his mouth, washing around between his teeth and gums, as he chewed and talked about the us we were now building. "Things are so *good*, now, with us, we're the luckiest couple ever." By the time the dessert arrived, the mania was gone. Disappeared into the future I hadn't believed in earnestly enough, into the bread that was too crusty, into the kiwi trifle that took too long to reach our table. As soon as we were back in our apartment, he headed for the bedroom, not a word to me since we'd left the restaurant.

"Hold it." I ran past him, turned, walked backwards ahead of him. "We're going to talk, okay? You can't just opt out, you can't just wait for me to say the right thing at the right time, then disappear when my timing sucks."

He let me pull him into the living room, but wouldn't sit, wouldn't touch my sleeve or let me hold his hands. I tucked one leg under my bum, shifted a cushion behind my back, pulled my leg out, rose to face him, caressed his shoulder, let my arm drop, stroked his upper jaw, let my arm drop again. A jolt of homesickness hit me then, and I missed him terribly before he even spoke. My hands stopped trying to paw him, and then he asked me, matter-of-fact: "Do you know what Muslims do when they wish for a divorce?" He didn't bark the question. Instead, the words rolled off his tongue like meet-and-greet small-talk.

"No, I don't. I doubt you do, either." Darius was, after all, still Mormon enough. He liked that when we first met I was on the cusp of non-belief. A believer ready to defect. Just for him. Half the time he was more Mormon that I was, half the time, more worldly.

"All Muslims do is repeat the words 'I divorce you' three times, and *voilà!*" He turned to face me. "I do, you know. I divorce you."

"Yeah, well, you'll have to marry me first."

"I divorce you."

"I question your authority on Muslim faith."

"I divorce you."

＊ ＊ ＊

Since arriving at to the hospital twenty-four hours earlier, Vera had sworn twice and punched the bed when the nurse told us "two centimetres" yet again. The nurse talked her into taking gas, but there was no sign of laughing that I could hear. Her labour had gone on and on. Nothing changed. Not even the nurses' determined manner, because they thought Vera had been indulged too long. Sleep kept pulling my legs from under me. Midnight shift change. Vera's door opened, the lights stabbed our retinas, the doctors and nurses multiplied.

"Maybe your water broke too soon," one doctor commented. I choked on his words. Could this be a perverse false labour? Did Vera still have months and months to go? She grabbed my arm just as I tottered. She'd been thinking the same thing.

"Don't be daft," I reassured her, my words easy now. "This kid's coming out tonight. Believe it." She even smiled, a real smile, not a pious Mormon smile. Vera and I. Alone. Together. By now, Darius was ensconced in his anaesthetist's house. No wife, no dog, no unexpected visitors.

After Darius had said his triple goodbye, he'd had no more

words for me. He would start house-sitting the next day, and I'd stay in the apartment. He'd still escort me to the airport for my Vancouver flight, as agreed. Vera and newborn would stay in our apartment until his boss returned to claim the house. Darius hated the way winter seized up his muscles, made his upper body too tight to lift weights. Weightlifters build density by lifting too much and too fast; their muscles tear, and the scar tissue adds visible bulk. But I couldn't bear the silence that meant we were already beginning to erase each other. So, because the dog was now a question in the "divorce," I asked Darius to take Circus for a walk with me. He nodded. Then, out in the December rain, away from our apartment, he tried out one sentence. And I blew it by retorting.

And Craig, sweet beautiful Craig, who sang crazy camp songs in the middle of winter, Craig had the indecency to abandon Vera by dying. Then Vera wouldn't speak his name out loud. Nor sing songs to the coming baby.

❋   ❋   ❋

Three nurses tried to coax Vera onto the bed. "No!" she screamed. "I can't stand the contractions lying on my back." It was 3:07 a.m. She grabbed bunches of the blanket, and I followed the brochure's advice to tuck tennis balls underneath her lower back, and prop a hot water bottle under her neck.

"We have to do a pelvic check," one nurse explained. To me. I didn't know who to trust, so I just held Vera's hand and let them lift the sheets over her knees. "Yep, ten centimetres," the nurse triumphant. "Time to push, dear."

"Push what?" I asked, thrusting Vera's hand away from my own, then quickly patting her wrist.

"But I don't feel like pushing," Vera bleated. She'd been waiting for the gradual mathematical progression: two centimetres, four centimetres, six, eight ... Wasn't there supposed to be the part where she wanted urgently to push and they wouldn't let her? How had she missed that part?

"Tough luck." The nurse was adamant. "Time to push. *Now.*" And Vera did. She crouched, lurched, hunched onto her hands and knees and blew her cheeks into a trumpet, the one she and Craig had practiced in prenatal.

"Push, grind, *blow!*" The nurses finally dropped the boredom act.

Only two more trumpet blows and they let Vera feel the crown of the baby's head. She was working hard now, I was just the cheering section. My eyelids glued open, my chest dry and vacant. I hugged Vera's shaking body and we blew that damn trumpet together. My eyes must have already been in dream land because when the baby's head appeared it was a sharp purple like I've never seen on any human being. A punk purple. A neon bulb purple. Vera squeezed out the rest of his body in one breathy expulsion, pale violet streaks chalking his arms and legs. She kept trying to push, her insides screaming, and the nurses busy fiddling with the umbilical cord while she was trying to deliver a baby.

The nurses lifted Vera's arms, wrapped them around a swaddled bundle of new-born purple people-eater.

Craig.

We both burst into laughter. We were laughing, and then singing summer camp songs. Two grownup women. And one very new, very purple, newborn.

Fireside

I miss the food. The stocks and stocks of canned tuna and asparagus tips and baked beans and peaches piled in cellars, the constant baking, the five-cent hamburgers for sale during church fairs. The eternal company of eating. Hoarding food and supplies for the Armageddon—a disaster so bad you won't want to share. "Organize yourselves, prepare every needful thing," Joseph Smith commanded.

Sheldon had a girlfriend who had a delicate face, but was too big. For a girl. She had her stomach stapled when she turned nineteen. Day by day, we watched her carefully overfeed the remaining stomach lining until she could eat all her favourite foods again. The three inches of stomach the doctors left her stretched and stretched until she could fit entire meals back into that space; her original stomach still attached, but flaccid and empty—hanging onto its cravings, sucking juices from its new-born twin, waiting. The pocket of stomach stretched and stretched until she could eat as much as before the operation. "I'm ready for another staple," she told Sheldon, "another great medical divider."

But the doctor wouldn't give her any more pockets. "You enjoy eating," he told her. "One fix-it per body." Shitty Sheldon broke up with her the next day.

Mormons know how to enjoy food, maybe because it's the only legal sin left: roast chicken in double gravy, roast beef with glazed carrots and onions. Pasta with shrimp and Alfredo sauce, double banana splits. Nothing too sharp and nothing too ethnic, but everything rich, filling. And excessive. Any kind of chocolate you can imagine, homemade cinnamon buns, candied popcorn balls, licorice drops, Saskatoon pies and coconut-drop cookies, meringue tarts, strawberry cupcakes. And almond brittle, a regular treat at the Kimballs', which I presented yearly at the annual Teen Centre holiday reception.

And I miss being able to recognize sin. Because it's easy to single out sin when you're stuck together in a group that knows right from wrong. You're never alone in a Mormon ward.

I don't miss the praying or fasting once a month. I don't miss the singing or sewing circles. I don't miss having to wear dresses that exactly cover my knees. Or bracing myself to spend all eternity in a different heaven from my family. Or having to miss school events because they're not faith-promoting. I don't miss sitting on a church pew, attempting a demure position. Or memorizing passages from the *Book of Mormon*. Or thinking that being Mormon means being American.

But I do miss believing.

❋　❋　❋

Boys grow mouthy in junior high school, rebellious in high school, then have to be tamed back into the Mormon Church. "Best way to convert a sinner is to make him preach," Brother Kimball says. The boys spend time after high school graduation earning enough to pay their own way through an eighteen-month mission. During their mission, the boys graduate into mature men. They attend college or university, the recommended programs being business and management. Girls go straight from high school to university, the recommended programs are home ec and music. At university, the girls attend classes with returned missionaries who are usually two years older than they are. The girls call their second year of college their "matrimony" year.

After high school, Vera enrolled in Brigham Young University, taking classes in art and music and home ec. I was still slogging through my last year of high school. Suddenly, we were years apart. Except for that one dance she invited me to when she was back for the summer, our exchanges became increasingly less frequent. Our short, sporadic letters now only mentioned the year in summary. By the second year, our postcards fit a correspondence-school model:

Vera: "I'm going to a dance this Saturday. It's the BYU annual coming home."

Me: "I have the same prof for social work as for intro education. He's going to hook me up working part-time with delinquents."

Vera: "Our house is looking at inviting some new girls in, and I get to vote in the lucky ones."

Me: "The engineers have painted the library rock sculpture again. Someone told me it has over 400 layers of solid paint, not including words."

Vera: "Craig and I are going on a second date—I could be married by this time next year." Except as a convert, Craig was behind the other boys, and still had to complete his mission, so their engagement put Vera over two years behind schedule.

Me: "Jana visited me on campus today—she said she was

there for nostalgia, but she went to Trent U. And she told me these are the 'best years' of my life. ~~God~~ I hope not; if this is the highlight, then it's all downhill from here."

And then a delivery of their wedding announcement. The reception set for Boxing Day. Mormons marry fast: "short courtship, long romance," or something like that. Even Mormons can only go so long without touching. And if they do succumb, then they only get a regular Mormon wedding at a regular Mormon Church. No way Vera would marry anywhere other than the temple. Vera and Craig met in Provo, but chose the Cardston Temple for their ceremony. He was a teenage convert, so had no family who would be allowed attend, and she wanted her Calgary Merry Miss friends to meet him all at once. For some reason, she wanted me around, too, though by that time, I wasn't temple material, and barely eligible to make it into the basement special-heaven.

❋   ❋   ❋

The August before their wedding, Darius and I threw a moving-in-together party. Vera didn't realize it was a sin party until she saw our shared bed. But instead of preaching about sex, she warned me against the dangers of the wine spritzers we served in a large punch bowl. I had a tall glass with ice, and Darius was slurping a grape slushee.

"But why not drink de-alcoholized wine?" I asked. "We have some. That would be okay, wouldn't it?"

"No. Mormons don't drink wine. God doesn't want us to."

"He let Jesus drink wine. He let the disciples." I tried using the Bible, though the *Book of Mormon* would have been better fodder. "Jesus changed water into wine himself."

"No, their wine was pure and holy. No alcohol in it at all. Jesus blessed the meal and then nobody got drunk." Vera was always able to take that one step beyond scripture.

"So, it was de-alcoholized wine," I said. "That's what I'm offering you, non-alcoholic alcohol."

"You're not Jesus, you know. You don't have magic powers like Jesus. You're not God's chosen one."

Vera always got the last word, which secretly relieved me. I asked the questions I knew Mutti would ask, with scorn in her voice, on the lookout for religious crutches. On the lookout for a Gabrielle-powered wheelchair to zip around the edges of Christianity.

After her "Dumbbells" show, Gabrielle and I met for coffee; I confessed my religious background, she bragged about her sexual conquests. The next coffee get-together, she told me I wasn't the only child with religious grandeur. "When I was eight," she confided, "I knew I was the next Jesus." She needed to arrange some new pieces for her show, and had invited me to keep her company at the gallery. "Or I thought so, because every Catholic image of Jesus showed him hooked up to a body brace." She popped a wheelie so she could back Emmanuel down a step that divided the gallery into two levels. "The nuns told me that my suffering body would lead me to a cleansed soul." She pointed to a row of seven paintings being hoisted onto the walls. They were a series of self-portraits of the subject masturbating in different wheelchairs. "The nuns knew nothing hurt, but they convinced me that I had the corner on suffering, anyway." She nudged the bottom of the first painting. "Me and Jesus."

At our moving-in-together party, Phil naturally glommed onto Gabrielle's wit. Which left Vera for Darius and me. I still longed for Vera and Mormonism to make some sort of pure and perfect sense—to be the logical science that kept the moon rotating with its face always toward Earth, its shadowed side always hidden, always turned the other way. As long as Vera had the answers, I could stay religious-by-proxy, I could keep revolving away from Mutti and her Earth logic. But I also couldn't back away, Not anymore. "In the *Doctrine and Covenants*," I said, "Joseph Smith didn't proscribe just coffee and tea, he counted *all* hot drinks as forbidden." I waited for Vera's response.

She winked at Darius, like they were on the same side. "Yeah, yeah," she said, waving her hand in front of her face, "and chocolate has caffeine in it—tell me one I *haven't* heard a million times." She shook her head at me, at the spritzer in my hand, at the whole party. "I know the Church is true," she recited. "And that's all I ever need to know."

I pictured her next words being a testimonial about the burning in her bosom that proved her knowledge.

"I agree," Darius cut in, the Jack Mormon holding out for religious extremes. "People should know what they believe. And *why*. Either drink or don't drink, but don't substitute fake imitations for the real thing." He smiled at Vera, and she took a deep sip of his purple slushee.

❋   ❋   ❋

In Philadelphia, birds-of-paradise wave against libraries, schools, shopping malls. In Calgary, when I buy one, the clerk at the florist's opens it for me by hand. "You don't want to rely on them opening themselves. They're finicky, you know, and if they don't open, then all you're left with is a beak." She laughs at this, but I admire the flower's beak, its protective shell harbouring delicate yet brittle orange teeth. A flower with teeth so sharp it can scratch the skin, but can't manage to blossom by itself.

When I fly down in January, it's winter in Calgary, but Philadelphia reinvents autumn. My host is originally from Finland. Donalda Lasker says she misses winter solstice, but that's what malls are for. By February, hearts decorate every window. Pictures of snow people dot the library where I research and attend lectures, endless lectures: "How to Control a Teenager's Environment," "The Teen Terror," "We Know Them as Our Kids," "Delinquent or Dilettante?" All the Americans want to believe in stories of snow and ice, igloos and polar bears. Who am I to retreat into the truth? They ask and I tell them: "We live in log houses; I ride a horse to work; Mounties deliver the mail by dogsleds; there is no litter in the parks; cars stop for pedestrians; I drink beer for breakfast; my mouth is shaped like an O." When I fly back into Calgary, the red-and-white hearts have been swallowed by the Ides of March.

✳   ✳   ✳

I want my mind to be as sharp as a lover's.

After discovering South Street, I walk back to work and notice the downtown Philadelphia I haven't seen yet. Large buildings plastered with murals, and bookstores crammed full of authors Mutti has never heard of. I go into one and pick up the latest Marissa Piesman—I've never seen her name in Calgary bookstores, and here she is, four copies of each mystery. I read them on the fifty-five-minute Septa ride to and from work. What I love about the hero Nina Fischman is that she doesn't solve the mysteries because of finely-tuned grey matter, but simply because she loves to gossip. Or sometimes her mother figures the case out. Or there isn't really a mystery, just a dead body and a likely and obvious suspect—always guilty—so the pleasure is not in the tricks, but in following Nina as she gossips with co-workers and potential witnesses, as she argues about which New York subway routes are fastest, and as she and her mother eat knishes on the sofa, chatting about who Nina flirted with that day.

I resist the urge to read as I explore the centre of town. On top of city hall stands a bronze William Penn, Quaker hero who created this town out of practically nothing. For over a century—right up until 1987, no building was allowed to be constructed higher than the brim of the statue's hat. I never believed stories like that when I read them in children's books, and now I'm in a city where what I think of as Mormon whimsy was law. The downtown is packed with buildings practically rubbing against each other, but Calgary's skyscraper heaven compared to here. Heading toward the hat (still easily visible from blocks and blocks away), I notice that some of the streets are only about six feet wide, barely big enough for a single auto. Bizarre in a city that was supposedly designed to combat the

London city layout so conducive to fires. Fires are nightly news fare in Philadelphia. Then I realize that these must be the servant entrances, and wouldn't have been taken into account in city planning. Downtown, the streets are numbered, and the road names are trees—Maple, Walnut, Elm. What were once servant entrances now lead into trendy apartments, improperly expensive.

When I retreat to my northern Philly residence, Donalda Lasker serves wine-red beet soup with German asparagus and waffles. I have never eaten so well or so much in my life. After supper the two of us leave her husband at the not-quite-cleared kitchen table, playing Patience. Though it's late February, she and her husband need to work outdoors around the trees and garden fences. We push open the screen door, and I see the compost heap overflowing with grass cuttings and squash rinds, and hear the wind rustle leaves onto their lawn. "Look," she takes my arm and guides my gaze upwards, and I see a pebble shoot across the sky. Then another, and another. "A meteor storm," she informs me, delighted. The nightly news informed me faithfully of yet another Septa train mishap, and how to secure my home against fires, but left out the sky. Now, I stare up at stars that, when I look at them, drop out of my peripheral vision. All the way from heaven, they burn off until they're just solid rocks. Flames, then crystal, then coal, then just part of the ground. A reverse evolution. Fallen stars magically transforming from fire into stone.

Two weeks later, I am the one who invites Donalda Lasker out into her own garden. "Look," I say, and point toward the moon. A fat star glows a faint blue beside its beam. "Jupiter," I tell her.

"If we get the binoculars, we'll be able to make out its moons." This time, I am the one pleased. She gave me vanishing stars and now I've presented her with a moon within stroking distance of other moons, the sky a reflection of this planet. The moons hugging each other gently, keeping each other close. Elohim sending envoys of spirit children down from Kolob.

Advice My Father Gave Me

"Don't ever tell them your grandmother was Jewish," Vati says.

"Who?"

"Anybody. Nobody. People say it doesn't matter anymore—that's what they said before the war. It mattered. Just forget it. You don't have to remember everything. Your mother never should have told you. Your grandmother was Hungarian, that's all you need to remember. If you tell them, people will think *you're* Jewish."

❊　❊　❊

I can't seem to put the pieces in order. I'm trying to confess but no one's listening. It's not that God's dead exactly, just that we've been cut off mid-conversation. The line has disconnected and I can't redial. I can't stop my insides telling where they've been. My blood follows the prairie tides. I sway in the middle of downtown, listing for God's ears. This is not the part where I start to hear voices. God is mute. But if you're chosen, God can listen. He's all eardrums and corti and anvil. I can tell him about the frozen peas I bought yesterday, frosted into stiff shells. I can tell him about Mutti's rose bush that was almost dead and now displays one proud yellow bud. I can tell him about Darius's 3-D postcard from Berlin that contained a piece of the newly-torn-down wall. Getting that postcard convinced me to take the Philadelphia gig. I couldn't read the signature, but the handwriting and the cement shard together signified Darius mailing bits of freedom to me. The Mormons had sent him to Germany for his belated mission; he was telling me he now understood my mother tongue.

God is all-listening, all-hearing. If you're a chosen one. If you're lucky enough to manage to believe. My words enter a wind tunnel, a Badlands coulee, the narrow passage between one stalk of canola and another. But these stories aren't narrow, they're expanding. And I can't keep up.

Heaven in a Handbasket

There are people who believe borders make romantic meta-
phors: the borders within us, that surround us, the borders of
friendship, the borders that keep us out. Or in.

I opted to make yet another road trip with Phil. Because of
his imagination.

In the four days I've been back, the snow has melted off the
trees and the sidewalks. Not that it won't snow again in May,
but spring thaw promises salvation from eternal frost. I'm relieved to be hanging clothes in my own closet, folding socks into
my dresser drawers. I plan to spend the entire weekend recov-
ering from Philadelphia, where I was in charge of convincing
Americans that helping teenagers changes the future. I've gone
for coffee with Gabrielle, but haven't even called Mutti yet. The
phone rings.

The telephone seduces and irritates me. My apartment is not
large, but the rooms are at strange angles and hide innumerable
corners. I have bought a cord with enough extensions that it
can reach any room, any one of those tricky corners. I like to be
able to walk around when I talk on the phone—what if I need a
pen or a recipe or want to match my socks while I'm gabbing? I
follow the ringing and the twisted cord and find the telephone
in the bathroom beneath last night's nightie and on top of a pile
of books on top of a pile of magazines. "Hello," I say breathily
into the receiver. I push the lid down on the toilet and sit.

Phil doesn't say hello or how are you. Like Mutti's phone

conversations, his voice simply plunges into the topic and I take a second to remember that I'm back in Alberta, but is he? Phil doesn't wait for me to catch up. "Let's do it," he says, his words reaching through the connection. "Let's drive out there." Where? Drive *away* from Calgary? Phil's voice continues, curled into my ears, slipping down through my bloodstream. "Let's go down to that temple town of yours, and see what's what. Don't you want to?"

I lean back against the toilet tank, trying to figure what game he's playing. "You're joking," I say. "I just got back to Calgary." And then, "Where are you calling from?"

"I'm in town," he says. "*C'mon!*" Phil, trying to convert me.

But why would I want to go back there? It's not *my* temple. It was my church, but it never was my temple. "For once I'd like to stay put," I say. The toilet roll is down to its cardboard skin; dust-bunnies the size of real bunnies rub up against the wall. I should rearrange the jumble of cotton balls, old lipstick cylinders, empty plant pots, and cleaning implements crammed onto the shelf behind the mirror.

I'd just seen Phil four days before, as he waved me through the gate at the Toronto airport. Since I had a stop-over, he'd driven to the airport for a hug, then nostalgia hit, and he started calculating how fast he could drive to Calgary on the late-March TransCanada. "I'll see ya soon in Calgary," he said when they called my flight, instead of goodbye. I thought he'd meant weeks, not days.

"Don't you still have geography in Ontario to cover?" Phil changes jobs frequently, but he doesn't quit mid-stream. And I thought this stint as a book jobber would last the longest. Phil lives on automobile air and car-seat posture.

"I'm taking a break," Phil said, holding on to my suitcase so I couldn't escape until he was ready for me to go. That was all the explanation I expected. Phil tells Gabrielle more than he tells me, but he barely even tells himself all the details sometimes. "I need to be home," he continued. "They agreed to transfer me out to Alberta. At least for the spring." He grinned. "Nobody else wants to drive the prairies. Nobody else wants the hours and hours of flat pastures." The joke's on them, Phil's grin said. "Chatting up bookstore owners is the job description, but driving from city to city is what I *do* all day. I may be a book rep, but I get to sit behind the wheel of a car all day, cruise the highways, while someone else pays my gas bill." He hugged me and then sent me in the direction of the plane. "I'll be there in no time," he promised. "We'll have a real road trip. The three of us." Phil nudged me toward my gate. The airport air was surreal: I was flying home from Philadelphia, with a stopover in Toronto to see Phil, who will meet me in Calgary, in order to drive with me away from that city. "Set something up," Phil said. "Make sure Gabrielle knows our plan." *Our plan*, as if I helped him concoct it, as if I needed to drive Alberta as much as he did. How to subvert Phil's take-charge stance? "I'll see you soon," Phil promised again, and gave me a signature A-frame hug: shoulders only.

True to his word, Phil phones almost the minute he crosses into Calgary's city limits, yet he's raring to drive off, again. And Mutti calls *me* the boomerang kid? "I clocked in last night at midnight," he says. "Slept like a baby cradled in the Chinook arch. I'll swing by in about an hour, okay? Right after I pick up Gabrielle. The three of us can make a picnic of it—wha'd'ya say?" Gabrielle loves to be a passenger, and it hasn't been us three together since before Phil moved to Ontario.

"Phil ..." It's a miracle I'm still wavering. His next work gig will have to be as a preacher. "I haven't even unpacked yet, you know."

"Yeah, yeah, me neither. We're only going out for the day," he argues. "And this is an *adventure*, right? Think about it: how long has it been since you delivered yourself?"

✳   ✳   ✳

I stay sitting in my bathroom, phone cord in hand, calculating how long before Phil shows up at my door. Phil must have driven from Toronto in a non-stop rush. Mutti will never believe I'm contemplating returning to the scene of my childhood. Instead of Vera, I'll have Phil and Gabrielle with me. For protection? Or to deliver me from temptation? Phil has been longing for prairies since he started driving in the eastern rolling hills. Maybe when he and Gabrielle get here we'll just drive out to Cochrane for a coffee and ice cream?

But: "Road trip," Gabrielle sings when they arrive, and that settles it.

"Okay, Cardston," I say, but Phil and Gabrielle don't trust my words. And the day, truly murky, is not fit for the mountains, or glacial lakes, or city walks along the Bow. "Okay, Cardston?" I repeat.

Now, they believe that I'm willing to be a tourist in Alberta. They believe me, but not *in* me. They ask why the Mormons have opened their temple to non-Mormon tourists. "Think of it as a kind of sale," I explain. "One day only, no returns: the Cardston Temple, through the divine intervention of a leaky roof, is open to the public. Sale ends today: come now or forever hold your peace." I am not holding mine. The bishop and deacon offices will be roped off, the ushers will direct in a *helpful yet firm* manner. I will not be allowed to peek behind curtains. I will not be allowed to rummage at *this* sale. "They have to desanctify the temple so workers can go in and out without desecrating the premises. Since it's no longer a temple until they bless it again after the repairs, may as well let the locals peek inside the magician's cabinet." This week, the Alberta Mormon Temple of Latter-day Saints is a mere tourist trap. They'll let any sinner in, even me.

Phil and Gabrielle and I as religion tourists. Cardston lies 240 klicks south of Calgary, but it feels like the trip could take years. My lifetime. I pack a knapsack with an extra t-shirt, the latest Marissa Piesman mystery, a thermos of hot chocolate, and several pillows for Gabrielle. She's not one for luxury, but she's no martyr, either.

Phil lunges out of his cramped truck and begins shovelling junk from it into my rust-bucket. Gabrielle lifts herself into the back seat, where Phil stashes a thermos and a box of mixed tapes, several maps, a paper bag filled with grapes and oranges, his jacket, and two garbage bags filled with beer bottles and cans that he'll recycle on our way out of the city. "Gabrielle's supposed to spend the entire road trip back there like *that?*" I ask, pointing at his two suitcases, a knapsack, a box of boots, and a metal toolkit. Where does he think we are delivering ourselves?

And for how long? "We're only going to Cardston, Phil."

"These are all necessary road trip supplies," he retorts. "Besides," he reassures me, "I am a master packer! I can fit this stuff into pockets of your car you didn't even know existed." He begins hefting Gabrielle's wheelchair into the trunk.

Gabrielle settles two pillows behind her back, one beneath her knees. I suppress a laugh, but Gabrielle doesn't. "If you're such a master at packing," she reasons, "why not just shove everything into *one* bag to begin with?" But Phil is not going to debate. He places his knapsack at Gabrielle's feet, gives me several pairs of boots and his toolkit to store in my apartment for the day, and then he insists on driving.

With all three of us in my car, we head south on Deerfoot. Cars barrel past on their way to downtown, to the industrial section of the city, to away. We pass an automobile graveyard, huge and packed full of yesterday's transport. "Super-size-me!" Phil says at all the enormous junk heaps, at the cars refusing to rust, waiting to be salvaged by a collector hunting for parts. The road curves away from the tangled metal and then we're in the prairies, windswept and bare; clouds touching the ground, March snow threatening our windshield. Gabrielle and Phil, friends who're willing to follow my adventure, before they quite know the Mormon details.

"We'll be there in no time," Phil promises.

"Only if you keep speeding like this. I thought I was the ve-locity maniac." Over the years, I've gained a reputation with my friends for having no patience. *I don't* want *to be contented* was my favourite line in my post-Darius days.

"Don't worry, I never get speeding tickets." Phil waves at Gabrielle in the back seat, elbows me in the ribs. Now he's done it.

"Watch out, you'll invoke Gabrielle's god."

"Who?" he tries for eye contact with Gabrielle through the rear-view mirror, but she hums, "touch-a, touch-a, touch-a, touch me." Phil elbows me to fill him in.

"You know, that straight old white guy in the sky who's out to get us all," I say. "You get too cocky and—*zap*—he gets you where you live." Phil stares at me for longer than any driver should look away from the road. "He's like Santa Claus," I continue. "He knows when you've been good or bad." This last part I sing, to get a giggle, or to make them think I'm only joking. I hope I'm only joking. "And he knows where you live," I finish.

Then Gabrielle pipes up: "Since when did *you* become such a believer? Time was, you told me there was no such thing as a god, mine or anybody else's."

"Well," I concede, "it's true I value my born-again atheism, never thought I'd practice *any* religion again. But you've converted me, Gabrielle, you and your Murphy's Law deity."

"Uh-oh." Phil takes his foot off the gas pedal, spotting a Mountie. "Guess I'm inadvertently one of that old white guy's chosen ones." He whistles as we glide unimpeded past the cops.

* * *

We pass the sign indicating Calgary's city limits. "Now kisses don't count," Gabrielle says.

252

I believe in loyalty and fidelity, and though Phil likes the idea that "kisses wouldn't count against you," he still wants to count them for something.

"Oh, kisses always *matter*," Gabrielle says, "it's just that when you cross a border, the rules change. It's not even that the rules don't apply anymore, it's just difficult to hold one person accountable to another person's customs. It's like being legal drinking age in one state but not the next. For all a visitor knows, not only might it be *okay* to kiss people indiscriminately in new territory, it might be *expected*."

We three decide that this is a spectacular idea, but which borders make a difference? Provinces? Countries? The Winnipeg Perimeter? The Cardston city limits? When one's in a new country, who knows the rules? Which laws apply to whom? Mutti taught me that when you enter other people's houses, you follow their rules. Who am I to argue?

We're almost at Okotoks. Jana used to call it okay-tokes. Phil speeds by remnants of haystacks, fences that need painting, and pulls parallel to a train just leaving the city. "Hey," I address them both. "Anybody make fun of your names when you were a kid?" I think of what a nightmare my last name used to be for new teachers. "I mean for fun, what kind of nicknames did the other kids give you?"

"Chink," says Phil, awfully cheerfully. He races the locomotive, which starts to pull ahead. Then the highway leans a bit to the west, and the train leaves us way behind.

Gabrielle looks at me, I stare across at the handbrake.

"I think," Phil sings out, "it's time for you to tell us a story."

❋ ❋ ❋

"Once Upon a Prophet ..." I begin.

"C'mon," Phil urges, "tell us about the Teen Centre." He flicks his hair over his ears. "You know, before they promoted your ass to management status."

"Oooh, speaking of someone's ass," Gabrielle perks up, "tell us about the Winterpeg conference." Shit, all her talk about border kissing, I should have seen *that* coming.

One January when I was still a caseworker, I attended a conference in Winnipeg called Teenagers Today. On the last night of the conference, a faction of us decided to explore "the 'Peg." I was all for dropping in on the teenage lock-up unit and asking the "inmates" to give us the lowdown on where the action was, but my Ontario colleagues had ideas about cowboy boots and western music. "We not in *Calgary*, you know," I told them, but they were dead-set on dancing in a place called the Gilded Lasso.

"The thing about country music," a woman I'd not even noticed during the conference said to me, "is you can either stand there all night with an ironic twist to your lips, or you can dance to every song."

I gave her an ironic twist of my lips, but she was right. Dancing in any crowded bar means paying more attention to the boom-boom-boom than to the actual lyrics. Three of us danced together and we danced every song until I hit overload, and went back to our abandoned table. Nearby, a guy sat alone at a table that mirrored ours. I wondered who dragged him out for a night of cowboy song and dance. Maybe he belonged here? Except he wasn't dancing, and he wasn't wearing the uniform. When he caught me staring, my eyes slipped past his forehead at the neon ceiling, the gun-shaped wall lamps, the horseshoe bar.

The only two people in the world who didn't dance the Macarena. I smiled, but forgot to put in the ironic twist. He moved his lips, but stopped because even with only a few metres between us, talking was out of the question. He lifted one eyebrow. I tried to lift one in response, but both eyebrows went up.

He flicked his thumb to invite me over, then pushed back his chair when I did. The stomping feet shooed us to the bar, and he curled his fingers into mine so we wouldn't lose each other, readjusting his hand constantly to make sure I was still attached to my own digits. I was checking out his ass and bumping into chairs. Without my brain sending a command, my thumb started stroking the tips of his fingers, which were rough and squashy all at once. I smelled him when I leaned over the bar to shout-order a drink: aftershave, sweat, something minty. Perhaps gum, though he didn't have any when I kissed him. His tongue was cool from drinking beer, and tasted a bit salty. I couldn't get enough of it, kissing him. Making out in a cowboy bar. Perhaps my body sensed there would soon be a drought.

I expected him to whisper something corny into my ear. A "howdy do, ma'am" drawl, or else a tip of his imaginary hat. Something that fit the bar, but also denied it. So we could continue to be paired together, even after the Macarena song ended. I wanted him to acknowledge that we were both tourists here, observing the local imitation of cowboy. But he just stroked my palms, and alternated between kissing me and taking sips of his beer.

"Don't tell me your name," I blurted out, then had to repeat it when he leaned forward for a closer listen. "At least not your last name," I added, wondering if he'd planned to give me any name at all. He fingertips wandered past my wrist to stroke my left forearm. I didn't want the music to end, didn't want us to belong—again—to other people.

"Let's pretend we met in a bar," I shouted. "Let's assume we're both married, we give each other first names only, and we start our affair right here, right now." Then I held my breath.

He took a long swallow of his beer—I was drinking something fruity, with an umbrella and a huge chunk of pineapple teetering on its edge—and kissed my ear, the cool breath of his longing rested on my earlobe.

The affair lasted three weeks. Two weeks and six days longer than I thought it would. Years and years shorter than his body promised. That night, confessing our cowboy backgrounds, we found out we were both from Calgary, that we could meet again, and soon. We stuck to my barroom bargain, didn't tell our last names or where we worked or how we lived. But we did meet two nights later in Calgary, at the rock-alternative Republik bar on Notre Dame.

Phil makes a sudden decision to pass the semi just ahead of us. The hills to our left lurch forward, then back into place, the other driver offers a loud honk, and Phil quickly returns to his original lane just as a Jetta speeds past us in the other.

"Darius and I used to have a deal," I now say to Gabrielle and

Phil as we approach High River. "If he ever slept with someone else, he had to tell me, but if I ever did, he didn't want to
know."

"And?" asks Gabrielle.

"I kept my end of the bargain."

* * *

We'd kiss for hours, Blaise and I, kisses that announced to me
how little of himself Darius let me taste. Blaise tantalized me
with his mouth, brushing his lips against mine sparingly at first,
a stuttering delight. His lips grazed my skin, my nipples, even
my fingertips, but he wouldn't let my lips touch his until we'd
already spent hours and hours in that night's ratty motel room.
I'd phone Darius when I got there, and then again just before
I left. He never called me at work when I worked night shift.
Blaise and I were in the midst of a tawdry affair, so chose motels with small and dank rooms, preferably located along the
TransCanada. My lips actually ached—like a thin electrical
cord vibrated them—from not kissing him. And when he finally
let me kiss him back, I always came. I came and came and came
inside those carbon-copy, drive-up-to-the-door motel rooms.

I came so hard I bit my lip once—to stop them humming, I
think—and got blood on my blouse. I told Darius one of the
kids at the Teen Centre had a nose-bleed, which was a mistake
because then he wanted to analyze it under the microscope.

"It didn't get on *me*," I told him. "Just on some clothes. I already washed my jacket and would have washed my blouse, if
I'd seen the drips." I tried to imbed little truths into the stories

257

I told Darius that winter.

"Not with your bare hands?" he asked, examining my fingers for cuts. What if he saw teeth marks? "Throw it out," he commanded. "Just throw the shirt away." In his voice, the ultimate suffering of the betrayed lover. *How could I?* the voice asked me, *Didn't I care about him at all?* Gabrielle conjectured that I began an affair just so that my actions would fit more accurately into Darius's constantly-affronted stance. But the truth is, I fell for Blaise's lips and his hesitant sentences. I became addicted to his kisses, couldn't stand the physical withdrawal as he quite deliberately drew away from me, his body disconnecting from mine, his lips retreating farther and farther. Retreating into past tense, into a story I could someday tell about my mystery man, about lips and their slow, deliberate retreat.

About breaking the rules for no good reason other than curiosity.

Curiosity killed the cat, but it didn't kill me, just destroyed me a little.

Blaise left. Turns out, he wasn't interested in the rules, or how tantalizing it might be to fracture them. He ignored the difference between whole and broken, but grew to anticipate more from me than partial fervour. He kissed me and kissed me, on my belly, on my elbows, on my thighs, for days and devoted days. Motel nights during my nights off, during his I-never-asked-whats. In the middle of me informing him that his kisses bestowed upon me a mystical experience, he bolted upright and demanded to know what my full name was, my husband's name. No way. I needed Blaise daydreamable, not populating my day life. After he'd departed, I lay on the bed skinned and panting, unable to come, unable to go after him.

"Don't kiss me right away," I tried instructing Darius, thinking I could trick my body with camouflage. "Hold back—make me crazy for a kiss." I thought we could pull it off, I thought I could keep playing, but under new rules. And Darius kissed me so seldom, perhaps if that was part of the plan his inhibitions would become sexy?

"Don't be such a traffic cop," Darius answered. "I'll kiss you now, because I want to kiss you now." And he did.

* * *

"Describe what was so special about his lips?" Gabrielle-the-artist asks. "Were they especially pink? Were they vulva lips?" Phil just about drives off the road.

At this rate, we'll have to drive to the Maritimes if they want the whole story. But of course they don't—who wants the *whole* story?—they want the juicy bits. They want the bit that takes the longest to chew and has the most flavour, and then you spit it out as soon as it loses its zing. How did I get from illicit Blaise to ever-so-*licit* Darius? They want the story of Darius storming away from the matrimonial bed, having discovered a single strand of hair that matches neither of our heads.

They want slammed doors and broken china. But Darius and I owned no china. And since he behaved as if I were constantly betraying him, it was quite easy to actually do so. I apologized guiltily when I was five minutes late picking him up, or when I called to say I had to stay on at work past my regular shift because a girl was vomiting into her closet. I did this to give him little grudges, stories he could tell his med-student buddies. It never occurred to Darius that I might really have an affair. Never even crossed his mind.

"It wasn't his lips," I tell Gabrielle and Phil finally. "It was the way he *used* those lips."

Phil bursts out laughing. "I knew it—sexual deferral!" He's mighty pleased with himself. "You two are always throwing multiple orgasms in my face as the ultimate female trump card, but this is just plain old masculine pleasure deferral." He shifts into neutral for a slight slope in the highway.

"Oh, Phil." I can't help laughing, too. Phil doesn't like to be trumped, even when the trump is played during a conversation he'd rather not be in. Especially then. "It *was* deferral, but not the way you think. Darius just didn't *like* kissing. He had a built body, a body that obeyed his instructions to lift this or cut that. A precise body, and one that worked all the time, in every direction."

"Ha," Gabrielle interjects. "You know athletes. They're so busy training their bodies, they ignore messages of pain and surrender. Darius probably couldn't tell the difference between sweeping you off your feet and trying to sweep 250 kilos over his head." Sadly, Gabrielle has a point. "Go ahead, tell Phil about the flagpole!" Now, she's gone past that point.

"Funny thing about those teenagers …"

"Not a chance, lance," Phil says, shunning my redirect. "I want to hear about the flagpole—what is that?"

"The flagpole," Gabrielle says, leaning forward so she can see Phil's expression in the rear-view, "was Darius's term for an excessively ridiculous gymnastic move." She demonstrates with my car seat, holding onto the headrest with her right hand and the adjuster lever with her left. Phil can't see her entire body, but he gets the gist. "You hold onto a pole—hence the name—with both hands, positioned about three feet apart." Gabrielle loves Darius stories, mostly because she only met him enough times not to want to meet him again. "Stop signs work best, but anything higher than your height and thin enough to grab will do. Now, you hold your arms straight out, no bend in them at all, and lift your entire body, feet out to the side, using only your arm muscles." I can hear Darius's voice in Gabrielle's words. She sounds as if she heard this lecture directly from the source. She's laughing, and Phil's laughing, and so I'm laughing, too. "I, of course, would have to hoist my chair up along with my legs, but young Darius merely had to levitate his own muscular body."

"He cheated, you know," I tell them. "He'd cup one elbow around the pole and grab it with his whole body. But then it didn't come off like a flagpole so much as a sailor in a 40s musical." This makes them laugh all the more, and I figure I'm off the hook about kisses for now.

"But what about the kisses?" Phil asks. "You're saying because Darius had a great body, the guy couldn't kiss?"

"Well, sort of," I confess. "Darius could kiss, but kissing wasn't his religion the way it was with Blaise. Blaise wouldn't let me kiss him on the lips till he'd kissed me on the *lips*. He'd kiss and suckle and drive me wild. And when our mouths finally met, I could taste *me* on his lips."

Phil, of course, retreats into proper gentlemanly silence. I turn to see Gabrielle Spock-raise one eyebrow at me. We are two women sharing a locker-room moment.

Darius, who barely wanted to kiss me anywhere, never tasted like me. Not once.

✳ ✳ ✳

Phil slows down and lets the car behind pass us. Since it's a road trip, I'm getting the munchies. Plus, my breakfast consisted of half a slice of defrosted yeast bread. I grab Phil's bag on a quest for chocolate, but find only bananas and yellow peppers and a jar of mustard. Huh, it's Gabrielle's bag.

"Don't tell me you're a vegetarian now?" I ask. So much for my sugar fix.

"What's it to you?" Gabrielle snatches back her bag. "My doc wants me to try a new therapy, that's all." The skin on her arm's speckled with paint, browns and oranges and yellows streaking across her forearms.

"Like what?" I ask, spotting Phil's knapsack behind one of the pillows. I hunch way over to the passenger side to rummage through it. "You need a potato masher on a road trip?" I extract the implement, wave it toward the back seat for Gabrielle to mock, but she's stoic. "What's this about a doctor?" Gabrielle never gets sick. "Why didn't you say something the other day?"

"Too busy talking about the girl," Gabrielle laughs.

"What girl?" Phil asks, "Why don't I get to hear about the new girl?"

"Just concentrate on the driving, Phil," I say, patting his knee, "or I'll go into details about what Blaise's lips tasted like after he—" I spare him from the end of that sentence, then notice there's a wedge of lemon rind on Gabrielle's dress; I hand her a tissue. "And since when do you wear dresses, Gab?" Like me, Gabrielle is a jeans and t-shirt kinda gal. "You're not working today, are you?" I get a picture of Gabrielle checking out the Mormon temple, playing the part of a new convert who forgot her "Temple Recommend" at home. I sometimes worry that Gabrielle will be hired to check out the Teen Centre, playing an enraged and betrayed parent. The place is great on locks and multiple corridors, and dorms with nothing in them but two bunks per room. But accessible it is *not*. No ramps, no elevator, no handrails in the bathrooms. We ever get a physically handi-capped kid in there, the staff will be totally stumped. Gabrielle would have a field day.

"I'm not working, dufus. I'm on a road trip with my pals." Gabrielle's eyes follow an empty barn-to-be wooden frame till the road curves. Phil changes lanes to be on the inside. "We're on some sort of pilgrimage, here, isn't that right?" She taps my shoulder for confirmation, then adds as an afterthought: "This dress was the only yellow I own."

"Spill," I say, reaching back and tugging the hem of her mus-tard-coloured dress.

Gabrielle rubs her head, and I see flecks of paint in her hair, too. "It's my doc. She says I need more yellow in my life." She taps at the window with her fingernail. "Look, I don't necessar-ily buy into this shit. But my doctor's very new age." She drills her eyeballs into the back of Phil's head. "She says colours are more important than we know." Then she adds: "Phil recom-mended her."

"Phil!" I tug at his green sleeve. "You sent Gabrielle to a quack?"

"Look, she asked, okay?"

But how is yellow going to help? And with *what* is yellow going to help?"

Gabrielle shifts her thighs further up the seat manually, tucks her legs under her sweater, and leans way back. Her body rarely fits neatly into this ableist world, why is Phil sending her off to some kook-physio? "I don't see why the world doesn't fit *me*," is her usual complaint. "I don't see why I should adjust *my* body to fit the world. The world wants me in it, the world can just suck my tits." She smoothes her dress over her legs and sighs. Gabrielle never sighs. "I've been having trouble with bananas lately. And my doctor thought colour therapy would work, okay?"

"Bananas?" The sun shines muted through the clouds. It's early spring, we're on a mission to recuperate my childhood faith, and Gabrielle's wearing clothing as medical prescription.

"It's just my allergies, nothing serious. But I've already had to give up cheese and mustard and bean sprouts and popcorn. And now bananas." The backseat's crammed with Phil's masterful packing; Gabrielle irons a crease on his jacket with her thumb. "The doctor says I need to reintroduce my body to yellow or I'll lose all the colours in that food group."

"Food group? Pigment is a food category now?" Usually, Gabrielle gets to poke at *my* ridiculous beliefs.

"I know, I know, but the thing is, I don't actually have any yellow in my life." She examines her dress, as if wondering how it managed to infiltrate her closet.

"Show her the medicine," Phil says over his shoulder.

"No." If Gabrielle's popping yellow pills because of their hue … "This doctor was *your* idea, Phil."

Phil grins, stretches his arm back behind the driver's seat, and yanks her jacket from under Gabrielle's legs. She tries to snatch it away from him, but Phil's strong for a pretty boy. He chucks it into my lap. "Look in the pocket." A thin square of cardboard paper, three centimetres by four. Yellow on both sides. Bright, bright daisy. "She's supposed to keep it next to her skin, and fondle it as much as possible." Gabrielle aims a loose grape at Phil's neck, but he doesn't stop. "I send her for allergy tests and she ends up worshipping a piece of cardboard!"

"Bored now." Gabrielle cuts into our hooting.

We're at the turn-off for Head-Smashed-In Buffalo Jump. "Any takers?" Phil inquires. "We're just entering the Blood Reserve and I know a *great* restaurant coming up."

"Yeah, I *am* dying for something to drink, maybe a glass of bright lemonade?" I get a yellow pepper aimed at my head for that one. The exposé of Gabrielle's yellow medication has made us hungry. Maybe it *will* take days or weeks to drive all the way to my Mormon upbringing. We nod and Phil slows the car and flicks the errant grape off his shirt collar. Half way to Cardston.

Phil pulls in at a trailer with a store at one end. Gabrielle lifts into her chair and the three of us weave our way to the store entrance. Five steps on one side and a tin-foil ramp on the other. Gabrielle zips up and in; Phil trips on the first metal step; I take the ramp after Gabrielle. We scurry past the milk and pop and rows of chips and chocolate bars and microwave popcorn, through the back storage area, into a tiny room big enough for only one lopsided table and four chairs. Gabrielle wheels to the wide end of the table and edges one of the chairs out of her way. "Best Chinese-Western Food in Alberta," the sign says, but the only "western" food on the sign-board is hamburgers and fries.

"What'll it be?" the cook asks from behind a cut-open counter, then sends her daughter out with drinks and paper napkins. "Been here for twenty years," she tells us, then the daughter brags about the restaurant being the best Chinese food south of Nanton. The walls are faded pink, with small yellow fleurs-de-lis sprinkled randomly throughout each square foot. We order, and then silently wait.

The cook makes ginger beef and tea-smoked duck for Phil and me, bamboo shoots—extra on the curry—for Gabrielle. She hands us our plates on her way outside to sit beside her daughter smoking on the trailer steps. The older woman reaches out and wipes crumbs off the younger woman's shoulder. The daughter tosses back her head, points out toward the mountains. They both laugh as they talk, but I can't make out the words. The kitchen looks ultra tidy, I see no sauces waiting on the counter, no pot full of rice, no other evidence that they expect more diners. And with the three of us and Gabrielle's Emmanuel in here, who else would fit?

It's not even noon, but we gorge ourselves. Good road trip eats. And I needed the intermission, haven't really faced what I'm facing, today. Driving to Cardston to say goodbye to a religion I broke up with fourteen years ago. Back in the car, Phil lulls us by staying in the same lane the entire straight-as-an-arrow way. The clouds are so low now, and occasional raindrops splatter across the windshield. I no longer see the mountains to our right, and the hills are grey to our left. The next sign says sixty-three kilometres to go. We'll be there in less than an hour.

❋   ❋   ❋

Whenever I slip into leftover God-speak, Gabrielle voices some rank blasphemy, but whenever I remind her that I'm an atheist now, she introduces her god into the conversation. I trust Gabrielle's taunts to maintain my balance, to keep each foot from slipping too far into or away from belief. God looks over my shoulder, and Gabrielle knows it.

Gabrielle isn't a know-it-all, she just knows it all. Could come from her job of pretending to be a strident and unwilling customer to salespeople who want a buyer but don't want *her*. Phil and I, we want her.

It's not that Gabrielle's idea of god is the best. Or even the worst. Once we have named what we believe, we face that name every morning, every night. My childhood was a chess set peopled by mathematical rules and an invisible being who hummed those rules against the back of my neck. Later, my atheism became a god to whom I pray often. Gabrielle's god is the latest. He doesn't like us much, and that makes the rules so much easier to follow. And to break.

"I'm done with the Teen Centre," I announced to Gabrielle one day. "Those kids are on their own. They can get along without me. I couldn't care less." This was right before I got promoted, when I still dodged grenades in the trenches, and just getting teenagers to stop hurling the words slut/fat slob/loser/wanker was a day's battle.

"Don't say that," Gabrielle admonished me. "Not out loud. God's listening, you know, he's always listening." She shifted her legs, then her butt with her hands. "And you love that job. You *adore* bratty fifteen-year-olds. You wouldn't know what to do with well-adjusted kids if they walked up to you in a mall and politely asked for directions." She moved her left knee with her right hand. "So be careful. God is Murphy's Law. If he hears you brag, or sing your own praises, or suggest too certain a finality, God will twist around and make you pay. He'll make sure you're right and truly screwed." A week later, I got promoted. And a few months after that, I got dumped. God, the landlord, treating me like just another tenant in arrears.

Temple T-shirts

Phil parks on the street, a couple of blocks from the temple, newly constructed and polished. Scaffolding and tools are littered everywhere, and there is a sinewy line of tourists. On Monday, the builders will begin to pack up, the roof repaired. Church elders will be eager to reinstate the blessing, fortify the passages, translate this place from building back into temple. Open only to the holy few. Although it's Saturday and muggy out, I notice men standing in pairs, pointing at the scaffolds. With suspicion, or perhaps envy. On Monday, I will return to work, an efficient administrator, write reports about teenagers in Philadelphia. I will visit Mutti, give her a point-by-point on the temple, maybe even offer her a souvenir to include in the scrapbook she keeps for each daughter. On Monday. But tomorrow, the workers will not pack up their tools and equipment. Tomorrow is Sunday, and on Sunday we all will rest.

❋   ❋   ❋

Except for the temple being polished white and new, entering it reminds me of heritage museums: all the good stuff beckons from the other sides of the glistening ropes. And they make us wear slippers. At the doorway, we must reach into an industrial-sized garbage bin and retrieve a pair of white booties, which will protect the temple from our bare, too-human feet, covered by socks, covered by shoes, covered by pillow sheets of one-size-fits-all. And Gabrielle? Should she wrap newly-washed sheets around her wheels? The guards—I mean ushers—expect her to put on the slippers, even though her toes won't touch the floor. They check for particles of dirt clinging to her metal frame, then allow us to enter.

I couldn't bring myself to wear jeans, so I sweat in wool slacks and a polyester shirt. The day is murky, but not cold. I am an idiot to believe in prodigal daughters—not even the Bible has faith in them. Not one of the people in this line-up, including my friends (especially my friends), is Mormon. If any of them were, they wouldn't be here. Except for me.

One usher for every turn of a corner: "No, we don't mind questions." "Sorry, please don't touch." "Nothing to see along that corridor, please keep to the official tour." We wind up and around, up and around, trying to strain our eyes past the comforting velvet ropes. Me, invited into the temple. I want to brush back the curtains that cover the walls, to leap into the baptismal and be surrounded—at last—by the intimidating and expectant marble oxen waiting.

I ask: "How many offspring, exactly, does a person give birth to in heaven?" And: "Call me a doubting Thomasina, but why do worthy males get to 'evolve' into Gods, but not females? Don't you consider women to be worthy?" And finally: "How do I permanently remove my last name from the genealogical index?"

An usher with an orange tie to match his hair comes alert at my eager anxiety: "A notebook? Is this a school project?" He assesses my age and my attire. "Perhaps you'd better wait outside." Then, true to his title, he ushers me out. But it wasn't really curiosity driving my questions—I didn't want to *know*, I wanted to *show*. Whether or not I request a name deleted, Vati's baptism will remain in their database.

My friends are traitors. When they finally rejoin me, Phil asks, "Want to line up and go on the ride again?" Ha. Not in this life, not with me deposited there at the outer edges, kicked out, waiting for my friends in what is obviously a pointed metaphor for second-best heaven. Again. Still. For all eternity. I heave myself out into what should be the sun and relief but is only grey clouds and grey tents set up outside the temple grounds for the post-tour tourist.

Booths manned with the most helpful of souls decorate the sidewalks: one to help us trace our genealogy, free. One for popsicles for the kids, eighty-nine cents each. One selling t-shirts that proclaim, "I've Been to Temple!" ($29.97). And a second, large depository for collecting our now less-than-pristine slippers. Everyone, it seems, obeys the rules: drop your slippers here, do not litter, do not remove. When I was six, my father wrangled me free ballet lessons from a famous Croatian ballerina. I insisted on doing all my exercises *en pointe*, though Madam Valda forbade it. The lessons lasted one month. Because I tried too soon for pointe work, the dainty shoes dictating my performance more than my instructor. Because not listening to ballet teachers is the ultimate transgression for little girls. That, and disobeying God's word.

I realize I have kept on listening for that word. I wanted to stop cocking my ears in anticipation of holier-than-thou echoes. I wanted to believe there was no need to believe, no need to feel slighted, stood up, rejected by God. Wasn't *I* the one who dumped *Him*? Didn't *I* stop listening first? That's what

Cardston is for, that's the reason my friends have invited and dragged and arrowed me toward this holy-land target. I'm on a pilgrim's quest to purge from my mind the sound of that listening ear. I'm an anti-pilgrim looking for a way off, a way *out*.

My temple slippers have gathered dirt and clumps of grass, so I tug them off my shoes. Pick them up by the heels. Then I slip them into my bag; I've earned them. My friends finish touring through the booths with postcards and miniature temple paperweights, commemorative magnets and ancestor computer searches. What I came for, I realize, does not reside inside those walls. Phil has my keys in his hands, points with them to the exit. The sun peaks past a layer of cirrus clouds, Gabrielle's chair reflects blue and white. This day is done; time to return to the present.

❋   ❋   ❋

I got left. I got found. Vera lives in Utah, married to Craig's newly-converted brother. It's too weird for words, as far as I'm concerned, but he's sweet like Craig, can't carry a tune for love or money, and lives for their four kids. Mutti visits Vati's grave on his birthday and their wedding anniversary. She does not believe in an afterlife, but she leaves a pebble on his tombstone to honour his ancestors and her own choices. Vati and Darius are both only photographs now, and Blaise a tongue-flutter against my skin. I long, still, to run into Tommy Cardinal again, even if he would barely remember me—even if I was only an irritating anecdote along his way—but I will settle for seeing Charlotte age out of the system, become the Alberta farmer she longs to be.

From across the street, the temple prevails: a fortress, a citadel, a fortified bank. An impenetrable, concrete vow.

URIM AND THUMMIM: ONE

Joseph Smith lives in a Magritte painting, trees bent behind his knees, trees crowd his praying hands. Joey's father gave him a stone that used to be a quail's egg, now the colour of the rust on their wheelbarrow. Was this a tool? Was this a delicacy? "Don't peer with your eyes." Each brother, each sister, prays in a different direction, Joey wants a *map*. The egg can discover water, or gold, but water is more precious on a farm. Joey's hand turns burnt orange in sympathy and the egg twitches in his palm, carving his fingers into a tight fist.

URIM AND THUMMIM: TWO

Each Sunday a different square-dance, a new caller. The Presbyterians tap their heels against wooden floors, the Baptists twist their necks against the chorus. The Episcopalians, Pentecostals, the Methodists revive nightly. The Mennonites, the Quakers, the Hutterites whisper in unison, pray in duplicate. Joey even test-drives the Catholics. Who is the best man to lead this song? Who dictates the dance? The world should *fit*, but Joey Smith asks too many fourteen-year-old questions, invites godshine through leaves, a pillar of light that shadows tree trunks. The pillar of light is both Father and Son, but neither has pockets. "Which one? Which one? Which one?" asks Joey. "My son," says the light. Joey peels an orange and trees crack open within his jaws.

URIM AND THUMMIM: THREE

The Angel Moroni opens the bedroom door, crawls into Joey's bed, pours God's words into Joey's eyes; Joey throws away his glasses, sleeps for seventeen Sundays. Books made from gold prove the dinosaurs didn't exist. Jesus the Son uses a thimble to help translate gold plates into paper print. "Hide these words in the earth," Moroni tells Joey. "Become a pilgrim; travel your neck, sightsee at a tilt." Joey's father points at Joey's bed, at the windowsill, at the hills, at the sky. Thinking, in which direction should he dance? Then Emma two-steps into the story and Joey wears the thimble to his wedding; neglects to invite Moroni, or his halo, to the dance.

URIM AND THUMMIM: FOUR

Sermons spew out of men from the belly through the throat. Joey tries to hold his breath, to force Moroni to enter his body from the skin down through his intestines. Joey avoids dark liquids to make his body transparent. God's plan includes translucent skin and Emma's thimble. Joey's map melts in his hand, same as the quail's stone. Blue lines for rivers and saffron for veins. The treasure remains buried, and now the well's run dry. "Do not ask, and thou shalt receive." Moroni takes a vacation in Mexico, forgets to flip the calendar to October. Time for leg-bail. Time for the next treasure-move.

URIM AND THUMMIM: FIVE

Joey's father says God sits on your shoulder and tastes the lentils in your soup. Ask James One, Verse Five. Pirates sail through crops when the ocean's too tranquil. Angels live inside hats and horseshoes, slap you on the back when you're skating, tell you to cough three times to the left. Moroni tries fourteen languages—first Hutterite, then Japanese—before switching to English. "Adam and Eve got evicted when they changed the name of Eden to Evil." Paradise doesn't have a name, not when you spell it backwards. "Esidarap." Oh, blasphemy.

URIM AND THUMMIM: SIX

"Chew these words and swallow your destiny." Moroni dreams Joey back onto the farm. Once a year they dig up the gold, a memorial to memory, and once a year they bury it again, X-marks-the-spot. Saturday has one too many syllables, better excommunicate its "turd": Sad-day. His mother's needlepoint writes the Bible onto their walls: "Do unto others ..." "... a tooth for a tooth." Sweet-tooth longs for honey, but the bees won't play. Their crops float by on Huckleberry Finn rafts. Now Joey's brother, Hyrum, wants to join the game.

URIM AND THUMMIM: SEVEN

In the Bible, wives turn into salt when they peer into their husbands' pasts. Joey tells Emma and Hyrum to turn left at Eden, and he'll meet them at the crossroads. Joey plays leap-frog with the bees. "Hard work never hurts, here's a bucket for the slop." Joey ties his horse to Moroni's tether, rides toward the chapel bells, except it's not Sunday. Trots toward the city where people drown inside people, that's how babies are born. Bend old railroad tracks into the wheels of baby buggies. Carrots dangle upside-down and grow toward the stars. If they grow too fast, chop them down like trees, too slowly and you'll wrap their jewellery round your neck. God helps Joey to translate, then doesn't. Lucy in the sky. The gold plates stay buried, just a little. Longer.

URIM AND THUMMIM: EIGHT

Harvest moon slips from the horizon to the sacred grounds, visits Persephone in her grave. Heathens paint their houses pumpkin and spaghetti squash and eggplant. Magic tonic can make hair grow or lice weary. Apples in the orchard fall from branches to the roots. Joey limps from his bed to the rooftop, from his window to the noose enticing him from below. Bad eyesight or bad temper, his quail stone quivers. Fingernails bitten to the quick, Joey transcribes Moroni's hum, "One church is made of stone and one is made of wood." The angel can't remember in English, but his pitch is pure: "Israel will invent inspiration, with a golden arm pointing to the clouds." Curses and perfections. Joey balances the stone egg between two palms. Presses.

URIM AND THUMMIM: NINE

Eyelids slam open the way Joey slaps brick onto sacred brick. Goat's cheese and pig's sausage and miniature eggs from exhausted chickens. "The holy kneel at the foot of the shoulders, suck greedily on blessed water frozen into carrot-shaped icicles." "And the littlest one said, *move over*." Beer spills out amber, not clear, all the better to clog your intestines. Abstain, abstain. Churches breed members, Temples breed saints. How do you like *them* apples? Joey swallows. Apple pie. Apple marmalade with raspberry extract and orange peel flecks. Apples and cream. Apple cheeks. Adam's apple. Ample time.

URIM AND THUMMIM: TEN

God doesn't make social calls, unless it's a new century. "Gather ye rosebuds and gather ye tulip-flavoured vinegar." Sunday follows the map of the week, but twelve farmers don't show up on time. Pews should be carved from rusted combines. The veins under Joey's tongue mirror Emma's dentata under the blanket. Where's Hyrum now? Away in a manger. More eggs when the chickens wake up, and fewer when they miss their mothers. A hop and a skip, and two jumps to the moon. Adam was born in Kansas City, but then he left. When does Joey get his own planet? Patience is godliness. Moroni is worse than an alarm clock, time to gather eggs, time to gather the lost unborn souls of this lumbering continent.

URIM AND THUMMIM: ELEVEN

Wash your face with corporeal light and scrub behind your ears. Pastors up in the apple trees contemplate diving. A two-hour countdown to the sermon allows for milking the cows or hatching a chicken. Balderdash and fiddlemagee. "Prodigal infants make enhanced parents." Moths and mosquitoes make a home inside Bible pages, flip to the chapters about Mormon crickets and locust infestations. Read them. Twice. Kerosene lights the evening when Moroni won't turn his insides on. His voice like leaves, Moroni leads Joey into their woods. "The thimble next to the plates inside a box beneath the hill." That's map enough for Joey. He marks his X. Begins to dig.

URIM AND THUMMIM: TWELVE

The theatre demands artistic fervour but doesn't pay in gold. Joey waves at Emma, wearing the thimble on both thumbs—a prayer or a butterfly? Moroni sighs his father's sigh. Tag, you're the one chosen to sit at His feet to leap into burning wheels of song to bury the gold plates to unbury the hatchet to walk west before sunrise to gather ye sons and ye sons' sons to blurt out exclamation marks and a stream of inky semi-colons to fight to flight to just stop hopping around for one Medamn minute and *listen*. Mark Twain invents an octopus typewriter, and the world spins another millimetre. Gold tablets, God tablets, await earthly salvation. Godspeed and fair's fair. Once, thrice, another time a plow-master. "Just dig."

URIM AND THUMMIM: THIRTEEN

Digging is the opposite of finding, but Moroni says holes build character. "A little to the left." Joey's shovel is a flagpole, waiting for its nation. In a minute, in a minute, in a minute. The treasure promises fourteen packages, delivered before next Tuesday. The Mark of Mormon touches Joey's chest, sinks past his ribcage, crawls into his heaving lungs. The divine plan shifts from the wings of the angel to the palms of a boy, limping his irregular gait toward Bethlehem. Rescue and retreat, rescue and retreat. Joey turns to today's pillar of light.

URIM AND THUMMIM: FOURTEEN

Moroni draws triangles and checkmarks, then buries the evidence. "Your turn," he chants, and passes the spade to Joey, still lit. But to catch a frog in June you have to sleep during the day, camp out during the night. Joey takes multiple naps, wakes before dusk. "Hi-ho silver!" He chucks the quail stone into an ocean gully where it floats then sinks and slips into the future. Moroni has been haunting this square inch of Eden since before it was Eden. He's slept in hollow logs, inside barrels of beans, beneath every hearthstone in the valley. Time for Joey to grow up. "Come on." Moroni waves his wings, "Just dig." One hundred and sixteen pages later, Moroni pulls himself out of a hat.

URIM AND THUMMIM: FIFTEEN

Mud clinging to his pants, Joey packs up his tools. Moroni took the thimble with him, and now Joey's thumbs have come undone. Praying is for heathens, praying is for men whose ankles are too weak to hobble home. Heel to toe and break your goodwill, Emma wants her thimble back. She joins her husband's sermon after Hyrum makes a pass. "No coffee, no tea, no cola." Silver sues gold, but only the posse know how to bet on tomorrow. "I'll see your additional wife, raise you a third-floor heaven." Still, "leg bail" don't come cheap, when it ain't what you bargained for. No time to pack up the curtains, Joey and Emma leave town in a hurry. In a hurry, Hyrum trails after.

URIM AND THUMMIM: SIXTEEN

By fall equinox, the frog population has tripled. The bees won't pollinate, locusts lay oblong eggs. Joey roasts carrot sticks for supper, tells Emma to boil quail stones for breakfast. Moroni shows Joey how to turn gold into paper. Emma, not amused, sips coffee in the middle of the night. Before his hat-trick, Moroni offered up Aaron, and men translate themselves into priests. Quilts and spelling bees and rugs hang from the rafters. Frogs with no legs hop into double-boilers. "Don't cross the street when an angry mob demands justice." Bible repeat. Silver crosses used to kiss collarbones, but now they're sins of language.

URIM AND THUMMIM: SEVENTEEN

Boys pan for gold inside a hat, thimble their own Eden, then revive the city of Zion. Eleven other men agree. Buried treasure can
be hung in trees or read in circles. Men know men. Joey prays
but Moroni lies sick in bed with a stomach-ache of continental
proportions, he may be transferred to another planet. "Four score
and seven years from now." Neighbours ask, why Masonic hand-
shakes? Why the elevator to heaven? Why magic underwear?
Why this rascal boss? Joey hides the hat inside books bound with
a halo. Emma steeps tea, pours hot water down the well.

URIM AND THUMMIM: EIGHTEEN

Stone spectacles help or hinder, depends what story you're re-
enacting. Jesus the daughter of Zeus until Demeter abandoned
him to Christianity. How many hands point to Heaven to entice
the sky away from blue? It's a boy! It's another boy. It's seven
more wives kneeling in the shade. The quail egg used to be
Indian, now it's a seer-stone from Moroni's Eden. "Leave me out
of it." A Lamanite remnant, speaking from its grave. Boxes and
boxes of words jumble together, struggle to climb out in order.
"One, Two, Buckle His Shoe." Journeys to salty lakes require
infinite words. "Binding, paprika, glue, blueberry stains." School
teachers lend a hand, but not a scythe; wives multiply, but do not
reap. Hyrum sits around, his own spectacles broken, bent, sev-
ered from his ears. Another Monday night in New York, Ohio,
Missouri, Illinois. Next.

URIM AND THUMMIM: NINETEEN

The laying of hands bubbles at the forehead. "Upon my fellow servants I confer the Messiah." Keys open locks in doors or caves or hair. Mostly, prophesies pass Go; don't stop at the corner or confer with whom's rulebook. "Formerly a Baptist, I'd like to introduce you to John." Three taps for a period, two commas for the next page. Fill up on the Holy Ghost, and there's no room for dessert. Hollow the name and hide the Father. A tarring and a hanging. "Bless me in a mask." Moroni shakes his chins, hikes up to new hills, a new lake, new sunshine in his old old hand.

URIM AND THUMMIM: TWENTY

The Price of Peril awaits no manger. Prophets need a stopwatch. Leap, don't look. I went down to Babylon and Eeyore was my name-O. Joey grows up in Zion's camp, a suburb of Kirtland. Saints thrive, then don't, then thrive, then unpack. Learn how to taste mustard on the roof of your mouth. Tip the tongue forward. You can always change where you're from, just ask your parents. Joey breaks a tooth, whistles till sunrise. "Don't give away secrets. They cost too much in the Testament." Joey studies the prez, the sheriff's pledge, the county jails.

URIM AND THUMMIM: TWENTY-ONE

Economics from the flipside of a matchbook make do in a pinch. "Pinch me!" No dreaming before bedtime, the cavalry approaches. Missouri was Eden and Adam was God. Don't forget the snowy underwear. Adam and Eve lived in the Missouri valley, then sneezed into the wrong hanky. No whites inside apples, the red carries crater lies. Havoc begets havoc, Joey preaches to the fleeing. "Burn the spare, spoil the rod." Court-martials lure company; executions beg firing squads. Joey gets neither, his neck hurts, his nipples bleed tears. Where is the fruitless Moroni? "Young man, throw 'em in the brig, steal their opera, marry an encore." Don't squadron, don't break, just sink into the spray of apple seeds nibbling at your neckline, fill your mouth to the brim with expired verbs. Pagan.

On Monday

My sisters have spread from Calgary outwards: Toronto, Paris, Israel, France, Taiwan. Big cities away from our home, away from the intersection of flat plain and rocky mountains. They left and I stayed. As often as my job sends me away—to Vancouver, to Montréal, to Winnipeg, to Philadelphia—it hauls me back again. I used to tell myself that Calgary's street kids needed me to come back and save them. But it's the Teen Centre's administration that claims me. The Church of Helping: another faith I have tried to cling to, determined to believe its doctrine, against all scientific evidence to the contrary.

On Monday morning I sit down to a stack of release forms, piled onto my desk as if I could forge through them in one go. The court docket is already set, the busses waiting out front, but a new kid was admitted last night and his paperwork is incomplete. I pull out his file, check my watch: 9:32. The temple is closed to the public again, but has not yet been rededicated for baptisms and eternal sealings. Monday. I need to get back into work mode. I need to get back into *Calgary* work mode.

The phone rings. My mother doesn't say hello, just dives right in: "You've been to the temple, *na*?"

"Mutti?" I ask, just to be sure.

"Of course, who else?" she asks. She doesn't ask why I haven't called her, she doesn't ask why I made my way to Cardston now. Instead, her words leap forward. "Okay, no excuses this time. I've got the tickets already. What do you say?"

I hate this game, always stumble over the rules. "Tickets where? Plane or theatre?"

"Plane tickets, of course. I've decided to return to Germany. To Friedrichsdorf."

"You're going back?" is all I can manage. "But you said you'd never go back. You said leaving was like sealing a letter and never mailing it." I feel my indignation on her behalf rise up. "You said your older brother made you embroider your only dress with swastikas. You said that friends disappeared in the middle of the school day. You said a building fell on you, and you were the only one to crawl out alive." My words stop me. These are her words, her stories, not mine to throw back in the middle of a half-assed work-day telephone conversation.

"Not on me," she says quietly. "It wasn't me. The building didn't fall on me."

This is a new version of the story, but I don't have time for it this morning. "When? When do you leave?"

"Next month. How busy are you in April?"

I should have known. Why didn't she just ask right away? Why am I always supposed to intuit her plans with my sisters? They've probably been planning for weeks, and only informing me now. Why do I always forget? "No problem, Mutti," I reassure her. "I can come over every day and feed the cat, water the plants. It's the least I can do." No problem at all.

"Oh, Schatz, don't be silly." Mutti's voice comforts. "I want *us* to go to Germany. You and me. Mother and daughter, together. Flying there with me will give you a chance to reconnect with your past people."

"You never wanted me to be German before."

She laughs, a short cough into the phone. "Well, people change when they stop being mothers, you know." When did Mutti cease motherhood? "Besides, I was talking about your Mormon heritage, not your German one."

"Huh?"

"The Mormons have settled in the small town where I grew up. There's a temple in Friedrichsdorf. Your uncle walked through before they sanctified it, the year before he died."

"I thought you two didn't speak."

"No, we just hadn't had a conversation since disagreeing was the only subject matter we agreed upon." No coughed-up laugh this time. "A long time ago, home was something to get away from. After the war, there was nothing left. Nothing. In Canada, your father wanted so badly for you all to speak Croatian, and you learned French in school—I thought one more language would just confuse matters. So I didn't teach you German at home. I always regret that." She has confessed, finally, her sin of omission. One of the omissions.

"But I thought we did speak some German."

"Oh, Schatz, I barely speak German anymore." Mutti starts cough-laughing at me again, at my false assumptions. "You nosed around your memorial shrine, now I need to poke at mine." I have years of built-up questions for Mutti, but her disclosure throws me for a loop. When Darius left me, with no story to tell about the *why*, I grew to understand how betrayal can sit on your shoulders larger than words, heavier than storytelling.

✳   ✳   ✳

After Darius and I "divorced," when I flew back from my re-
prieve in Vancouver, I wasn't sure where I lived anymore. Vera
and baby moved back to Utah to be with Craig's family, and
Darius had given notice on the apartment, with no forwarding
address. I had a week of holiday time to rush through the place
and claim my property. I sorted through his abandoned boxes,
his now outdated medical textbooks, his muscle magazines, to
find my social work manuals, the art I bought at Gabrielle's
advice, the gardening tools Mutti gave me every birthday. I'd
thought Darius and I had seamlessly meshed our lives together.
But it turned out to be terribly easy, after nearly a decade together, to separate our stuff. I shoved bulging garbage bags into
Mutti's car, drove to the nearest "basement for rent" sign, and
unloaded everything into the bedroom. When I returned the
car, I didn't stay to chat. Our Xmas rites that year consisted of
Mutti giving me books I'd never read, plates and bookshelves
for my basement apartment, a coupon for a new bed, and pouring more *Glühwein* into my glass every time I took even one sip.
I gave her souvenirs from the Vancouver airport—maple fudge,
and candy-smoked salmon, and a paper yo-yo. Neither Ruth nor
Jana made it home that year. It was the silentest night we'd ever
celebrated. When I borrowed her car two days later, I couldn't
speak for fear that saying the words aloud would damn near
break me. And who knew what truths would emerge once I
started to confess? Until I allowed for it, Mutti made no comment, though she and my sisters must have built up hefty phone
bills discussing my *plight*.

After months in that basement, I started searching for above-
ground apartments, and faced up to sorting through some of

the garbage bags. I decided to return the gardening tools to Mutti as I seemed destined for apartment life.

I didn't bother ringing the bell, but curved around the house to the backyard where I knew Mutti would be bent over her not-yet-planted garden, weeding last year's rotting stems and leaves. I squatted beside her and saw a few pea pods still hanging on from last August. I plucked them and chewed three fat wrinkled peas. A bitter taste shot through my mouth; my eyes welled up. "Oh, Schatz," my mother said, yanking at a stubborn clump of grass, "he never will be worth these tears."

"Easy for you," I babbled. "You don't know what it's like when someone you love is gone, just *gone*." Then I hiccupped my ridiculous sorrow, aimed at a woman who'd been a widow for longer than Darius and I had been together. Crying me: pining for the touch of a man who wouldn't touch me even when we were together.

"I lost more than my brother in the war," Mutti says, surprising me. And of course that halted my silly lament, how can breaking up compete with both parents and a brother dying? That day, even inside my own pathetic grief, I asked Mutti about her brothers. She told me a bit about her younger brother who died at the Russian front, but nothing about the older one. I knew he lived in the same village they'd grown up in, had worked in a hospital during the war, had three children, and was now retired. But I hadn't met him, had never flown to Europe on any of my work trips, didn't know if my cousins spoke any English.

"My parents died when I was in my teens," she said, grinding her trowel around a patch of dandelions. "He was the oldest and became my sort-of father." She paused to choose her words carefully. "You might say we had an enormous father-daughter falling-out." She stood up. "Enough weeding for one day, come and have some peppermint tea." Two grown women sipping children's tea.

✳ ✳ ✳

Now that she's planning this trip for us, I understand Mutti's words from that day aren't the end of the story. Mutti loves words too much to offer so few at one time. But back then, I was too busy crying over Darius's retreat to make much of hers. I'd tried different tactics since then, but always got the same rehearsed speech. No real details about either brother, no new stories about the one who lived. After Vati died, Mutti strode forward, away from the dead in her life, and chose to walk instead with my sisters—three women, together carrying on. With Darius gone, I could've joined the coven, but I didn't quite understand the customs. But Saturday at Cardston, I confronted a large piece of my past devotion, or at least the oppressive stone building that represented a past faithful me. Monday may be a day for avoiding file reports and court forms, but I need to ask Mutti about the secret she's never told me, the story I've always been too youngest-daughter for, the childhood *she* escaped from. Right now, on the phone, somewhere inside her invitation is a clue to the rest of the story.

"Tell me," I say. "I won't even consider flying there if you don't tell me what happened to you in Germany. Everything."

I can tell that Mutti is trying to find the words to the story she had decided she'd never tell me. Her breath comes out choppy and for once words desert her. I wonder if she's already told my sisters, if I am the last one in on this secret or the first to break her self-imposed gag order. "Okay, tomorrow, come for supper," Mutti says. Her offer comes with food. "But until yesterday, you don't want to hear." Then a click.

I've been to the temple and I've convinced Mutti to divulge family secrets. Hanging up, I reach for the top file: Tom Cardinal.

Often, as a caseworker dealing with children and their grim futures, I would think the kids being admitted into the Teen Centre were kids I knew from high school or from kindergarten or even just from the neighbourhood. I thought I saw Corey once, right ear and both eyebrows studded with stainless steel rings; Tracy Alekhine waltzed in with a bruised cheek and tattooed lips; I'd already spotted Tommy Cardinal seven or eight times, each kid a finger-twirling replica of the eleven-year-old boy Vera and I used to play with. Or avoid playing with. I'd see Tommy's face, and have to swallow my greeting—again and again—because none of these boys could be Tommy, the Tommy I'd known was just another grownup out there in the world, not in here clutching a police officer's hand. He was working at a dry cleaner's or an insurance office, applying for grad school, or taking his own kid to the movies. The Tommy Cardinal I'd known wasn't standing in the lobby of my work place, wasn't waiting for me to rescue him.

"Did you ever see Tommy again?" Gabrielle asked me the day before I flew off to Philadelphia. Such a tiny sentence, such a large question.

My hands tremble as I open the file. Eleven-year-old boy,

riding the city trains without a ticket—the usual excuse for
bringing in runaways. Wouldn't tell the cops where he belonged.
I hope not fostered out to a family who expects to love him for
needing rescue, for skin dyed the colour of the lost tribe, for
his flock of dead Lamanite relatives, queuing up to be saved.
Tommy and Vera. Darius and Blaise. Mutti's lost brothers. My
surreal sisters.

"No," I replied to Gabrielle's probe. "No, I never did."

Tomorrow after supper, I'll stay until Mutti fills in those ever-
widening blanks. Mutti doesn't want me simply listening to
this story, she wants me to crack its code, detonate its grenade
crammed with shrapnel narrative. A barbaric story, but one I
need to hear, one Mutti needs to divulge, no matter how untel-
lable its ending.

Cross Your Heart

Eva grips Horst's neck with both hands. His arms are strong, so she won't fall, but her right stump bumps uncomfortably against his left hip. Horst shifts her so she leans against his chest. She can smell apple-core soap, poke a finger through the hole in his sweater just below his neck.

She gets to go to work with Horst! She gets to skip school and ride the train—she hasn't been on a train since her parents took her to München, where her father worked at the railroad. Shhh, don't think about that day. Eva has begged to skip school, ride with Horst all the way to the Wiesbaden station—"the prettiest city in all of Europe," Horst says—let him carry her up the winding hill with a hospital perched on top, like a castle, or a fortress. But Mam always says, "Don't be silly, Horst, *Eva* in a *hospital*, what are you thinking? Not over my dead body, that's what I say." Then she shuts the kitchen door so Eva doesn't hear the arguing. Mam has rules, and without rules a household is just a house, held by no one.

Horst jokes back, "That can be arranged," and he laughs because you shouldn't joke about dead bodies during war. But Mam doesn't laugh. Eva hasn't heard Mam laugh since Horst started inviting Eva to accompany him to his workplace. A girl can't be shielded from real life her whole life. On the way to the station, Horst tells Eva that today he'll need to lift some thirty patients from their beds onto chairs, onto examining tables. He gives her an exact weight of each person—twenty-six kilos, thirty-eight kilos, twenty-two kilos—you'd think the adults would weigh more, but Horst says in this hospital, some patients don't know enough to chew and swallow.

All the way up their road, with the trees gone, Eva can make out each house. In front of the Rueters, a tiny woman the size of Eva's pinky sweeps the road. "It may be war," Frau Rueter always says, "but all the more reason to sweep away rubble." Eva agrees. Eva's breathed in enough rubble to last a lifetime. Swish, swish, swish, Frau Rueter convinces the dust to move a few centimetres to the left. And there's Mam. She pokes her head out the kitchen door to call Eva. Her auburn hair curls off her shoulders. She looks over the fence, as if she's hunting Easter eggs, then dashes out the gate when she spots Eva. She's yelling at her, Eva can see Mam's lips widen, but Eva can't hear, Horst has walked such a distance in such a short time. Eva used to run from their house to the train station to meet him after work, but now it takes her too long, even with the wheelchair Mam and Dieter made for Eva when she got back home. But Horst's strides are long and confident, he's halfway to the station by the time Mam sees them round the corner. He walks as if running, no fair, Mam will never catch up! Eva giggles, and imagines the train waiting for them to board. She peeks her head above Horst's shoulder to look back.

Mam will never catch them. Eva hears the train whistle just as Horst steps onto the platform. Eva waves, but Mam is running too hard to wave back, her hair uncurling and dragging itself around her shoulders. "Bye, Mam," Eva calls out, though only Horst can hear her. "See you for supper!" she snorts because no peeling onions tonight, supper will be ready when she gets home, just like supper waits for Horst. Eva's going to work today!

"You'll stay in my ward," Horst tells her, as the train pulls away from their station, and that's when Eva knows she's not just visiting, she's moving.

Their car rides away from the platform before Mam even reaches the edge, her face splotchy from running, falling hair making her head appear lopsided and dopey. Horst nods at the conductor and pays Eva's ticket. "My daughter," he says, and the conductor nods sympathetically, gives Eva a smile like she's two. Or maybe seventy-two. When they get off the train and Horst tells her she's staying at his hospital from now on, Eva buries her face in his dank sweater. She's mad at him for not letting her bring Anna-Banana and not letting her say goodbye to Mam and Dieter.

"We're your parents now," Horst proclaimed nearly a year ago when he brought her home from *her* hospital, not the one where he works. Her brother Horst, no longer her brother, her sister no longer her sister. "I'm your father and she's your moth-er." He pointed at himself with his thumb and at Eva's sister with his chin. "Call her Mama, call me Papa." Horst pulled a blanket over Eva's waist without looking at the space that used to be her legs. "You're not an orphan. You're our daughter now. War changes everything." And then Horst sat down for supper. Marga—she means Mam—had cooked yams and boiled eggs and fresh rye bread and strawberry jam, Eva's favourites. Dieter, Eva's other brother, pulled Eva's chair close to the table.

"What about Dieter?" Eva asked. "Is he my father, too?" She tried to throw the scratchy blanket off her legs, she wanted to keep looking down, past her thighs, past one knee, till she got used to seeing how her legs now ended. Anna-Banana told Eva she liked her new legs, liked the extra space to curl into, but Eva wasn't used to them yet, and she wanted to look at what wasn't there. She learned a new way to go to the bathroom, new ways to get dressed. She still expected her body to be *longer*, and she needed to recognize herself. She needed to *see* her body to understand how to *move* it around.

"No, you can call Dieter, Uncle. We're your parents," he said again, and Eva saw her ex-sister and her new uncle roll their eyes at her new father.

"You think she'll forget about our real parents?" Mam demanded of Horst, after they sent Eva to bed. "You think that's even a good idea?" Mam started sweeping the floor, as she did every night. Eva fell asleep to Mam's swish-swish.

"Don't you get it?" Horst asked, trying hard to explain the rules to Mam—Eva wondered if they were married now—to explain how families work during war. "There were no casualties that day. *No* German casualties, just one English lady. Every news announcer carried the story: Germany got bombed by the British and *no* Germans died. The British are so bad at fighting, they kill themselves for us." Horst puffed on what used to be their father's pipe.

"And our parents," Mam corrected him. "They managed to bomb the hell out of the shoemaker's shop beside the railroad. Why won't you let us say our parents died?"

"Because I see more than you see. You want to march into the offices of the Gestapo and tell them? You have no sense," Horst said, sounding disgusted. "I'm helping this family survive this

296

war, even if I have to drag each of you kicking and screaming through to the other side." And then Horst was done talking, but Mam kept sweeping and sweeping into the night.

Mam took care of Eva like a real mother, helping her learn to use the bathroom again, sewing new clothes, tutoring her when Mam's own school work and chores were done. Eventually, staying home from school so supper didn't wait till night to get eaten. Dieter was shyer. Like Horst, he wouldn't look at her legs, but he built her a chair from old bicycle wheels and a tractor seat, and Mam painted stripes on it by mixing together berries and oil, and in a few months Eva could zip around their yard, and eventually to school.

Now, when they enter Horst's hospital, Eva remembers her chair and panics because she doesn't like to crawl in buildings until she knows where she's going and who might see her, but Horst says, "Don't worry, they've got lots of crutches here." He takes Eva to a bed. "This is yours now, don't let anyone else sleep here," he says, then leaves her there. Why would anyone try to sleep in her bed? Eva wonders. She wishes she could lay Anna-Banana on the pillow. *Her* pillow, *her* bed. She's not going to cry. The last time she cried, she woke up without—Eva scolds herself for thinking about that day!

The room Horst has left her in is as big as their kitchen at home, but filled to its edges with beds. There's moaning, and one patient is singing. On one side of Eva is a bald woman with cracked lips, and on the other, an open-mouthed woman lying on top of brown splotchy sheets. Six patients have dirty diapers piled in a bucket beside their beds. Eva wrinkles her nose. Can't these women smell? This must be why Horst has to lift so many patients every day. She tries to turn away from the stink, but it's no use. Several children play in the corner, they didn't stop when Horst walked in with Eva, and they don't see her now when she pushes herself up for a better look. Three boys and four girls. The girls are young, two of the boys are her age, but one is much older, at least by two years. They play together. They each have a piece of clothing in their hands—one a faded orange scarf, one an undershirt, three hold one shoe each, but none of the shoes match, and the oldest boy holds a long wig, tied in a ponytail. Eva watches as they pass the items back and forth, the oldest boy writing down the score on a piece of cloth. Eva has played games at school with all sorts of made-up toys—fence slats for field hockey, train stubs for card games, real charcoal for drawing class—but she can't make out the rules for this game.

"I'm Eva," she says through the thick air filled with groaning patients, and one woman praying out loud, the same words over and over, "I will lift up mine eyes unto the hills, from whence cometh my help, I will lift up mine eyes, I will lift up mine eyes." But the children in the corner say nothing, just keep passing around the clothing items. *What now?* Eva wonders. Will Horst come back after he's talked to the head nurse, or has he already begun his shift somewhere in the hospital? The people lying down look so frail, like if Horst tried to pick them up they would dissolve into dust. One woman with an eye missing wanders around the room plucking flowers from her elbows, gathering them into a bouquet she presents to a figure lying down, heatedly arguing with Jesus' brother. Maybe that's what you do during war, Eva thinks, pretend to be crazy so you get to stay in hospitals where you'll be safe. They talk, but not to each other, not to her.

Maybe Horst left her in the deaf ward by mistake. Except the circle of children in the corner move their lips, nod their heads together. Nobody's winning their game, as far as Eva can tell. She has been here for less than half an hour and already she wants to go home. Even school would be better. Nobody ignores her at school, not even the teacher when she wants him to. Maybe Horst is joking that Eva has to stay here. Maybe Mam grabbed the next train, is right this minute walking up that winding hill, with just as many curves as Horst described. Mam will walk through the door any minute with her lopsided auburn hair and sour cherries as a treat. Eva closes her eyes to picture Mam's huffing face at the train station.

No.

No Mam will arrive to lift her out of this messy room filled with ugly people. Ugly and old and sick and crazy. Horst is her father, Eva is his daughter. He wouldn't bring her here if it weren't the right place to be. She grabs the edge of her mattress and uses her arms to lower her body until her right stump touches the floor. So what if those children laugh at her? She'll crawl to them and stuff herself into their middle and they'll all play together just like her friends at school. For weeks following her return to school from the other hospital, the boys stared and the girls pretended her desk still sat empty. Finally, Eva crawled right up to Jürgen Tolz and asked if he wanted to see her stump up close. Then all the boys begged her to let them touch. Friedl, too, her friend since Eva introduced Anna-Banana to Friedl's Baby Heidi in kindergarten. Even in this place, Eva may be different, but after a while these new kids won't remember that they each have one and a half legs more than she does. Her stump hits the floor, and Eva begins a long sticky crawl toward the corner of her new home.

But before Eva makes it across the floor, Horst scoops her up and chastises her for getting her dress smudged. When Horst frowns and points his chin at her dress, Eva feels like she soiled herself. But how's she supposed to get around without her chair or Mam to carry her? She sees no crutches anywhere, despite Horst's promise. After he brushes off her dress, he carries her into a room at the end of the corridor to introduce her to the head nurse. The room is the tidiest Eva has ever seen, and each book on the bookcase lines up with the spine of the others. A perfectly solid green rock secures a pile of folders on the desk. Horst tells her later that the rock's name is Jade. Eva would like to introduce Anna-Banana to Jade, they could play games together. The only dirt is a pile of ashes in the ashtray. The clear glass ashtray and the square block of jade are both exactly the same distance from the edge of the desk. Perhaps they hold the desk in place, not just the paper? Head Nurse sits behind her desk.

"So, you're Horst's," Head Nurse says with a smile bigger than her face. Eva recognizes the pity in it.

Horst nods, as if owning Eva is, indeed, his latest accomplishment. "Eva, this is Head Nurse—she runs the entire hospital. Despite what the doctors may say."

Head Nurse stands abruptly, her uniform unwrinkled, her cap floating centimetres above her perfectly smooth hair. Eva wonders, how does it know which direction to float? Is it attached by a string, like a balloon? Horst is ready to leave, and Eva reaches her arms up to him for wherever they're going next.

"No, young lady," Head Nurse says. "You'll not rely on this good man so much while you're in my care." Her lips change to the colour of white asparagus, and she turns and gives Horst an asparagus-tip nod. Horst sets Eva down on the floor to find her own way back to her room. Time for Horst to work. Time for Horst to get busy, to help all those patients reaching their tongues toward Heaven.

Back home, right behind their yard, Apple Heaven. Dieter gave it that name the first time he helped Eva climb the fence using only her arms and one stump. He lifted her into a tree and let go. Eva grabbed at the branches all around her, and the tree hugged her back. Her weight kept her balanced.

The apple trees behind their house belonged to the man who grew strawberries in the field outside town, and before the war surrounded the houses near the school with apple and pear trees. Dieter and his friends stole fruit after school, but the owner never chased them. "There's too much to sell, anyway," he shrugged, when Horst took Eva to apologize for trespassing. "Go ahead, swing from the top branches for all I care." He blinked at Horst when he said this. "Just don't come crying to me if anybody gets hurt." His eyes slipped toward Eva's lower body. "I mean, hurt *more*."

So Eva and Dieter played Catch-Me in the apple trees. By November the fruit was too shrivelled to eat, but the branches were strong enough to carry even Dieter's weight. The rules were you had to slap your palm against the other person's back or shoulder, so when Dieter swung too close, Eva turned to face him at the crucial moment. When Dieter tried to reach his arm over her head to pat her back, Eva swung to a lower branch and flipped around until she was behind him. *Tag, you're it!* Then she somersaulted through the tree until she was part of the leaves. School was for learning, and after school was for playing and helping Mam. And if it weren't for the war, Eva wouldn't have to be sad, ever.

Often at the kitchen table, Horst counted his money to see if it would be enough for the following month. He counted it almost every day and Eva would laugh except Horst got angry when his own daughter ridiculed him. His eyeglasses were too old and he squinted when he read with them, so he put his mother's reading glasses overtop. Eva *did* laugh the first time she saw Horst wearing two pairs of glasses, and Horst smacked her with the accounts book. "Just wait till you get older and you need tools to improve *your* body," he snarled.

When Eva still lived at home and went to school every day, Monsieur, the teacher, gave the students multiplication and drawing and language conjugation and history. History started out with the French poet Baudelaire and his poems about how rebuilding cities meant widening the streets and eliminating the poor people. But then history kept reeling backwards. Monsieur showed them pictures of paintings by Vincent van Gogh: women picking potatoes with their bums in the air. Monsieur told the class that Baudelaire was so poor he was buried with his parents, and Eva giggled out loud because he was stuck sleeping in their bed forever. Shhh, don't think about that day. Then they only studied the ancients—how Romans spread their soldiers like jam across the whole of Europe, and if people were better bred, Germany wouldn't need to re-spread the jam.

Now, weeks since Horst has brought her to this ward, Eva scuttles from room to room, her fingers inked with dirt and glue from the floor. On her second day, Eva found a room filled with crutches, and she thought she'd died and gone to hospital heaven. Eva picked two crutches that didn't match, one slightly longer, the other a bit thicker.

The room was full of canes and slings as well as crutches hanging from the walls, and she thought how fun it would be to turn this room into a gymnastics room—it even smelled like the sweat in the wooden basement they used as a gym at her old school. "Horses sweat," Monsieur would say to them, "men perspire." Etiquette and gymnastics went together. Geography and history stayed way back in the past, but proper manners never went out of style.

"What about girls?" Eva asked Monsieur, but he just clapped his hands together. You could only go so far with etiquette, to look at Monsieur's reddening face. "What about girls?" Eva asked again, but this time to Mam, at home as they peeled potatoes for supper, the boiling water steaming both their faces red.

Mam chuckled into her peelings, left to dry out on the counter, then used for kindling in the morning. "Women *glow*," Mam told her, and they both laughed at the glow soaking their armpits, the glow dripping from Mam's forehead, the glow that always found a way to dampen and stain the crease at the bottom of all Eva's dresses. Between Mam and Monsieur, Eva would learn about the whole world. If the war ever let history catch up to the present.

The crutch room *is* just like the gym at school, and Eva will use the slings and bandages to rig the crutches to the wall. If she invents a climbing game for this room, maybe the other kids will play with her. Or at least say no. Eva so tired of kids facing their backs at her, as if she doesn't exist. Like Eva, the kids don't seem sick, just different. The oldest boy, Landau, lives here because he's a *Mischling*. Eva didn't know you could cure Jewishness, but Head Nurse says there's a cure for every ailment. There's a boy with lips that leak all over his face, two blind girls, two brothers who are extra short, and a girl with perfect sunflower hair, perfect daisy teeth, perfect legs and feet, but she doesn't move her arms.

When Eva asks Horst about the new playroom, he tells her there's a war going on, and patients need to contribute, too. Eva knows all about the war, it's why Mam can't go to school anymore and cooks for Horst and Dieter, but not Eva anymore. Eva sips the thin beige soup from the hospital kitchen, just like a real patient. The war also meant that Mam and Horst fought all the time, at night with the doors shut, when they thought Eva and Dieter both slept.

"Germany can't afford *useless eaters* when our boys have to be provided for," Eva would hear Horst say, in the middle of her dream about growing thick hairs on her regrown feet. "We need to protect the food supply, why can't you understand that?" During their fights, Horst sounded less and less like family, and more and more like a teacher whose student wouldn't learn. "Soldiers before the asocial, strength before feebleness," he recited.

"It's nonsense," Mam spat out. "What do you think such policies will lead to? Der Fury needs healthy boys for killing or dying, and you call it medicine." Eva, awake, wished she'd woken up sooner, as she couldn't make out what part of the war they were arguing about.

"Watch what you say, sister," Horst warned. It must be serious, if Horst forgot that Mam wasn't his sister anymore.

"You're the one," Mam said indignantly, "who's always saying the war is almost over, that Germany is gaining ground. And now suddenly there's not enough food for everyone?" Mam exhaled noisily. "It's nonsense. You're speaking nonsense and it's making us crazy."

"Don't say crazy," was Horst's only reply. "War isn't crazy."

The War is why Mam doesn't visit because Eva lives in another city now, and the war keeps families apart. The pacing woman in Eva's room says, "War keeps families from finding each other, keeps us apart, keeps our eyes pointed toward the sky." The woman doesn't stop pacing or even look down at Eva, so Eva scrambles back and forth with her across the floor. "My sister will come," says the woman, chewing on her nightie strings. "Your mother, too," she says, finally acknowledging Eva crawling beside her. "No mother would leave her child in a hospital, not this one." The woman spits out the nightgown string, but then pulls a bit of lace from the sleeves into her mouth, chewing at the holes in the fabric.

Only crazy people eat their clothing, but Eva wants to hear again that Mam will come visit, because the crazy woman says that Mam will march up to the hospital doors, past Head Nurse's office, nod at but not speak to Horst, and pick Eva up off the filthy floor and carry her all the way home, even if she has to walk for three days straight. Eva's first father had to walk for three days once, before the war. He was heading home, already out the door, and safely halfway down the street from his office when a trolley slid off its tracks, slammed against his left side, and threw him against the cobblestone so hard that he went to sleep. When he woke up, he was in another town, lying in a cow field decorated with dandelions. He picked up his boots and his work cap—his briefcase was gone, and his key, and his money—and he walked three days till he was home again. Eva's first mother fell down when she opened the door and he was standing there clutching the mail. "I thought you were dead," she said. "I thought you were dead," and her voice sounded like when she told Eva to go pick some cherries for the pie, or put Anna-Banana in her room and get ready for dinner, or asked Horst what time his shift began the next day. Then she fell over and the bowl of mashed potatoes she'd been holding crashed out of her hands and all over the floor.

Eva's father came home and her mother fell to the ground and Eva wasn't going to remember about any other explosions near her father. Shhh, just don't think about that day.

For weeks, Eva explores the wards of Horst's hospital. He gives her a strong squeeze on her shoulders when she leans upright, no wall for support, on her new crutches. She watches him pull an empty gurney from the basement up to the third floor. She follows him into the stairwell up to the second floor. She can't keep up, even though Horst pulls the gurney alone. On the second floor, she helps Cook pass out cracked plates and bent forks. She can grab two in one hand and still manage her crutches. Going downstairs is too hard, so Eva drags her crutches behind the heavy doors, and props them up for later. But when she comes back, her crutches are gone, and Head Nurse has locked the room full of more crutches. Eva doesn't ask Head Nurse for another set, because when kids complain they get called to the main office. Eva has seen them head down the corridors and not return. Punishment lasts a long time in this place. If she never gets to go outside, Eva doesn't *really* need crutches. Her hands will get dirty, but she's dirty already—war time means not enough water for baths. Eva will find another game, she only needs the right equipment. She crawls off her bed, down the corridor, turns before Head Nurse's office, around the cabinet, into the room with books. Mostly, they show pictures of patients and describe things like how to treat malaria, but Eva has also found a slim recipe book with writing in the margins. Every day she allows herself to read one recipe, won't even turn the page to peek at what's cooking tomorrow.

Today it's Potato Pancakes.

Eva has helped Mam cook them a million times, but this book has a twist. She peels seven large potatoes, setting the peelings to one side to dry into kindling. The book doesn't say this part, but the book doesn't know it's wartime now and every bit counts. Her fingers remember peeling, she could peel potatoes in her sleep, she could peel potatoes with one arm, with her feet if she had feet. Eva grates the potatoes, one two three four five six seven, until each potato is a mush of starch and liquid in the bowl she clutches against her belly. She sprinkles a bit of flour into the bowl to absorb the water. At home, Mam always used the wooden spoon she inherited from Eva's first mother, with a painted elephant on its tip. But here in the hospital, Eva stirs with a pencil she snitched from Head Nurse's desk; she can crawl most places without any of the other nurses noticing her. For the bowl, Eva's grabbed one of those shoes Landau plays with. She doesn't even care if he gets mad. The other kids can't exactly ignore her *more*. Eva grates a giant onion into the potatoes, then smells her fingers for the whiff of its skin on her own.

Beat two medium eggs lightly, add to potato mixture. Eva lingers over the rich orange yolks, the delicate transparent jelly protecting what it thought would become a baby chicken. Mam used to have two chickens running around the backyard, but one got loose and zig-zagged under the wheels of a military car, and Horst decided they'd better eat the other one before owning a chicken got them all arrested. Eva giggled at a chicken arresting them, but Horst yanked at her chair and she stopped. Mam wanted to keep collecting eggs, but Horst said "roast chicken," and roast chicken was what they had for supper the very next day. "It may be war," said Horst, his mouth shiny with chicken grease, "but you can still buy eggs at the market. Besides, it's been a year, everybody knows the Reich will triumph soon enough." He sliced himself another helping. "The fighting won't infect Germany, no need for us to watch a chicken starve to death because we want its future eggs," he said.

But since Eva started living at the hospital, the war has stretched its mouth wider and wider to swallow up more countries, more soldiers. She heard the nurse with braces say, "If

Der Fury keeps this up, my brothers will have to fight the Americans, next." Horst tells her that Dieter's been shipped to the front. The front of what? Eva wonders. She doesn't know where the back or middle of the war might be, either. Add salt and pepper to taste.

If this were back home, Mam would drip the batter into heated oil and Eva would watch the pancakes bubble lacily and their edges brown as if they were beginning to burn. But before she can start cooking—Eva's using the floor heating grate as a grill—this book says to grind four garlic cloves into the batter, and so she does. Their neighbour, Frau Rueter, would raise her eyes to high heaven if she smelled garlic coming from their kitchen. "Only Gypsies cook with that stuff!" she'd shout at them, then slam down her window in case the Gestapo smelled foreigners and came looking. But this book has shepherded Eva through weeks of lukewarm soup, no meat in the broth, no dessert, not a drop of fat in their meals, barely any salt. Besides, Eva likes the plot-twist: *four* cloves of garlic, the smell alone gives her shivers.

Eva reads the measurements again. The previous owner has scrawled a note beneath the instructions: "And let cool before eating, plain or with applesauce." Eva licks her finger, tastes green apples from Apple Heaven behind their back fence. She closes her eyes, rubs her palms against the tree bark. The sun stokes her face, and the dirt under her bum is apple orchard warm, not a ripped-up hospital floor. Tonight supper won't be watery soup, but this exact recipe from this exact page, and Mam will make her peel potatoes and stir the applesauce, because supper won't cook itself.

After reading the recipe seven times—once for each potato—
Eva returns the book to the shelf and crawls out the door. If you
sit in one place too long, Head Nurse finds you and sends you
with bandages to another ward, or to carry the laundry, or bring
an extra meal to the shuffling patients who go outside to hammer repairs after their morning medicine. Then Horst scolds
you for getting in the way, keep out of the way, Eva. If she were
sick, the nurses would like her better. She's seen them sit by the
beds of children too weak to move, too sick to drink more beige
soup, the nurses sit there even when the child dies and it's time
for Horst to remove the body. Eva doesn't like to stay in the room
when a patient dies, but sometimes it happens at night and she
wakes up to the smell of asparagus, and she knows there's been
too much pee for a night accident, somebody died and her last
supper flushed out of her. So far, Eva's friend the crazy woman
is still strong enough to pace their room. Sometimes, Eva pours
beige soup from her own plate onto her friend's; Horst brings
Eva sausages from home, or a boiled egg. Yesterday, Head Nurse
walked into each room and made the same announcement: they
may transfer patients to make room for injured soldiers. Eva
crawled after her, but stayed several hops back. The patients
didn't move, didn't even tilt their heads to listen. Eva saw that
older boy writing down notes, a cheat-sheet? The other nurses—holding bed pans, syringes, patients' wrists—turned to each
other, the war on their shoulders now, even Head Nurse's uniform doesn't smell as freshly starched as usual.

But if soldiers come, where will they put all the patients? Eva
knows the rooms are overflowing with straw mattresses, most
on the floors, buckets between beds for patients who can't make

it all the way to the bathrooms outside in the hallways. Maybe Dieter will get just a little bit hurt and he can come here so she can sit with him and feed him—Potato Pancakes and hard-boiled eggs and smelly hand cheese. The book will have a recipe just for Dieter.

Eva crawls out the door, turns right, sticks to the wall so that the nurses won't notice her. The male nurses always use the south stairwell to go up, and the female nurses use the west stairwell. Eva doesn't know if it's habit or schedule. Mostly, the nurses don't look down. They walk from room to room with syringes, vials of Luminal, tattered clothing donated from the outside. Horst sees her, though. Sometimes, he'll pat her head, other times he'll frown his vegetable lips down at her. "Nurses here know you're my daughter. They'll treat you better if you stay upright. Or stay on your bed." Horst lifts her easily, swings open the stairway doors, brings her back to her dorm, kisses her forehead, goes back to work. Eva sees him throughout the day lifting patients, injecting needles, pushing bodies out of the rooms and away from the hospital. But Eva isn't sick, she doesn't need to stay in bed. Why doesn't Mam at least send her some books to read? Why hasn't Mam written? Or visited? Or sent Anna-Banana?

Eva remembers more of what Mam said to Horst when he first brought up the idea of taking Eva to visit his hospital. "Hasn't she seen enough of hospitals? Really, Horst, where's your head?" Eva suddenly pictures Horst searching through the cellar for his lost head, two sets of glasses awkwardly perched on his neck. Horst never wears his glasses at the hospital. Good thing he doesn't need to read here, just gives the patient the injection Dr Schmidt prescribes, carries sick men and women to other wards, transfers children, loads up the grey buses, follows Head Nurse on her rounds. He is her number two man. "A hospital is no place for a sick person," Eva heard Mam saying the next week. "You know that better than any of us, Horst." Eva waited for Horst to assert how important his job is, especially now that it's war, waited for him to brag about the gun he'd been assigned, she saw him stash it under his mattress when he got home from work the day before.

But Horst didn't say all that, just scraped his chair as he got up. "The law is the law," was his only reply, chewing his apple strudel, pushing his empty plate toward Mam.

"What *are* you talking about, Horst?" Mam grabbed the plate and started washing. The running water made it harder to hear, so Eva slipped down another stair. "We can take care of Eva here, you don't even have to do anything, why do you want her with you at work? She's not *sick*." Mam threw the plate back onto the table, but it didn't break. Horst pushed it aside, like he was full all over again.

"Pick it up," Horst said.

Mam took a big breath instead. "When Eva was in her hospital after the explosion—" No. Eva climbs the stairs away from their conversation. Shhh. Don't think about that day, don't talk about explosions. Too many noises crowd her head. She goes back to her room, sings to Anna-Banana in as loud a whisper as she can.

The day after Horst brought her to his hospital, Eva had a runny nose that wouldn't stop. Head Nurse offered her a hankie, but within a few days, Eva woke up and it wasn't tucked into her shirt pocket. She wiped her nose on her nightie, like the other patients. But no matter. Her nose never runs anymore. Even though the patients drink nothing but beige soup every day, Eva feels drier and drier. She stops wiping her nose, stops sneezing, stops needing to swallow. No matter how much soup she slurps down, Eva can feel her body drying from the inside out. If Mam were here, she'd slide cucumber skins along Eva's arms and forehead and neck. Eva would kiss the soft meat of the peels and her lips would spring back from where they stick to the inside of her mouth. But now Eva is all dust, where she used to be eyes and nose and mouth. At night, she reaches out for Anna-Banana, but her fingers miss the woollen strands of hair, the embroidered eyes that she can trace in the dark. Anna-Banana sleeps in Mam's house and waits for Eva to come home from the hospital. Anna-Banana remembers when Eva went to a hospital before. She only stayed three weeks. Eva will be home soon, and Anna-Banana will drench her cloth face with banana-shaped tears, but apple-flavoured.

❋ ❋ ❋

By the fourth week, Eva works in the garden with the other children. One day, she crawls to Head Nurse's office and listens under the door. She can only see feet, but she hears Horst say how he doesn't want Eva to work, that he wants her to get more food than the other patients, that he thinks she should get her crutches back. But Head Nurse doesn't give in to Horst the way Mam and Eva do at home. "If she's healthy, she should work, like the other patients. There's a war on, Horst. Healthy patients need to work." Head Nurse sounds like her tongue has a paper-clip stuck to it. "We don't have much of a budget here. You know every resource is going toward helping the war, helping *us* win. Every effort makes a difference, every task has an ambition." The backs of Horst's heels are scuffed. "Der Fury says that every person can make a difference, even children, even the elderly." Eva sees that the toes of Head Nurse's shoes are white as flour. Head Nurse opens the door so Horst will know their time is up. Neither of them see Eva because she has scampered behind a pile of dirty shirts waiting to go to the laundry. Eva still hides from Head Nurse, who has eyes like potatoes. But she doesn't bother hiding from the other nurses. They don't notice Eva crawling or patients who call out for more food please. The nurses talk about beds and transport and medication, but they only see patients when there's a bare arm in front of them and a syringe on the tray beside the bed. A dying child. Maybe the garden will have some potatoes leftover from fall. They'll be chalky, but Eva can slip one or two into her sewn-up skirt and use the pencil to mash it up in the shoe.

Except the garden is for flowers and shrubs, no vegetables in sight. "Shouldn't we grow carrots and cabbage?" Eva asks, but Gardener does not answer, he tells them what to weed and where to bury ground-up eggshells and cucumber peelings for the compost. And then he watches them work. The other children work faster than Eva, but they don't smile as much. She's outside! She's holding a passion flower in her hands! It's blue, with white-tinted edges, and its middle fans out away from the other petals. Gardener tells Eva to pluck it for Dr Schmidt's office, but she doesn't know where that is. Besides, the thought of this intricate flower shrinking and fading inside the grey hospital makes Eva want to throw a trowel at the ground. When a bus with grey windows drives onto the hospital grounds, nurses run to unlock the gates. An old man stands on the outside, but nurses don't let him in. Eva hears him ask for his daughter, but one of the nurses with a kind voice says, "Please, go home, your daughter died weeks ago." She reaches a hand toward his shoulder. "Patients are infectious, even the clothing is infectious, go home, sir." The man tries to enter the grounds with the bus, but the nurses block his path. "There was nothing Dr Schmidt could do," the nurse says, pushing him gently backwards and away.

In the garden, the kids work quickly, and throw small objects toward Landau that they unearth while weeding. Eva doesn't see what they're throwing, so she moves one row over. She digs for something to throw, but only finds worms and pebbles the size of her knuckles. Maybe she'll be assigned a better row next time? Eva doesn't try to make friends anymore, too many patients know that Horst gives her sausages. He sits on her bed now and watches her eat them so she can't share with her friend the pacing woman. Pacing Woman still talked to Eva, right up until she went home, but the other patients turn away when Horst enters the room smelling of cooked meat. Eva's belly hurts after she swallows. Why can't everyone in here have a brother/father like Horst? Eva sticks her nose into the earth, smells winter coming. When she raises her head, she sees Landau eat a tulip head. He chews so fast that Gardener doesn't see, but Eva sees and waves to him when he looks around for witnesses. She waves and Landau turns back to his patch of earth, then faces her again and points to the shed. Gardener always goes to the shed just before Cook calls lunch, and then the kids huddle together for the length of a cigarette, their backs to the hospital, their backs to Eva. But this time Landau has invited her. Eva has watched them play their clothing game according to whatever rules Landau announces. A month is a long time to explore on your own. Eva jabs her trowel at the dirt and unearths a dead bird. Its feathers so dirt-encrusted that Eva can't see what colour it was originally, can't see if its wing is broken or merely bent from being buried. Did someone plant it here, a quiet grave beneath the beauty of the tulips and the passion flowers? Eva doesn't think this is the sort of treasure that Landau collects, so she buries it again. That morning, Gardener tossed a pigeon he found on his way to work into the incinerator. Eva's sharp intake of mourning made him laugh. "Burning doesn't make it any more dead," he told her, and pointed to where she should overturn the rich, dark earth. Now, Gardener heads for his shed, and Eva and the two short brothers and the blind girl and the girl with the sunflower hair circle to where Landau sits with yet another piece of the clothing puzzle. Landau found it before morning bells, hid it inside his pant leg until Gardener's smoke break. This time, what the children pass around is a pair of goggle-sized eyeglasses with one arm missing.

✳ ✳ ✳

They're not playing games.

Eva learns this in the huddle. It's no game at all. "And I also found Anika's shirt," Landau whispers, and he pulls out three centimetres of red cloth with a purple tail hanging off its edge. "She was wearing it when Head Nurse called her to the office." Landau held the wrinkled bit of cloth out for each one to hold to their eyes, then put it back inside his shoe. "She said she'd never let go of her dragon tail, that she'd never pass it on to another kid," he told Eva, who didn't know Anika, had never seen this shirt, but still tried to follow the rules of this complicated activity. Then Gardener emerged from the shed, stomping out his cigarette butt, and they all lined up for lunch.

Now that Landau talks to her, the other kids explain the rules.

"Every day, patients come into this hospital," the boy with scabby lips whispers to Eva during lunch. "Every day, patients leave. They get transferred to another ward, to another hospital. Into the bus, out of the bus. We can't keep track." He finishes off the last of his beige soup. "Nobody ever visits, nobody sends a letter, or a postcard even, not when they've promised." Then the boy slips away. Eva wonders if talking hurts his lips. "Your father is a nurse here," he'd said, when he first sat down next to her. "What does he tell you?"

Eva tries to explain that Horst tells her weight scales and calculates how many patients he lifted that week, but never tells her where he lifts them *to*. They listen to her catalogue how much Horst doesn't say, then Landau tells her the ghost story of how patients disappear. "Not at night, like you'd think," he confides, "but during the day. Nurses show up in the hallways, gather enough patients to fill the bus, then off they go, one nurse hanging on to the doors, waving to the soldiers marching outside the hospital gate." A fairy tale.

Mam used to call to Eva, "Come in! come in!" whenever she heard the rumble of a bus. "If you see a bus with its windows painted grey, get out of the street." Eva tried to tug free, she wanted to play Apple-Tag with Dieter. "I mean it, sister!" Mam said with icicles in her voice. "You see that kind of bus, you stash yourself away. You hurry home, if you can, but if not, head for Frau Rueter's, or Frau Hoffman's, or Herr Munster's." Mam let go then, but she wasn't finished. "Eva, nobody sees inside those painted windows, there must be ghosts riding around in them. I don't want to lose you in there." Then she let Eva go play in Apple Heaven.

"It's not a game," says Landau.

On Tuesday, Eva recognizes Pacing Woman's chewed lace nightie; she sees a new patient wearing it in their room. The new patient faces the wall, mumbles into her cot, kicks at Eva crawling next to the patient's bucket that hasn't been changed since she arrived. Eva's pacing friend went home to her family and must not want that old nightie anymore, Eva thinks. She gave it away before she left. Eva didn't see her leave, couldn't ask Horst to send a passion flower with her friend. On Monday night, the bed was empty, and on Tuesday morning the nightie reappeared, but this time on the kicking woman.

Landau has explained the rules four times. The grownups in this ward are too ill to play, the children keep track of who belongs to what. Landau has scarred the pattern of an "M" into his underwear, using cigarette butts Gardener left smouldering beside the shed. Head Nurse would notice a burnt shirt, but she doesn't touch the patients and won't see anything beneath his clothes. None of the nurses here touch the patients. Until they need to be moved. Each child marks a piece of clothing, so the others in the circle will recognize its owner. It's the only thing they can think of to ensure they leave evidence of themselves. That's how they play detective. "No, it's not playing," Landau reminds her. Over and over, Landau repeats the final rule in their game: "No matter what, don't let anyone take your marker away from you. Keep it as ID, hold onto it. Don't let them pass you on."

Mam still hasn't come. Eva asks Horst why, but he says not to think about that home, this is her home now. "I'm your father," he repeats. "I'm your father," he says when he goes off shift, when he arrives in the morning, when other nurses walk onto the wards with handfuls of patient files. "When the war ends," he says, "when Der Fury conquers his enemies, *everyone* will return to a better home, to an improved world."

One day, Eva sees Dr Schmidt in her room. Because it's war, the hospital can only afford one doctor. That's why Head Nurse knows so much. When nurses carry patients out, some of the patients scream and grab onto their beds. They scream harder when they see the grey busses. Sometimes Horst has to drag patients on board. Eva watches from the garden, but Horst doesn't see her. Eva hears one woman call out from inside the bus, "Open your eyes, Frieda, it's the last time you'll see God's sky. Take a good, long drink of blue." Then Horst pulls and lifts at the same time, and Frieda's head goes bump-bump-bump up the bus steps. Horst jumps out and the doors close.

Horst never goes with the grey buses. Never.

Eva tries to wave to the patients in the bus. Horst says patients don't like to be moved to other hospitals, because they get used to where they are. So Eva waves to the scared patients, but Mam was right, the windows are painted, the patients' faces already lost behind the grey windows.

* * *

Underneath the cots, Eva plays hide-and-seek. Only three children still live at the hospital, the oldest boy Landau, the boy with the lips that never heal, and Eva. She doesn't want to play their boring detective game anymore. She wants Anna-Banana and Mam and Monsieur's history, and Apple Heaven. Eva's hiding. She knows Landau will begin looking in the stairwells first. That's when she sees Dr Schmidt's feet. She knows it's the doctor because he doesn't wear white shoes like the nurses, his shoes are shiny shiny black. Black and so shiny, Eva thinks his shoes might be purple. She reaches to touch. She shouldn't, but it's been so long since she stroked anything not covered with dirt or grime. Even their daily ration of beige soup has a layer of dust floating on the surface. Cook says it's extra protein, but Eva can taste sand slide down her throat. The doctor's shoes are bright, so bright they shine like velvet. Or skin. Eva traces from the toe to the heel, and the doctor hauls her out from under his feet.

"A cripple?" Doctor Schmidt asks Head Nurse. The sound of his voice matches the feel of his shoes. "You let this poor child crawl around in filth?" He lifts Eva into his arms and gently places her on the newly-empty bed. Strokes hair out of her eyes. "The war has turned us into animals." He shakes his head at Eva, like they have landed in a pickle together. Then he pulls

off her homemade skirt, examines her one stump and one nothing. He only touches her at her remaining knee, very softly.
"Hmmm," he says. Eva thinks maybe she smells and tries to
pull her undershirt lower again. The doctor doesn't lean toward
Head Nurse the way Horst does and wait for her eyes to tell
him okay. "Why is she here?" he asks Head Nurse, but his eyes
never leave Eva's legs.

"One of the ward nurses brought her," Head Nurse points
behind her, as if Horst will walk onto his shift exactly now. She
waves a finger at the doctor, but his eyes are fixed on Eva's dirty
collar, on the ripped hem of her skirt that used to tuck neatly
under her bum. "She's a ... she's his relative," Head Nurse says.
Eva can see each word limp toward the period, slump down in
relief when they finally come to a full stop.

"I don't care if she's Der Fury's goddaughter," the doctor announces, and several nurses jump as if they've heard a gunshot
in the courtyard. "This hospital is no place for a child, especially
a mutilated one. I want her transferred immediately." He pulls
Eva's skirt back over her bum, and walks toward the door.

"But doctor," Head Nurse tries one more time. After all, this
is *her* hospital, these are *her* patients. The doctor only shows up
to sign papers. "She wasn't born deformed, she's a war injury."

"All the more reason to get her out of here," he answers. "A
life in this place isn't worth living. Take her away." He then
stares into Head Nurse's eyes until she is forced to retreat in
the face of his healing gaze.

✳   ✳   ✳

The bus ride is short, even with three stops at other hospitals. At every stop, the bus picks up children, but Eva doesn't want to play with any of them; she wants to hold her breath until she can no longer smell hospital oxygen or patients or syringes or this bus. Eva thought it would take hours or even days to drive back to Mam peeling potatoes in the kitchen. The knife will drop when she sees Eva, her hair coming loose as she runs into the street to carry Eva off the bus, away from the burnt soldiers Eva sees hovering above the patients, the ghostly odour of their smouldering clothes covering the windows until they are a grey so dark Eva cannot see out, cannot tell the difference between sky and buildings. The inside of the bus looks like when Eva was buried underneath … Shhh, no more bad days!

She's been in the hospital for so long, she doesn't recognize her town anymore. What used to be houses and a bakery and the post office are now rubble. Streets run up against piles of rocks and then just end, nowhere to go. The bus drives slowly, and then Eva remembers she's supposed to poke holes in her skirt. Landau said to stick her fingers inside the seams and leave gaping eyelets for him to discover. She'll ask Mam to send the old skirt back to the hospital so that Landau can keep playing. Eva's skirts don't need markers anyway, Mam tailored these clothes for Eva alone.

When the bus stops for more patients, the invisible burnt soldiers float around the bus until Eva chokes. Smoke travels through her veins. They never go past her house, why is this trip taking so long? Then it's the final stop, and the Hadamar hospital looks like another fortress on a hilltop. Nurses come to the bus, sign for their new charges, then watch the bus drive away empty of passengers, except for the floating soldiers who continue to choke the windows from the inside. The nurses lead or carry each patient, no screaming, off the bus, into this hospital, and down the stairs to its cement basement. Eva clings to the nurse who looks like her first mother.

Mam says it's okay to talk about their mother, but don't let Horst hear. "Shhh," Horst says, "shhh, shhh, shhh." The nurse's arms are covered with scratch marks and freckles and her skin glistening from how hard she works all day, just like Horst. She puts Eva down gently. The basement is cold cement and not much light. The patients huddle in a line while nurses take their clothes, fill boxes with torn slacks, bent hair pins, mismatched socks, glasses, fraying bras. The woman in front of Eva sits down on the freezing cement to take off her underwear. "I can't balance with these ankles," she apologizes to the nurses, to the other patients. "My ankles are no good." Many of the patients can't stand, but there are no chairs in the basement, no beds, no crutches. Eva feels the cement freezing on her stump and beneath her bum. She pushes her body up and away from the cold, but then her hands freeze, her fingers too numb to unbutton her shirt when it's her turn. She starts to cry. Everyone's going to think she's a baby, Eva thinks.

"Shhh," says the nurse who looks like her mother, "don't cry. You get to go home soon, so soon." Then she smiles at Eva, down the entire line of naked patients, including the woman hunched forward, one hand over each breast. The children grab at grownup ankles and knees. Eva wants to touch someone's skin, feel a body warm in her hands. The nurse points to the shower room. More patients start crying, it's been so long since any of them had a shower, not even a sinkful of water for a cat's-lick. One older man carries a scrub brush and a sliver of soap he must have been saving since hearing about the showers. Eva has been drinking tepid leek soup for over a month and today she'll feel hot water wash down her dusty back, around her unglowing armpits, over her dry and earth-encrusted hair. Warm water she can swallow, and it won't taste like sand! A hot shower to drown the dust beneath her skin, dust that's ground into her greying bones.

But it is still war, and there is not enough water for patients to shower one at a time. The nurses herd the patients into the shower room. If they all stand, everyone will fit. The man with the scrub brush starts humming and the woman who can't stand on one leg tries to sing words with him. People's faces disappear and Eva sees only legs, an orchard of legs in front of her eyes. The shower room has new-fangled electric lamps that show off the brilliant white ceilings and the sharp, white walls. The line snakes forward. Eva crawls up the two steps and a man with no fingers lifts her so she won't get trampled by the never-ending snake. He tries to hold her away from his own nakedness, but the line snakes and snakes and Eva gets pressed up against the bodies of other naked men and women and against children's foreheads, so she doesn't even need the man to hold her anymore, she stays up in the air just from all the bodies pressing. Eva's caught in the folds of skin and elbows and poking fingers, her shoulders squished against the others so tightly she hangs above the glowing white-tiled floor.

"When you're finished cleaning yourselves, you'll all get clean clothes. New clothes," a nurse announces, retreating up the basement stairs. Why don't the nurses just stay down here and wait?

From inside the snake's tail, Eva glimpses a long hallway leading from the back of the shower room to what must be a doctor's examining room. She can't move anymore, she's so tightly squeezed in by the other patients. She smells the same soup emanating from the skins of patients from four different hospitals. She hears singing and moaning and suddenly remembers the walls falling in on Eva and her first mother and father. "SHHH!" Eva tries to scream, but she doesn't remember how to stop thinking about that day. She stares down the other hallway, notices that the floor is only tiled along one wall, the other side is bare cement. The tiled part is a slippery arrow, pointing their way out. Inside the shower room, Eva can barely twist her neck, sees only the showerheads above, and tiles that reach from the floor halfway to the ceiling. There're no windows, just a rectangle of glass inside the shower room door.

Finally, when Eva's lungs kiss her ribcage, the people crowded into the snake-shape stop, and the door with the window swings shut. Outside, a doctor's face peers at them through the glass. Even in this basement, he wears his white lab coat. Nobody moves, nobody cries. Eva hears a sound like air rushing out of a balloon, except it must be a giant balloon because the whooshing doesn't stop. Her stomach heaves and her lids scratch the insides of her eyes. A boy beside her vomits onto her stomach, the man with no fingers moans, a toddler starts to sing a lullabye, but then coughs and coughs. "Shhh," goes the whooshing balloon. "Shhh."

Eva is suddenly, so violently glad that Anna-Banana *isn't* here with her, isn't breathing poisonous air, isn't going to be dragged out the door, down the tiled side of the corridor onto a dissection table, then thrown onto a stove and burnt down to nothing.

Horst always tells her he's her father, and not to think about bad days, not to think about how a building could collapse on top of you and your parents. On that day, she walked into a shoemaker's with her first mother and father, and the ceiling exploded. Horst tells her, "Don't remember them dead. Don't think about being buried with them." Just like Baudelaire, Eva was buried with her parents. An entire building on top of her chest and waist, but not her legs, her legs somewhere else. The roof dropped on her legs and she woke up missing body parts and family parts. "Shhh, Eva," is Horst's fatherly advice, "think about your new father and your new mother. Don't talk about the bad days."

But Horst was wrong.

That day, Eva looked up and saw a hand reach out of the ceiling and down her throat. It took what it wanted, snatching the flesh of her calves. Today, squashed between a shaved chest and the boy throwing up, Eva wishes she'd thought about that other day, every day. Her first mother taking her on the train just for new shoes, her first father accompanying them on his way to work, the shoes to be blue with orange flowers. Eva wishes she could hear his voice say, "Not too fancy, war's coming." In the white light of this white room, Eva remembers her mother wore a navy dress, shoes bent at the toes, and when she walked, Eva saw they were the same colour as the street.

Eva's head is getting too heavy to hold up, and all the naked bodies pressing against her are sagging. Eva tries to figure out what Mam's hair looks like when she lets it down on purpose, when it stretches all the way to her bum. Eva's hair won't grow past her shoulders. She cut Anna-Banana's hair, too, and keeps the wheat-coloured yarn tips in a locket, stashed at home under her pillow. Eva's eyes close, her stomach heaves, but she swallows and opens her eyes; stares at the skin pressed against her face. Blinks. Her father's cane tapping against the cobblestones, her mother checking the grocery list, Eva running into the shoe store, pulling Father behind her, Mother opening her mouth wider and wider, trying to swallow the collapsing walls.

✳ ✳ ✳

After, when the gas has leaked and leaked and leaked into the room, the man watching through the window will wait extra long, to make sure not a muscle moves on the other side of the door. He will wait another hour to make sure there is no gas left for *him*. Only then will he heave open the door and pry apart bodies that have died hugging each other. Will pry a child with auburn hair and no legs, drag her along the tiled side of the floor, flop her onto one of the examination tables. He'll match her name to the photo nurses took when the patients were naked, will write down the diagnosis: "Feebleminded." He will then close Eva's folder and send it for filing to Tiergartenstraße-4.

"She watches you, our real mother," Mam promised Eva, the night before Horst took her away. Eva asked and asked about her real parents, but only when Horst couldn't hear, couldn't stop the words she coaxed from Mam's lips. "Our mother is up there watching you right now," Mam promised.

327

At this moment, Eva fervently hopes not, hopes her real mother is truly dead, too dead to behold *this* awful day. Her body shudders one last tremble. But even with her eyelids closed, she sees a wisp of Mam's hair escape into the air, hang above their frozen heads. The gas has swollen Eva's tongue and chases wires from her fingertips to her waist, from the nape of her neck to toes that aren't even there.

Eva's last act in this world is gratitude that Mam doesn't have to witness her sister-daughter inhale the ultimate cure.

Castle on the Left

"Horst didn't know," Mutti reassures me. She prepared broccoli in black bean sauce and garlic chicken. I made rosehip tea for dessert, but neither of us ate once Mutti started telling. "He never suspected what might happen, what *would* happen." She's trying to apologize for him. Her words tumble out crookedly, it's taken too much jawbone to tell me she had a sister. I had an aunt. I should have had an aunt.

Mutti inhales deeply. "Of course, he knew. How could he not know? He loaded the buses, he wrote letters of condolence to the families. He labelled phony urns." Her hands are streaked with dandelion juice, her fingernails crusted with earth from a day outside in the sun. "'They're better off dead,' Dr Schmidt told the nurses. 'Eva's better off in an institution,' Horst parroted, like any good Nazi." She takes her fork and stabs at the strawberries in her bowl. "No," she corrects herself, "he wasn't a Nazi, I could understand better if he had been a party member, a true believer, but he was just another follower." And she gets up then, to clear our plates. I've heard the whole story in one evening; enough is enough. I offer to wash dishes, but when Mutti says, "No, no," I shrug on my jacket instead. At the door, I take a bundle of letters she hands me. "The doctors thought they were gardeners, weeding out diseased plants. They decided that if they wore white coats they had the right to kill instead of cure, that killing *was* cure." Mutti shakes her head, this story is still science fiction, even though it happened fifty years ago, even though it happened to her sister.

"But if she hadn't inherited her condition," I start to protest: to get more words? To make the story keep going until a better ending appears? "If it was because of injury …" I stop because there is no justification, no logic behind medical cleansing. Mutti shakes her head, eyes dry, bony hands gently guiding me out the screen door, into the splendid, clear night.

When I get home, I crawl into bed and pull Mutti's collection of papers toward me. A letter from Bernberg, saying Eva died from pneumonia, her ashes to be delivered at a later date. Another letter, exactly the same, identical handwriting, with a different name signed at the bottom. Eva died at Sonnenstein, two weeks earlier than her other death, from tuberculosis, her clothes burned, her sister not allowed to retrieve the body. But the family would receive the ashes in an urn. And sixteen letters Mutti wrote to Eva while she was in Horst's hospital. Opened but never replied to, several containing stamped return envelopes with their home address already filled in. I can't stand to read in bed anymore, this is not a bedtime story. I get up, but can't make out Mutti's German handwriting.

The hard part is that this story isn't finished. Eva died *before* the war encroached on regular German lives. There was plenty of food, plenty of hospital space. Killing patients was target practice. This was 1941; there were still fours years of horror left. Mutti went to Hadamar after the war, made Horst tell her one thing, just one detail. After months of her nagging, he gave her the name of a nurse. Mutti went from Friedrichsdorf to Hadamar, and three days later to the Frankfurt train station. She stayed in Paris until she had money to pay for passage across the Atlantic, landing in New York, marrying Vati there, then making their way to Canada together. Mutti never went home again, was never willing to see Horst's blameless expression, his determined face, never willing to hear him say again, "She's better off dead."

*　*　*

I procure a vacation from staffing, from time-tabling, and from paper pushing so I may journey to Germany with Mutti, meet people I don't know, yet am curiously related to. Horst's children. My cousins. Eva's nieces and nephew.

"Always secure your own oxygen mask before assisting a fellow passenger," the taped announcement says. Beneath the right wing of the plane, a Rolls Royce insignia peeks out. I marvel at how my chest opened when the plane rose above the clouds. Just before we boarded, I presented Mutti with a bunch of Michaelmas daisies, her favourite flower. She tucked the brilliant bouquet into the pocket of the seat in front of her, and the petals bow over her knees. Persephone's song catches in my throat as a thin cloud of frost drowns earthbound clumps of tenacious April snow. The fog beneath the plane layers Vera's God's world below us. A river cuts into the dry chiselled banks of the Badlands. Where the devil lives.

I shall fly with Mutti into tomorrow. In a minute, she'll pull down the shade and adjust her headset for the first of several in-flight movies, *Harold and Maude*. "You'd think they'd play a recent film," Mutti will complain, switching her headset from English to Deutsch. "But who can resist the appeal of a wizened

broad, eh?" Her eyes will crinkle. She'll think she's embarrass-
ing me.

"I agree," I'll say, plugging in my own headset. "I'm looking
forward to corrupting a few youths when I reach your age." And
she'll slap at my shoulder, but gently, and then we'll both sigh
at the same time, mother and daughter, holding hands to keep
the plane aloft.

When we reach Friedrichsdorf, Mutti's hometown, Mutti and
I will stroll past the Mormon temple, curious tourists, casually passing by *Der Tempel Kirche Jesu Christi der Heiligen der
Letzten Tage*—the forty-first in the world to be dedicated. When
we approach the path that displays the angel Moroni trumpet-
ing his heavenly song, I'll snap a photo and continue sightsee-
ing. And then, arm in arm, Mutti will point out the house where
she and Horst lived during the war, her parents' cemetery, and
Eva's favourite apple tree. She'll greet widows and orphans from
her other life, and we'll eat the town's world-famous Zwieback.
I'll hear about the Jewish shopkeeper who remained in this
town right through to the end of the war, relinquishing his son
to the German army, and about the people who waved when
they should have saluted, *heil-Hitlered* when they were too ter-
rified to wave. I will encounter my grandparents' neighbours
who survived the war, who survived its aftermath, townspeople
who greeted the US army wildly, and who four years ago permit-
ted the Mormons to dedicate a temple in the town where my
aunt Eva was born.

If the Mormons find her name in a church registry, they will
baptize Eva by proxy, just as they have baptized Dieter, and
Mutti's parents, and a generation of Holocaust victims, and the

war's German and French and Italian and Greek dead soldiers. They have baptized Hitler and Eva Braun, Napoleon, Albert Einstein, and many Popes. They'll baptize Horst and, one day, Mutti and me too.

Mutti and I cleave together, taking photos of cobblestone lanes, mediaeval barns, and the paternoster elevator in city hall—a rosary of linked compartments—whose chain heaves from the basement to the top of the building and around again in an endless loop. We hop into one of the gaping wooden cubicles, ride around twice, then hop out at the café on the top floor, where we order *spaghetti-eis* and drink *Milch Kaffee*. I kiss Mutti's grizzled knuckles when she pulls out Anna Banana, all Horst's children have left of Eva.

Mother and daughter, discrete links. We shall saunter through the streets that all—in this small town—lead toward home.

ACKNOWLEDGMENTS

Excerpts of this novel have previously appeared in the literary journals *Alberta Views*, *Other Voices*, the anthology *RE:generations*, and the chapbook *Eaten of Worms*. I thank the editors of these fine publications.

I gratefully acknowledge the public funding I received from the Alberta Foundation for the Arts while working on an early draft of this novel. I am indebted to the faculty research award from the academic organization, DAAD (Deutscher Akademischer Austausch Dienst) that I was awarded to study Disability Studies and the Legacy of Eugenics in Germany (Sharon Snyder, director; David Mitchell, co-director), research which figures prominently in this novel. And I am grateful to continued academic support from the University of Windsor.

I thank Yvonne Markotić and Martin McSween, for inviting me to assist them during two childbirths (and Jaffra and Joa, for getting born). Pat Couture, for the story of yellow. Greg Gerrard, for wine and other encouragement. Lori Hogg, for literary tattles about some few ego-driven med-students. Dot Webster, for incredible "books" assistance. And the many chess players, child-care kids and workers, and Mormons I have met over the years, for sharing their passions.

I thank the editors and the entire fabulous Arsenal Pulp Press team, who doled out wonderful feedback and high expectations for this book.

Huge thanks and gratitude to: Louis Cabri, for mulling over various openings and endings. Louis de Bernières, who gave excellent advice early on in the manuscript. Suzette Mayr and

Rosemary Nixon, for editing and commenting on a plethora of versions. Aritha van Herk, for discussions about early drafts. And Suzette Mayr (again), for an eleventh-hour meticulous reading of the entire thing (again).

Finally, I thank Robert Kroetsch, for always insisting I could write this book.